SECRET AT DARK CASTLE

Prickly Hawthorn Village #1

KAREN DEAN BENSON

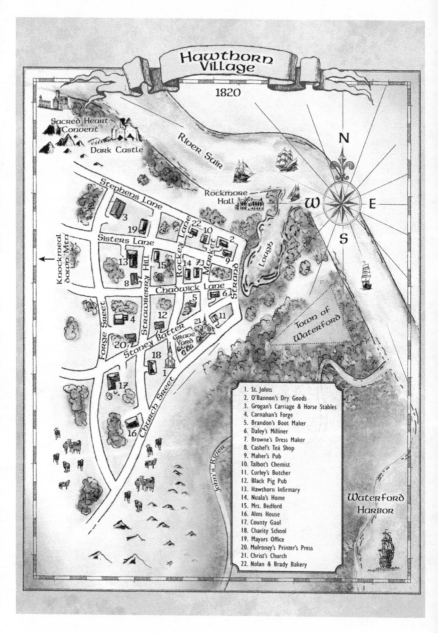

Hawthorn Village

1820

Sacred Heart Convent

Dark Castle

River Suir

Stephens Lane

Rockmore Hall

Knockmeal down Mtn

Sisters Lane

Lough

Chadwick Lane

Strawberry Hill

Rockery Lane

Market

Strand

Forge Street

Stoney Batter

Grave Yard

Town of Waterford

Church Street

River Suir

Waterford Harbor

1. St. Johns
2. O'Bannon's Dry Goods
3. Grogan's Carriage & Horse Stables
4. Carnahan's Forge
5. Brandon's Boot Maker
6. Daley's Milliner
7. Browne's Dress Maker
8. Cashel's Tea Shop
9. Maher's Pub
10. Talbot's Chemist
11. Curley's Butcher
12. Black Pig Pub
13. Hawthorn Infirmary
14. Nuala's Home
15. Mrs. Bedford
16. Alms House
17. County Gaol
18. Charity School
19. Mayors Office
20. Mulroney's Printer's Press
21. Christ's Church
22. Nolan & Brady Bakery

Charlie, you make it all fun!

ACKNOWLEDGMENTS

A story happens when a village of book lovers comes to the rescue. My publisher Nancy Schumacher's enthusiasm makes it all possible. A cast of readers whose opinions I appreciate are Ellen Simmons, Dee Williams, Ruth Hartwig, Judy Dickinson, and Sarah Zulewski. Very special thanks to Tina Wainscott for keeping me rational with her wisdom of all things authorly, and Nancy Mayer of Beau Monde, a Regency Researcher, with faultless peerage knowledge. Graphic Artist Susan Shaw, whose fantastic creativity turned my exceedingly primitive drawings into the map of Hawthorn Village, and the lineage chart of the Darnley's. Last but not least, my writing partners, Karen Auriti and Doris Lemcke whose support is priceless and thankfully endless.

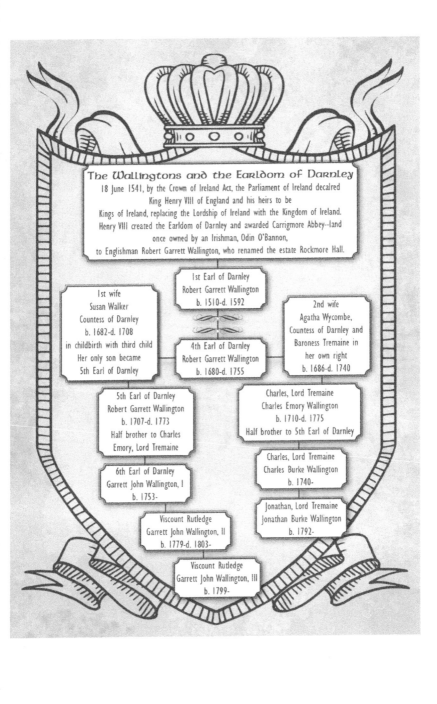

The Wallingtons and the Earldom of Darnley

18 June 1541, by the Crown of Ireland Act, the Parliament of Ireland declared King Henry VIII of England and his heirs to be Kings of Ireland, replacing the Lordship of Ireland with the Kingdom of Ireland. Henry VIII created the Earldom of Darnley and awarded Carrigmore Abbey--land once owned by an Irishman, Odin O'Bannon, to Englishman Robert Garrett Wallington, who renamed the estate Rockmore Hall.

1st Earl of Darnley
Robert Garrett Wallington
b. 1510-d. 1592

1st wife
Susan Walker
Countess of Darnley
b. 1682-d. 1708
in childbirth with third child
Her only son became
5th Earl of Darnley

2nd wife
Agatha Wycombe,
Countess of Darnley and
Baroness Tremaine in
her own right
b. 1686-d. 1740

4th Earl of Darnley
Robert Garrett Wallington
b. 1680-d. 1755

5th Earl of Darnley
Robert Garrett Wallington
b. 1707-d. 1773
Half brother to Charles
Emory, Lord Tremaine

Charles, Lord Tremaine
Charles Emory Wallington
b. 1710-d. 1775
Half brother to 5th Earl of Darnley

6th Earl of Darnley
Garrett John Wallington, I
b. 1753-

Charles, Lord Tremaine
Charles Burke Wallington
b. 1740-

Viscount Rutledge
Garrett John Wallington, II
b. 1779-d. 1803-

Jonathan, Lord Tremaine
Jonathan Burke Wallington
b. 1792-

Viscount Rutledge
Garrett John Wallington, III
b. 1799-

Late September 1799
County Waterford, Ireland

Shanna O'Key, known for her damaging gossip and bitter tongue, made her way on the well-worn path past the hulking ruin called Dark Castle. The shadowy entrance faced west, and the last rays of the setting sun caught a cloaked figure scurrying from the gaping entrance.

She froze, thinking of the ghosts said to haunt the castle. Specters were silent, however, and this one disturbed the eventide quiet with his rush to leave. Moments later, she recognized the second man—Lord Darnley's son, Lord Rutledge. Hardly over her shock, a woman obscured by a cloak, scuttled out of the ruin with a babe in arms.

At fifteen years of age, Shanna knew the makings of a good tale when she saw one and squinted into the growing darkness. As the woman flitted around the corner, Shanna damned the babble about hauntings and stalked to the passageway. The scent of beeswax drew her to a far chamber. The thick candle she found was warm to the touch.

Picking off the lid of a jar, fragrance of pine and wood musk swirled in the air. Sacramental oil? Frankincense? A babe in arms? The Anglican lord's son? And, most likely, a Catholic wench?

Shanna's breath caught in her throat with the realization that she might have just witnessed an illegal, papist baptism.

Spring 1816
County Waterford, Ireland
Rockmore Hall

Witham, Rockmore Hall's butler of thirty-four years, yanked on the lower drawer of a chest, unable to dislodge it, and concluded that something was wedged against the side rails. Muttering, he straightened, hands on hips, and glared at the inert piece of mahogany. As far as he knew, other than dusting, the drawers had not been touched since the demise of Lord Rutledge thirteen years previous.

Unwilling to allow a piece of furniture to get the better of him, he attacked the six-drawer chest as if an adversary. Bracing the toe of his leather shoe against its leg, he grasped the handles and yanked with vigor. A mere creak, it instantly gave up the drawer, sending the butler flat on his derrière, the coffer landing on his outstretched legs. A box within, its lid askew, held letters, brown with age, that scattered.

Long ago, every item of Rutledge's personal effects had been removed and stored. This discovery caused Witham to bite the side of his cheek with uncertainty. Reminding Lord Darnley of the great loss of his only son, and heir, might not be prudent.

He returned the letters with the wispy penmanship to the box and clasped the lid. Brushing off the backside of his worsted wool, he made his way down two flights to Lord Darnley's library, a sanctuary where his lordship resided at this time of day.

After knocking lightly, he entered waiting to be recognized.

Lord Darnley looked over the top of his spectacles. "What?"

"This was in a drawer in Rutledge's old room." Witham stepped forward and placed the box on the desk. "Apparently, we weren't entirely thorough in the cleaning." He glanced apologetically at his lordship. "It contains letters to his lordship."

Lord Darnley returned the quill to its inkwell. "What do they say?"

"I would not have intruded, my lord."

"In Rutledge's old room, you say?"

"Yes."

Settling into his chair, hands clasped over his waist-coated belly, his lordship asked, "Whatever made you look there?"

"Lady Duncamden's arrival. I considered putting her up in a room with a view of the fountain and gardens."

"She would enjoy that." His gaze on the box, he speculated. "These must have been written before Rutledge left for university." His interest fell to the crossed fingers on his belly. Witham appeared uneasy, and Lord Darnley clearly understood why. "You needn't think I'll slip into despair, Witham. Lord knows these past years have brought me peace and distance."

He couldn't help but think of his namesake and heir, the beloved son lost in a storm on the stretch of water where St. George's Channel meets the Celtic Sea. He'd been sailing from Wales back to County Waterford and Rockmore Hall. Shortly after his death, Mr. Franklin Hagadorn, the family solicitor, delivered a life-changing packet.

The lightning bolt of news contained a certificate of marriage between his son and a woman whose name was initialed F.O., signed and stamped with a Roman Catholic priest's seal. A letter explained Rutledge fathered a child with this woman, whom he secretly married. The woman was unable to keep the child, and Rutledge placed him with the Molloys, cottiers in the village on land owned by Lord Darnley. Rutledge compensated them handsomely for raising the boy, whom he named Ayden.

Thoroughly investigating the whereabouts of the priest, Darnley discovered he passed away three years previous. Before that, a fire destroyed the rectory where the documents were kept. He also discovered that Fr. Damien went about Ireland performing many such marriages between Protestants, and Catholics, seeing it as his duty to make sure innocent children were not born illegitimate, and therefore providing them with an acceptable place in Ireland's society.

Children born of a mixed marriage would hardly be acceptable if not illegitimate. The realization that he'd an heir, a grandson, was beyond anything he could have desired. The preparations he carried out before meeting the four-year-old involved the entire staff of Rockmore Hall. He provided a room on the second floor with southern exposure, in the same wing as his grandfather. His living conditions improved with indoor plumbing, a fireplace in each room, and marble floors to mention a portion of a long list of conveniences. Darnley did not want his grandson deprived of social regard befitting his title and station. He was not a snob, but his grandson hailed from a long line of Englishmen who, over generations, evolved into Irish noblemen, descendants of title and land awarded in 1541 by Henry VIII.

Now, thirteen years later, the handsome young Lord Rutledge, renamed Garrett III, was a man of seventeen. Nearing the end of his education at Eton and usually visiting Rockmore Hall on holidays with a few friends adding to Darnley's delight.

Stirring from his memories, Darnley leaned away from the small chest, casting a forced smile at Witham. "I'll let these sit a day or two. It shouldn't matter, considering how long they've been stored."

Witham bowed and closed the door, worried if perhaps he should have read them before handing them over. After all, he had been with his lordship since 1773, a time when the nobleman came into his inheritance at the age of twenty. Forty-three years passed since then.

He made his way below stairs in search of Mrs. Atkinson. Either talking about his concern with the housekeeper would make him feel better or he would rue the fact that he confided in her and feel miserable.

It was nearing luncheon, and Witham found the slender, salt-and-pepper-haired housekeeper in the linen room showing a new maid how to fold and store sheets. He breathed deeply of the scent of lavender before interrupting the instructions.

Mrs. Atkinson glanced up, humor crinkling the corners of her gray eyes. "What can I do for you?"

"I'd have a minute of your time when you are free." He glanced at the housemaid, who ran an open palm across the fold of a newly ironed sheet with what looked like a great deal of pride. Perhaps her first time to iron.

Mrs. Atkinson nodded to the maid. "That will be all, Olive. Mrs. Hill will have luncheon prepared."

The maid curtsied and left. Mrs. Atkinson turned her attention on him, an eyebrow raised in question.

"I found a packet of old letters and gave them to his lordship. The look that came over him had me doubting my decision," he gushed, clearly seeking approval.

"Isn't it a little late to ask what I think?"

With a sheepish shrug, he nodded.

She set the hot iron in a metal plate for safekeeping. "You could do no less. They are his property. Where did you find them?"

"In Lord Rutledge's old room."

"Ah, you are expecting to have it cleaned for Lady Duncamden?"

He nodded. "They tumbled out of a stuck drawer." He ran a fingertip across his brow as if smoothing the furrows. "I could tell looking at his lordship he fell to momentary sorrow."

"We feared Rockmore Hall would never climb out of the crushing loss. You are a good man, Witham. You lead with your heart." Her calm voice was reassuring.

Embarrassment over the flattery, he cleared his throat as he glanced at the highly polished tips of his black shoes.

"Are they from that time, could you tell?" Mrs. Atkinson asked.

"Yes, that's why I doubt my actions. I'm afraid of what they hold."

"Ah, well, that might change things a wee bit. We'll keep an eye on his lordship, then."

Witham nodded. "That I'll do. He did mention his intention to set them aside for a while."

A loud bang, followed by a screech, came from the direction of the kitchen. Witham stepped aside to allow Mrs. Atkinson's quick strut toward the upset.

☙❧

As Darnley reached for his quill, his gaze caught the wooden cask Witham left on his desktop. His heart beat fast and he could no longer finish the letter to his cohort in Dublin. The quill returned to the inkwell, he reached for the box with an unsteady hand, curiosity getting the best of him.

Passing the box under his nose, he breathed deeply, hoping for the scent of his son but found only the musk of old wood. His fingers slid over the surface as if touching his small son's cheek. Remembering their years together, he turned his head toward the giant hawthorn outside the leaded windows and the rolling hills beyond. The tree would bud soon. His son always delighted in the pink blossoms against the blue sky.

With the reservoir of untold memories in his lap, he resigned himself to the inevitable and flipped the lid to reveal a small stack of history. What news did these letters hold? What earth-shattering, heart-wrenching information would they reveal? Of a certainty, his son would not be returned to him. That, more than anything else in the world, was what he wanted.

S keptical as he was of the heartrending lore in the old letters, Darnley read them all but needn't have gone beyond the third. The nugget, the sole reason at this moment his carriage swayed over the ribbon of well-worn road, was the name *Mairéad*.

White stockings flying, the four matching blacks trotted toward the convent of the Sacred Heart of Jesus. Darnley's heart quickened at the possibility of what lay ahead.

A handful of nuns lived in the restored fortress. Their Christian works aided the poor in the bleak months of winter and early spring before crops were harvested. Under English rule, Catholic nuns could keep their convent, and the Church of Ireland allowed them to service the poor, providing they did not try to persuade conversion. It was a far more lenient application of the law than in the previous two centuries, when practicing Catholicism was punishable by death.

Darnley rested his arm along the top of the bench, tapping the tooled leather with his fingertips. He prided himself on a calm manner, but in this instance, doubt troubled him. Was he a foolish old man to interrogate a nun?

"Only time will tell," he muttered to the velvety cushions of the otherwise empty interior; time and perhaps a great deal of fortitude. He certainly had an abundance of both. After all, wasn't he still alive?

They slowed, and Darnley braced himself for what was about to occur. Outside the window, a stone wall about eight feet high rose up from the sod. Large carved doors built into the castle-like structure were the only opening. He stepped down from the carriage and told Huet, his driver, to stay put as he banged the metal knocker twice.

Several minutes passed before a small, carved portal opened. A black-veiled nun, white wimple circling her long, thin face, said, "Good morning, sir. What may I do for you?"

"I wish to speak with your Mother Abbess."

"She'll need your name and reason for calling."

"Garrett Wallington of Rockford Hall, and my business is for Mother Abbess's ears only."

She seemed unaware of the title he would carry, attesting to her unworldliness.

She answered, "You will have to wait there." Her gaze swept the path upon which he stood, lingering a moment on the door of his carriage where the Darnley crest was embedded. As if she was caught eavesdropping, she abruptly closed the small portal.

With no alternative, he did just that. His glance slid to the high wall extending from both sides of the entrance. The fortress was part of an old Norman stronghold, a fact he knew because Rockmore Hall's western boundary abutted this property.

Darnley clasped his hands behind his back and strode a short distance alongside the wall, kicking up a stone here and there. He never paid attention to this convent, tucked as it was between two hills on a rocky patch. The top floors long-since rotted away, and at some point, a roof was built over the ground floor rooms.

He was a foolish old man to come here. With nothing more to go on than a letter sent to his long-dead son, he was in search of anything that might link him to the secrets of his son's life. If the letter led to discovery of any sort, he would be grateful for

England's laxity in enforcing the penal laws against Roman Catholics.

County Waterford was unusual, in that it escaped grueling religious antagonism. He knew that the Catholics expected immediate emancipation about ten years ago with the promises of British and Irish ministers ringing in their heads. Instead William Pitt, *the younger,* suddenly and shamefully broke his word and continued to enforce restrictions on the papists.

At the sound of footsteps tapping on cobblestones, he turned back to the large wooden doors. The heavy mahogany creaked open, and the nun who peered through the peep door bade him enter. "I will take you to Mother Abbess, my lord."

She gave a respectful bow, closed the door behind him, and led the way. Their steps echoed on the slate of the hallway. Mother Abbess must have alerted the little nun to his title.

They came to a sparsely furnished room. The convent's superior turned from the window to greet him. "Lord Darnley." She walked over to a group of four chairs with cushions and extended her hand, indicating that he should choose one.

Her tunic was black, as was her veil, relieved in its severity by a white scapular and wimple covering her shoulders and framing her face. Green eyes sparkled with interest. After taking a seat, she folded her hands neatly in her lap and said, "Sister Catherine is bringing us tea. In the meantime, my lord, what brings you to our modest convent?"

He attempted to relax against the back of the cushion, his hands falling on the curvature of the chair's arms. He was about to ask what was perhaps one of the single most important questions of his life and was baffled how to phrase it.

He met her questioning gaze. "Have you...some years ago—" Clearing his throat, he continued. "Was there an infant left on your doorstep?" He let out a breath, his fingers tapping the hand-carved ends of the armrest.

Sister Catherine's entrance almost masked the gasp that

escaped the abbess. The cups rattled as the nun set the serving pieces on a table between the chairs.

Mother Abbess's voice was crisp with the nun. "I'll manage." She turned to him. "Cream, sugar?"

"Both, please."

As the door to the office closed behind the retreating nun, and his heart rate calmed, his apprehension about the absurdity of his question faded. He reached for the cup and saucer she held out.

Mother Abbess sipped, then set her cup down. "It is the policy of our order to protect the identity of our community members. I am simply not allowed to answer your question."

Darnley set his tea on the tray with a great deal of resolution. "I have reason to believe an infant, a girl child, was left on your doorstep in the late autumn of 1799. Mairéad."

Though he spoke Gaelic only sporadically, he knew the correct pronunciation was Mow rae, with the long sound of A at the end. He pronounced it to himself a dozen times on the ride to the convent.

Her hands pressed tightly together, and the play of emotion on her stern features convinced him she knew of such a child. He added, "My information is that a note accompanied the basket in which she was swathed. It read that she was not meant for vows."

The abbess was clearly hiding something. Was the lass here? Had she taken the oath? What was he to do with a child who was a nun? He was Protestant and wondered if one could void Catholic religious rites. Would it be a crime against Christianity to do so?

"You need be forthcoming, Mother Abbess. I have no wish to cause a scene, but if this young woman is under your roof, I intend meeting her."

Casting a nervous glance about her office as if she looked for an answer on the walls and shelves, she said, "You are a man of power, my lord. You come to my convent, demanding something of me that will break my heart." Barely whispering now, she added, "I feared this day would come. Now that it has, I hardly know how to cope."

Darnley stood. Her declaration eased the concern that the colleen wasn't on the premises, yet caused him remorse, for doing what he intended would upend the lass' life forever and obviously break this religious woman's heart. Nevertheless, now that he knew, there was no turning back.

"Show her to me." He turned away from her to the garden area that roused from winter with green sprouts poking through the earth.

Her voice, thick with fear, curled across the room to him. "Who is she to you?"

He glowered over his shoulder at her but could not give her an answer.

She straightened her back and came off the chair, almost as if ready to do battle. "How did you come by the knowledge she is here?"

A tic near her mouth revealed her anxiety, and he returned his attention to the garden. A high wall at the entrance made of rough stone wound its way for as far as the eye could see. Several arched passageways relieved the wall of its prison-like feel.

The whole of it, getting his hopes up, the possibilities he allowed himself frustrated him to the core, and he barked at the nun, "Letters that wasted away in a box all these years. Until yesterday, I had no idea she existed."

"You are here out of curiosity." Accusation and condemnation were crisp in her voice. "Is this an experiment? Checking her worth for your lofty consideration?"

He spun back to her. "Egad, I'm not inhuman. I've lost three children. Two in the 1783 epidemic and one as an adult. Certainly, I have questions and a great interest. Her name appeared in a letter to my son dated seventeen years ago. I intend to find out why."

Mother Abbess struggled to regain composure. Her hand went to her scapular, and she fell back a step, shock and fear again registering on her features. "You must admit her name is fairly common, my lord. She knows nothing of her parentage and dresses as a postulant. Our way of life is all she knows. She was baptized Roman Catholic before she was left with us."

To his own ears, his reasoning held as many holes as a sieve. However, her continued reluctance irritated him. "I have no doubt she was baptized, and I do not care a fiddle-dee-dee about her clothing. What I desire at this moment is to look upon her. Meet her. Talk to her. I hadn't presumed it would be a hindrance to her well-being to do so."

He had begun all wrong with this woman. He hoped he would not regret his impetuosity.

She pulled on the bell cord hanging on the wall behind her desk. The convent was quiet. The ring came from somewhere far off in the nether regions of the old castle. A look of sorrow darkened her light eyes. Of course, there would be a deep emotional connection existing between this woman and Mairéad.

A nun knocked, and Mother Abbess shifted her attention to the slight, elder woman. "Is Mairéad at lessons?"

"She is painting."

"That will be all." The Abbess's chin rose, and she folded her hands within the sleeves of her tunic. "I'll take you to her."

Locking gazes with the nun, he said, "I want to be clear that the lass is not to be told why I am here. That is privileged information for you alone."

"You can be sure I will not reveal your reason. As, even I am not sure what it is." Her voice held sorrow that mingled with the slight click of rosary beads dangling from her waist.

He deserved the caustic remark. His actions mocked the demeanor of a gentleman. "I hope you can accept my apology, Mother Abbess. I am not usually so gruff. The letter was found yesterday, and my desire was to arrive last evening."

"I am grateful you tempered your enthusiasm."

He chuckled. "You are kind. The possibility that this young woman could be a part of my family overwhelmed me."

She looked straight ahead, chin up, nothing of modesty in her manner as she said, "I see nothing of her in you. Nothing a'tall. You are wasting both our day with this folly."

They passed through a pointed stone archway covered in ivy, along a well-worn path to another building. A loggia on the south side of the ancient structure led them through a small courtyard to a door on the other side.

The Abbess pulled the latch, and they entered a room with two small windows. Easels with drawings clamped to the surface showed various stages of development, while a strong smell of turpentine rent the air. Walls lined with shelving were weighted with jars of various colors, brushes, writing tools, a box of sponges, and books.

Mother Abbess sent him a look of warning as she nodded for him to follow. "Mairéad, I've brought someone who is interested in your work."

A veiled head rose above the worktable as the nun drew the lass's attention from her work. Lovely delicate features, dark eyebrows above almond-shaped green eyes, and a ready smile greeted him without pretense.

Immediately entranced, he stepped forward. "You are an illuminator?"

The nun introduced them. "Lord Darnley allow me to present Mairéad. Though young, she has taken to the art skillfully."

Setting her pen down, the lass slipped off a stool to stand next to her easel and gave him a slight curtsy in greeting. She was not much over five feet tall, he guessed. "Do you have work for me, my lord?"

Her cultured articulation in the Queen's English, not quirky Irish, was quite acceptable to him, nothing like the rigid demeanor of her superior.

"Ah …. perhaps. I am thinking a biography I wrote could do with enhancement." He forced his eyes from her to glance at the work in progress. "Will you show me your present work?"

Mother Abbess interjected, "She is setting the lead, readying it to receive the pigment." Her arm spread outward over the two rows of easels. "These are examples of the various stages of completion."

He looked back at Mairéad. "Where did you learn this art?" Though he cared little about who might have taught her, this young woman enchanted him with her feminine features, full pink lips, and winged brows over those serious, focused eyes. In her humble serenity, he sensed intelligence, curiosity, and vitality fluttering beneath the surface of her modesty, as if his blood recognized her.

Void of breath, overwhelmed with the discovery, he called himself a fool. Reaching back into his dead son's life caused the old vulnerability to surface. As Mother Abbess so cryptically pointed out, she looked nothing like him. The lass' speech was refined, reflecting this convent community of learned women.

She pushed the veil from her shoulder with an ink-stained hand. "Sister Boniface taught me. I am still learning. It takes years and years. Did you bring your biography with you?"

Her questioning prompted him. "No. I ... I wanted to meet you, judge your work." His gaze shifted to the nun locking him with a disdainful glare. He reminded himself that he did not have to answer to her.

Mairéad asked, "Do you wish to begin chapters? Or enhance your heraldry?" She moved toward another easel. "This is going to be a family crest that will illustrate a book about the coat of arms for a lord who lives far away." She turned to her superior. "Dublin, isn't it?"

He was surprised she did not know how far Dublin was from the convent. How could one not know that? "Have you not been to Dublin?" he asked.

"No, my lord."

"Waterford?" Surely, she'd been there. From the convent it was little more than an hour's ride to Rockmore, and Waterford was barely beyond that to the east.

Pursing full pink lips, she shook her head.

Turning back to Mother Abbess, he asked, "Has she been outside these walls?"

The nun crossed her arms, shoved her hands into her sleeves of black wool. She surely wanted this to be over and him gone. Her eyes momentarily closed, and she slowly shook her veiled head.

What *did* he want? Why exactly was he here? Mairéad was merely a name in a letter written to Rutledge before he died.

Never in his life had he done anything quite so harebrained. Seeing this child close enough to touch, he found himself longing for a deeper understanding of her whys and wherefores. She was not just a name on a piece of old parchment—she was as real as he, though locked away in this nunnery.

A sense of foolishness washed over him. "Why have you not left this convent?" He caught himself in the nick of time, grateful he'd not said drafty tomb filled with dried-up women.

She leaned on the stool next to her easel. "All I want, and need is here, within the walls of the Sacred Heart of Jesus." Her ink-stained hand waved out over the easels.

Of all answers, he did not expect solitude, a lifeless life. There was a huge world to embrace. He had the means to show her that world. His world.

He touched the page she was currently working on, trying to come to grips with a decision that was forming, and suddenly blurted, "I am hiring you to work on my biography."

Her lovely features widened with a smile of delight. "That is most kind." Her gaze shifted to Mother Abbess, and back to him.

"I intend that you live at Rockmore Hall as you work on the manuscript." Lacking forethought, he shocked himself almost as much as he did her—if he rightly understood the look that transformed her features into incredulity.

Her cheeks flushed. "How can this be?" Glaring at her superior, she demanded, "I am to take my first vows this autumn. You promised."

The older woman, lips in a thin line, arms withdrawn from the sleeves, hands shaking, seethed, "You intrude on our lives with your bombast. The girl has no preparation for such a move, no desire to embrace what you offer."

Mairéad quickly moved behind Mother Abbess, as if to hide from him, eyes wide with fear and something else. A flicker of defiance?

He would not tolerate defeat. It was time these two learned that his will prevailed over a nun and a young convent lass. "This is for your own good, child. In time, you will learn the why of it. For now, you will be able to carry on as you do here. Paint and illuminate. Your life will not change so much at Rockmore Hall."

This spit of a young woman surprised him again when she left the nun's side and stood in front of him. Anger lit a fire in her black-rimmed emerald eyes. "I will not leave the convent to satisfy a whim of yours."

While the abbess' pinched features glowed prideful with the lass' defiance, he seized the moment with an authoritative bark. "Will you force me to use my power to make this happen?"

Capitulation did not come easy to Mother Abbess. She was used to caring for many nuns, managing this convent. He assumed the child meant a great deal. He gave her a moment to collect herself.

Shock and fear shone in her eyes, followed by a reluctant acceptance that tugged at his heartstrings. She slid her arm around the slim shoulders, drawing her toward the windows, murmuring to her, running a fingertip across her cheek, swiping at a tear. The gray veil shook in denial. Finally, the lass spun from Mother Abbess and stomped her foot. Her refusal turned to anger, and a part of him respected her defiance, nearly making him regret his actions. Nearly.

If this religious woman ignored his wishes, he'd be bloody damned. Invigorated by his desire to show the lass a world she was missing, he pushed forward with modified tone. "My manuscript is rather large. It will be a better use of your time to live at Rockmore Hall until it is finished. You will be comfortable and well cared for, Mairéad."

There, he said her name for the first time since meeting her, allowing the long A sound to linger in the charged air.

Both women stared at him as if he had two heads, their combined scorn radically obvious. He'd had enough. "Pack your personal items. I'll send Huet for your brushes and whatnot before the end of the week."

The Abbess's hand wavered in the air as if she might pull the lass behind her.

Mairéad's watery grimace tugged at him. Her chin rose, and with a shaky voice she promised the abbess, "I'll work fast. It won't be long before I'm back where I belong."

❦

Huddled in a corner of the opulent carriage, Mairéad grasped the leather strap. Clinging for security lest the swaying carriage caused her to slide to the floor. Something inside twisted with anxiety, and her mind raced with fear of the unknown. She held to her superior's last words: "Pray to the Blessed Mother for comfort and guidance." They promised to write one another.

With her attention fixed on Lord Darnley's polished boots, it occurred to Mairéad that she'd never been alone in the presence of a man before. He separated her from the dearest Mother Abbess, her mother in all but reality. At least, he hadn't forbidden they write.

Her gaze slowly lifted from his boots to the large hands clasped at his knees. She was loath to look him in the eye. A gold ring with scrolls and a blue stone glistened on his left hand. She turned to the window and settled her gaze on the rolling hills shot with rugged sandstone crags, grazing sheep, and wispy clouds floating on the gentle breeze.

Sister Catherine sobbed her good-bye. Sister Helen hugged her close and slipped two ginger cookies, fresh baked and wrapped in a cloth, into her hand. There was no time to say good-bye to the others.

Mairéad had never ridden in a carriage before. The horses' pounding hooves on the earth raced like the beat of her heart. Sensing that her companion drew one arm off his leg and placed it atop the bench, she did not look up, afraid what she might see in his eyes. She believed the heart of a person showed in their eyes. What might she find in his? He intended she practice her art, yet it gave her little satisfaction. At least she would earn much needed income for the convent.

Curiosity finally gave her the courage to peek at him. Were his almighty eyes shut? *Was he napping then?* Irate that he could be so cavalier about whisking her from the convent, she withdrew her hand from the strap and clapped. Twice. Sharply.

His eyes popped wide, and he cleared his throat as a slow smile spread across his features. "Did I nod off?"

"What manner of person causes aching upheaval in the lives of others such as you have done?" Her hand gripped the strap again, as if it were a lifeline. His smile turned to a gaping grin. How dare he amuse himself at her confusion, her displacement? "You are a mean sort to take me from my family. It is expected that you bring your manuscript to the convent. Have you no feelings that you have set me adrift?"

He shifted in his seat. "Ah, you do have spirit. Not a worrisome sort who cries and wails at life's inopportune changes."

"You name this abduction inopportune? Do all men of your position have such light consideration of others?"

The grin vanished. His bushy gray brows narrowed, and his hands again gripped his knees, though his tone was conciliatory. "I hope you choose to believe me, Miss Mairéad. I, too, am perplexed at my actions. From the moment I set eyes on you, I wanted to protect you, give you shelter, care for you. To share what I have with you, as an uncle would a niece, a loved one, certainly. I can tell you no more than that. How you decide to make yourself comfortable at Rockmore Hall is your choice. All will be at your disposal, and it will be yours from this moment on. I hope you come to accept the wisdom of my decision."

Her heart thumped. She took a deep breath and looked straight into his gray eyes, admitted to a kindness and concluded he was not a fabricator. What might he feel tomorrow? She did not know, but sensed he revealed what was in his heart today. What she said, however, was quite different.

"One simply does not tear another from loved ones on a whim. Furthermore, I will illuminate for you as payment for my keep. How you intend paying for the actual work will be between you and Mother Abbess. When I am finished, you will return me to the convent. Do we have an agreement?"

His eyes sparkled when he smiled. "Indeed, Miss Margaret, I accept."

Lifting her chin, she remarked. "I prefer the Irish."

"Then let it be so, Miss Mairéad."

"I have never been addressed as Miss."

"You will be while you are in my employ."

She reached across the aisle and accepted his extended hand. His chuckle warmed the air.

I mbued with a dash of independence, Mairéad felt comforted. Though biding her time until of age to take vows, this lordly man was not going to disrupt her future. The more quickly she worked on his manuscript, the sooner she could return to where she belonged.

Trepidation turned to wonderment as the carriage passed beneath a leafy arbor of trees, a great tunnel the color of limes.

"If you lean toward your left, you will catch a glimpse of the Hall." Darnley's low voice charged with pride.

Words failed her as Rockmore Hall came into view. Four floors high with wings branching off each side of the middle part. Fronting the hall was a green park with a lough dotted by—she was sure, they were swans, two sets of swans. She'd seen pictures.

In the middle of the rippling water, a fountain spurted into the sky. Tearing her gaze from the glorious scene, she met his stare. He clearly expected her to say something.

She blustered past her amazement. "I'll get lost. I will not see you for days and days. Perhaps that is what you wish."

"I'll have Mrs. Atkinson appoint a maid for you."

She protested, "I would not know what to do with a maid. She will be grateful for the day I return to the convent. Of that, you can be sure." None too soon, she thought.

Darnley's fingers thrummed on the bench, as if he fell to deep contemplation. Well, then, so be it. She straightened, squaring her shoulders. Her gaze shifted to the passing landscape. He would learn quickly enough how unpleasant she could be. Had not Mother Abbess's litany of wrongdoing reminded her often enough?

Rockmore Hall loomed up as if a giant as they emerged from the tunnel of sun-dappled lime. Stately, glistening in the waning light, windows reflecting the golden sunset, it overwhelmed.

She gulped down the knot in her throat as the four blacks were reined to a stop in front of the hall. Six people, wearing black, with pristine white blouses and shirts—the same colors as convent garb —lined up on the steps.

"The staff of Rockmore are welcoming you," he answered her unspoken question. "It's the custom."

He must have intended bringing her back, then.

When the carriage door swung open and a step was put in place, she shoved down her discomfort at being in this strange place. Lord Darnley descended first, nodding at a man he called Witham. Turning back, he held out his hand for her.

Promising herself to show some of her superior's dignity, she brushed the veil ends off her shoulders. Firmly clasping his hand, he became the only familiarity amidst this vast oasis of rare beauty. She clung to him.

Her blood thrummed as he introduced the man, Witham, as the butler who gave her a nod of welcome.

As Mairéad had not released Lord Darnley's hand, she kept in step as each person's name was announced. Mrs. Atkinson, the housekeeper, Tench, Lord Darnley's valet, Mrs. Hill, the cook, Rodney, the under butler, and Ryan, a lady's maid. Each gave a small curtsy or a slight bow, as if she were someone of importance. Shocked by the notion, she involuntarily jerked her hand from Lord Darnley's.

He reacted with raised brows, followed by a quick smile. "Are you ready to come inside your new domicile?"

She wanted to remind him that these arrangements were temporary. Rockmore Hall was *not* hers. However, prudence stilled her tongue. This was a conversation needing privacy, and best not shared with the stiff, black line of staff.

As if the approach to Rockmore Hall and meeting his household had not twisted her insides into a knot, the interior of the hall certainly did. It glistened. There was no other word. Pure and simple, it glistened. Like her illuminations, or the way she always imagined heaven would look, shining, bright, and clean. However, she doubted heaven had a stairway of marble and gold with a carpeted runner of reds, blues, and cream that wandered upward and off to the left and right.

Lord Darnley glanced at the housekeeper, who kept pace behind them, "We will take tea in the library." Then he asked, "Has the rose room been prepared for Miss Mairéad's arrival?"

"As you requested, my lord." Mrs. Atkinson smiled at her. "I think you will be quite comfortable. Allow me to offer my personal welcome to Rockmore Hall, Miss Mairéad." Her shoes softly tapped on the marble floor as she left to prepare tea.

Lord Darnley led the way to his library. The room must be where he conducted the daily business of managing his estate. Far grander than Mother Abbess's library, the walls were lined with several hundred books and a ladder that scaled one of the walls.

Overwhelmed with the possibility of a great opportunity, she blurted, "Until I return to the convent, will you allow me access to your reading room?"

He waved her to a chair, as he sat in its companion, a table between them. "You may come into this room at any time and peruse. Most young women are not of a mind. However, with what little I realize about you, your interest doesn't surprise me." He shifted in the chair, crossing his legs. "Mother Abbess mentioned your enthusiasm for learning."

Surprised that her superior would mention this, she smiled inwardly, comforted by Mother Abbess' compliment.

He had more to say regarding Mother Abbess's advice. "She said you don't need to be challenged, that you rise in the morning with a great deal of enthusiasm for what lies ahead."

Her superior had not seen fit to say anything of the sort to her, ever. What compelled her to say such to this man? Restless, Mairéad's attention turned to a large bank of windows framing a lovely hawthorn tree on a small rise. Butterflies flitted, and a blue jay sang from somewhere within the pink flowering clusters.

Darnley shifted in his chair again, and Mairéad turned from the pastoral scene. This room, his manner, the servants, her gray tunic and veil, all converged in her brain like a storm of confusion. She blurted, "Why did you really bring me here?"

Darnley drew in a breath. It appeared she was not going to let go of the notion that he held an ulterior motive. Mother Abbess warned of her tenacity. Truth be told, his actions were surprising. Right now, he intended to understand her. He sensed she belonged more to this life than in a convent.

"I am not sure. When you looked up from your easel, I was reminded of a time long ago. I could not let go of it. A lovely time, when innocence and uncomplicated lives made the days simpler. Then you spoke, and your voice molded that past into a sharp image."

He did not intend to reveal the letter to her. He might never do so. After all, other than the mention of her name and the convent, it gave no indication of her importance. As far as he was concerned, she was naught but a foundling with a talent for illumination.

"Like a ghostly apparition?" Her tone changed from confrontational to eager, surprising him, and he chuckled.

24

"I don't believe in fairies and leprechauns. However, something similar, I suppose. Do you believe in them?"

She fussed with a pleat in her skirt. "Not really, but I have read our Irish lore." She glanced out the window behind him. "That hawthorn has tales associated with it. Do you have a broken heart?"

What an upstart question. She was full of surprises. "Me? Now, what would you know of broken hearts, young as you are?"

She appeared surprised by his ignorance. "It is ancient lore that the hawthorn heals broken hearts, and I can see that someone who lives here knows this. When the turf was cut, a wide swath was left tall so as not to offend the little ones."

He harrumphed. "In what manner does the hawthorn accomplish such mending?"

The length of Mairéad's veil slid off her shoulder when she shrugged. A glimmer of the woman she was to become flashed at him. She took obvious pleasure in informing him of the hawthorn's benefits. In the moment, he grasped a childlike awe, though clothed in convent garb, almost as if she played at being a grownup.

"The hawthorn is an emblem of hope. Maybe, in that regard, if one hopes, one can heal." She was direct—uncomfortably so.

He asked, "Are you suggesting I have a broken heart?"

"Far be it for me to suggest such a thing, my lord. I do not know you at all. I would not attempt to speculate about your state of mind or heart."

Mrs. Atkinson arrived with the tea tray. Setting it on the table, Lord Darnley raised an eyebrow at her. "Have you poured before?"

"No, my lord."

"Would you like Mrs. Atkinson to show you?"

She glanced at the housekeeper, clearly struggling with curiosity about this new life, despite her intention to return to the convent.

He said, "Why don't you show us, Mrs. Atkinson. I'll pull over a chair for you."

Mairéad's interest in the exchange between Lord Darnley and his housekeeper gave her a bit of insight in the running of the Hall.

Of a sudden, the great clock in the corner chimed six, causing her sudden panic. She stood. "How could I have forgotten Nones? I do not want to miss Vespers, too, my lord. Excuse me, please. If someone will show me, I need to go to my room."

Mrs. Atkinson also stood. "I will show her." She smiled at Lord Darnley. "Excuse us, my lord."

He sipped his tea and nodded. She spoke of prayers. She was a faithful young woman. This was obviously the result of convent life with the nuns. He needed to keep that in mind.

❦

Mairéad followed Mrs. Atkinson up the grand stairs. They turned to the east wing, which meant she would have morning sun. All her life there was one tiny window in her cell high above, where she could see the sky. The view was a privilege, especially in prayer, because the saints were up there amongst the twinkling.

Mrs. Atkinson broke the silence. "We have a lovely little chapel. Would it suit you to use it for your prayers? I can show you tomorrow if you like."

"Would I be interrupting others? I would not like to do that."

"A woman, Miss O'Bannon, uses it from time to time. Just slips in, and then out again. She lives in Hawthorn Village. Every so often I've seen her in the graveyard, too. Beyond that, I know of no others who use the chapel."

They walked halfway down the hall and entered a room facing the back of the estate. It was truly a rose room, decorated with brocade drapes of rose and cream at the windows and matching colors on the bed. A fire crackled in the hearth, its glow accentuating the rose-hued papered walls. Mairéad was immediately drawn to the four windows. Her breath caught, and her fingers caressed the leaded crisscrosses.

A glorious, beautiful world stretched out before her in the fading light of day. She faced the grounds overlooking the back of Rockmore Hall. A huge park spread its emerald grasses to a forest in the west and stables in the east. Beyond the center of the park a small lake surrounded a mound of sod upon which a roofed structure held upright with eight Doric columns proudly invited one to venture forth. A quaint bridge provided access.

The pastoral scene matched a painting on the wall of Lord Darnley's library. Did he, too, paint? The next opportunity she had she would look for a signature.

Mrs. Atkinson came up behind her. "If you look to the left, you'll see the steeple in amongst the treetops."

It was hard to spot in the fading light, but she did see it and knew spending time there would be grand. Her wonder almost overtook her disquiet about the upheaval in her life. She swiped at a tear that dribbled. Uncomfortable, she shied from the housekeeper and turned away from the view. The crackling fire, the rose walls, the draped bed—could she rest her eyes on something simple? Was it going to be possible?

Mrs. Atkinson stood with her hands on the back of a chair positioned before the grate. "Coming here must be the hardest decision of your life."

She snapped, "If it had been my decision, I would not be here."

Mrs. Atkinson pursed her lips just the tiniest bit.

Mairéad said, "I'm sorry to be so plain spoken. Excuse my rudeness."

"It must be terribly hard to consider life beyond what you've known."

Sympathy. She gulped and turned away from the housekeeper. "I'll manage. It is not forever." Her voice lacked conviction, even to her own ears.

Mrs. Atkinson patted the upholstery of the chair. "I don't want to keep you from Vespers. Shall I come back later and help you unpack?"

Mairéad did not turn around. She could not. Her struggle to maintain dignity would be lost. "I have so little. I can manage. Thank you."

"All right, then. Supper is at eight. I'll return for you."

"That won't be necessary. I'm sure I can find the way."

Mrs. Atkinson's skirts rustled as she moved toward the door. "It will be my pleasure, Miss Mairéad."

The door closed with a gentle click.

She glanced at the darkening outside the leaded panes and moved in front of them as if she could embrace them. Her reflection startled her. The veil and tunic of a postulant, her face and hands quite visible. This was the first time she saw her image as others might. It was a pleasant surprise. She supposed she could be mistaken for a nun, although her veil was short and gray, as was her tunic, not the black of the Sacred Heart of Jesus community.

She intended to be consecrated a postulant, but Mother Abbess said she was not ready. Because there was no other clothing at the convent, as she outgrew donated children's wear, it seemed easier to use what was at hand. This autumn, her dream would come true. She would be eighteen in September, old enough to take her first vows.

The splendor of four windows was hard to overcome. She forced herself to look away and bite back tears that threatened. She never cried. She hadn't known how vulnerable to vanity she could be, either.

After evening prayers, she unpacked her belongings, which took up all of one drawer. The fire was welcome as she waited for Mrs. Atkinson. Rockmore Hall was quieter than the convent. The luxury of beautiful woven carpets spread over marble floors and silk draperies at the windows most probably contributed to the hushed atmosphere.

At a light knock, Mairéad jumped and opened the door. Mrs.

Atkinson entered with a vase of lilacs and greenery bringing a most welcome presence.

Setting the floral arrangement on the table in front of the chair, the housekeeper said, "If you are ready, we can be on our way."

As they descended the stairs, Mrs. Atkinson said, "His lordship has requested that I find a room for your painting. On our tour of the hall tomorrow, I will show you two, one that faces east and another that faces west, and you can choose which you might prefer."

Mrs. Atkinson directed her to a parlor decorated with glistening mirrors at each end with large baroque frames. Lord Darnley waited for her with a drink in hand. "Good evening, Miss Mairéad. What can I offer you?"

Mrs. Atkinson excused herself, but not before suggesting to Mairéad that she might like to try a soda water.

Lord Darnley handed her a glass with fizzy water that tickled her nose when she sipped.

Witham announced dinner, and Lord Darnley held out his arm. At the puzzled look on her face, he told her, "A young lady needs to be escorted to the dining room. A gentleman offers his arm where she may rest her hand."

Her eyes widened with the wonder of it all, and she placed her ink-stained hand on his arm, regretting she hadn't scrubbed harder. They walked along the marbled corridor covered in a blue and maize runner. She would need to watch how he ate in case etiquette here was different from the manners at the convent.

Delicious aromas escaped the open doors as they entered the dining room. Candelabra flickered with light, which glistened off water goblets, a remarkable sight. Uniformed footmen pulled out gold cushioned chairs for them.

Lord Darnley lifted his goblet, filled with red wine, and toasted her. "Welcome to my table, Miss Mairéad. May you be so comfortable here that it will be hard for you to leave."

She smiled at the Irish greeting known to her from years in the convent and lifted her glass to join his as a gesture a guest would make.

Throughout the meal of a saddle of venison, fluffy mashed potatoes, sautéed mushrooms with peas, and bread stuffing. Cook also provided a tarty crabapple and sloe jelly to add flavor to the meat.

Mairéad tried not to embarrass herself. To her great relief, eating customs were similar to those in the convent, and she relaxed and enjoyed the meal.

Lord Darnley was inquisitive. "How did you find your room? Adequate, I hope?"

"Far different from what I am used to. The fire is cozy. I did not have such luxury at Sacred Heart."

"Which suggests," Lord Darnley interjected, "your illumination equipment will arrive by week's end. Enough time to have an easel set up. Would you prefer several of them for your process? I noted there were six drawing boards in your workroom." He bit into a forkful of stuffing.

"The process would go quicker if I had at least three easels. It will depend on the amount of work you have for me."

A commotion from the front of the estate echoed down the marble floor into the dining room. Witham strode in, then came to a rigid halt, announcing, "The Right Honorable Countess of Duncamden, your lordship."

At his heels, two little dogs scampered into the room, one white with a black face and the other fully black, like two balls of lamb's wool, only not so tightly curled, and full of energy. They tore one after the other around the table as two footmen scurried to gather the mischievous pets.

A tall, reed-thin woman leaning on a cane entered the room. His lordship stood, and Mairéad followed suit. A footman immediately began to set another place.

Lord Darnley hugged the woman, bussing her on both cheeks, then turned, "May I present Miss Mairéad. My sister Philomena, Countess of Duncamden."

She gave a tiny curtsy and wondered if more was expected. "Pleased to meet you, my lady."

Lady Duncamden patted her bosom, searching for the quizzing glass that hung by a silver chain around her neck, and lifted it to her eye. One magnified, pale blue eye searched Mairéad's length, noting the woolen tunic and veil, and then came to rest on her face.

Lord Darnley said, "Miss Mairéad is a young woman I've taken in to illuminate the biography I've been working on."

The dogs scampered away from the footmen, circling Mairéad's sandals. She wanted to scoop one into her arms, yet the scrutiny from the quizzing glass caused her to stand rigidly.

"Eh, Margaret then?" The countess's eye grew larger as she leaned in.

Mairéad said nothing. His Lordship, however, spoke up, "She prefers Mairéad."

A footman grabbed up the white dog, holding it with both hands. A tiny pink tongue tried to lick his face as the dog wiggled to be set free.

The quizzing glass came close to her face. A long moment passed before the countess tapped her cane on the floor and said, "So be it."

Mairéad breathed slowly, sensing she had passed a test but not at all sure what it was. The black dog jumped at her tunic, clearly wanting her attention. She was reaching down for it when another footman snatched it up, holding it at arm's length rather than chance having his face licked, she supposed.

The countess lowered the quizzing glass. "I'll take my place, and we can get better acquainted over supper." The silver chain of her eye glass sparkled in the candlelight as she waved at one of the footmen. "Take those curs for a walk. I've my fill of their bustling nonsense. Keep them in the kitchen for the rest of the night."

They all took their seats, and the glasses were refilled, all this in a matter of moments. The countess searched the table with her quizzing glass for food that looked palatable, no doubt. "I'll have some peas." She waved her hand at a footman to serve. "A piece of meat, a spoon of potatoes, and a drop of the jelly." With that, she tucked a napkin into the neck of her cream and lace gown and turned her attention to Mairéad.

"What is your age, my dear gel,, and where do you come from?"

Her ladyship's mobcap was extravagant, and Mairéad could hardly take her eyes off the puffed-up top, featuring a lovely blue ribbon woven in and out of lace ruffles at the crown.

In its simplicity, Mrs. Atkinson's cap could not compare. It came down to one's station, much like her own gray tunic and veil and the nun's black. Realizing her ladyship waited for an answer, she stammered, "I admire your head wear, my lady. I am seventeen, and today have come from a convent community."

Totally ignoring Mairéad's compliment, her ladyship turned to her brother, thin gray brows rose over pointed features. "What is this convent? Which one?"

Lord Darnley said, "It is Roman Catholic. The Sacred Heart of Jesus, toward Portlaw along the Suir. I believe it was something of a castle and fell to ruination until a number of years ago when it was rebuilt to make it fit to occupy."

Those thin brows knitted, and the countess turned the looking glass back to Mairéad. She had lost all interest in eating. "You are a nun? Quite young to be, aren't you? Isn't there a period of grace before taking final vows or something or other?"

"I am not a sister of the community."

"You wear the garb of such. Why not?"

Mairéad looked to Lord Darnley. He winked at her and took a sip of wine. He was not going to help her explain anything to his nosy sister. Obviously, advanced age gave her allowance for rudeness.

"Well, Margaret, what have you to say?"

Whatever should she say, under the circumstances. Most likely the truth. "Mother Abbess would not agree to my taking vows. She said I was too young to make the decision. This fall I will be of age and will take my novitiate vow. The reason I am dressed as a postulant is that I've lived at the convent, and there is no such thing as extra anything, including clothing. I wear what is available. Makes me fit in, almost like the other sisters."

Her pale blue eye, magnified hugely by the glass, glared from across the table. "You are a foundling," she said, almost as if the magnification unearthed the truth. "Is that why you do not have a surname? Why, your hair is not cut?"

Mairéad assumed she had only one parent, the one who left her on the step. There would not be a surname for her. Mother Abbess felt certain she was conceived outside wedlock. She lived with women who had only one name, so it hadn't occurred to her that she needed a surname. As for her hair, Mother Abbess would not allow her to cut it. That was part of the ceremony, a rite of passage, when taking vows. None of this, however, was something she wished to discuss. Awash in shock and humiliation at the affront, Mairéad felt heat flush her skin.

It was a good thing Lord Darnley's goblet was pewter, because he set it down rather hard. "Philly leave her alone. She is not hours out of the place. Let her catch her breath before you badger her about this and that. Besides, your supper is getting cold. It won't even be fit for your bitches."

The countess gave her brother a scathing glance. Then turned her attention to Mairéad. "I am a fussy old woman, my dear. Now that I know somewhat of your circumstance, I will help you. Nothing like a purpose in life to make one want to get up in the morning. You will be my purpose, Margaret. We'll begin with fittings for a wardrobe." With that, she picked up her fork and knife and began cutting the turkey skin away from the white meat.

Grateful for the lapse in questioning, Mairéad cut into her portion of turkey.

When Lady Duncamden finished peeling skin off the meat, her gaze landed on her. The turkey speared with a fork, she asked, "What kind of painting do you do, my dear? Do you specialize?"

"I illuminate manuscripts, my lady. It is a means to earn money for our convent."

Clearly surprised, her ladyship set her fork down and took up her goblet. "How enterprising of you."

Lord Darnley seemed a touch agitated. "Her work is impeccable."

"Well, I, for one, marvel at her ingenuity." She smiled at Mairéad before taking a sip.

Mairéad couldn't guess what part of the conversation caused Lord Darnley to be upset. A bit grieved that she may be the source of his discomfort, the distinct sound of barking rolled into the dining room. It crossed her mind that she might play with the puppies this evening.

Lord Darnley said, "Philly's estate, Duncamden, is west of County Waterford, not too far from Lismore and along the banks of River Blackwater. I rather think she got a late start considering the hour of her arrival."

He knew the Georgian behemoth filled with family treasurers from seafaring adventures was drafty and rather lonely. Though Lismore was a small market town, Philomena always considered it romantically situated, lying as it did on the southern bank of the River Blackwater. The fine stone bridge, erected by the late Duke of Devonshire, was a gateway to more than three hundred estates nestled into the cheerful, thriving hills.

Glancing at his sister, he sensed her mind was a whirlwind of activity about the coming days. Which would now include dressing his young artist in something other than nun's garb. Philly enjoyed a good, long visit at Rockmore from time to time. Her journey began at the east end of County Waterford. The route gave her plenty of scenery to enjoy. She caught glimpses here and there of the Celtic Sea, winking its shimmering waves as she rambled toward his estate. He knew all this because she would invariably retell him of her journey in the days to come. It was somewhat of a ritual between them.

Not able to sleep, Mairéad tossed and turned, her mind abuzz with all that happened that day. It hardly seemed possible that just last night she'd crept into her little cot. She snuggled under far different linens this night and didn't miss her woolen blanket that barely warded off the chill seeping into her room.

Last night she fell asleep dreaming of what color to paint the robe of a mighty lord sitting in the curve of the letter G. The manuscript was Lord Groversham's admirable account of his father's military service.

She fussed about tomorrow, sensing that it would present itself with plenty of problems. For one, she had no desire to change the way she dressed. It would be useless. She was not staying at Rockmore Hall beyond her birthday, the twenty-first of September. Since this was mid-April, she had six months to accomplish her work. It was not a lifetime.

After Lady Duncamden declared that she would change her mode of dress, Mairéad decided she needed to discuss the matter with Lord Darnley. The elder woman, imbued with vim and vigor, clearly employed a mind of her own. In some ways, she reminded Mairéad of the elder nuns, Sisters Constance and Davideena. Those two put their noses into anything that was not their business. She noticed Mother Abbess rolling her eyes a time or two at their meddling.

What was she to do about Lord Darnley's sister, who meant well, but clearly wanted to be involved where it was unnecessary? It was also obvious she must endure the English of her name rather than the Gaelic. Apparently, thoughtlessness was a reward of age.

Perhaps part of her problem was the pillow on her bed. At the convent, her pillow was thin. This pillow was permanently over fluffed. Sleeping on it would put a kink in her neck. She tossed it to the other side of the bed, which was also a problem. The bed was big enough for three, mayhap four people. Her cot was a perfect fit. From her toes to the top of her head, she fit perfectly on the mattress pad. Not so in this monstrosity.

Giving up, Mairéad threw the covers back and slipped from the bed, using the step to get to the floor. A shaft of moonlight cut through a small gap in the drapes. Pulling them open, she stepped inside the drapes in front of the windows. A half-moon shadowed the breathtaking view. A small herd of deer, one with antlers, grazed near the lough. A foggy mist crept along the grass. The steeple on the little church caught a shimmer of moonlight.

Overwhelmed with her plight and the sight of such loveliness, she whispered, "Dear Mother of God, guide me. Help me make the proper choices while I am in this place. Keep me near to your heart. My faith is strong, but I have never been in such circumstance. And, please love me despite my failings."

Comforted, she watched the deer graze and gambol near the lough, frivolous like the puppies. She returned to the bed and the heavy blankets that would keep her warm. Reaching for the pillow, she drew it close but hugged it rather than put it beneath her head.

The next morning, Mairéad woke as Mrs. Atkinson entered the room. Another woman, who wore a small white cap and apron and carried a tray, accompanied her.

"Good morning to you, Miss Mairéad. I've brought a lady's maid, Ryan, to assist you, and a tray of hot chocolate and wafers."

Mairéad pushed herself upright, hair tangled about her

shoulders and arms. She was regretting the laziness of not braiding her nearly waist-length hair. Peeking through the heavy strands of dark auburn her nose tweaked with a fragrance she did not recognize.

Ryan, a chamber maid perhaps ten years older than she, stood near the bed, ready to assist. "Good morning, miss."

She pushed the hair off her face. "Good morning to you and Mrs. Atkinson."

The housekeeper crossed the room after scattering coals on the fire. "How did you sleep?"

"It took a while to get used to the bed." Realizing she still hugged the pillow; she punched a fist into the softness. "And this fluffy monster took a bit of patience. As you can see, I eventually settled." Ryan drew the covers back, freeing Mairéad's legs. More aware of the exotic scent, she said, "Something smells delicious."

"Hot chocolate. Is it new to you?" Mrs. Atkinson handed her a shawl.

Her eyes opened with wonder, and she nodded as the maid wrapped the shawl about her. She padded across the carpet toward the kindled fire and the tray.

"How did you begin your day in the convent?"

"Prayer, tea, strong, biscuits and on Sundays, jam."

"Well, you may never go back to tea again." Mrs. Atkinson motioned for her to sit. "Enjoy your chocolate. Ryan will straighten things and put out clothing for the day."

Mairéad adjusted the shawl and sat in the chair, tucking her feet up under her. The lady's maid opened a large storage unit with two doors, then closed it and shrugged her shoulders at Mrs. Atkinson.

Mairéad held the cup of chocolate in both hands, savoring the fragrance and the misty heat. "Hmm. Lovely." She gestured toward the dresser with her pinkie finger. "My clothes are in the second drawer."

The housekeeper mentioned, "His lordship has assigned Ryan

to help you in the mornings with your clothing and your hair. She will also assist you in the evenings when you're ready for bed."

"I am capable of dressing without assistance."

Without saying a word, Mrs. Atkinson's gaze swept over her hair.

She licked the delicious chocolate off her upper lip. "I'm not usually so unkempt."

The fragrant cup was half-empty. She held it to her lips, taking in another long, satisfying sniff. "This is wonderful. Thank you."

The two women stood before her, and it suddenly dawned on her she'd interrupted the routine of their morning. "I am unused to assistance of any kind." Her disdainful remark in the carriage haunted her thoughts. She needed forgiveness for her caustic tongue.

"I know." The housekeeper's benevolent smile meant she understood the strange situation in which Lord Darnley placed her. The woman added, "The contradiction of your current arrangements, however temporary, compared to the stringent life you have led, would appear overwhelming."

Setting the empty cup on the tray, Mairéad said, "I intend to do my best and quickly complete Lord Darnley's manuscripts. Then I must return to the convent. It is clearly where I belong." Her gaze drifted to the tray. "Though there are some things I will dearly yearn for."

She glanced at Ryan. "It would be nice to have help with my hair. I struggle with the tangles." She threaded her fingers through the heavy auburn mass hanging past her shoulders. "I can't believe I forgot to braid it last eve. All this will be shorn when I return to the convent."

Mrs. Atkinson sent a sharp glance her way with a tiny shake of her head as if she wanted to say something. Ryan busied herself pouring hot water from a pitcher in a wash bowl.

Reaching for the door latch, the housekeeper said, "Well, then. I will let the two of you acquaint. Breakfast is in the dining room.

After you've eaten, I will show you about the hall. And, I'm quite sure you're anxious to visit the chapel."

"You are kind, Mrs. Atkinson. I hope His lordship knows how fortunate he is."

A pink flush spread across the housekeeper's cheeks. "His lordship is of generous disposition. I've been fortunate with my employment at Rockmore." A click of the door latch and she was on her way to other duties.

Even with Ryan tending to her thick hair, it took longer than usual to untangle. The maid drew the length back, fastening it with pins, so she could wear the veil.

When she was not feeling rushed, Mairéad usually gathered the length in a bun at her nape. In winter, she left it to hang down her back. It warmed her as she bent over an easel. Ryan's pampering made her feel special, reminding her of when she was little and fussed over by the sister charged with her care.

Ryan offered to show her the way to the dining room, but Mairéad intended to retrace her steps of last eve on her own. She strode the corridor lined with benches and tables laden with urns of fragrant flowers. Two flights later she arrived on the main floor.

As it turned out, the aroma of breakfast helped her find the dining room. A mirror framed in gold above a long, dark mahogany cabinet sparkled with flickering candelabra. A green and white liveried footman stood against the wall ready to assist. Gold buttons on his sleeves winked with light as he lifted each covered dish. Bacon, potatoes, strawberries, rolls, butter, two different kinds of jam, fluffy eggs, made her think of the twitters that would come from Sisters Davideena and Constance if they were with her. She smiled at the thought.

"I think I'll have a glass of juice, a roll, and some jam. Looks like marmalade to me," she said to the footman.

His response was to hand her a gold-edged plate. It was far larger than she needed, but she knew from supper it was the norm at Rockmore. Among several items, she took a piece of crisp bacon as she never tasted it before and simply could not ignore the delicious scent. They raised pigs at the convent to sell, not to eat.

Sitting near the end of the table, she drew a napkin to her lap and enjoyed the luxury of the morning. By this time of day, were she still at the convent, she would have already accomplished nearly two hours of painting, besides morning prayers, all before breakfast. She took her time, enjoying the solitude and the gentle ease of the morning. Slathering a wedge of soda bread with butter and marmalade, Muffy surprised her by scampering into the room and jumping at her tunic. Laying down the knife, she grinned at the insistent bark, wagging tail, and twinkling black eyes that demanded her attention.

Scooping up the black ball of fur, she received a rough-edged lick on her cheek. "How did you manage to escape?"

A footman, out of breath, rushed in from the direction of the kitchen. "Escape she did, miss. I'll take her." Reluctantly, she handed the black ball over. "Are they allowed outside?"

"On a leash, else we'd never find them. They can be gone in a second and don't mind at all."

"I would like to take them out when I have extra time. Should I speak to you or Lady Duncamden?"

He tried hard not to grimace. She could see he had a thought he did not want to share. "I think it best you check with one of us in the kitchen. We seem to be in charge when her ladyship visits."

"I'll come around when I have time. Thank you."

Tucking Muffy under his arm, the footman made his dignified way toward the hall that led to the kitchen. She could not help but giggle at the curly black tail that wagged from under his arm.

As she savored the tart marmalade, Mrs. Atkinson entered the dining room. "Will you be ready in fifteen minutes? I have two rooms you might like to use for painting. We'll see which one suits."

A short while later, the two women climbed the stairs to the third floor. Mrs. Atkinson showed her a large room in the corner of the east wing, windows on the south and east walls. She would have morning and early afternoon light. Perfect. The view was of the front of Rockmore to the south, while the east windows overlooked part of the park and the stables and cottages beyond. Her bedchamber was one floor below on the north side.

"I'll show you the other room, in the west wing."

Mairéad pronounced, "You need not bother. This is perfect."

"You're sure?"

"The light, the size of the room, it is going to be quite nice."

The women descended the stairs, and Mrs. Atkinson took her through the kitchen on the ground floor. Mrs. Hill, whom she had met yesterday, was elbow deep in flour. The cook glanced at them, red-faced and smiling, as they approached.

Not in the least hungry after the filling breakfast, she realized the cook was preparing dinner rolls. Pursing her lips, she knew that if she tasted all the delectable foods presented at each meal, her tunic would need altering. She'd begin to look like several of the nuns at the convent.

Mrs. Atkinson accepted the cook's offer of a cup of tea before they continued their walk to the chapel. Intrigued by the bustling of several maids, Mairéad glanced about the well-ordered chaos. Sacred Heart's kitchen hardly compared. A maid drew bread from a baker's oven built in the side of a huge fireplace. The aroma of warm yeast filled the air. Several steaming pots hung on iron hinged hooks, no doubt preparations for the next meal. She stepped aside as a tall, pock-marked lad laid an armful of dripping wet vegetables on the long table situated in the center of the room. She guessed he must have cleaned off the dirt at the well outside.

Oatmeal biscuits with nuts accompanied tea. Mrs. Atkinson moved to the servants' dining area adjacent to the kitchen, setting the tray down on the large table. A jar of vanilla-scented orchids adorned the table. With eight chairs on each side and one at the ends, the table was larger than the convents. Mairéad realized that it must take a great many servants to run Rockmore. Why, it took two stern-faced footmen just to care for Muffy and Sassy.

Tea and three biscuits later, Mrs. Atkinson, house keys jangling at her waist, suggested they begin their walk. In the park, Mairéad took note of the overcast sky and wind brewing. She was grateful for the suggestion of a shawl, as her woolen tunic might not have been sufficient.

A lovely courtyard lay just outside the kitchen door, no doubt busy with deliveries for the household. A lovely ivy trellis, already full of rosebuds, covered the stone edifice.

As they made their way along a gravel path toward the forest and chapel spire, Mairéad looked to the right toward a beautiful grassy park in the middle of the lough, a wee croft. "What a pretty sight."

"We refer to it as the summerhouse. What with half walls, when else could you use it? I believe it was the fourth Lord Darnley who increased the size of the lough and built the bridge and the small, open-sided building to afford a view of the surrounding area. We can sit a minute or two before going on to the chapel, if you like."

Beyond a rolling hill and to the extreme right, Mairéad spied a walled area. "What might that be?"

"Ah, a garden."

Pensive for a moment, she asked, "What a shame to keep a garden walled."

"I agree, but it keeps out all kinds of animals who nibble their way as if a banquet is laid for them. The walls also protect the flowers from the wind and storms that occasionally ravage the land."

"Animals are a great nuisance at the convent. Sister Davideena tries to outsmart them, with about as much success as failure. Her reaction is always 'Fatten the critters for our table or leave the vegetables as they are. One way or another we'll get both.' "

"She sounds a pragmatic sort."

"Else she would go crazy over it." Mairéad chuckled at the image of Sister Davideena swatting the ground with a broom.

With a sense of pride, the housekeeper said, "It was either the fourth or fifth countess who built the walled garden. Her husband was permissive in the extreme."

The flutter of birds overhead took their attention skyward. She placed a hand atop her veil and watched a flock of cranes. "I've much to learn about life outside the convent. It has not been a whole day away, and everything is new. An exciting adventure. My stay will go quickly."

Mrs. Atkinson did not respond, and Mairéad ventured, "I am not ungrateful. Mother Abbess does the best with what she has to offer all of us. No one is treated any different than another, and if food isn't as plentiful, we share that in equal measure as well."

"I understand. Those of us fortunate to have employment at Rockmore Hall feel the same as you." She cast a wistful gaze. "My background is not one of affluence, either. What made me decide to work for Lord Darnley was knowing the hardship of the earlier generations that built this place, stone by stone, and the care his lordship takes to preserve it. Almost makes me think of it more as a museum than a residence. When the land was first cultivated, it wasn't by Wallingtons."

"When would that have been? Early on, I suspect."

"I've read the history. The O'Bannons were first, in the late 1400s. When King Henry VIII was declared King of Ireland in 1541, he took land from the Irish and gave it to his Englishmen. Much of County Waterford changed hands at that time. Rockmore went to Lord Darnley's family, the Wallingtons. That's when the Earldom of Darnley was begun."

Their attention followed the flight of two cranes as they landed in the marsh at the edge of the lough and stood statue-like, waiting to catch a meal.

Mrs. Atkinson whispered, "Those are common cranes. Oh, and look to the left in the weeds, crack cranes. Seldom seen, a treat for you, then."

After a few minutes of espying the leggy birds, they left the summerhouse, making their way across the bridge toward the forest and the chapel. A fox ran from one side of the path to the other.

Mairéad commented, "No telling what the dogs will scare up when I take them out."

"They need the energy of youth. I would tire."

She modestly suggested, "You talk like an elder."

The housekeeper chuckled. "I'm twice your age. I could be your mother."

Ignoring the comment, she asked, "How long have you worked for his lordship?"

"Oh, my, eighteen years almost. Time moves faster each year." She lifted the hem of her skirt to better navigate the ruts.

Tree growth grew dense taking them into a gloomier realm. Mrs. Atkinson glanced over her shoulder, and Mairéad followed her line of vision. "Do you think we should turn back?"

"No. There's a basket of candles inside. It can't be two o'clock yet. I hope a storm isn't brewing."

Then, there it was, in all its miniature majesty—the chapel. Constructed of clay bricks and small stones, with a stained window on each side of the entryway. Welcoming and inviting, it stood as a symbol of hope for miles around. Its crowning glory, the steeple with a cross at the tip, poked a hole in the canopy of elm and oak reaching for the sky. Gray clouds tumbled overhead. The air was alive with the awesome rustle and whisper of the breeze turning the leaves.

Mrs. Atkinson lifted the latch, the door opened inward. A waft of musk, born of sacramental oils, washed over them. The nave contained three rows of pews on each side of the aisle that led to the altar.

Two windows on each of the outside walls allowing light were inlaid with colored glass to match the two by the door, all bearing scenes of saints and forest. A marble altar in the sanctuary gave the appearance of expectation, as if it waited for a priest to say Holy Mass.

Of interest, even though the outside light was darkening by the minute, was the artwork on the windows. Mairéad stood in front of the first stained glass and admired the workmanship. Mrs. Atkinson handed her a lit candle.

"Thank you," she remarked as Mrs. Atkinson took a place in the nook of a pew.

"Take your time. I'm going to sit quietly for a bit and clear my head."

Appreciating her consideration, Mairéad touched the lower portion of the window, running her fingertips along the leaded lines, admiring the workmanship. She was sure that on a bright day the windows would sparkle. The one she stood in front of was of Saint Brigid and imprinted with 423–524 AD, Kildare. She had read the life of this saint. A brave, simple woman dedicated to helping others.

Holding the candle high, she stepped back to better view the second window, a forest scene with a stag and a shaft of sunray shooting down from an opening in the clouds that landed on a cloaked figure, his sword drawn. No date, no name, but nonetheless beautifully depicted. A staunch believer in God, no doubt, ready to defend his faith.

She marveled at the lovely sanctuary. Running her palm over the smooth marble of the altar, she was hardly able to fathom the number of prayers that must have been whispered within these walls over the centuries.

She glanced at the housekeeper, her head bowed, resting or praying. Not wanting to disturb her, Mairéad moved closer to the windows on the other side of the nave. One was of two women holding hands, the other another forest scene. Upon closer inspection, she read the inscription beneath the women, Fionnuala and Mairéad O'Bannon, 1134 A.D.

Delightfully surprised that the likeness of her name was etched on the glass, she ran her fingers over the letters. She loved her name, coming as it did from the parent who left her on the steps. She had not run across the usage anywhere before. In some ways, her life was so sheltered, seeing the likeness gave her an immediate sense of pride. Then quickly, she reminded herself that Mother Abbess preached that pride goes before a fall. She drew her fingertips off the glass, curling them into a fist.

Left on the doorstep of the convent as an infant, Mairéad grew up with no knowledge of her background, save her name and that a Roman Catholic Priest baptized her. The note also stated that she must not enter the order of religious, with no explanation as to why. Yet, Mairéad knew that when she reached the age of reason, she could, of her own volition, become a nun. Mother Abbess told her so.

Her palm inadvertently went to her left breast. There was one other tiny piece of identification, a small heart scratched on her skin. A mark a mother would be aware of on her babe. Whether cut on her skin purposefully or a natural birthmark, she had no idea. Either way, the woman who birthed Mairéad surely knew of the mark.

It was with shock when, at about seven years of age, she inquired of Mother Abbess about the mark on her chest and was met with a stern reaction. She *tsked*, saying something about an abomination to one's self. God's holy vessel should not be defiled, a work of the *divil*, she muttered, vowing with vengeance, "Thank the Almighty it is on a part of your being that cannot be seen by others."

To this day, she remembered that scene. Mother Abbess with plenty to say about the Celts and the pagan Irish legend. She believed the pagan rite led to the defiling scar. Part of Mairéad's reasoning to enter convent life was to purify herself from the heathen symbolism.

In her earlier years, she begged God's mercy. Maturity and forgiveness allowed her peace. She took solace in that, despite the defilement of her body, she would be allowed to become a novitiate.

Yesterday, when Lord Darnley entered her workroom at the convent, she'd sensed Mother Abbess's anxiety and instantly recalled the discussion so long ago. Her defiling scar was why she'd refused to leave the convent with his lordship.

Then Mother Abbess's firm decision that she must go with him was an order brooking no refusal. The nun's turnabout shocked and confused her.

Mrs. Atkinson's voice drew her back to the moment. "I had forgotten that inscription."

Mairéad's gaze flickered to the stained-glass window. "You mentioned a woman, O'Bannon, who uses the chapel. Also, that the O'Bannons were first to dwell on this land."

Mrs. Atkinson shifted in the pew. "I didn't put the two together. It's a common enough surname. Who knows if she is related or not? I doubt even she would know."

She slowly glanced about the chapel. "I can understand her wanting to come here. It's beautiful and peaceful. Yet, I also feel a sense of urgency. Do you feel it?"

"The fairies have touched you." The housekeeper cast a slanted eye her way. "Is it not so?"

Mairéad smiled, knowing Mother Abbess would surely have a retort that might burn the housekeeper's ears.

"I must say," Mrs. Atkinson folded her hands, giving the distinct impression she was being deliberate, "I was surprised his lordship hired you to work for him here and not at the convent."

"Lord Darnley insisted on it. I was surprised when Mother Abbess relented to his wishes." Shrugging her shoulders, Mairéad continued in a wistful voice. "I've never been away from the convent."

"Never?"

Shaking her head, she cast a sideways glance at the woman. "Though I believe the bargain made between them is to my benefit. This is new to me, living in a household. I can't quite fathom that it's real. That I would have a bit of an adventure along with the work that is so dear."

Snuffing the candles, they returned them to a shelf on the way out.

She kept abreast Mrs. Atkinson as they trod the path. The wind fluttered her veil off her shoulders as she noted the housekeeper's little smile.

"Lady Duncamden is a kindly woman and means well. I overheard her questioning you. You must have been a bit unsettled. The truth does work well on her. You calmed her enough that she offered a generous addition to your wardrobe." Mrs. Atkinson turned a raised brow on Mairéad.

"It will prove a foolish expense. I do not expect to be here beyond the summer."

Mrs. Atkinson pursed her lips as they approached the backside of the estate and the red doors of the kitchen. The lough with the summerhouse to their far left, the walled garden even further in the distance, and the expanse of the park's verdant hills rolling all the way to the four-storied hall was a panoramic wonderland. Activity was taking place at the stables where two men walked steeds on leaders, one a beautiful roan, the other black as midnight.

"Have you learned to ride?" Mrs. Atkinson asked.

She couldn't squelch the spurt of a giggle. "Can you imagine convent life with sisters riding? Veils flying in the wind?"

"I guess it does seem improbable, but what about you? Do you think you might enjoy trying?"

Astounded, she turned to the housekeeper. "How would it be possible?"

"Oh, now, Miss Mairéad, I can't imagine Lord Darnley would deny you anything." Mrs. Atkinson picked up her pace as they made their way toward the kitchen entrance.

Mairéad fell behind as she attempted to sort out the housekeeper's remark. She had not expected to be treated with partiality. Moreover, why would his lordship consider doing so? Above all else, why did Mrs. Atkinson make mention of the possibility? Gathering up her skirts, she quickened her pace, by this time Mrs. Atkinson gained the red door.

S he called out to the disappearing housekeeper. "Would it be all right if I sat awhile in the summerhouse?"

Mrs. Atkinson raised her hand in farewell. Mairéad intended to contemplate the whole of the morning. Usually alone for the better part of the day, she was unused to company, and therefore craved quiet in a place to meditate. Nestled on the bench, against the railing, she sat in the shadows and looked at the back of Rockmore Hall, searching for the windows in her new bedchamber. It was about this hour yesterday when Lord Darnley entered her life.

Her daily praying was all askew, certainly not intentionally. Now that she was familiar with the chapel, she would make good use of its solitude. Her gaze swept along the roofline of the estate. It was magnificent, the stone edifice a solid and secure stronghold against the world. Perhaps similar as when the convent might've been when it was a functioning castle in Viking and Norman times.

A flapping on the water turned her attention just as the long-legged birds took flight, soaring above the forest where the spire shone. This was a peaceful, delightful world, and she knew she would enjoy her stay. Lord Darnley was a kind man, despite her first impression. Yes, she was puzzled to what his real purpose was

KAREN DEAN BENSON

to bring her here. She assumed it was the illuminating, but it didn't make sense. Giving a nod to her overactive imagination, she clapped her hands together. *Mairéad, the fairies have indeed taken hold of your thinking.*

Not one to let dust settle, as always reminded by Sister Catriona, she decided at this moment to find her benefactor and ask him straight out why he brought her to Rockmore Hall. As she stood, something in an upper window on the far side of the estate flashed in the sunlight. Drapes opened. She was being watched.

As she made her way toward the kitchen, she glanced again at the far window. A woman looked down at her. Not Lady Duncamden, she stopped and gazed at the figure. A bright red shawl around her shoulders, the woman waved, and Mairéad returned the greeting. Someone she had yet to meet. This was a busy household, indeed.

As she knocked on the library door, which was open, Lord Darnley glanced up from his desk. "Come in, my dear. How fares your visit to the chapel?" He came around his desk and joined her in one of the chairs.

"I enjoyed a bit of a history lesson from Mrs. Atkinson about the O'Bannons and the Wallingtons."

"What did you think of the windows in the chapel? With your artist's eye, they should have caught your attention. The building is an original to the estate, built sometime in the late 1400s by the O'Bannons. The Wallingtons came a hundred and more years after."

"A pleasant surprise, the likeness of my name written in the Irish dated 1134."

"It is a beautiful name. Rather popular in Ireland's history. It must make you feel connected in a way."

His interest made her more aware, his perspectives insightful. She found she enjoyed his company. Squaring her shoulders, sitting straight as a pin, hands nestled in her lap, sandals barely touching the floor, she faced him. "Why did you bring me here?"

His chair creaked as he adjusted his posture, not looking at her. "To illuminate some of my work. What makes you ask?"

"I've always worked from the convent. You insisted, and I think the least you should do is explain why."

He locked on her without a word coming forth, his grey eyes intense, searching. What was behind his scrutiny? She waited another moment or two.

Nothing.

"Have you no answer for me?" Her hands clutched, waiting. Mother Abbess used to say, *be careful what you ask for.*

The lids of his eyes shut, and he stilled. Was he hiding something? She continued to wait.

Finally, his inspection focused on her again. "I am an old man, my dear. The only family I have is a grandson who visits from Berkshire at whim." His lips twitched, almost as if he tried to hide a smile, "Of course, there is my sister, Lady Duncamden, but most of the time I am lonely. I have some precious material that I have always wanted illuminated, and I learned of the nuns at Sacred Heart of Jesus's ability to transform pages. You were a surprise with your enthusiasm, your wit, your ladylike appearance. I knew in a moment you would be the one to accomplish the embellishment. Despite your age, your work is rather accomplished."

Easing up a bit, she picked at a speck on her tunic. "You have not quite answered my question, my lord. Why could I not have accomplished such at the convent?"

"But I did answer you. I need to be about my estate and, yet, I am lonely. You can do so here and keep me company when you are not in your workroom." He spread his arms wide, encompassing the whole of Rockmore Hall.

"Truly?" The puzzlement on her veil-framed face caused him to laugh.

"It was an epiphany for me. Which is why I broached Mother Abbess with my idea."

"In all truth, you blurted it out in front of both of us, as if it came to you in that instant on the wings of a bee filled with nectar."

The space between his eyes scrunched. His thumbs circled each other. "I plead guilty, my dear. That is exactly how it happened, on the wings of a bee."

She rolled her eyes, something she would never think of doing. Was he wheedling her?

It looked to her as if he bit the sides of his mouth. His voice sounded stiff when he asked, "Did you just roll your eyes at me?"

An instant flush rose up her neck. Flustered hardly explained her feelings. "I ... well, you ..."

She could see him struggle with something, and then suddenly he burst forth, practically guffawing. "My dear Miss Mairéad... have you not been teased?" Tears were sliding down his ruddy pink cheeks. He took out a handkerchief and swiped them away. "I haven't had such delight since my sister's pups–ah, well, I won't go into that right now."

Did she bring him merriment? Was he making fun of her? Ridiculing her? A mixture of humiliation and confusion brought her to her feet.

His big hand reached over circling her wrist. "You bring me pleasure, Miss Mairéad. I am delighted to have you at Rockmore Hall. I am guilty of teasing, but it was not meant to disarm you. Please do not leave."

She locked gazes with him, behind which hid something much deeper than this, but exactly what, she'd no idea. "I should not have rolled my eyes. I don't think I recall doing that before."

"We're even then?"

She regained her seat and smiled at him. "For now."

He guffawed once more, heartily.

"There is one thing. I am unsure how to handle ..."

Swiping his face with the handkerchief, he asked, "My sister?"

Her eyes squinting, she nodded.

His hands spread wide. "Nor do I. You may have to give in, if only a little, simply to quiet her. Could you perhaps do that as a

SECRET AT DARK CASTLE

favor to me? At my age, I do not want to listen to her complain that you won't accept her offer. You have only just met and can see what it is I am up against each time she visits. Projects are her specialty."

Mairéad shook off his lament. The poor man, she did understand his plight. His sister was a force one could not easily put aside. "I'll do my best. It will be hard to change the way I dress. I suppose if I had already taken vows, I would have to deny your request, but under the circumstances, I can make the adjustment. It will only last through the end of summer."

Lord Darnley put his hands on the arms of the chair and pushed himself up. "My instincts about you do not waver, my dear. You are as compassionate as your superior mentioned."

"She said so?" A trickle of pure pleasure skimmed through her.

"Indeed, she went so far as to say you were a special young woman, and I was to care for you as if you were one of mine."

Feeling as though she walked on a cloud, she went into the kitchen and asked to take Muffy and Sassy for a walk, with leashes, of course. Out the door they went. It took Mairéad a few minutes to figure out how to keep the leather strips from tangling as the black and white balls of fur scrambled back and forth in front of her, then behind. She intended to return to the summerhouse, but the curs sniffed the stables and pulled her in that direction.

As she approached the red brick wall surrounding the stable yard, commotion caused by a coach laden with parcels made her wary of getting too close with the inquisitive dogs. Four dark brown draughts with huge hooves snorted and stomped, their yokes jingling with the shake of massive heads. A passenger threw open the door, calling out for the step. One of the drivers yelled, "We're here but a minute, sir. Get back in."

The driver climbed down, unstrapping a box of some size from the rear. A man clad in a leather work apron and wiping his hands on a cloth came forward, accepting the box.

Mairéad had little choice but to scoop up a dog under each arm. They yipped and wiggled to jump from her hold.

"Here, miss. I'll take them." A young man approached, holding out his blackened hands.

"No need. I have a firm grip. They could get stomped if I gave them rein."

"You're new, then, aren't cha? The lass from the convent, then. Me name's Mikey."

"I'm Mairéad."

"Will ye be with us long then?" He wiped his hands on the sides of his pants. The driver returned to the coach and snapped the reins. The crunching of wheels and hooves against the gravel took her interest. Sassy and Muffy wiggled and struggled against her until the coach made its way to the roundabout and on its way. Then, she set them on the ground. Eager to be down, they strained against the leather leashes, intending to scamper after the coach.

"Through the summer. His lordship has need of illumination for some books."

Mikey scratched the back of his head, pushing his tam down on his forehead. "I'll not know what you're talkin' about, but it sounds like work to me."

Another man, large and muscular, came toward them. "Takin' your break, Mikey?" His scowl told her Mikey probably took time from his chores whenever possible.

As if he did not understand the sarcasm in the man's voice, Mikey answered, "Just passin' the time with the convent lass. Her name's Miss Mairéad."

The stable man nodded to her. "I'm Shamus. I'll be the one to get your kit ready when ye want to ride."

"A pleasure to meet you, Shamus. However, it is a futile offer, for I cannot ride." The dogs took a sudden interest in sniffing the men's shoes. Muffy jumped at Mikey's trousers. He bent over and scratched her ears.

"A shame 'tis. Some of the most beautiful land to be seen out there and more to the eye if seated atop a horse. His lordship came out this morning and picked out a mare, should ye be interested."

This was a surprise, for he'd not uttered a word to her. Elated at his overt care, she wanted to jump with the excitement that tingled. Instead, she squeezed her eyes shut, lest tears spring forth. Surely, she wanted to ride, but she was insecure and a bit frightened. Looking at her hands gripping the curs' leads, she mumbled, "I would not know the first thing about riding."

"His lordship was anxious ye should learn and asked me to set aside time each day to be your guide. Ye come around early afternoon each day, and we'll see yer progress. I've no doubt."

Gulping with the wonder this could actually happen, she said, "Why, certainly I will come. Tomorrow then? Will that do? What should I wear?" Her enthusiasm dwindled as she glanced at her gray tunic.

Shamus shook his head. "I'm thinkin' Mrs. Atkinson can fit ye out. Tell her you're havin' a riding lesson tomorrow. She'll come through for ye."

He placed his large hand on Mikey's nape. "Now we'll get on with our duties, won't we, lad?" He winked at her. Mikey waved as he was pushed through the iron gates that separated the parkland from the stable area.

She watched them as they entered one of the arched alcoves leading into the interior of the large stable. A tower at one end spewed black smoke. The convent did not have horses. Every week Mr. Chiley brought a pony trap around, inquiring of Mother Abbess if she needed to go to market or town. It was always a great convenience. Mr. Chiley also took charge of delivering Mother Abbess to the dispensaries in both Hawthorn Village and Waterford. There she provided love and care to the sick and infirm, greatly appreciating his weekly kindness.

Tugging on the leather leashes, Mairéad diverted Muffy and Sassy's attention toward the summerhouse. It was a slow walk as the dogs sniffed along the parkland. A V formation of geese landed in the lough, and the tug on the leashes reset the pace of walking.

The cur's activity immediately set the geese in motion, and the dogs yapped and jumped as they did so. Ah, if they could only fly, the geese would be in trouble.

Large splats of water dropped from a dark cloud, and she hurried the dogs toward shelter under the roof of the summerhouse, where they could wait out the passing rain. Sitting on the bench, she drew the dogs up and was rewarded with enthusiastic licking of her hands. Their warmth felt nice as they snuggled against her.

The geese returned just as the rain let up. Muffy and Sassy flew off the bench, Mairéad after them. Somehow, she let the reins dangle off her wrist.

Halfway across the park, she called their names to no avail. A patch of hawthorn bushes caught their attention as the birds took flight. Their leashes tangled on the thorns. Aha. She whispered a little prayer of thanks, grabbing them in a conquering fist.

Coaxing the dogs back to where her veil flew off, she awkwardly settled it on her head. As she did, her gaze was drawn to the woman in the window from this morning, still wrapped in the red shawl. Mairéad waved and received a wave in return, then the woman withdrew from sight as they neared the entrance to the hall.

Mairéad handed over the dogs and leashes to one of the footmen. He led them, tails wagging and little mouths panting, to a water bowl in the corner of the slate-floored kitchen.

Mrs. Hill chuckled. "Not as easy as it looks, eh?"

"How right you are." She glanced at the pots steaming with delicious scents. "It smells like curry."

"I hope you like shrimp. And would you be enjoying a nice white sauce over rice and peas?" She bent over the steamy pot.

As busy as the cook was, Mairéad nodded but did not bother her with the knowledge she had never tasted shrimp. She knew they were a crustacean from the ocean.

These twenty-four hours showered her with newness. It would be impolite not to adjust to Rockmore Hall's way of doing things.

In truth, she found herself eager to experience it all, but there was something else going on inside her as she struggled with her conscience. She needed time to think it through, perhaps when next she visited the chapel.

In the privacy of her room, she collapsed in a chair and enjoyed the sight of the blue sky and passing clouds. Sometime later, a knock at the door and Ryan's entrance, arms full of clothing, caused her to sit up.

"A little nappy does no harm. Sorry to have bothered you, miss." Ryan laid the bundle on the bed and began sorting the clothing.

"What are you doing?" Mairéad glanced at a lovely assortment of colors and textiles.

"Mrs. Atkinson suggested I search through some trunks. These are more for the fit than for color or frill. They've been aired though a bit of mint might still linger. Oh, and a suitable outfit for riding, as she mentioned you might be interested."

Mairéad felt a lump form in her throat. This was too much, too fast, and unnecessary.

A maid entered with a tea tray, then curtsied and left. "That was quick," said Ryan, as she poured and prepared her a cup, remembering she liked both sugar and cream.

"I'm not going to enjoy this alone, Ryan," she admitted, taking the cup.

"It is most unseemly, miss. I am but a maid."

"What am I, then?" Her question fell on deaf ears as Ryan stooped to pick up a gown that slid to the floor.

Long minutes passed. After the spotty rain of the day, rays of sunlight were welcome. Mairéad ran fingers over a particularly lovely bit of yellow froth as Ryan laid them out. "I am unused to this way of living."

Ryan shifted her weight from one foot to the other, finally declaring, "As I see it, you've only just arrived, and who could expect that convent life would prepare you for such as all this."

"You are right in that."

"Perhaps there is another way to look at it. This could simply be an opportunity for you to learn about life beyond the convent. Perhaps to ready you for something bigger than a life filled with prayer. I mean that kindly. Prayer works wonders but doing also brings surprising alternatives."

"How do I reconcile changing my mode of clothing. 'Tis all I've known." Mairéad's brow furrowed. She did not want to offend but was maddeningly confused.

"My guess is you needn't wear any of it. It's your choice. I think Mrs. Atkinson was trying to assist you with blending in while you are here." Ryan took a deep breath, then plunged in. "I don't think there is anything in the world that can change who you are inside. Certainly, clothing cannot do that, no more than what you eat or if you take the dogs for a walk."

With a tenuous smile, Mairéad said, "The bacon was quite tasty. How did you know?"

The maid's cheeks flushed. "Cook mentioned you took a second helping. She was mighty pleased. We're thinking your life at the convent was sparse. Afterall, it's what you've known for all your years."

Mairéad caught a glimpse of the lowering sun. "I am making too much of it, aren't I? It's everything new, sweeping across me like a broom getting rid of my old self." She turned and fixed her gaze on the maid. "If I am truly honest, it's been a lovely day. I slept in the bed of a princess last night, then there was breakfast, the lovely chapel. Beyond wonderful is Mrs. Atkinson, and Muffy and Sassy are fun." She wrung her hands together. "I have done nothing to deserve such enjoyment. It is unearned."

Ryan took a step forward, then stopped almost as if she needed to remind herself of something. "Such a quandary. I tell you what. I will hang the clothes in your press, and they can wait a day or two for when you are interested. Mrs. Atkinson runs this household, has for years before I came to be here, and she's always taken a special interest in anything to do with Lord Darnley. As for the pups, they need your youth and vigor. The kitchen staff noticed you and jabbered in delight as you walked and ran with them, getting them out from underfoot. You were a sight to behold from the kitchen."

Mairéad wiped at her teary eyes, self-conscious to be sharing her emotions with another. "It is more like they took me for a walk. To the stables, then the geese, then the summerhouse, then more geese. I was exhausted."

As Ryan hung the gowns, Mairéad, slanted a tiny grin at her. "Mayhap, you should leave out something for me to wear for a riding lesson tomorrow."

"Now, doesn't that feel right as rain?" Ryan added "would you like your hair brushed out before supper?"

"I would indeed," and sat on the stool before the dressing table. She could see Ryan's reflection in the mirror. The maid gathered the length off her nape and began stroking it with the brush.

"You've a fine color and texture to your locks. Many a girl would wish for just the same."

"It can get unruly. The time will come when I won't have to worry about it anymore."

"May I ask you something?" She twisted the length about her fist and brushed the ends out of the auburn strands.

"Surely, anything."

"Curious of me, but have you a room of your own at the convent?"

"Yes, each of us have our own cell. I'm luckier than most, I've a window."

"So, much like here, then?"

Mairéad sputtered, "Hardly. I couldn't find the chamber pot and searched every conceivable nook. In desperation, I opened that door assuming it was a passage to the rooms next door. Can you imagine my surprise, a grand bathing room with a copper tub large enough to sit in, a small bench with a round wooden seat upon which to sit for necessity, a bowl, a mirror, and clean linen."

Ryan bit her lower lip trying not to laugh. "Mrs. Atkinson didn't show it to you?"

"She may have assumed I would know of it."

❦

Later, during supper, Mairéad became acquainted with shrimp. She found the succulent bites swimming in a savory cheese-curry sauce and rice mixed with vegetables quite delicious. Lady Duncamden plied her with questions.

"I understand the little beasts kept you busy."

"We enjoyed an hour or more in the park. A lot of diversions caught their attention."

"I've readied a letter to my dresser." She sipped her wine. "I've never understood why my brother has not employed a seamstress. Most manors do, if only for the daily wear for staff." She fluffed out her napkin and adjusted it under her chin. "An inconvenience to be sure."

Lord Darnley ignored his sister's pinched grimace and asked of Mairéad, "I believe Mrs. Atkinson would know of someone in the village. Did you ask her?"

"Well, I can easily do without——"

His imperious sibling picked up her fork, interrupting Mairéad and said, as though she had not heard the question, "Your cook seems to educate herself in the culinary arts more with every visit."

With a twinkle in his eye, he teased, "She wishes to impress you."

She wiggled a tiny bit in her chair, giving a confident nod of her head as though agreeing with him.

Mairéad hid a grin at the transparency of her ladyship's delight. She seized upon no better time to confess about the clothing situation than right now. "Mrs. Atkinson found some gowns that just might fit, and I would like to spare you the expense of employing a seamstress."

The elderly woman's gray brows rose as she glanced down her nose. "Are they satisfactory? Should I look at them?"

"Ryan is airing them. I can't imagine they would not suit while I am here. I dislike thinking you will spend good money when I need gowns for only a short stay, though your offer is kind and most generous."

Her ladyship harrumphed as a footman took the empty plates from the table and delivered raspberry pie.

Lord Darnley, having been rather quiet throughout the meal, made an announcement. "Rutledge has written. He expects to arrive toward the end of next week and is bringing Innisbeck with him. Tremaine also has leave from Edinburgh. They plan to meet up in Waterford and arrive together." He asked his sister, "Do you recall meeting either of the young men?"

"Is Innisbeck the red-haired young man who brays like an ass when he guffaws?" she asked as she delicately patted the sides of her mouth with the napkin.

"I believe you have caught the essence of him, yes." Darnley grimaced and asked, "Of course, you do recall Tremaine?"

"Is this a test of whether or not I'm daft? Jonathan Tremaine is the grandson of our father's brother." She smirked at Mairéad. "He thinks to put me in one of those horrid places, all rotted and crumbling."

His gaze turned askance. "Take note of how she accuses me," he said to Mairéad. "I do not usually have a witness to her sharp tongue."

Her ladyship obviously intended to prove her keen memory. "Already at university, isn't he? And rather interested in medicine, I also seem to recall." She tasted another piece of the pie. "I am pleased cook wants to impress me. She has certainly outdone herself with this pie. By the by, lass, Tremaine is quite popular with your sex."

"Philly. Honestly. Your talk is gruesome."

"I thought I'd enlighten her. She might not be aware how women act who have no scruples."

He gaped at her, "Why would she know. She's been in a convent her entire life."

"Precisely," she sent Mairéad a wink.

Enjoying their interaction, Mairéad felt the tug of merriment at table, which was unheard of at the convent during meals. Usually, one of the sisters read from the Bible as the others ate. In all her years, she experienced no less than four complete readings of the Bible.

Lord Darnley explained, "Tremaine's family and ours are not only distantly related but have been friends for many years. He is the older by a few years than Rutledge. He was the draw for Rutledge to decide on Eton, and for that, I am grateful. My grandson's inclination is not learning. Tremaine attended Trinity. He left there after three years and has since transferred to Edinburgh Medical School. Very bright young man.

"Eton is where my grandson also met Innisbeck. The three have maintained a close friendship." He bit into his pie, before adding, "We will have a lively table in the evenings. Rutledge likes to tease his great-aunt."

Mairéad inquired, "Your grandson lives in England, then?"

"Berkshire and is expressing an interest in Cambridge."

A curt edge to her words, Lady Duncamden interjected, "My brother always hoped some of Tremaine would rub off on Rutledge. We have yet to notice an influence. Darnley attended Trinity in Dublin, but his grandson has airs about him. Not good enough. His current intention is to get into Trinity at Cambridge and begin a new tradition for the Wallingtons."

Mairéad sensed a tension, possibly regret, in Darnley's voice when he spoke of his grandson and asked, "You would like him to choose Trinity, I take it. Like his friend?"

His jaw tensed, and he set down his fork. "Since the Third Darnley, we have all been educated at that fine university. This rascal of mine sees fit to change our history."

An edge to her ladyship's tone she urged, "Tell her that's not all he wants changed."

He cast his sister a dark look, and she turned her attention to finishing the raspberry pie, perhaps realizing she erred.

Mairéad changed the subject. "This is delicious. As it is early in the season, these berries must have been put up last summer. They still have texture and sweetness."

With a sigh, he laid his fork on his plate and asked, "Seeing as how you will be in company with Rutledge, might you have questions?"

It was almost as if he could read her mind. She drew her hands to her lap and gave him her full attention. "I do wonder if you have other grandchildren."

"Rutledge is my only one. His father died when he was young."

"Is your grandson's mother gone, too?"

Lord Darnley forked another piece of pie but did not put it in his mouth. His gaze on his plate, he whispered. "The boy never knew her. It is one of his deepest regrets. He reminds me of it on occasion, too."

She put her hand on his arm. "Such a sadness. He is fortunate to have you. I hope he realizes that."

Lady Duncamden harrumphed.

Lord Darnley glanced at his sister. "Yes, well, we've made up a kind of family for him, haven't we, Philly?"

"And done a fine job of it, I'd say. *When* he applies himself, he earns honors in all his classes. Though my brother bails him out on occasion. He seems to think the world is his oyster and he can do no wrong. Pure foolishness on the boy's part." With a brief glance at Mairéad, she continued. "You, my dear? The little I know of you I sense you've done well with your learning at the convent."

Her question caused Mairéad a comical tweak of memory. "I've many teachers. Each one with a specialty eager to impart. It was like having a dozen or more mothers." Talking about her life reminded her of the sisters' likely concern for how she was doing and whether she was well. She stated, "I would like to send a letter when the carriage retrieves my paints."

Darnley set his fork down and leaned in. "The driver will go over on Friday. If you give your post to Witham, he will pass it on."

Supper finished, Lady Duncamden excused herself to write letters, and Lord Darnley excused himself to finish a report he was working on for the minister of land grants in Dublin. Mairéad went to the kitchen in search of Mrs. Atkinson.

Directed to a sitting room in the servant's wing, Mairéad found her with a book in her lap and feet on a stool, looking rather content.

"I am sorry to disturb you."

"You are not disturbing me. How was supper?"

"Interesting. Lord Darnley talked of his grandson. Lady Duncamden suggested a troubled relationship, and I noted his lordship appeared to despair over their conversation."

Though not invited to, she settled on a stool.

Mrs. Atkinson began. "Rutledge has suffered a bit. He never really knew his father, who died quite young. He was fostered to a cropper family on the estate and given the name Ayden. When his father died, at twenty-four, the child's existence came to light, and Lord Darnley brought the nearly five-year-old Ayden here, changed his name from Ayden Wallington to Garrett III, and made him his heir. Eventually, once his legitimate birth was accepted by the crown, he was given the courtesy title of viscount and named Lord Rutledge."

Mairéad was thoughtful. "A shame, he prefers to be elsewhere, when he could be here with his grandfather?"

"He isn't the most ingratiating young man. I think there is a lot of anger and unresolved issues. I was here when they brought him from the cropper's cottage. We could not console him. Nothing worked. His lordship, God bless him, just lost his son and heir. When he discovered the presence of a grandson, he was ecstatic. The young Ayden wanted none of it. As far as I know, he has never changed his mind."

"I do understand being taken from your home. I was not given a choice about coming here. Knowing I will return at the end of the summer eases my mind."

The housekeeper folded the book in her lap. "Rutledge is expected next week. You will meet."

"I am not sure I look forward to it after all I heard at table tonight." She smiled at Mrs. Atkinson. "But Lord Darnley will not be the wiser."

"We all cosset him. It seems, you have begun, too."

"He is a kind man. His generosity has allowed me privileges I will never forget. I wonder, do you know where I might find writing tools? I have many sisters expecting a letter from me. I need to settle their curiosity."

Mrs. Atkinson pursed her lips. "You fit in here so nicely, I forget where you came from. There is a desk in your room. Let Ryan know if it's not stocked with quill, ink, and parchment."

"Thank you and for the clothing, too."

"Are they a fit?" Mrs. Atkinson's lively countenance was pleasantly framed by dark hair streaked with a little gray and rolled into a bun. Mairéad sensed her devoid of strife and agitation, as if the roof could cave in and she would simply take care to put it to rights. Her comfort with the housekeeper helped a great deal with settling in for the summer.

"Ryan believes they will do nicely. I'm...well, tomorrow I have a lesson in riding. Shamus..."

"Ah, you'll learn quickly with him. He's quite knowledgeable. Taught the young lord many years ago, who is a skilled horseman, winning Hawthorn Lough's races for several years now."

"I hope to stay put on the saddle. Though it may be a useless pursuit. The convent does not own a horse."

"My dear, once learned you'll carry the knowledge and always be able to ride, should the occasion present." Mrs. Atkinson took her feet off the stool and set her book on the side table. "I'm not one to share family tales, but since you will be meeting Rutledge next week, I think you should be forewarned of his singular mind. His interests concern himself. His lordship is usually not one of them. What Rutledge wants he's not denied. I feel I can be forthcoming with you because it will become apparent."

Mairéad listened carefully. It surprised her that Lord Darnley would allow contemptuous behavior in one of his own. She knew Mother Abbess's response to such and could not imagine Lord Darnley allowing his own grandson to have fits. "I am sorry his lordship must put up with it."

"I think his lordship is burdened with a measure of guilt. Rutledge holds a load of anger over his grandfather. Blames him for his early life, his father's death. You may hear arguing and tantrums while he is here. Keep your distance is my suggestion."

"Thank you for the warning."

The housekeeper chuckled. "I'm fairly certain talk at the convent never goes above moderate."

Mairéad's mood lightened. "Perhaps not, but there is stomping of shoes on the cobbles and the occasional slamming of a door that suggests someone didn't get what they wanted." She gestured toward the book Mrs. Atkinson placed on the table. "I've taken you away from your reading, and as Muffy and Sassy tired me out today and I have a riding lesson tomorrow, I had better begin dreaming of how that is going to happen."

She left Mrs. Atkinson chuckling about her remark.

6

R yan shook the dark-blue twill. "This should suit for your lesson. There is a jacket to keep you warm. It promises to be overcast today."

Mairéad stood before her in a shift, putting all modesty aside for this change of attire. Ryan allowed that sitting sidesaddle would not do with wide petticoats, so the twill would work nicely with a simple underskirt rather than petticoats. Drawing it over her head, Ryan buttoned the sleeves and back.

Finished, she asked, "Seems a good fit. How does it feel?"

Mairéad took a few steps, let her palms slide down the material on her sleeves and skirt and touched her neck, feeling the collar. "I think I like it. What do you say?"

"Ah, look for yourself." When she opened the door on the clothes press, a mirror fastened to the length of the inside revealed Mairéad in her riding gown. No veil, no gray tunic. She saw a waistline, and a slightly billowed skirt. The tips of her sandals peeked beneath the hem.

What really surprised her was how she looked without a veil. "I am to be a completely different person, am I not?" She caught Ryan's expression in the mirror.

She could think of no words to describe how she looked and

sought confirmation of some sort. "Will this do? What do you think?"

Ryan's eyes widened. "I think you look like a young lady about to venture into the world for her first riding lesson. You are lovely, miss. I don't know if it's the style of the gown, leaving off the veil, or the dark blue, but the gown is suited to you."

"Will I be able to ride in this?" Her palms smoothed over the skirt again.

"Women do all the time. The fit of the saddle makes it easier, from what I have heard."

With that, Ryan helped her into the jacket and tied a small hat upon her head. Earlier, she brushed her hair into one braid. Mairéad started toward the door when Ryan stopped her. "We ... I forgot something most important. Your sandals. You need boots to keep your foot in the stirrup."

She drew out a black pair from the floor of the clothes press. "I'm hoping they are a fit. I will put some cloth in the toe if they are too big."

The boots ran partway up her calf, with a bit of a heel that she was not used to, she shuffled about determining they were not going to slide off. "Heavier than my sandals to be sure, but I believe they are the right size."

"Enjoy your lesson. I'll be anxious to hear about it."

"Unless I end up on the ground."

"Shamus would not let that happen to you. He's a grand and careful man."

Mairéad's ears perked up at Ryan's change of tone, sounding as if she revered him.

In that moment, her glance fell to the red shawl draped over the chair. She had not noticed it earlier. Her finger trailed over the fabric, soft like silk. Yesterday, the woman on the fourth floor was wearing a red shawl. If this was hers, how did it get here?

She glanced up to ask Ryan, to find her gone. Perhaps she brought it in as part of one of the outfits and forgot to mention it?

Shamus greeted Mairéad in a clean shirt and shaved face. She was so surprised she almost didn't recognize him.

"I see ye are ready, lass."

"As well as can be. You have a willing pupil, but that doesn't address how I shall take to the experience."

"Let me acquaint ye with the saddle. When Lady Darnley rode, she used a seat made special for her that others have since used and find safe and comfortable. I have no reason to think ye'll find it any less."

As she tagged behind him into the cavernous interior of the stable, the scent of fresh hay and manure bit at her nose. A few horses colored tan, cream, black, and reddish were in stalls with a half door across each entrance, their names quaintly displayed above each stall. Carrot, Snowflake, Fizz, Star, Hungas, Hegarty, and Aggie. For the most part, she could understand the names. Carrot's coat was reddish. Hungas whinnied and stomped his hoof as she walked past, obviously vigorous. Star was a small horse with a white patch on her dark brown face, and Mairéad guessed Aggie might be short for Augustin, because he lifted his head and looked down on her with a kind of majesty as she walked by.

Following Shamus along the wide dirt floor, he spoke over his shoulder, "I haven't lost ye, have I?"

Quickening her pace, she allowed, "I'm reading their names. Does his lordship ride?"

"That he does, on occasion. He prefers Hungas, the one that stomped as ye walked past. He wants yer attention, that one. You're ta try out Caomh, 'tis the mare his lordship picked. She's here at the end." He lifted the handle on the half door and went in ahead of her. He talked gently and patted the neck of a light tan horse with a black tail and mane. "I've brought a lassie for ye, Caomh. We think ye'll get along fine when she knows the way of ridin' ye."

He gestured to her saying, "Take this carrot and hold it at the end for her."

She eagerly took the vegetable and did as told. The mare eyed her with beautiful dark liquid brown eyes. A lump formed in her throat. It was almost as if Caomh wanted to be friendly with her. Delicately, the mare took the carrot with her thick brown lips and chewed, never blinking those huge brown eyes.

"Go ahead, lass, run your hand over her face. She won't bite."

Mairéad took her glove off and did so, along the velvety length of her brow where a shock of black hair hung between her chocolate eyes and long black lashes, then down to her nose. The mare snorted, and she jumped back. "Oh."

Shamus chuckled. "She's lettin' ye know she likes ye and thanks for the carrot. Ye'll get used ta the ways of her, as she'll get used ta ye."

Leaning against the stall wall, a hand to her chest, she breathed, "This is thrilling."

"I ken your excitement. We'll take it slow. Come, let me show ye the saddle then."

She started to leave and on impulse caressed Caomh's neck and whispered, "I'll be back."

She followed Shamus to what he called the saddlery, a room at the end of the wide dirt hall. Saddles, leather straps, and bridles hung from a horizontal post. He patted one and beckoned her close. "This is her ladyship's saddle."

Running her hand over the seat part, she tried to make sense of how to sit. He must have read her mind. "Your right leg fits between the two pommels and your left leg goes on this side." He held up a length of leather with a metal hinge. "And your left shoe slips in this. 'Tis a stirrup."

"How do I actually get in it?"

"The beast will be saddled up and taken to a box. Ye'll climb up on the box, and sit, and adjust your legs. All right and easy like, lass. Though I'd easily hoist ye up and into it." He grabbed a blanket off a shelf. "I'll be with ye through it all and keep the reins and we'll stroll about the yard at first. When the time comes, we'll ride together. Slow and easy, as his lordship directed."

Happiness swept over her like sunshine, and the drum in her chest and the ringing in her ears quieted. "I think I can do this, Shamus, I truly do."

"You're a bit of a thing ta put the saddle on, so watch me." He reached for a bridle and the saddle, and they returned to Caomh's stall. He was whistling. She had not heard whistling but one other time, when Mr. Chiley brought his pony trap to take Mother Abbess to town. It made her think of the convent, and what an adventure this would be to write about.

Shamus clasped the saddle to Caomh's middle, put the bridle in place with its brow band, throat latch, bit, and the reins. She noted the security of it all. Eventually she hoped to handle this herself and followed Shamus as he led the pretty mare out of her stall and down the aisle to the box.

Seating herself was surprisingly easy, though she realized it might not be if it was necessary to do it from the ground with no box upon which to stand. In any case, she put her hands on the pommel of the saddle and adjusted to the feel of the saddle and the mare.

"How is the weather up there?" Shamus grinned.

Glancing down at him, her delight bubbled. The world was a different place from where she sat. It made her feel adventurous, perhaps even triumphant? Yes, she liked triumphant. "I've never been this tall. I like it." Caomh shook, and her silky mane brushed against her wrist. She reached over and patted the mare's neck. "Are you ready to take me for a ride, Caomh?"

Shamus interjected, "It'll be ye who takes her for a ride, lass. Ye are in charge, not the horse. Something to remember for the future."

Having said that, he began walking them as he held the reins. The sway of the mare was a gentle roll, triggering a swell of passion for the experience of a lifetime.

After they made several laps around the fenced-in yard,

Shamus offered her the reins. "If ye want her ta turn left, give a slight tug on the left, same goes for the right."

Reflexively, her thighs tightened about the pommels. Her boot in the stirrup firmed. She clasped the reins. Shamus warned, "Loose, easy like, lass. Try to relax. Caomh is sweet. She won't do anything to hurt ye, and I'm right here."

Mairéad took a deep breath, casting him a nervous smile. Grateful for his confidence, she loosened her hold on the reins, patted the mare's neck, and with a tiny nudge of her leg urged her forward, as if she'd ridden her entire life. One step, and another, and another. Around and around and around, turning right, turning left, even bringing her to a halt, and then urging her on again.

Shamus laughed. Several stable men stood at the fence, watching. One of them shouted, "Ye're a natural, miss."

Unbelievable. From her lofty perch, a panorama beyond the yard, across the lough, to the forest, and the emerald hills to the west caused her heart to soar.

࿇

The week flew by with the delivery of her paints and brushes. Lord Darnley's valet, Tench, delivered and set up three easels in her workroom. A stool for each easel and a manuscript not quite finished were also delivered with great care and a note from Mother Abbess that she needed to finish the project. Tench was quite solicitous, asking if there was anything else she needed.

She quickly finished with the project that was left at the convent, and Lord Darnley arranged for its return to Mother Abbess. Then, she settled her attention on Lord Darnley's biography. He was most thorough in what he wanted. As was usual when a client requested illumination, the page was already scripted, but with a large square in the upper left corner blank for painting.

The first step was to smooth the parchment with pumice in preparation and dry it with bone powder. Next would be tracing

72

his idea on another piece of parchment the same size as the space allowed on the page. This drawing would be transferred to the manuscript with chalk via a series of holes punched through the original parchment. She intended that Lord Darnley look at the punched model made with the pricked holes before she began on the scripted document.

Right now, however, a beautiful cream-colored mare waited for her. She untied her apron, snagging it on a hook, straightened her brushes and jars, and then closed the door on her workroom.

৪৯৪৯

Mairéad and Caomh fell easily into a daily routine. Shamus's confidence encouraged her to ride out alone. He said she took to riding like a swan to water. The end of summer might come a bit too quick. Unsure how she was going to handle the loss of such pleasure, she intended to enjoy this experience as often as she could until it must come to an end.

The routine at Sacred Heart was consistent. Bells that rang for rising and at prayer times throughout the day, tending to chores, and her illumination was never ending. She obediently stopped what she was doing and went to chapel as did all the nuns.

Now, the direction of her day was administered by her own conscience. However, creature of habit that she was, she rose before dawn, said morning prayers, dressed, and drank her chocolate. Usually the first one to arrive in the dining room, she ate, chiding herself for taking a strip of the tasty bacon each day. Then she went straight to her workroom, brilliant with morning sun, and spent the next four hours or so plying her craft.

Her work on the manuscript done for the day, she changed into her riding habit.

৪৯৪৯

Caomh whinnied and shook her mane, her soft lips reaching for

73

the daily carrot Mairéad offered. "You are greedy, missy. Here you go."

Shamus stopped to chat a moment. "Where to, lass?"

"Good day, sir. Perhaps we could explore the lough, riding around the perimeter? What do you think?"

"It'll be wet in the lower parts, especially the closer you get to the river. Better you stay to higher ground."

"We will be beware of bogs, now, won't we?" She patted Caomh's neck.

On her way to the woods, she directed the little mare north along the river. Glancing back, Shamus continued to watch from the stable doors flung wide, hands on his hips as though mulling an idea. She knew him well enough by now to understand he cared about her welfare.

The buckskin cob kept to a worn path around the perimeter of hillocks and an ancient earthen ruin, mayhap a castle from days of yore. Someday she would stop but would need to reseat herself if she did.

Caomh cantered over the land, and Mairéad pondered a casual remark Shamus made several days earlier in reference to Lady Darnley. It occurred to her that the woman in the window on the top floor of the west wing might be her, but if so, why did she not come to dinner? There had never been a mention of Lord Darnley's wife, so it was an awkward question to ask. Perhaps she could inquire of Mrs. Atkinson.

Shamus also mentioned Caomh's intelligence and that she loved to run. Over the last two weeks, as Mairéad gained confidence, more and more she spurred the mare to a trot. Delighted and feeling a bit daring, she tapped the mare's flank with her quirt. The response was a longer gait, robust.

Riding south, they reached the far end of Hawthorn Village and its lough, which shimmered with brilliance in the breeze. She took the opportunity to dismount onto a rock wall about two and a half feet high. She held to the reins, talking aloud, feeling somehow that the mare understood her. "This will be a bit of a test for us. I plan to reseat after a nice little stroll. We'll come back to this wall."

Caomh gave her a tiny nudge, making Mairéad think she understood. "You are a clever one. Smart indeed."

The wind off the land smelled sweet with ripening hay. A few clouds swept shadows across the rippling wave of growth. Leaning her head against the mare's neck, she patted the soft buckskin. A confidence and peacefulness settled on her.

It was odd to feel so comfortable here, and she cast off the wee inkling of being a traitor. Was she an ungrateful wench, who initially longed for autumn and the return to convent life, but now was not in such a rush?

As far as the eye could see, County Waterford's hills trundled across the land. In the west, a fair distance away, yellow gorse burned brightly, its pungent coconut scent, released by the warmth of the sun, drifted on the breeze. Thanks to the clear, bright day, beyond the gorse was a remarkable though faint view of the Knockmealdowns of Tipperary.

To the east, pink and lavender rhododendron rolled in wild abandon across the hills, beyond which the Village of Waterford snuggled against the River Suir.

County Waterford's map, displayed on the wall in Lord Darnley's library, allowed her this perspective. Envisioning her location on that map gave her a keen awareness of the countryside. She certainly was not lost.

Off in the distance, three riders disrupted her musing. They raced, leaning into the effort, urging their mounts. It appeared they were taking the route toward her rather than veering off in the direction of Hawthorn Village. She began walking the buckskin toward the rock wall.

The riders gained on her as she attempted to reach the wall, and the sound of pounding hooves closed in. She would feel better atop Caomh. Even if she stepped up her brisk pace, she knew there was no way she would reach the wall before they were upon her.

Pursued and vulnerable, she tried to calm the thrumming in her chest.

With all the land open to them, why would they come directly toward her? The staccato beating of the hooves slowed, and she turned to the sound.

The rider in the forefront jumped off his moving steed, landing on his feet, allowing his horse to slow and stop a few yards beyond. His behavior dramatic and a bit breathtaking, he swept off his hat and made a leg, saying, "At your service, my lady."

The other two riders also slowed their pace. They climbed off their mounts and gave her a nod, obviously waiting for the first rider to do something, a fact that designated him their leader in her mind. She looked him in the eye, clutching the buckskin's leads.

"Allow me to introduce myself, Ayden, and my friends, Innisbeck and Tremaine."

Her inspection narrowed on Innisbeck. He did have a shock of red hair accentuating his plaid jacket, which meant that Ayden must be Lord Darnley's grandson. Why did he call himself Ayden? Then she glanced at Tremaine. He was tall, flaxen hair curled about his high collar, escaping his queue, no doubt from the ride. Dressed in buckskin breeches, black waist jacket, and riding boots, he appeared the eldest of the three, certainly in manner if not dress. He met her glance with an easy smile, which produced little crinkles in the corners of his blue eyes. His disarming smile caused her to lower her gaze. He was quieter and rather handsome, though she was not sure she could be a judge of such.

"Cat got your tongue?" Ayden quipped and reached out, running a gloved hand along Caomh's rump as he stepped near.

His swagger instantly irritated her. Was it the combination of what she already knew and his pushy, demanding nature? Or was she being overly sensitive?

Ayden flashed a grin at his companions, his dark hair curled about his oval face. "You are amusing us with your neglect of an introduction."

"Your amusement is of no concern to me." Her fist tightened on the reins.

He stepped closer, disturbing her sense of decency. Defensively, she stood her ground, Caomh's breath on her back. He reached out to the mare, running his palm down her nose. The mare whinnied in response.

Ayden must recognize the mare. Mairéad did not like him. He was too forward, too rakish and aggressive. He reeked of hostility. Mrs. Atkinson warned her.

His hand drifted from the mare's forelock and landed on her arm. Startled, she jerked away. The mare sidestepped. Innisbeck immediately confirmed Lady Duncamden's description of a braying ass. She tried not to snicker, though her disdain was immediate.

Tremaine called out, "We are expected. We should be on our way."

Ayden held up a hand to quiet him, never taking his eyes from her. "You live in the village?"

"Where I live is none of your concern." Caomh pulled on the reins as she stepped back.

"Sassy and pretty. Tell me where you live, and I'll make it a point to visit while I'm in the area."

A nervous laugh bubbled out of her. There were sons accompanying fathers as they delivered needed items to the convent. A time or two she watched them unload as they labored. They did not begin to compare in dress and manner to these three, and most especially this one.

He flashed a big white smile, his gray eyes glistening. Eyes that matched his grandfather's. He said, "Tell me where to find you, pretty lady. You intrigue me."

Tremaine spoke, his voice heavy with command. "Ayden, we must be on our way."

Innisbeck stuck his thumbs into the sides of his vest, one leg cocked, as if he watched something of great interest. "Leave him be. I'm of a mind to witness this test of wills."

Mairéad glanced at Tremaine. His mouth was tight. He was clearly not a proponent of Ayden's manner. Innisbeck displayed the opposite. She turned her unease on Lord Darnley's grandson. "I prefer to be left on my own. Why not do as your friend suggests and be on your way?"

He reached for her arm again, encircled it, and drew her close. She kicked him in the leg, glad of the boot she wore. He laughed. She tugged on her arm. Tremaine jumped close, grabbed Ayden's hand as it grasped her, and peeled his fingers off. "I apologize for this, miss."

He elbowed Ayden out of the way and put his hands on her waist, effortlessly lifting her into the saddle. "He's a lot of bark. Now be on your way." He backed away, giving her a slight nod, and slapped Caomh on the rump.

The buckskin took off, her mane flying in the wind and quickly put space between them. Hammering in Mairéad's chest had her gulping for air as the mare loped.

Glancing back, she could see off in the distance that the three riders took a direct route toward Rockmore Hall. Once she gained space, she calmed and took a circuitous path back to the hall, approaching through the woods behind the chapel. Tying Caomh to a limb, she stalked inside the quiet, cool interior, seeking to ease her nerves and piece together what had taken place out on the grassy slope of hill.

❦

Later, after she left Caomh at the stables with Mikey and took the back stairs to her room, she waited for Ryan's assistance. Sometime during these past several weeks, she began to rely on the maid's handiness.

With a knock and the opening of her door, Ryan's welcome smile eased her jumpy nerves. "Which gown this evening, miss?"

"My veil and tunic." Standing at the window, she turned in time to catch the surprise on the maid's features. "I feel the need of my things about me. I am but a visitor who works here. I'd almost forgotten." In her continued upset, she was taking it out on this woman, whose brow wrinkled with confusion.

"I'll put them out for you." Ryan went directly to the large chifforobe.

The clock struck the half hour. On her way to the parlor, Mairéad grew anxious thinking about the inevitable discovery his lordship's grandson was about to make. She arrived to find Lord Darnley and his sister seated with refreshment in hand. Ayden and his friends were not about, and the tension she harbored washed away like rain washes the air. Greeting the elderly pair, she was grateful she would not be alone with the three men, most especially the grandson.

Lord Darnley began, "I've good news. Rutledge has arrived. He's brought a pair of friends, and they should be joining us any minute."

Lady Duncamden's raspy voice scratched Mairéad's frail sensitivity. "You've worn your convent clothing. Where are the gowns your maid found?" She sighed as she squinted through her glass. "No matter, my dear. Darnley, give her that lime drink she enjoys."

Mairéad stood with her back to the room, looking out the window. "I will go without tonight, thank you, my lord." She glanced at the sky's fading pinks and oranges, the last of the sunset leaving the earth. Usually deer frolicked at this time of eve. With a keen ear for the sound of distant commotion, her skin prickled at men's laughter and conversation and heavy footsteps the carpet runner on the marble floors did not disguise. She took solace in the darkening sky with its bands of pink and orange stretching across the sky and did not turn around as they entered.

Lord Darnley's voice filled with cheer as his grandson and friends greeted him. She saw the mirror image of them reflected in the window, each man greeting Lady Duncamden, taking her hand, small pleasures exchanged at seeing one another again, and her ladyship's delight at the fuss they made over her. What Mairéad really wanted to do was sink into the floor or hide behind the drape. She felt a fool to put herself through this. Why had she not demanded to stay in the convent? This was not where she belonged. Clearly at a disadvantage with her convent upbringing, she didn't know how to handle the arrogant grandson.

The moment his lordship talked, she dreaded what he would say. "Miss Mairéad, come here, my dear. Meet my grandson and his company that I've been telling you about."

She turned from the window. Her gaze sweeping each face. Their recognition took a moment. Ayden's came with a grin from ear to ear. Innisbeck followed with a guffaw as Lady Duncamden predicted, an ass. Tremaine narrowed his vision then a small rise of his brow and a tiny lift of one side of his lips. She thought he mocked her.

Lord Darnley brought her within the circle surrounding her ladyship, who sat on the divan. "This young lady is painting for me. She is an illuminator, working on some manuscripts of mine. Miss Mairéad, may I present my grandson, Rutledge."

Rutledge stood tall above her. A slight mocking grin reaching to his gray eyes, and it sounded as if he clicked his heels when he bowed. "Margaret, how pleased I am to meet you."

She hoped for a scrap of sincerity, respect for her person. She was about to correct the English use of her name when Lord Darnley said, "Lord Innisbeck of Berkshire."

Innisbeck nodded to her. At least he showed respect and did not tuck his thumbs in his waistcoat and look her up and down as he did earlier. "Good evening." It was all she could seem to muster after his rude behavior earlier.

Lord Darnley's voice took on a gentler tone when he said, "Lord Tremaine, back in the county from Edinburgh University, and it remains to be seen what his future holds, when he completes his medical studies."

Tremaine's lips spread across white teeth, and his chin lowered as he smiled down at her with startling blue eyes. His baritone like a warm breeze, "A pleasure, and a delight, Sister Mairéad. I don't ever recall meeting a Catholic nun."

Obviously full of mirth at the gathering of his small family, his lordship was quick to respond. "As she has not yet taken vows, you still haven't, but the time will come, sometime this fall, I believe."

Tremaine tilted his head to one side, eyeing her. "You are to be commended devoting your life to God."

Dratted heat crept up her neck, and she dearly. hoped it would not reach her cheeks.

7

W itham announced dinner in his usual stoic manner, with a slight nod of acknowledgement as Rutledge escorted his great-aunt to supper. Lord Darnley and Tremaine, intent on conversation, left Innisbeck to offer his arm to her, proving he was not quite the oaf he appeared earlier.

Rutledge vexed her to the core. Her inexperience with the male gender did not prepare her for the irritation she felt. She hoped dining would not prove a disaster. His grandfather's presence surely would keep him in check. Sister Catriona used a phrase, arrogance will be rewarded. She always said it with a wink. Mairéad could only hope.

Innisbeck's etiquette toward her changed. Perhaps, now that he was in Lord Darnley's manor, Rutledge's influence waned. "You appear recovered from our acquaintance earlier."

Because he was at the least a foot taller, she hoped he would not detect her disdain, though her voice might give her away. "I was surprised it was not mentioned to his lordship. I assume that was because of the inappropriate behavior of his grandson."

She expected he would guffaw. Instead, he appeared flummoxed.

Designated seating with Lord Darnley at the head of the table placed her on his lordship's left and Rutledge on her left. Lady Duncamden, across the table, took the chair between Tremaine and Innisbeck.

Raising his goblet, Lord Darnley's steely gaze settling on her, then Rutledge, then back to her, as if he knew a secret. Had someone told him of his grandson's disrespect? Her heart flipped. She did not want this lovely man knowing the crudity of the grandson he loved.

His lordship went on to make deliberate eye contact with each of them as he offered, "Let us toast togetherness, friends, and family."

৩%৯

Lord Darnley intended to inquire of Miss Mairéad why she would wear her nun's outfit now, of all evenings, especially since she began dressing as other young women.

No matter, she was here by his side. His old heart swelled with love, though her parentage was unknown. If he could not have his own children about him, he could bask in the borrowed.

His sister's lively spirit sparkled as she engaged in verbal combat with Innisbeck. By the clear delight in her voice, he supposed she looked forward to this with eager anticipation. Tremaine, to her right, gave his attention to Rutledge, who attempted to bring Miss Mairéad into conversation. It was clear there was an edge to her. Perhaps her sheltered life? She may not have sat at a table with young men before. Ah, that must be it. He sipped his wine mulling the thought.

Footmen presented platters of roast duck, mashed potatoes, some kind or other of a rice concoction with green and red pepper mixed in with the sauce, and oat bread, deliciously reeking of yeast and slathered in soft butter. He hoped the aromas enticed an appetite in his grandson, whose goblet was on its third refill. Rutledge's attention was riveted on the lass as he leaned forward and spoke in a voice only she could hear.

83

She screeched, and a reflex jerk of her left arm caused the contents of Rutledge's goblet to spew onto his face and clothing. She leaned toward Lord Darnley, causing her chair to move away from the table and tip over.

Laughter from Rutledge mingled with astonishment as he cursed.

Springing to her feet, the look of horror on her face. Tremaine almost toppled his own chair as he moved quickly to her side. Footmen scrambled, in a state of confusion, unsure what to do. What happened?

In a matter of a second, Tremaine escorted Miss Mairéad from the room.

Lord Darnley hadn't moved a muscle. His fork was stilled halfway to his gaping mouth. His shock shifted to his sister, who mirrored his own. Innisbeck, eyes wide as saucers, muffled a snort.

Darnley dropped his fork and jumped from his chair. "What just happened?" he shouted, jolting himself. He *never* raised his voice.

Innisbeck, laughing, pointed at Rutledge, who shrugged his shoulders, a lurid gleam in his eye. Red wine dripped from his face and coat, while footmen wiped him down. He grinned like a baboon.

Lord Darnley narrowed his vision on his grandson. "What did you do?"

Rutledge's shoulders shook with jocularity an inebriated grin slashed across his face. He locked eyes with Innisbeck, who seemed to join in the hilarity of the situation. Until Lord Darnley shoved his chair back and leaned in on the table, his fingers tenting on the cloth. "What, in the name of all that is holy, did you do to that young woman?" The angry tone of his voice was unfamiliar, even to him.

Rutledge struggled to stand. Placing his fingers on the tablecloth, he fumbled in his attempt to mimic his elder. He raised his right hand, making a claw as if groping.

Darnley's blood pounded at his temples, so concussed was he. His sister gasped at the crude gesture her great-nephew depicted.

Innisbeck came around the table and grabbed Rutledge by the shoulders, shaking him hard. "I'll take care of him for now, my lord." He nodded to Lady Duncamden. "Sorry, my lady. Sorry you witnessed such horrid behavior. You won't be seeing him again until he is able to apologize."

He grabbed Rutledge by the arm and drew him forward. Rutledge's feet stumbled over each other, but he was able to keep pace, mumbling as he did so. His arm rose up in a feeble attempt to wave good-bye to his grandfather and great-aunt.

Silence filled the dining room, until his sister let out a low long breath. "I am afraid for him. He has become someone I do not know."

Darnley stroked his brow with a shaky hand. "I must go to her. I hardly know what to say."

Color returning to her cheeks, his sister said, "He shows no respect for the foundling."

Anger, swift and roiling, filled him and he blurted, "No woman should be disrespected, foundling or otherwise." He stumbled past his chair, taking part of the tablecloth with him. Untangling himself, he left her to sift through the tawdry last few minutes.

At Darnley's gentle knock on Miss Mairéad's door, Ryan opened it slightly. "'Tis you, my lord," she said and opened the door to admit him.

"How is she?" Darnley asked, then saw the lass in front of the grate, weeping into her hands.

Ryan's sad face and pressed lips reflected her distress.

He said, "I'll stay with her for now. I'll ring when I am ready to leave."

"Yes, my lord," she said and closed the door quietly.

He walked across the chamber and stood with his hands folded, desiring to comfort her, but unsure how she might respond. "I am appalled at my grandson's behavior, my dear. I am stricken with bewilderment at his actions." His arms and hands opened to her. "Is there anything, anything I can do?"

Raising her face from her hands, red, swollen eyes filled with sorrow. She futilely endeavored to gain control. Finally, she flung herself into the fold of his embrace. "There, there, now. I can't apologize for his crass behavior, but I can promise you it will never happen again. You have my sworn promise, Miss Mairéad."

Her sobs shortened, eventually coming in long breaths that seemed to ease. As she wiped her face with his handkerchief, he guided her to one of the chairs before the fire, then sat near. "I am trying to understand how a sheltered young lady handles something like this. His crudeness is despicable. Beyond being outraged, I want to have him thrashed."

She twisted the handkerchief with her fingers. Gaining a modicum of control, she lifted a teary gaze. "He ... he shocked me. His hand on my leg was-was vulgar."

Darnley could only imagine her tender heart's devastation.

"I didn't know what to do, my lord. It was so...I was mortified."

"You carry no blame, my dear. If you remember when you first met Lady Duncamden, we discussed Rutledge, hinting at behavior for which he has been reprimanded many times. Mind you, I'm not excusing him. It is just that this is not the first time he has done something crude."

She rested her head against the back of the chair and closed her eyes, her hands limp in her lap. "I am the one out of place. I need to leave."

He blurted, "You are where you belong." His definitive tone accompanied his fist pounding on the arm of the chair.

❧

Mairéad opened her eyes. Lord Darnley's shoulders slumped in distress with obvious concern, certainly not the person who had taken her from the convent. Compassion flooded her heart. His devastation etched in the leathery crevices of his face. She reflected on the many emotions that bombarded her since he had first walked into her life. It was almost too much, though most of it was joyful and exciting.

"What would you ask of me, my lord? Rutledge is your grandson, after all."

"That you will allow me to make amends for the injury committed against your feminine self. To ensure it will never happen again and to promise you safety always."

He offered her a choice.

"Then I must tell you tonight was not the first time Rutledge and I met. When I was out riding this afternoon, he and his companions came up to me as I walked Caomh near the far side of Hawthorn Village."

Lord Darnley's chin rose, and his mouth slackened.

She nodded slightly in anticipation of his thinking. "He grabbed my arm, and Tremaine stepped between us, lifting me onto Caomh's back, allowing me to be on my way."

A deep sigh as he guessed, "You wore your habit to dinner thinking to cloak yourself with your desire to become a nun."

She nodded, fingers twisting the handkerchief in her lap. He was vulnerable to the problems of the temporal world. She ached for him. He was becoming dear to her.

With his shoulders slumped and his chin nearly resting on his chest, he said, "I am so sorry. It is not the meeting for the two of you of which I dreamed. Not by far, my dear."

Her compassion for him far exceeded fear for herself. "I will stay and complete your paintings."

"I am grateful for that," Darnley said, with the first glimmer of hope she heard from him since he entered the chamber.

"I do this for you, my lord, because you have been so kind to me. The fact that you have treated me as a guest rather than someone who works for you has made me quite comfortable."

He started to say something, then pursed his lips, a bit of color and vitality returning to his features.

She added, "Tremaine was kind. He brought me to my room and rang for Ryan."

"Not all men are scoundrels."

"Another lesson I am learning on this side of Sacred Heart's stone walls."

They stood up, and she hugged him. "I care for you, my lord. You matter to me."

His eyes reddened, and his gray brows rose up his forehead. He took the twisted handkerchief from her hands and dabbed at the tears escaping her eyes. "I am heartened you did not demand to be returned to the convent."

"We should probably go back to the dining room. I wonder about Lady Duncamden. And I know you have not finished eating. We'll end the evening on a friendly note."

He sighed, brushing her forehead with his lips. "You bring me ease, my dear. I am sure Philly is in a twist. She will need to satisfy that you are recovered."

☙❧

The next morning Rutledge's absence at breakfast brought Mairéad a sweeping sense of relief as she took note of Innisbeck, Tremaine, her ladyship, and his lordship.

Both Tremaine and Innisbeck stood when she entered the room. Tremaine settled his gaze on her as if inspecting how she fared after last eve, his greeting a smile and nod.

Her ladyship obviously hadn't resolved her issues regarding last night's supper. She barked, "Where is that great-nephew? He should be shamefaced after last night, ruining our pleasant company and dinner, but I know him and think not."

Though she hadn't aimed her question at anyone, Tremaine and Innisbeck exchanged glances, then Tremaine spoke. "He is abed, my lady. We expect it will be dinner at the earliest."

"Hmm," she murmured, maybe thinking it best. Glancing at Miss Mairéad, she added, "I like you gowned like a proper young lady. That blue suits you. Tell Ryan to get rid of the drab convent fare."

"As I will return to the convent at the end of the summer, my lady, I'll have need of my things." She bit into a scone generously slathered with soft butter and raspberry jam.

Lord Darnley inquired of Innisbeck, "Do you have plans for the day, sir?"

"I'm of a mind to lay low, perhaps read if I may peruse your library, and check in on Rutledge from time to time."

"The library is at your disposal, young man, and thank you for your attention to my grandson." He turned to Tremaine, "What about you, sir? Do you have plans?"

Dragging his attention from Mairéad to his host, Tremaine said, "Nothing that can't be changed. Do you have a suggestion?" He stirred sugar into his tea.

"I would regard it as a personal favor if you came by my study when you have a moment or two. Some documents arrived regarding a penitentiary to be built in Waterford. I'd like you to look them over and offer an opinion."

Forking a slice of sausage, Tremaine said, "It would be my pleasure, though it's been awhile since I've read any scuttle on the matter."

Relieved to hear that Rutledge would not be joining them for breakfast, Mairéad drifted into her own thoughts of the day ahead. She missed Sassy and Muffy due to her enthusiasm for riding. They might be a balm for the afternoon. First, however, she needed to get in several hours of work.

Since yesterday morning, when the red shawl appeared in her room, she hadn't a moment to indulge a whimsy. Paying a visit to the woman who waved several times seemed most appropriate.

Midafternoon, Lord Darnley gazed over his desktop as the door to the library opened. His grandson strode across the room, the pallor of his skin ashen, witness to the excess of drink. From the looks of it, what he consumed at table was a prelude to a night of drunkenness. Smudgy circles under his eyes, a slight waver to his walk, and the fact that he did not show for breakfast. His guests did, clean shaven and courteous.

Darnley waited for him to begin. He set his reading material on the desk and, leaning his forearms on the top, entwined his fingers.

"The lass, is she a by-blow?" Rutledge dropped into the chair in front of the desk, legs sprawled in front of him.

Darnley clenched his fingers, taking an immediate offense at the unscrupulous suggestion. "Is this how you talk about a guest?"

"If not that, then what? I did notice your attention. Clear enough even through the wine."

"Miss Mairéad is a skilled painter of manuscripts, an illuminator. I hired her from the Sacred Heart Convent to finish a biography."

"Protected by her craft. Nicely done, Darnley. A little surprising, though. How is such a thing possible at your—"

Slamming his fist on the desktop, Darnley stood. "I've enough of your innuendo and unprincipled opinion. Leave, return to school, or hold your filthy tongue and act like a gentleman."

"You mean like your son the *gentleman* who left me in a pigsty to be raised by illiterates and went off to his fancy life in Cambridge?" He jumped up, fists at the ready, legs spread as if he might bound across the desk and assault his grandfather.

Clenching his teeth, Darnley shook his head, turned his back on his grandson, and faced the hawthorn tree. *If you possess miracles, I could use one right now.*

He turned about, his grandson's anger clearly a weight on his own conscience, and asked, "Why does it always come to this between us?"

"Why is it my father didn't feel he could tell you he sired a son. Instead, shame ridden, he handed me off to cotters. The irony being they work for you." His hand swept through his hair. The other slipped to his waist.

It pained Darnley that his grandson roiled with anger barely held in check. "The moment I learned of your existence I went for you. Had your father seen fit to share your birth with me, your life would have begun differently. I am not accountable for what your father did, only what I could do."

At his side, Rutledge's fists opened, closed, stretched wide again as if he were trying to decide if he should use them. "Easy for you, isn't it? Exonerate yourself as you've done most of your life. Shift blame to others, turn away from responsibilities."

Darnley's breathing came hard. Hostility rose against this self-pitying young man. "You are given every opportunity, far more than most. You turn it into someone else's fault when your grades do not measure up or your drunken escapades cause others great inconvenience."

"That's what I've always been—an inconvenience. To my weak parent who wanted nothing to do with me. To you, shipping me off to Berkshire. Did it occur to you I might have wanted to spend more time with you?" A hiccup sent gin-charged fumes into the air.

Pointing a finger at his smirking grandson, Darnley raised his voice. "You are a scoundrel, and until you can see yourself as others do, you are no longer welcome here."

"Dashed old man, don't get all foxed." Rutledge came at him with open hands. Darnley winced, thankful the desk separated them. "I belong here, you said so yourself. You can't make me leave."

"Your vile behavior toward that young woman was despicable. Have you apologized? Did it even occur to you that she deserves respect?"

Rutledge swept a palm through his dark hair. "She's a sham, wearing a veil without vows. I'd guess she might earn her keep on her back, but I'm not sure you can get it up anymore."

The blood whooshed from Darnley's head. With a deep, clipped voice, he said, "I have spoken for the last time. I'm an old man and want nothing to do with your debauchery, lies, and lack of credibility with your schooling. Get out. Go back to Eton, where you are the darling of the self-aggrandizing crowd."

Rutledge stepped closer; hands fisted. "Bastard you are. High and mighty self, lording who I am, demanding me to be like the man you claim was my father. I want none of it, hear me. The title, money, land. Keep your filthy piece of glory." His nostrils flared with the malice he spewed.

"Out! Now!" Darnley yelled, surprising himself with the venom in his tone.

Rutledge took a step backward, blinking. For a moment, he held his breath. The look of disbelief changed to red-faced anger. "To hell with you. I don't need anything you've got to offer. Nothing." He stalked to the door, gripped the latch, and yelled, "I'll get my things, and the next time I set eyes on you, you'll be in a box ready for that hill out there where you put a stone with my father's name on it. The grave is as empty as your promises to me." He threw the door open. It banged against the wall as he stalked away.

The shock caused Darnley's heart to pound, but just as he took a breath, Rutledge returned, a fist in the air. "I'll have the last word, old man. You won't even be cold yet when I take over Rockmore Hall. Let that sink in. I hate this place and relish the thought of taking it apart piece by piece." Spinning on his heel, he stalked out.

Tench, who heard the exchange, entered immediately. "Can I do anything, my lord?"

Darnley waved his hand as he fell into his chair. "Go after him and see if you can assist in getting his things together."

❦

Mairéad finished reading the first paragraphs of Lord Darnley's chapter on his son, Garrett John II, who died in 1803. She then spent several hours drawing an identifiable figure on the historiated initial *G*, which would begin the chapter. It helped for her to look at Garrett II's full-length portrait in the gallery, fleshing him out in her mind. Because he was such a central figure in Lord Darnley's life, she intended using gold leaf as a special touch.

Setting this aspect of her work aside, she created a new outline with graphite powder dots, readying her work for tomorrow, and then went to her room to get the red shawl.

On the fourth floor of the west wing, she knocked on the door at the end of the hall. Smoothing the shawl across her shoulders, she knocked a second time, this time a bit harder.

A maid answered. "May I help you?" Her gaze fell to the shawl about Mairéad's shoulders. One could hardly overlook the red silk.

"I've come to meet your mistress. I believe she gifted me with this beautiful shawl."

The maid opened the door and allowed her to enter. "If you wait here, I'll see if Lady Darnley is accepting visitors at this time."

Lady Darnley? Mairéad glanced at a landscape on the wall. A rendering of the chapel, beautifully done. The treetops barely reached the eaves, clearly showing the box on which, the steeple rested; the date on the painting was 1568. Mrs. Atkinson told her the chapel was original to the property.

"It's lovely isn't it?"

Mairéad spun about. A delicate woman with pure white hair, not old, not by Mairéad's definition, but elderly, stood behind her. Her beautiful smile and bright pale blue eyes twinkled as she said, "You may call me Lady Adrianna, my dear."

"I am Mairéad. I wanted to thank you for this." She spread her arms wide, allowing the silk to dangle in all its splendor. Though invited to call Lady Darnley by her first name, she could not bring herself to do so.

"I know who you are, dear. Darnley told me. Come, let us enjoy the sun. Sit with me in the parlor. It overlooks the park where you walk the dogs. Cindy will bring tea."

Mairéad followed her ladyship through several rooms, another parlor, and a library, noticing the sun pouring into a lovely room at the corner of the Hall. It was from here she waved. "You live here?"

"I do." She seated herself, and Mairéad turned from the bank of windows and perched on the companion chair.

The maid set a tray on the table. "Will there be anything else, my lady?"

"This will do nicely. Thank you, Cindy."

Her mobcap bobbed as she grinned at Mairéad, curtsied, and left.

Lady Darnley said, "I am glad you responded to my invitation."

"The shawl? It would have been unkind not to, my lady. It is lovely."

"I notice you riding. Spending time at the chapel."

Mairéad was not surprised that her habits were on display. The park was a vast, lovely expanse of nature that spread out against the backdrop of the manor house. "When Shamus was teaching me to ride, he mentioned Lady Darnley. At the time, I thought he talked of someone from the past. It must be your saddle I use."

"Darnley had that made for me years ago. I rode most days in the sixties and seventies. It gives me pleasure to watch you." She poured tea and handed cup and saucer to Mairéad. "I would like to learn more about you. Darnley has told me a little, but my curiosity pesters me."

"I lead a simple life, my lady. I was left on the steps of Sacred Heart Convent as an infant. My life is there. Sister Boniface taught me to illuminate. I do not pretend to be the best, but I enjoy the detail, setting the colors, especially drawing."

"Will you bring me a sample the next time you visit? I would enjoy seeing the progress as you work."

"Perhaps you would like to come to the workroom and see for yourself."

Lady Darnley set her cup and saucer on the tray her keen pale eyes directed at Mairéad. "Oh, no, my dear. I do not leave my apartment. Peace and tranquility is here in abundance. The outside world does not intrude on me. I simply do not have it in me to leave here."

Caught unaware by the declaration, Mairéad asked, "How was this in my room?" She lifted a corner of the shawl.

"Cindy runs all my errands." A smile brightened her delicate features.

"Then I shall bring some of my work to you after it has dried. There are steps to illuminating. I have only completed the second step for his lordship thus far. I have a finished piece ready to return to the convent. Mother Abbess sent it with my things when Lord Darnley brought me to Rockmore Hall."

"Yes, he told me how he rushed you." Her bright eyes narrowed. "Shame on him."

Though agreeing, Mairéad could hardly believe her ears.

Cindy entered the sunny parlor. "Anything more, my lady?"

"This is Cynthia's polite way of telling me it is time for my afternoon rest. Would you be so kind as to visit me again, my dear? The sooner the better would suit me."

Filled with unasked questions, Mairéad was thrilled, "It will be a pleasure, my lady. Thank you for the beautiful shawl and the lovely tea."

8

Leaving Lady Darnley's apartment, Mairéad had three choices —riding Caomh, walking Muffy and Sassy, or sitting quietly in the chapel. The majestic yet humble chapel won. Mulling over her nearly two weeks at Rockmore Hall, she was certain about one thing, so far. Each day presented an unforeseen thunderclap of bewilderment. Half of it she could not put in writing or Mother Abbess might show up and force her back to the convent.

Once inside the stone and wooden nave, she drew the shawl up over her hair and walked to the window with her name imprinted. Well, it wasn't *her* name, but it fascinated her to discover it in a church built several hundred years previously. Who was Fionnuala? In all the prayers to saints over the years, never did she recall hearing that name.

Kneeling, making the sign of the cross, head bowed over prayerful hands, she began *Nones*, along with a litany of thankfulness for these past two weeks because, despite Rutledge's behavior, everyone else treated her with kindness. She was not going to allow his crudity to cast a pall over her time here.

The wind increased and branches scraped the outer wall of the chapel. Finished with *Nones*, the ninth-hour prayers, she rested against the pew. Mother Abbess had not answered her last missive.

She knew the convent was expecting two novices from Dublin to join their community, and if they arrived, acclimating them to the ways of convent life would occupy a large portion of her attention.

Her musing drifted to her ladyship. She assumed Lord Darnley was a widower. No wonder she sometimes caught a wistful look on his features. Lady Darnley made the comment that she preferred to live quietly, but Mairéad was uncertain whether her husband agreed. Was he not a consideration of his wife, or did he approve her choice?

If she, Mairéad, had a family—*No*. She absolutely was not going there. Her good fortune lay with those who cared for her and loved her. Who her parents might be was not within her power to question. A fact that turned her to considering the rascal grandson, Rutledge. He cared so little for others. What could possibly have happened to him that caused such discontent? His behavior went deep into his soul.

Cupping a hand over her mouth, muffling disgust, she mustn't analyze the actions of Lord Darnley's grandson. He paled in comparison to his friends in any case, more so Tremaine than Innisbeck.

A cough startled her. Skewing about in the oaken pew, a sudden flush heated her neck.

Tremaine's deep voice filtered to her, "I did not wish to disturb you, but it's pure foolishness witnessing your mutters and snuffling."

Jumping off the pew, adjusting the shawl, making sure her head remained covered, she sputtered, "I most certainly did not."

His lips pursed in a grin, and with brows raised, he nodded assurance.

Crossing her arms defensively, she made her way toward the door. He stepped into the aisle, halting her advancement.

"I know what I heard, and it sounded like whispering, muttering. Do you often argue with yourself in a holy place?"

"It's none of your concern." A sense of shame washed over her that he witnessed her struggle—brought on by *his* friend.

"When someone enters a chapel, their endeavor is to pray, concentrate. I find you a distraction." His grin brought crinkles at the corners of his eyes.

He made fun of her, what is more, her own ruffled emotions were a private matter. "Step aside. I'll leave you to your solitude and *prayer*," she retorted, chiding herself for the sarcasm. Living on the outside of the convent walls put her at a disadvantage.

With a slight bow, hat in hand, he pointed toward the door. As she took a step forward, he whispered, "Do you not know when you are being teased?"

The look on her face must have surprised him, because he changed his tone. "Forgive me, Sister Mairéad. I'm used to egocentric individuals. You are tender-hearted, and I have bruised you. Please accept my apology." He straightened, holding the brim of his hat in both hands. It was plain he expected a response.

Her chin rose as she slanted him a narrowed glance. "Are you suggesting I am self-absorbed?"

"Not at all, fair damsel. You are the complete opposite."

She found herself biting her bottom lip, something she never did.

He asked, "How long before we arrived had you been at the hall?"

"Two weeks." She made to leave, and again, he stopped her.

"Lord Darnley is quite happy you are at Rockmore. He mentioned it this morning. He finds you a shining light in his household."

Not used to compliments, she was stunned. "His lordship actually said that?"

"He did. He is grateful you are here for the summer."

A sense of wonder came to her, salted with guilt. "If you must know, I had no say in leaving Sacred Heart. I was fairly ordered to come here."

"I'm sure Lord Darnley prized your talent."

She shrugged. His inquisitiveness boarded on prying.

"I have a splendid idea. What if I accompany you on a walk, and we acquaint one another?"

Stepping toward the door, she said, "I am not interested. You are the friend of a man I do not like, and that poses a problem for me."

Following in her wake, he said, "Rutledge? Our families joined long before either of us was born. I can't make apologies for him, and I doubt he does for himself, as I mentioned last evening when I escorted you to your room. Please do not make the mistake of thinking that I in any way condone his behavior, for I do not. What's more, he is aware of my feelings on the matter."

"Generations are binding." Before opening the door, she added, "I think it a shame after years of your shared relationship, you apparently have nothing in common with him. It must sadden you a great deal."

"Which is why knowing you would fill that void to some degree." The glint in his eyes brought a smile to her.

"You are persistent, Lord Tremaine. A short walk, then."

He reached behind her opening the door to a rush of fresh, clean air and brisk wind. A shaft of sunlight dowsed them, and it took a moment to adjust to the light.

"Are you a native of County Waterford?" he inquired.

"I was left on the steps of Sacred Heart as an infant. All I own was my given name and a note that read I was not to enter the religious order."

"Yet, you will do so this fall?"

As she stepped onto the gravel path, she clung to her shawl lest the breeze send it windward. "I'll be of age in September and it is what I know, after all."

He did not put his hat on, surely because of the wind. His thick flaxen hair, slipping from its queue, framed his head like a wild halo. His stark blue eyes searched her face. Puzzlement creased his brow. "That is your decision because you were left as an infant?" He cocked his head and locked his gaze on her.

She did not know what to say. In her growing years, there was never any conversation on the matter. It was just to be.

"Come, Miss Mairéad, help me understand. I feel you owe me considering I've acted as a friend on two occasions now, rescuing you from Rutledge."

He had dropped the use of *sister* when saying her name. The heat of a blush rose up her neck. She glanced at her fingers clutching the shawl. Was he right? Did she owe him? She said, "Other than with Mother Abbess, I have never discussed the matter. She refused to talk about the possibility occurring until I turn eighteen. Why wouldn't I? My whole life has been at Sacred Heart. The women are my family."

"Ah, but now you are discovering more about life on the outside, are you not? New things to consider? Secular attitudes, a difference in perception?"

Caomh and hot chocolate came to mind.

He took one of her hands from the shawl and held it in his larger one, halting their progress. "I would be honored to be your friend, Miss Mairéad. I must leave early in the morning. Duty visits to my family. My family home is an hour from here, toward the Knockmealdowns. I plan to return next week to join up with Innisbeck and Rutledge."

A sudden sense of loss came over her. What was wrong with her? Tears threatened, and she should have turned away, but her hand felt so natural in his. She gulped at the knot in her throat, and softly mentioned, "I am pleased to be friends with you."

His smile was, well, the word *charming* came to mind. It lit his eyes and made them sparkle. And, of course, the crinkles in the corners of his eyes added to the warmth of his nature.

His dark brows rose adding disappointment to his words as if he expected her to reject him. "I can't explain how I feel. Yesterday, you made me breathless with anticipation. I felt as if I've known you forever." He tugged on the hand he held. "Don't you think that odd, when we've never met?"

Captured by his sincerity, she stumbled over the workings of his mind. "I... well I have never had a friend my age. I suppose it is the same as having one that is older, and I have more than enough of those." She grinned as a picture of the nuns came to mind. She knew full well that she was the topic of conversation now that she was gone. "The sisters of Sacred Heart, we live together. They are my family. So, no, I don't believe it odd we should become friends."

He drew her hand to his lips and pressed a kiss against her knuckles. "I am honored to be accepted as a friend of your age."

Her laughter eased the knot in her throat and mixed with the wind. His friendship offered her a complexity she'd not dealt with before, but a whisper in her ear told her it was a fine thing, and quite dandy to have this nice man, near her age, be a friend.

When they arrived at the hall, Mairéad and Tremaine parted, he to check in on Innisbeck and Rutledge, she to find Lord Darnley. She knew he was most likely in the library, where he liked to sit and look out at the hawthorn tree and the pastureland waving in the breeze.

She found him right where she suspected. His chair at an angle to the desk as if he'd been enjoying the landscape, eyes closed, but not napping. She tiptoed near, quietly asking, "Are you asleep, my lord?"

"No, just thinking." His eyes opened, and a slow smile spread across his face at the sight of her.

She sat across from him. "Do you have a minute or two to spare?"

"It would appear I do," he acknowledged, followed with a chuckle.

"You told me your grandson was your only family and included Lady Duncamden as you said such."

His left hand reached onto the blotter of his desk, toying with a paperweight. "Ah. So, you've met Lady Adrianna, have you?"

"Did you think I would not?" She straightened in the chair, knowing full well her voice held censure.

"I wasn't sure. Her ladyship's moods change." Darnley's gaze fell to the floor, his chair remained askew.

This man was full of surprise and depth, with feelings he harbored that perhaps he didn't easily share. "I'm sorry. It's been said I'm meddlesome and am oft criticized for it."

He turned the chair to face her. Put both arms on the desk, twining his hands. "I will answer anything you care to ask, my dear. I did not tell you about Lady Darnley because I am not sure how long you will stay at Rockmore. She never leaves her apartment, relying on her servant when she needs to communicate.

"Years ago, more than I like to remember, a fever claimed the lives of our two youngest, Robert and Dorothy. Our eldest, Garrett II, Viscount Rutledge, was away at Eton, or he might have succumbed as well. Lady Adrianna could not bear to walk the halls, sit in the dining room and parlors. Wherever she went, reminders of our children caused her to sob and mourn. When Mr. Stuart, our doctor at the time, suggested she live in another part of the hall, it was meant to save her sanity. I thought it temporary, but she's never left."

The utter sadness in his voice touched her deeply. She didn't know how to respond.

Not finished with the telling, he continued. "She always appeared to revive when our son returned from Eton. He had a way with her that I'd lost. Her laughter was music to me when he visited. She'd become the gay woman I adored. Then tragedy struck again. He was swept away at sea on a return trip from the continent. He was only twenty-four."

Mairéad could hardly grasp such loss. "What of his wife and your grandson? Do they not bring her joy?"

"We knew nothing of them at the time. We learned about his secret life in the weeks that followed. After Garrett's death, a solicitor delivered a letter in which the mother was referred to with initials on the marriage certificate. Their child, a son, had been given over to cotters on our property. Naturally, I immediately brought him to Rockmore Hall. Lady Adrianna refused to meet him. She has never set eyes on him that I know. Except perhaps out her windows."

Struck by the sad circumstance, she could relate in that she hadn't a family.

"I know what is running through your mind. I don't condone her refusal. I believe she is deeply afraid she will lose him and cannot bear another broken heart."

He had lived a long time with this tragedy. In the few weeks she spent with him, she'd seen the clouding of his eyes, and concluded his thoughts drifted to times past. "Could it be possible that your grandson's behavior is rebellion? His way of lashing out against the loss of her friendship. After all, he is without a mother. A grandmother would be a wonderful replacement. Her refusal could give him cause for feeling rejected."

"You are wise. Yes, that occurred to me, but I can't force a relationship." He sat back in his chair, drew his arms off the desktop. "There should come a time in a young man's life when he makes a decision to grow beyond disadvantages and adversity. My grandson doesn't seem capable of or willing to do that. It's as if he is frozen in the past without the ability to move forward."

Darnley stood and turned his attention to the hawthorn, folding his arms across his chest. With his back to her, he asked, "Take yourself, for example. Do you even know your parentage? Do you wallow in that lack of knowledge? Of course, you do not. You are devoted to good works, you've learned a trade, you think of others. Perhaps I should not have done so, but I have drawn a comparison of you two young people, and it does not bode well for Rutledge. I hope my banishing him from Rockmore has him digging deep into the man he needs to be." When he turned to face her, animosity and disappointment etched his countenance.

"You sent him away? Because of what he did? Oh, my lord. Not because of me? I intend to return to the convent when my work is done. Please do not make me the reason you cast him out. Please." She stood and leaned into the opposite side of his desk. "I beg of you."

"It's done, Miss Mairéad. Enough said on the matter. I can only hope it is the spur he needs to look inward."

During their lively supper, Tremaine entertained Lord Darnley and Lady Duncamden with stories of their shared past. Mairéad recognized in her new friend an ability to comfort, far different from Rutledge's anger and the foolishness she sensed in Innisbeck. Like Lord Darnley drawing comparisons, she found herself doing the same.

His lordship mentioned Innisbeck and his grandson left earlier in the day. He assumed they were returning to Berkshire. Tremaine did not inquire why they left without a good-bye, perhaps drawing his own conclusions.

In the parlor after their meal, Tremaine offered to play whist. Her ladyship announced that Muffy and Sassy had exhausted her and all she wanted was to sit before a fire with a glass of sherry.

His lordship grunted, "I'll join you in the sherry."

Not giving up, Tremaine turned to Mairéad. "Dice or cribbage, then?"

Forced to admit she had never played, Lord Darnley chuckled, "Seems you'll have to play solitaire or simply enjoy a quiet evening with us in the parlor, sir."

Tremaine responded, "As I must be on my way early, that is the most sensible option." His blue eyes twinkled in merriment when he glanced at her. "So, I will spare you the humiliation of a good trouncing."

Mairéad's raised brows were meant to challenge. "At some time in the future then?"

He laughed outright. "I take it you intend to learn?"

Her ladyship's gravelly voice chimed in, "I'll make sure she is a worthy opponent. Cribbage will be her game."

Mairéad readily decided Tremaine was a cheerful man, with a sense of fun. Why could Rutledge not be like this?

It was clear the day had caught up with her ladyship. She looked tired. Mairéad knew the elderly woman was familiar with her brother's moods regarding Rutledge and figured she deliberately requested Muffy and Sassy join the small group as entertainment and diversion. Sassy begged her way onto the elderly woman's lap. Muffy toured the room, sniffing the shoes of each, and then circled the area in front of the fireplace before curling into a small black fur ball. Obvious to her, this was a family truly caring for one other and felt a sense of honor to bear witness.

Tremaine offered, "Seems we didn't pass the test."

"An independent lady. A lot like her owner," quipped Mairéad. That drew a smile from Lady Duncamden who looked cozy, a wrap across her lap, sherry in hand, and Sassy snuggled close.

Within the hour, Tremaine made his good-byes. He planned to be on the road early. Mairéad also retreated to her chamber. Though restless and unable to settle, she needed time to herself. Dismissing Ryan from her chamber before readying for bed, she stood at the windows. A full moon lit up the park. A stag and his small herd grazed near the summerhouse, their moonlit shadows long against the grass already wet with night mist.

Another shadowy length presented itself across the park. The deer moved slowly away, not startled by the cloaked figure. With purposeful stride, the person turned onto the path leading to the chapel. Immediately, Mairéad recalled Mrs. Atkinson telling her about the O'Bannon woman.

She grabbed up the red shawl and hurried from the chamber.

❧

The further Mairéad trod along the path, the less light there was from the moon. Within a few minutes, she approached the chapel. Opening the door, she slipped inside lighting a candle. When her sight adjusted, she knelt in the nearest pew. It was too late for *vespers* and too early for *Complines*. Making the sign of the cross against her chest, she quickly whispered prayers in the hope they would take care of both obligations. Within minutes, crossing herself, she stepped outside, asking for forgiveness for treating night prayers so casually.

As she followed the path around the chapel to the graveyard, sticks and brush snapped under her boots, thin soled but better than sandals. Within a short distance, and barely visible, sat a woman leaning against a headstone, her soft voice wistful with song. It seemed her loss was so deep, she comforted herself by spending time with the bones of someone from her past. Loathe to intrude, Mairéad regretted her approach.

Pausing to consider the woman, she wondered whose stone she visited. If she, Mairéad, lost Mother Abbess surely, she would do the same. Suddenly the idea of losing his lordship blew into her musing. Ah, most certainly, she would, and it struck her so deeply, she shook the notion away, fearful of the image that sprang to mind, and turned toward the chapel.

The snap of twigs made her edgy. She was about to run when a voice said, "You have come to visit someone, then?"

Obscurity ran deep where Mairéad stood, and she suddenly found herself nearly shoulder to shoulder with the woman.

The woman's cloak covered her hair, but a speck of moonlight revealed a pleasant, even-featured face and mayhap sorrow in her eyes. Her voice was soft, full of worship, "You have the privilege of praying in a sacred place, hundreds of years old, built before my *seanmháthair*, who was verra old when she passed. This place was verra old, even then."

"You are able to trace your grandmother? Would you be an O'Bannon, then?"

"That I am. You would know the history?" She nodded toward the chapel.

"I've learned a little staying at the hall. The O'Bannons built it."

The woman said, "That would be near about 1300s. My ancestors were invaded by the Normans. Pagans who wanted to learn about God from us." Her sorrowful gaze swept over the stone walls. "The Christianity they discovered allowed this holy place to be built. Ye've seen Saint Brigid's window, I'll be thinkin'."

"It's lovely. Also, the window of the two O'Bannon women."

The woman's work-worn hand sliced the air. "No more. I've happiness in my heart. I'll be needin' to keep it, not brush it off with the ghost of sadness." She turned in a flurry, warning over her shoulder, "You'll be gettin' on, too. I smell rain."

Mairéad kept an eye on the retreating figure as she fled along the path. Clouds passed in front of the moonlight, glistening now and then on the dew of the park. The scent of rain came to her, too. Before leaving, she wanted to look at the stone where the woman sang.

Garrett John Wallington II, Lord Rutledge. Mairéad's fingertips traced the etching on the stone. Curious as to why the woman would sing to a stone, she glanced back down the path and then back to the stone. This was Lord Darnley's son, who was swept away at sea. Though marked with the years 1779 to 1803, this was an empty grave. She felt sorrow for the woman, for she knew there must have been an attachment between them for her to come here at night and sing to emptiness.

9

Mrs. Atkinson knocked gently on the workroom door before entering. Mairéad looked up from the table. "Good morning."

"And to you. Laundry wants you to wear these when you paint." She waved half sleeves at Mairéad.

Setting her paintbrush down, Mairéad lifted her arm. "I'm afraid the damage has already been done." Drawing a sleeve over her hand, she covered the cuff of her gown and repeated the effort on her other hand.

The housekeeper walked behind the stool where she perched and curiously inquired, "What have we here?"

"Lord Darnley wanted his family initial to begin the story of–let me see where I put the other pages."

"I didn't intend interrupting your progress." She pointed to the letter W that turned into an ivy vine spreading its tendrils across the page. "This looks intriguing. Stands for Wallington, I take it."

"The vine symbolizes the story he wrote of his ancestry. I've just begun treating the parchment. You can see the sage paint, not yet dry. When it is, I will embellish it with a touch of gold leaf. Finished with that, I'll add flowers. I'm thinking a likeness of him would be most appropriate."

A neat, bushy brow rose as she complimented. "You have a gift for this."

Mairéad was about to disagree when the housekeeper said, "Accept the compliment. Your talent is worthy."

She slid off the stool breathlessly admitting, "I met the O'Bannon woman."

Mrs. Atkinson's interest turned from the painting to her. "When was this?"

"Last night outside the chapel."

"Did she set your curiosity to rest?"

Mairéad grinned. "Ah, so I'm fairly obvious. I came upon her as she sang to a marker. She was quite alone, yet content from what I could gather."

"I told you this was her ancestors' land. Some graves are from centuries ago."

"She was singing to the stone of Garrett II."

"Hmm." Mrs. Atkinson turned her attention to the window. "I think you may have been cooped up in the convent too long."

Mairéad knew what she saw and heard, and quickly changed the subject. "Shamus sent word this morning that Caomh has missed me. How would he know that?"

"Shamus knows his horses I will tell you that. I'm certain he is grateful you are assisting with their exercise. You have a busy day ahead. I will leave you to finish and get on with your four-legged adventure. Just remember to wear the sleeves and quiet the rumbling from the laundry."

Later in the afternoon, tired from her afternoon gallop with the buckskin, Mairéad returned to her chamber to find a letter from Mother Abbess. She plopped in the nearest chair, tearing the seal from the fold.

Dear Mairéad,

Sister Catriona sends her regards for the charcoal drawing of her feeding the chickens. Well done from memory. You are missed, but we all concede the work you are doing is valuable to Lord Darnley, thus making your absence one of need.

We enjoyed your observation of the puppies. I believe you took them for a walk when they ran off. Be grateful for your youth that allowed you to go after them.

As I write this, the two sisters from Dublin are delayed once again. A fever is claiming lives in the boggy section in the south of the city, and they are desperately needed, as one can only surmise. We pray to spare their lives in the aftermath of the scourge. On my visits with Mr. Chiley into Hawthorn Village, we have not seen any indication of the fever spreading about the countryside. For this we are thankful.

Give my regards to his lordship, and gently remind him you are missed here at Sacred Heart. We all send our love, Sister Eleanor Anthony Eustace.

Her absence was one of regret, but not of her doing, and as the days passed the weight of her contrition lessened.

Mairéad realized she must have dozed off. Ryan was taking a gown from the mahogany chifforobe

"What time is it?"

"Half after six." Ryan also mentioned, "Lady Duncamden will be leaving tomorrow."

❧

With Ryan's assistance, Mairéad was able to arrive in the parlor before the clock struck seven.

Lord Darnley greeted her with the lime drink she preferred. She went directly to the divan where her ladyship reclined. "It'll be a sad day tomorrow with your leaving."

"It's past time. You know, like fish ..."

Lord Darnley interjected, "Your three days passed weeks ago, so you can't use that old herring."

Ignoring her brother, she bustled with energy. "I must know. You met Lady Adrianna? How did you manage that?" She held her quizzing glass, watching Mairéad with one enlarged blue eye.

"A pleasant visit, considering I was unexpected. She ordered tea, and we made small talk. She's asked me to return."

"I do not seem to get on so well with her. Snippy."

Which one would be the snippy one, Mairéad wondered? She quickly drew her lime drink to her lips, hoping for a pucker.

Lady's Duncamden lorgnette bobbed on her ample bosom as she breathed, "Out of the goodness of my heart, I give her license to act as she does, but enough is enough for anyone to endure. I am more concerned with Darnley, and the ruckus with Rutledge. It's worn him down."

"Don't use me as an excuse, Philly." her brother cautioned from the window where he stood. "You know as well as I, Lady Adrianna suffered to the brink of near catastrophe. Her living arrangements are a panacea for which I am grateful."

Mairéad listened to their back and forth, enjoying their sibling banter. They must have had a wonderful childhood enduring into their harmonious and sympathetic elderly years.

Witham announced dinner and the women put their hands in the crooks of Lord Darnley's arms as they made their way toward supper.

As footmen brought around trays of poached salmon in a buttery fennel sauce and potatoes and cabbage, her ladyship inquired, a quirky lilt to her amused features, "I am curious. What made you visit Lady Adrianna?"

"I found a beautiful red shawl in my room. The only time I noticed such a shawl a woman on the fourth floor waved at me and was wearing one. I took it upon myself to knock on her door."

"She never gifted me with such." Those pale blue eyes twinkled with deviltry.

His lordship swallowed a forkful, chewed, and then asked,

"What are you up to now? You never needed an invite. Miss Mairéad will doubt her actions."

Mairéad teased her. "Whose feathers will you ruffle when you are in your castle? Your staff?"

Lord Darnley almost choked on his wine. "Her staff? They absolutely adore her. It's-it's sickening. They fawn and fetch. 'Tis the reason those curs act the way they do, fussed over as if they were her children."

His sister's chin rose. Though not unusually tall either seated in or out of her chair, she appeared to look down her nose at him. "Better the kind I have than to put up with Rutledge."

Mairéad caught her gasp before it escaped.

Lord Darnley grew quite serious. "First of all, he is a grandson, not a servant. Furthermore, I followed an age-old recipe for reform. We will see how it works in the months to come. He will either sink or swim, as they say. Whatever he does, it's within his power to do it."

His sister lifted her glass of wine. "I drink to you, Wally. You are a prince among men, figuratively speaking, of course. I know what it cost you to banish him and fully agree with your method. I just don't know if I would have had the strength, were I in your shoes."

He turned to Mairéad and winked. "This is why I allow those curs here. She comes with them."

◈

The next afternoon, after several intense hours of painting, Mairéad was delivered of a note from Lord Darnley saying he would ride with her this afternoon. He probably missed the company of his sister, who had taken her leave immediately after breakfast.

Shamus greeted her at the stable door, Caomh saddled and ready.

Lord Darnley's voice boomed from the interior as he appeared with his steed in tow. "We'll be having a time of it today, won't we? Have you met Hungas?"

"On my first visit to the stables. He seems quite spirited, like his master if I'm not mistaken."

Caomh whinnied, eager to be on their way. Mairéad climbed the two steps up the box, put her left foot in the stirrup, and settled comfortably in the saddle. Taking the reins from Shamus, she announced, "Let the afternoon begin, my lord."

"Have you ridden along the Suir toward Waterford?" he asked.

When she shook her head, he said, "Then that's where we'll ride. It's a lovely day, and it's been an age since I've been out and about."

As he took command of his steed, she followed suit. They left the stable yard, turning north toward the ancient River Suir. Both the mare and the stallion were able to trot, the mare stepping up her pace to keep abreast Hungas. Nearing the lowland, they came in sight of the river. Lord Darnley slowed his mount to a jog. Caomh followed suit without Mairéad having to tug on the reins. She guessed his lordship intended giving the mare a rest. The stallion snorted and stomped his hooves in irritation.

She leaned over and patted Caomh's neck. "Isn't this a nice little break for you?"

Chuckling, his lordship said, "Hungas doesn't think so. Nevertheless, I am a bit winded. It's been too long since I've ridden."

"We can go back, my lord. You needn't think I'll be disappointed."

"You are a kind soul, young lady."

They were on a rise that overlooked the rolling beauty of the emerald island. Off in the distance, a light mist hovered over the ribbon of water that created the boundary between the Counties of Waterford and Wexford. To their left, the river veered west. To the right, it meandered sharply toward the bustling village of Waterford then flowed south toward the harbor where the Celtic

Sea met St. George's Channel. She knew the layout from the globe in the library.

"Perhaps I'll take you up on a return. I'm a bit winded."

Without showing concern, she was alerted that this was not his usual demeanor. Astride a horse, she had no comparison, but certainly, in his daily activity, he would have made no such request. Tugging on the mare's reins, she guided her back across the hill at a walk.

Hungas snorted. "Now, now. We'll run out your energy another day."

They kept up the easy three-beat gait until she noted that Lord Darnley's face grew quite pale. He could not seem to catch his breath. "You are faint?"

He turned to her, white as a sheet, and gave an indication that he was. A hand went to his chest. She reached over, grabbing Hungas' reins, bringing both horses to a stop. "What must I do to help?"

He garbled sounds then sagged in the saddle against Hungas' neck and did not move. The stallion stomped his hoof and snorted. She glanced about, getting her sense of direction. They were, at the least, a half hour from Rockmore.

Fear pounding through her senses. She gingerly walked both horses, side by side, slowly, to keep Lord Darnley seated. Systematically they made progress. Prayers fell from her mind to her lips. She was grateful the stallion seemed to sense his rider's predicament, whatever it might be. If it was in her power, she intended Lord Darnley reach assistance, medical help.

Dear Mother of God, please do not let anything happen to this wonderful man you have brought into my life. He has had his own heartbreak and does not deserve to die out here, alone, without family.

The words whispered aloud struck her. He was not alone. With her fists tight about the reins of both horses, she vowed, "I'll get you to the manor, my lord."

Like the howl of death, her thought at the graveyard that if he died, she would visit his stone came back to her. A feeling of dread crawled over her, as if that had been a portent, an omen. *We Irish are a strange lot.*

As prayers fell from her lips, she was dreadfully aware that his lordship could slip from the saddle. She kept the horses at a walk, hoping his body would be less likely to slide. She would have to leave him and get help if that happened. Little by little they closed the distance between them and the hall. The large oaks and hawthorns came into view. The tip of the chapel sparkled, and the twin towers of the stable loomed on the horizon. Gradually, Rockmore Hall grew larger and closer.

His lordship moaned, and his right arm started to move. In a firm voice she assured him, "My lord, keep still until we get to the stable and assistance. Do not move about. Please."

Gardeners worked along the small lough of the summerhouse. She yelled, "Help! Get help!" She could see them, hands cupping their eyes, cutting the sun's glare. "Get help! Urgent!"

One of the gardeners stepped forward, the other grabbed his shoulders and pointed to the stable. He turned and ran.

Within a minute, Shamus took one glance and turned on his heel. Riding bareback, he galloped out of the stable yard. Tears sprang to her eyes.

Occupied with the reins and the dear man next to her, she continued to pray, whispering words of desperation and concern. In that moment, she realized how truly scared she was.

Shamus slowed and came alongside. "What happened?"

"He mentioned he did not feel himself and then collapsed."

Shamus walked his mount close along the other side of Hungas. "You're doin' fine. Head for the kitchen. We'll have willin' hands to carry him inside."

She tried to stop the tears.

Shaumus' gaze spread over her. "You're a brave one, ye are, lass. You're doin' fine. We're almost ta home."

Witham, alerted and prepared to help, stood in the cobbled courtyard along with several stablemen eager to be of assistance.

Shamus slid off his horse, giving the reins to a yard boy. As he moved to Hungas' left flank, ready to catch the dear man, Witham wiggled between Hungas and Caomh, drawing his lordship's boot from the stirrup. "He is free."

Mairéad stilled with fear he might slide to the ground with his perch against Hungas' neck most precarious. Her little mare seemed to understand the importance of her role and stood firm.

The sight of Lord Darnley's limp body tugged at Mairéad's heart as the stout arms of four men eased him down and into their firm grasp. A moan passed his lips, his eyes fluttered, and then closed. Witham directed the men to his lordship's chamber. His voice steady, considering the circumstances.

Witham had already ordered Mikey to the village to fetch the doctor. "Tell him it's a dire emergency."

Of a sudden, Mairéad found herself alone. The buckskin shied and nickered as if she understood her responsibility ended. Numb, she led the mare toward the chapel. When inside the comfort of a place to pray, her grief knotted in her throat. Tears loosened their hold on her fear as she begged for his lordship's return to health.

The cool and quiet of the sanctuary gradually eased her uncontrollable trembling. Images of what could be flashed in her mind. She needed to compose herself before returning Caomh to the stables. As time passed, Lord Darnley and his grandson came to mind. Their tenuous relationship swam in the abyss of her meditation.

She would never presume to take Rutledge's place, but she could certainly care for the dear man in her own way. With sweaty hands clasped in worship and petition, she begged for the opportunity to care for Lord Darnley.

When she returned Caomh to the stable, Shamus informed her that two doctors had been with his lordship for some time now.

An older man, tam scrunched in his fist, approached her as she left the stable. "Miss, a word with ye, please?"

Holding a hand over her eyes, shielding the bright sun, she said, "Yes?"

"Molloy, miss. I work for his lordship and live over there." He nodded beyond the stables where the cottiers lived. "Will ye let him know we're prayin' for him. Worried we are, as he's a lovely man ta us all."

His sadness and sincerity struck her, "You may call me Mairéad, and I will make sure he knows how you all feel. When I know more, Shamus will most likely be informed."

"Bless ye, miss." He placed his tam atop the bald spot on his head and lunged away, no doubt toward the other cottiers who waited with their prayer beads sifting through their fingers.

She walked across the park to the back of the hall. Glancing upward, she noted that Lady Darnley was not at the window of her apartment. She was concerned how Lord Darnley's illness would affect her ladyship's tenuous hold on normalcy.

Lord Darnley's chamber was on the second floor down the west wing. Benches and commodes decorated the long hallway. As she approached what must be his suite, Witham and Mrs. Atkinson huddled against the wall in whispered conversation. The dark, wood-paneled door stood ajar just enough for Mairéad to notice two men, whom she suspected were medical men. The four-poster was draped with heavily embroidered curtains, which were drawn aside enough to allow her a glimpse of Lord Darnley sitting on the edge.

A low sigh escaped, and her palm spread across her heart, as tears stung. The sight of him immediately calmed her of the notion he died.

Mrs. Atkinson turned to her. "Mighty brave you were, Miss Mairéad. I can't imagine the courage it took to bring him back. How far had you ridden?"

She must have been holding her breath as a gasp of relief escaped. "Lord Darnley means a great deal to me." Surprising herself with the admission, she stammered, "We-we were on a hilltop overlooking the Suir where it bends upriver when I first noticed how pale he had become."

Mrs. Atkinson put her arm about Mairéad's shoulders.

Witham cleared his throat. "We are waiting for the assessment to be done. It is clear you saved his life."

Her knees gave out, and she dropped like a sack of potatoes onto a bench. If she had known the dire circumstances, would that have rattled her common sense? Casting another glance inside the chamber, her gaze feasted on him sitting on the bed and not lain out–dead. A knot in her throat hurt.

One of the men stepped into the hallway, smoothing his palm over his vest. He appeared tired as his gaze lingered on Mairéad before he sought out Witham and Mrs. Atkinson.

Witham said, "Mr. Martin, this is Miss Mairéad. You may speak freely in front of her. It was she who brought Lord Darnley back to us."

Mr. Martin said, "Your quick attention minimized the damage." His features eased a bit as he added, "I won't confuse our findings with medical talk. Plainly, he has suffered apoplexy. His sense of smell is altered, though hearing and vision are not impaired. There is a drooping of the left eyelid and a weakness of the left arm and leg. Breathing and heart rate remain steady to an almost acceptable rate. Slurred speech is due to the tongue's weakness. He is confused about details leading up to the attack, but that should resolve in time."

Witham asked, "What course of medical action do you intend?"

"I am of a mind to bleed the bodily tension. My associate, Mr. O'Reilly, disagrees with me on this. We will see what tomorrow brings and come to a meeting of the minds at that time."

Mrs. Atkinson's frown increased as the doctor spoke. Her arms folded across her chest; head bowed.

"Do you know what caused the apoplexy?" Witham glanced at Mairéad before shifting his gaze to Mr. Martin.

"We know it can be the result of an internal maladjustment of the body system. Another seizure could happen."

Desperation forced Mairéad to challenge him. "How do you know?"

Startled, Mr. Martin scowled at her. "Years of experience."

"I am not doubting you, sir. I simply need to understand."

His cold gaze slid down on her. "Medicine is a science. We look for signs. Though one of his eyes is weakened, neither are sunken, his ears are not cold and clammy, and the skin on his face is soft, not stretched and dry. If present, all of these are clear signs that death is near."

Mrs. Atkinson perked up. "Then there is hope?" Her fingers twisted to the point they were white with tension.

Mairéad covered her gaping mouth, hoping for the best but finding it hard to put faith in his reassurance. Tench paced back and forth until Witham snapped at him to do so somewhere else. Leaning against a far corner, Tench sighed, clearly distraught.

Mr. Martin took his fob out flipping the spring on his watch. "If Lord Darnley continues through the night without another episode, his chances of near recovery are excellent."

Tears sprang to Mairéad's eyes. "I want to stay with his lordship."

Witham said, "I don't believe——"

Mrs. Atkinson spoke up. "I'll stay with her. You have an estate to manage. Lord Darnley would expect nothing less of you." Her chin rose as if she dared him to refuse. "And, of course, Tench will be with us."

"Very well, then."

Mr. Martin said, "I'll return by eight at the latest. Otherwise, if there is a change, send for me immediately."

Witham gave a slight nod. "As you wish, sir."

The second doctor stepped into the hall. His gaze swept past the three of them and locked on Mr. Martin. "His lordship is resting peacefully. He was able to swallow a small drop of laudanum. He is quieted and restful. I see no reason to bleed him tonight."

Mr. Martin's jaw firmed, and his eyes slanted to his colleague. "We cannot know what morning will bring, O'Reilly. Reserving your opinion would be wise."

Mairéad could wait no longer. "Excuse me, doctor. May I use compresses on his forehead, and talk to him if he wakes?"

"Primitive care, but I suppose it will make you feel useful, and it will do his lordship no harm." His icy gaze swept over her; his disdain as clear as if he slapped her.

Witham inquired, "What else might be done?"

"The dose of laudanum should keep him quiet for the night. Now, if there are no further questions?" His left brow chased up his forehead, perhaps trying to touch the top of his hairline, as he again, glanced at his watch.

Perplexed over his imperious demeanor, Mairéad questioned, "I feel Lord Darnley is receiving casual attention. Shouldn't one of you offer to stay the night?"

A gasp came from Mrs. Atkinson, and Mairéad knew instantly she'd overstepped.

Mr. Martin pocketed his watch, cast her a dark look, and said, "Limit her time with his lordship. Seems she hasn't the sense God gave a goose."

Witham said, "I'll see you out."

The men departed, following the butler along the hall. A servant lit candles in the hallway. The evening came on quickly. Mrs. Atkinson motioned for Mairéad to enter the bedchamber ahead of her.

Mairéad inched her way bedside. The dear man lay on his back, both arms on the outside of the covers. Her fingers found their way to his arm, and she curled the limp hand into her own, rubbing it against her cheek. "I prayed for you," she told him. "I know you will return to health."

Mrs. Atkinson whispered over her shoulder, "Your heart is true, Miss Mairéad. You gave voice to what we were all thinking, but not the nerve to say. If nothing else, his lordship may well respond to your warm nature. He's known precious little of it from others."

10

Appearing to be asleep, the slow movement of Lord Darnley's chest was comforting.

Mairéad whispered, "He looks so peaceful."

Mrs. Atkinson nodded. "You prayed at the chapel?"

"With all my heart."

"Well, then, he is in good hands." Mrs. Atkinson moved away from the bed as a maid entered.

Mairéad slipped onto the chair, putting her hand over his. Warm skin, not clammy, Mr. Martin had said. He was alive, and tears stung her eyes again. She wasn't prepared to lose him. In the few weeks since they'd met she felt a part of his life. Her stay at Rockmore Hall carved memories to recall the rest of her life.

His thumb caressed her fingers, he mumbled, and something akin to adoration flooded her being. Did he know it was she? All else ceased to exist, but that this dear man should come back to health.

Mrs. Atkinson brought a bowl of tepid water and a cloth, setting them on the bedside table. Mairéad wetted the linen and patted his face. She paced herself, saying ten Hail Mary's, then rewetted the linen, placing the freshened cloth on his forehead again.

Humming a tune from long ago that Sister Catriona had taught her when she was wee, was comforting. A bit timid to do so and have Mrs. Atkinson hear, she kept the words soft and whispery, just enough to reach his ears. Her hand occasionally slid up his arm, patting him, then returned to his hand. His thumb had not moved since the first time, but that was enough. She knew it was a sign from heaven that he would recover, believing in miracles as she did.

Ministering to him and herself as well. His strength washed over her through their joined hands. Even though he was an elder man, his moral character was as rigid as his durability. He could make himself well, unless his heart was broken with the dismissal of his grandson. She swallowed the lump in her throat.

Mrs. Atkinson came bedside. "I think you will be all right if I leave you for an hour or so." She placed her hand on Mairéad's shoulder. "Ring the bell for the kitchen and I will come immediately. Knowing Witham, he will check on you and his lordship, too. Even Tench is at wit's end. There is so little he can do for Lord Darnley. He is used to being busy. He is at loose ends and will be in and out, spending his energy in pacing until this takes a turn for the better."

"Your faith increases mine."

Her hand slipped from Mairéad as she turned to go and then glanced back. "You are good for him, miss. He needs you in his life, especially since the dispute with Rutledge."

The housekeeper's words lingered in the room for her to rummage through. It might appear that she needed him, too. The difference between a convent full of women and a household with a caring sire, a patriarch, struck her as vital. Until he brought her here, she did not know the wonder of such a relationship.

Tench entered the chamber with two pair of Lord Darnley's boots and asked, "Is there any sign of wakening?"

"When I held his hand, his thumb moved."

"His right hand?" He walked into the dressing room and rather quickly returned, free of the boots. Poor man, he was attempting to keep busy. The boots could be used as a looking glass.

She nodded.

"It is his left that is impaired, but a good sign, nonetheless."

"Tench, do you know why Mr. Martin seemed cross with Mr. O'Reilly about the matter of bleeding his lordship?"

"It's gossip, Miss Mairéad, but Mr. Martin knows Lord Darnley's caution on drawing out humors and yet suggested he might do so anyway. It's Mr. O'Reilly who shares Lord Darnley's contempt for bleeding."

She leaned back, looking up at him. "Yet Mr. Martin would do such a thing? It will be allowed then?"

"He is the doctor. If Lord Rutledge were here, he would have the right to decide. The rest of us do not."

As the evening wore on, a maid brought her refreshment, and she continued to pray and refresh the linen. She sang to him in a stronger tone with none to cluck at her for such foolishness. As she caressed his hand and arm, her mind drifted to a dangerous place, a dark cloud where she put images of a father she would never know.

She must be careful not to replace that man with this one. Lord Darnley might not recover, and then what would she do with her broken heart?

The truth was her dreams already began to shift. She bent over, placing a kiss on his hand, rubbing her cheek against its soft warmth.

Sometime later, Mrs. Atkinson tapped her on the shoulder. Mairéad opened her eyes. She had fallen asleep, her head on the bed cover, her hand clutching his lordship's.

"It's almost eleven, Mairéad. Get some sleep. I'll stay now."

In the early morning Mairéad returned just as the sun opened the sky with light, Mrs. Atkinson asked her to assist in moving his lordship on his side. "Physical change is a good thing. He'll have to be kept still after the bleeding, so I want to change his position beforehand. Mr. Martin should be here any time now."

He moaned as they rolled him, and Mairéad couldn't help but frown.

"Perfectly normal. He is alive. I intend he stay that way," Mrs. Atkinson mumbled.

"Can the doctor be stopped from bleeding him? Tench told me how Lord Darnley feels about the procedure."

Before Mrs. Atkinson could answer her, as good as his word, Mr. Martin arrived at eight. He immediately rolled up the linen on Lord Darnley's left arm, tapping the skin, running a long finger up the vein, and readying the area for bleeding the humors.

Not able to contain herself a moment longer, Mairéad scowled, "I understand you are aware of Lord Darnley's sensibility on bleeding. Is that not so?"

The look he gave her would have been funny if the situation were not so dire. "A child, questioning me?"

Disdain thickly coated her words, "I am hardly a child. If you didn't know his feelings, that would be one thing, but you do, and I am questioning your lack of respect for his lordship." She crossed her arms, fuming with ire.

The doctor straightened up from his posture over his patient's bed. "What is your position in this household?" He glanced about for the housekeeper, who momentarily stepped out of the chamber.

"I am an illuminator of Lord Darnley's biography."

He growled. "That makes you an expert. Leave the business of healing to a learned man."

Anger sparked her tongue. "When he recovers, I intend he know you were informed of his abhorrence for the procedure, yet you blatantly disregarded his wishes."

He turned away from the bed and faced her, clearly disgruntled. "You're not meek as a lamb, now are you? *If* he recovers, you may so inform him." He raised his arm, making her think he might strike her.

"Now, get out of this chamber or button your sass. This is a delicate procedure, and I do not want a distraction. I need my wits."

Clamping her mouth shut, nothing on this earth would make her leave his lordship.

Mr. Martin proceeded to spread out a cloth beneath the patient's left arm and pulled a small pointed object from his bag. He ran a finger over the arm until he found the spot he wanted to puncture. She held back a scream as he dug the sharp instrument into flesh, drawing a rivulet of dark red blood along pale skin that collected in the pan upon which his arm rested.

Aghast by the sight of the blood oozing along the curvature of his arm, Mairéad felt a buzzing like a nest of bees fill her ears. She couldn't recall hating anyone before, but she was certain that is what she felt for this doctor. How long she stood there, glued to the sight of the runnel of dark blood, she did not know. Mrs. Atkinson came up behind her, placing her hands on Mairéad's shoulders.

"Come away, Miss Mairéad. Look out the window instead."

It was a bright morning outside, bright and alive with the sound of birds in the trees, nary a cloud in the sky. But her attention returned to Mr. Martin as he spoke.

"It is a concern that Lord Darnley has not opened his eyes. His skin feels warm, which is good, the heartbeat is strong. Draw the drapes and keep a high fire in the grate." He strode to the first of four windows and jerked the drapes shut one by one, as if the household deliberately intended to injure his patient.

He packed his black bag, snapped it shut, and said, "I have another visit to make north of here, I will return this afternoon on my way back to the village. The bleeding should have begun to work. He may revive at any time."

Mrs. Atkinson said, "Thank you, Mr. Martin. I will see you out."

His hand on the door latch, he said, "No need." His heavy footfall led out the door.

With her hand, Mairéad fanned her face. "I have never seen a bleeding. It was all rather matter of fact."

"I am not in agreement with the procedure, but then I am not a doctor." Mrs. Atkinson fussed with the coverlet, tucking it over him, drawing his bled arm carefully atop a folded pillow to raise it up.

"It was apparent last night that Mr. O'Reilly shares your opinion."

"Hmm. Disagreeing with Mr. Martin isn't my place. I was hoping his colleague would lend some weight to our thinking." She turned an intense glance to Mairéad. "Are you able to stay with him for a bit?"

"I cannot paint knowing he lies here. Yes, if you need me. I'll ring the kitchen if anything changes."

A brief smile swept over Mrs. Atkinson's face, and she toyed with the ring of keys at her waist. "I'll have a tray sent up. We can't have you growing weak." She turned to go, then stopped, a brief sigh accompanying her declaration. "You are a very determined lass. I bit my cheek to keep from encouraging you. He will recover. He's a strong man. Hardship he has known, but it has never bested him." With her hand on the latch, she added, "I'll close the door, and you can sing as loud and long as you wish."

For the first time in almost twenty-four hours, a spark of joy inserted itself. Tugging on the heavy drapes, she drew them open against Mr. Martin's orders. Giving her irritation with the doctor a further nudge, she cranked open a leaded-paned window a few inches, letting in the fresh air and bird song of nesting.

The morning passed with neither eye flutter nor thumb movement from him. Tunes from childhood came to mind as she sang. Prayers in between songs whispered from her lips. A knock on the door brought concern that she was too loud.

Mairéad could hardly believe her eyes. Her ladyship, frail, red eyed, dabbing her face with a lace kerchief, rushed forward. Cindy, her maid, following close behind her, offered her a chair, which Lady Adrianna refused.

Mairéad immediately stood, marveling at the strength it must have taken for the woman to leave her gilded post. Lord Darnley's possible demise obviously overrode her aversion to death and grave illness.

"Did I hear singing?" She swiped at the corners of her eyes, a continual stream of tears wetting her cheeks.

"Yes, my lady. I believe Lord Darnley can hear, and I want him to hear something cheerful."

The delicate woman absentmindedly nodded, obviously intending to talk of something else. "Tell me what happened after you rode out. He hasn't taken Hungas out in months."

Mairéad glanced at his lordship, searching for any sign of recognition to his wife's voice.

She grasped Mairéad's arm, her ladyship turned to look directly at her. "I must know how this happened."

"Please, my lady," Cindy said. "You can see his lordship is resting peacefully. I am sure Miss Mairéad will tell you all, but you must calm yourself." She pulled the woman toward two chairs in front of the blazing fire.

When seated, her ladyship continued to wipe away the never-ending tears.

Mairéad sat in the adjoining chair. "He appeared fatigued as we rode. Then he collapsed. Thankfully he was well seated and collapsed against the stallion as we slowly made our way. A gardener, quick to note our distress, ran for Shamus, who rode out and flanked Hungas with his steed until we reached Witham and three others, who carried his lordship to bed."

Her ladyship's face flushed, either by the fire or her worry, it was hard to tell. "What did that horrid doctor have to say on the matter?"

Mairéad let the remark about that odious man go. "Lord Darnley has experienced apoplexy, my lady, but the doctor does expect a full recovery."

A sob came from the frail woman, breaking Mairéad's own delicate composure. She could only imagine the woman's pain after so many losses, and now this, the fear of her husband joining all those stones in the graveyard.

"Should we order tea?" Mairéad glanced at Cindy, who pulled on the bell.

The swish of her ladyship's gown as she leaned over her husband's bedside, her soft voice pleading, struck Mairéad deeply.

"Come back to me, Garrett. I have been so foolish and wasted all these years. Come back to me, and we will begin anew." Her thin body trembled.

Cindy was immediately at her side, hand on her arm. "There, there, my lady. A wonderful decision you have made, without doubt."

"Did he hear me?" She turned back to Mairéad, her pale blue eyes searching for an answer.

Cindy tried to calm her. "'Tis a sure thing he hears you. Now all he must do is rest and then wake. The same as you must rest."

She allowed Cindy to direct her back to the chair.

The experience of witnessing her ladyship's devotion twisted Mairéad's heart. When the serving maid arrived, her instant shock seeing Lady Darnley, quickly vanished beneath her manners. However, Mairéad knew her ladyship's presence in her husband's chamber would spread like wildfire.

The three women sat in silence, all looking at the bed with its precious, beloved inhabitant, the slight movement of his breathing giving them hope.

"Sing to him."

At her ladyship's request, Mairéad turned to her with brow furrowed in question. "I've not the voice of a learned singer, my lady."

"Do this for me. Teach me how to comfort." A broken sob accompanied her declaration.

This was a request Mairéad could not refuse, and she went to his bedside. Reaching for his hand, she began a lullaby sung to her by Sister Constance, who had told her it was as old as the hills of Ireland. The whispered lyrics floated lightly about the chamber. *May love and laughter light your days and warm your heart and cottage.* After a few stanzas, she hummed the rest in a soothing lilt.

A sigh escaped her ladyship. "I must write to Rutledge. He needs my sincere apology. Has he been notified of his grandfather's illness?" Her gaze settled on Mairéad.

The unexpected announcement caused Cindy to glance at her mistress, her mouth in a perfect O shape. She, too, glanced at Mairéad.

With both women's attention on her, she fumbled for words. "I don't know. Would Witham?"

"Ring for him," ordered Lady Darnley, her determination becoming clearer by the minute.

Cindy went to the bell pull.

Witham arrived like a leaf in the wind. Out of breath, tugging on his waistcoat, he strode into the room.

Mairéad said, "My lady wishes to speak with you."

Complete bewilderment flushed his cheeks, and for a moment he almost lost his masterly demeanor. "Yes, ma'am."

"Has Rutledge been informed of his grandfather's apoplexy?"

"Not to my knowledge. However, I will check with Mrs. Atkinson."

"Do that. Then bring me writing material, for I will inform him myself. I want him to take a leave from his studies and be with me through this time."

"As you wish, my lady."

He was about to leave when she added, "Witham, ready my old room and have my things brought down. I intend to have access to his lordship day and night during this crisis. Cindy will help you with the details."

A gust of fresh air blew into the room, stirring the ashes in the grate and increasing the flickers of the fire. Mairéad silently thanked the Blessed Mother for reuniting these two. A wonderful glow warmed her on behalf of Lord Darnley.

When he returned, Mr. Martin was not accompanied by his younger partner, Mr. O'Reilly. He glanced at the open drapes and the dying grate. A stern edge to his voice. "What have we here?"

With her disdain for the doctor bothersome, Mairéad, who had begun singing again, stopped, rose from the chair, and went to a corner of the room. She could not summon a feeling of respect and she thought it best to hide her attitude.

Lady Darnley greeted him with a cheery voice. "Good morning to you, Mr. Martin. It seems Garrett might be coming back to us. His thumb moved."

With a sly twist of his lips, the doctor countered, "I would hope you are not fantasizing about something you wish to happen." He pulled open the flaps on his black bag and drew out his bleeding cup, a tourniquet, and other necessary items.

Mairéad's side glance at her ladyship revealed a clear look of disdain on the thin face. She might be elderly, and she might have been confined for years, but there was no doubt she was of sound mind.

The doctor misread the look, or chose to ignore it, because he added, "Perhaps you desire to leave the room, my lady, along with the maid." He cast a disdainful gaze toward the corner where Mairéad stood, arms folded, mutiny brimming.

Lady Darnley spouted, "The *maid* is a valued member of our household. You will address her as Miss Mairéad, and at the same time pack up that evil little bag of yours. There will be no letting of blood in this room."

As if a hand swept over his face, a forced smile appeared, and conceit crinkled the corners of his eyes as his thin lips curved. Straightening his back until he was as rigid as an oak, he gave her a look radiating authority and a good dose of condescension.

"Now, now, Lady Darnley. You are of a delicate nature and should not pretend otherwise. I might have to perform the procedure on you. When you allow humors to grow, it compounds sickness within. We do not want that, do we?"

His flippant disdain caught up with him. Lady Darnley drew

herself up and slipped her hand beneath her husband's as it lay on the cover. "*We* ask you to leave. Inform Mr. O'Reilly *we* prefer his presence in attendance on Lord Darnley. Do *we* make ourselves perfectly clear?"

Mairéad turned into the corner. She tried not to make a sound, but a snort of delight escaped. The bleeding bowl pinged as Mr. Martin plopped it into the black bag, and then Mairéad heard the snap of the bag's closure.

Mr. Martin rigidly declared, "I will so inform Mr. O'Reilly. Good day to you."

When the door shut with a thud and Mairéad turned about. Her gaze met her ladyship's, and they both burst into giggles.

Mr. O'Reilly made house calls twice each day, in the morning and again in the midafternoon. He encouraged the women to keep vigil, reminding them they would not want to miss when he woke. Mr. O'Reilly's wisdom encouraged a positive reaction from both Lady Darnley and Mairéad, even spreading to Mrs. Atkinson, Cindy, Tench, and Witham. It might be another week before Rutledge arrived. It all depended upon how fast his grandmother's letter traveled to England's Bristol shore and on to Eton in Berkshire. In the meantime, the two women determined to stay at Lord Darnley's bedside.

Two days with no further physical reaction from the patient increased the anxiety level within the walls of Rockmore Hall. Only the slow rise and fall of Lord Darnley's chest continued to give hope. Lady Darnley was now fully ensconced in the room next door, with an adjoining dressing room and bathing area separating the two bedchambers. Cindy took up sleeping on a palate in the dressing room, to be near Lady Darnley, fearful she might collapse beneath the emotional stress.

As her ladyship rested, early in the third afternoon, Cindy confided to Mairéad the wonder of it all. She confessed being with Lady Darnley for years and likened her to a butterfly fluttering out of her chrysalis into life. With the little Mairéad knew about the situation, she had to agree with the beautiful image of Lady Darnley as elegant and delicate.

The sun lowered into late afternoon as Mairéad sat at his lordship's bedside and sang the words to a lullaby in a low voice. Suddenly his eyes rolled beneath thin, parchment-like lids. She sang her tune a bit louder, leaning closer. There was a definite reaction. His thumb moved. Lady Darnley gasped as she noticed.

Mairéad continued humming and stood. Easing Lady Darnley onto the chair and entwined their hands. Mairéad backed away. Though she continued to sing the words, *let no ill dreams, our souls alarm, no power of night approach to harm.*

Lady Darnley whispered, "He is responding to you." Tears stung Mairéad's eyes and made her throat clutch so that singing became difficult.

Her ladyship smoothed a hand against his forehead. "My dearest, Garrett. Can you hear us? We are waiting for you to wake up. Rutledge is on his way, too. Oh! It-it moved. His thumb moved." She leaned in caressing his cheek. "You hear us. Mairéad is right, you do hear us. My darling Wally."

Mairéad knew it was her pet name for him, and said, "He responded to your words of endearment, my lady."

Her heart filled with the joy of the moment, she allowed it to sink in as she watched her ladyship soothe him, comforting herself at the same time. "Shall I inform Witham and Mrs. Atkinson of the change. And have a tray sent up for you?"

"Cindy is probably on her way up. Why don't you take some time for yourself, dear? Ride if you like or paint." She glanced out the window. "Though I believe it's too late for either. You've spent three days without leisure. And I haven't sung in years. It is about time I give it a try. Now be off with you."

11

As the days passed, Lady Darnley showed no stress whatsoever. It was clear she adored her husband and perhaps was attempting to make up for the years spent in her apartment.

The household waited for word from Rutledge. Lady Darnley sent the letter to Eton, not knowing for sure if that was where he had gone.

Jonathan, Lord Tremaine, sent word he would arrive on Thursday. The only other letter she'd received was from Mother Abbess, and though she was grateful to receive hers, she was most excited to read his.

The pitter-pat of her heart caught her by surprise. She had begun to think Tremaine forgot his promise to return on his way to Scotland and university, but today was Thursday. She could hardly contain herself.

Ryan took extra care of her hair. Mairéad chose the blue gown with the square-cut neckline and lace inset. It'd made her feel special. Which was curious. When she wore it to dinner with Lady Duncamden and his lordship, her only concern was she'd put aside her veil and tunic.

This was different. Her reflection in the mirror told her so, as did Ryan as she twisted lengths of her dark auburn hair about her ears.

"Won't I get this tangle to do what I want? I promise it will be right as rain, miss."

Mairéad grinned at the maid. "Or what? You'll cut it off as will be done this fall when I take vows?"

"We'll be seeing about that now, won't we?" Her tongue caught between her teeth as she pinned the strand of braid in place. "Like a crown. Hmm. I'm of a mind to pat myself on the sleeve, I am."

"If the sisters could see me, they would gasp." Mairéad turned her head and glanced at the sides. Never wearing her hair up, her neck felt as barren as the back of her hands. With her hair shorn this fall, at least she would feel the cloth of a veil against her skin.

"You are a sight, miss. It would be my wish Lord Darnley could see you, too."

"I am to relieve Lady Darnley this morning. Each day with him brings gratitude for his murmurs. Even with his struggle to talk, it is foretelling of his eventual wellness."

Ryan folded her sleeping gown and other articles of clothing, mumbled as she did so.

"Did you say something?"

"You are devoted to his lordship. We speak of it in the kitchen. Never did we think her ladyship would come out of her cocoon. And aren't we all happy you'll have your own company soon enough."

"You give me approval to which I am not entitled. If you speak of Lord Tremaine? He is not my company."

Ryan gave her a slanted look. "Whose name was on the letter that arrived yesterday?"

An instant heat spread to her cheeks. "Is nothing a private matter at Rockmore?"

Ryan attempted to disguise a blatant grin. "Where you are concerned it is not, miss. To us you are like sunshine."

Tremaine neared Rockmore Hall, arriving by coach. After more than a week at his family home, he was eager to return to school, but not before spending several days at Rockmore Hall. He planned to leave Monday for Dublin where a ferry would carry him to Glasgow. Five coaches a day ran between Glasgow and Edinburgh, so he would not have to put up at an inn. The forty-two-mile journey usually took twelve hours over rutted roads. He was familiar with each curve in the road, and all stops to refresh the horses before arriving at university, highwaymen being the only probable danger.

For now, he was looking forward to his visit with a certain miss who, with beguiling inexperience, quite captured his imagination. He glanced out the window catching the approach of Rockmore Hall.

Witham showed him into the library. "As it is almost three o'clock, a sherry, my lord?"

"Thank you, I'll wait for ..."

Mairéad, gowned in a stylish, blue day-dress walked toward him her arms outstretched.

He grasped her hands. "You look lovely."

A pinkish blush on her cheeks, and sparkling eyes were the greeting he hoped, as she bade, "We are glad you made time for us. I'm afraid I've unpleasant news with which to greet you."

He drew her to a settee. The lids of his eyes lowered with skepticism. "It's not hopeless, is it?"

"Lord Darnley has been brought down by apoplexy. It involves his left arm and hand, left eyelid, and tongue. The doctor is predicting a complete recovery but explains it will take quite a while."

For a moment, Tremaine said not a word, thinking the household must be in a quandary, with Lady Darnley forever withdrawn and this young woman perhaps shouldering more than she bargained for. Rutledge? He didn't want to even ask where the bloody hell he was.

"May I go up?"

"He is sleeping right now, but Lady Adrianna will send Cindy when he rouses."

"When did this happen? You could have posted to me."

"I know how much he means to you. Please accept my apology. It was very confusing at first. We were riding when it happened. Speculation centers around his disagreement with Rutledge and the anger between them too much of a horrid burden."

He withdrew his hold on her hand, resting his elbows on his knees. "And Rutledge?"

"We've not heard a word since his lordship sent him away. It's assumed he's returned to Eton. His lordship took ill soon after you left."

"What is being done for him?" His mind buzzed with concern. His mother's medical problems allowed that two maids were in constant attendance on her. Her illness was one of the reasons he was in medical school.

"Mr. Martin bled him. Oh, and Lady Darnley has moved back into the apartment adjoining her husband. She banned Mr. Martin when she learned what he did without her approval. It was quite something. Apparently, the doctor knew of Lord Darnley's disgust with bleeding and still performed the procedure. Lady Darnley ordered him from Rockmore and told him to send Mr. O'Reilly in his stead."

Tremaine ran a hand through his blond hair and let out a breath of grave concern. "I've walked into a real quagmire, haven't I?"

She smoothed out her muslin overskirt, glancing at him. "Everyone is concerned. As you are aware, he is a greatly beloved man. Your presence is truly appreciated. Her ladyship was relieved you planned to spend some time here before returning to Edinburgh."

"And you? Are you pleased?"

Lowering her lids, she nodded, and the blush returned.

He cupped her hand and softly chuckled. "Good, because I hope to spend the next few days getting acquainted."

She shyly glanced up, "I would like that, too."

"In a short time, Lord Darnley has come to mean a great deal to you."

A mixture of emotion pierced her green eyes, furrowing her brow. She was obviously troubled, but her voice was not weepy. Her strength of character held her together through the trauma.

He said, "Has anyone told you that your eyes glisten with attention? I suspect you are a rarity. The young women I know are involved with dancing, gowns, and marriage."

"I've lived differently than you."

"What do you think about my world, *Sister* Mairéad." He settled back in his chair, his hands dangling over the ends of the carved mahogany arms.

"Bewildered and regretful. For instance, Rutledge thinks of himself and not those who have cared for him, loved him. He crushed his grandfather, and Lord Darnley's distress was that I would return to the convent."

"You aren't to blame for any of what happened, my dear. You can't reconcile Rutledge's anger toward his grandfather, especially considering if circumstances were reversed, you would never behave in that way."

She stared at him, but he couldn't discern her thoughts.

He asked, "What are your plans?"

"I'm not near finished with my work, and Lord Darnley is fragile and needy. As is Lady Darnley in her loving concern for him." She sprang to her feet and paced across the room. "I've seen the deep, abiding love between them. It's remarkable to witness. It touches me to the core. He responds to her. It is slight, but it is a beginning. I am honored to have seen such love between two people."

Her declaration brought an emotional stirring in him. He reminded himself of her life. "The truth is there's been little love here. What you've told me is remarkable. Something makes me think you are behind it all."

She glanced out the window at the far-off grasses bent with a wind, hills rolling against the sky where the emerald green met lapis blue. He wanted to go to her and put his arm about her, give her a feeling of security. He stayed the impulse and quietly listened as she continued.

"If it weren't for the sadness brought on by Rutledge's behavior and then Lord Darnley's illness, I would be nearly done with his biography by now." She turned to him, hands folded, dainty chin firm as she declared, "I'm not ready to leave him. Which is why I cannot concern myself that my work hasn't moved along as quickly as Mother Abbess originally planned."

He moved to stand near her. "You have discovered the friendship of a great, comforting man, and you aren't ready to give him up in his time of need."

"I believe you are right."

He touched her cheek and slid his fingertips up to lightly touch the auburn crown of braided hair.

Witham entered with a silver platter. He presented Mairéad with a letter, glancing apologetically at Tremaine.

"Do you mind?" she asked of Tremaine.

He nodded and turned to the shelves of books, respecting her privacy.

Her voice drifted to him from across the room. "This is in response to one I sent informing Mother Abbess of Lord Darnley's illness. She is arriving in the morning."

The tension in her voice was obvious. She was clearly torn between her superior's desire to take her back to the convent and her own need to stay. Tremaine did not dare offer advice, for it would not be objective. Selfishly, he wondered if he would have any time a'tall with Sister Mairéad.

Cindy arrived with an invitation from Lady Darnley to bring Tremaine up to his lordship. Mairéad bade him go, she would join them in a little while.

Late the next morning, the distinct swish of rosary beads came to Mairéad. Mother Abbess must have left the convent before dawn, well before *Lauds* to have arrived so early. The prayer beads tinkled against her tunic as she walked along the hall toward the workroom. For a moment, the sound clutched at Mairéad's heart. She sorely missed the nun.

As Witham announced her, Mother Abbess entered the room. Mairéad glanced up from her work. Brilliant sun washed across the easels pinned with her earlier labor.

Slipping off the stool and placing the paintbrush in its dish, she grabbed a cloth to wipe her hands as the nun came toward her.

"I've brought well wishes from all. Lord Darnley and his household are included in our daily prayers, and Sister Davideena devoted her time to a novena for Lord Darnley."

Hearing this caused her to want to hug the Abbess but knew she was not inclined toward physical contact.

"Would you like tea? Have you eaten? You must have left quite early."

The abbess glanced about the room, no doubt noticing how bright it was. She crossed the room to the bank of windows in the work area taking in the view from one end of the park to the other. Her voice came across as strained. "A hot cup of tea would be appreciated." She sighed and turned from the glorious sight, centering her attention on an easel holding yesterday's drawing. She ran a finger across the dried paint. "You are not as far along as I would have hoped."

Mairéad nodded to Witham who waited for instruction. "We will take tea here, please."

Then she turned back to her guest, ignoring her remark. "How was the journey?"

"Bumpy. Mr. Chiley was happy to oblige. He has a niece nearby and needed to deliver a chair and table from her mother. It all took place quickly, and I did not have time to give you much notice."

Mairéad walked to the windows and glanced at the park, recalling her own fascination with the sight when she first arrived at Rockmore.

Mother Abbess appeared unsettled. It would have been an uncomfortable journey in Mr. Chiley's cart. However, she sensed it was something else and asked, "Do you wish to sit with Lord Darnley for a bit?"

"Is he accepting visitors?" Her eyes narrowed, as if dubious.

"He isn't aware enough for that, but his eyes flicker, and he knows Lady Darnley."

"From your letter, I'd say her ladyship has made quite a change in her own life." Mother Abbess's critical gaze swept over Mairéad's gown, which she chose because Tremaine was visiting. Her superior's reaction had not come to mind.

A surge of defiance set her jaw, and with a deep breath to ease anxiety, she wrapped her arms around her waist. Rebelling would be unseemly. "Yes, I would say, from what little I discern, Lord Darnley is content. Part of his mouth smiles at her, and her ladyship is highly attentive to him."

"That must be helpful to you. I gather you were at his bedside for a number of days, keeping you from your work."

"He is helpless. Why would I not?" Needing to shake off her defensiveness, she reminded herself this woman was here because she cared. "Do you recall Sister Catriona singing to me when I was little?"

The nun gave her a side glance. "Indeed, and always off key."

"Well, I sang to him. The songs I could recall. I set children's rhymes to a singsong and psalms I memorized and was rewarded when his thumb moved across my hand. Lady Darnley overheard, and then she began singing to him."

"You are a pair of songbirds, are you not, then?"

Mairéad looked at her left wrist and pulled on the cloth as if it was snug. She hardly knew what to say. Surely, Mother Abbess meant that as a compliment, but the nicety did not extend to her voice. This was not going to be an easy visit. She was grateful when a knock at the door announced Mrs. Atkinson entering with the tea tray.

Mairéad introduced her to Mother Abbess, who inquired, "You are the housekeeper?"

"Yes, and is there anything else I can bring you? I know you've had a long morning's journey." She folded her hands, a smile on her face. Mairéad hoped she would stay but was not sure how to ask her to have tea with them. It would most likely be improper. Furthermore, she did not want Mother Abbess to snip at the housekeeper.

"I require little, Mrs. Atkinson. However, it would be my pleasure to meet her ladyship, if possible. I will not visit Lord Darnley when he is so greatly indisposed. As Mairéad is my responsibility, it would ease my mind to meet her ladyship."

Mrs. Atkinson's eyes widened a tiny bit. "Of course, I will see to it myself. May I ask how long you have?"

"Mr. Chiley will return for me at four."

"I will bring you an answer as quickly as I have one. The two of you enjoy your visit. Miss Mairéad, ring if you need anything."

"Thank you." Not meeting her superior's expectations made her feel immature. Reminding herself she hadn't asked to be planted in the middle of a way of life she never envisioned. Mother Abbess' presence threatened her tender feelings toward the Darnleys. Her caring was made to feel insignificant.

The conversation lulled as they sat in companion chairs, sipping tea before it cooled overmuch, when suddenly Tremaine burst through the door.

"Oh, excuse me, ladies. Ah, Sisters. I intended to catch Sister Mairéad at her painting." There was a mischievous glint in his eye. "Shall I leave?"

Mother Abbess spoke up. "Not on my account. Please come in."

Mairéad introduced them, expecting her superior's barrage of questions, which took but a moment to begin. "You refer to Mairéad as sister. Why?"

His eyes lit with humor. "Is that not her chosen future?"

Silence skipped across the space. Had he rendered the Abbess at a loss for words?

A moment later, Mother Abbess inquired, "Are you a member of this household?"

"A distant relative of the Wallington's. I've news of Lord Darnley's latest achievements for Sister Mairéad." He turned a mischievous glint on her. "Both eyes are open and even winking on command with his right. He can slightly raise his right hand and leg. Mr. O'Reilly has ordered him into a chair and that he attempt to feed himself broth, for starters." He grinned with the delivery of such great news, taking in the two women, who simply stared at him, teacups balanced on the saucers in hand.

Mairéad set her cup down. "I am so grateful. Her ladyship must be ecstatic."

"I believe she might have danced about the room if I hadn't been there. She did clasp her hands and cry." He added, "Tears of relief, I am sure." His engaging smile, along with a lock of flaxen hair hanging in disarray, eased Mairéad's trepidation a wee bit.

With his hand on the door jamb, he said, "I'm on my way to the library. There is an article in yesterday's *London Times* about England's dedication to locomotives that I think he might like." He gave a slight nod to the women. "I hope you enjoy the rest of your visit. Nice to have met you, Mother Abbess. Sister Mairéad speaks of you lovingly. I'll leave you to the conversation I interrupted in my excitement." He gave a rather gallant bow. "Mother Abbess, if you are staying for dinner, I look forward to it."

He was out the door quickly, and Mother Abbess did not answer him. Her voice, when she spoke, was pleasant. "A nice young man. A relative, he said. Does that mean he spends a great deal of time at Rockmore?"

"He is in medical school in Edinburgh. Rockmore Hall is

situated on the journey between his family home and school. It is convenient for him to visit as he travels between the two."

Mother Abbess's lids lowered over her eyes as she listened. The look on her face was one of displeasure.

A maid entered. "Mrs. Atkinson sent me with word that her ladyship will see you in the parlor at two." Curtsying, she left.

"Tremaine is a relative on his father's side. Their estate is west of here. Lord Rutledge, Lord Darnley's grandson, is also expected at any time from Eton."

"Grandson?" The nun's eyes practically bulged the cup rattled against the saucer.

You would have thought Mairéad said the devil himself was coming. "What is so surprising about that?"

"I was under the impression Lord Darnley did not have family. After your last letter, I discovered that his wife is alive. You tell me Tremaine is a relative. Now I learn Lord Darnley has a grandson."

Mairéad did not understand Mother Abbess's confusion. She was clearly rattled. Then it dawned on her. Mother Abbess was questioning why she needed to stay here when family was in attendance.

Owing the woman truth about her newfound feelings, she stated, "I enjoy the time I spend with his lordship, reading to him, singing. He responds to me, and I find it fulfilling."

For a long minute, the elder woman set her gaze on the windows hardly blinking. When she spoke, her words were measured. "We must not become too attached simply because we assume a role of vague importance, when most likely it is servitude that is required."

Mairéad knew the tone and understood the intent of what she said. Valiantly setting aside her hurt, she tried to consider what her elder's feelings might be. The nun had taken in an infant, cared for that child, taught her, fed her, and clothed her. Guilt pressed upon her, adding to an already heavy burden.

Until two months ago, she'd been unaware of the emotional

wall between the two of them. The realization came about after Lord Darnley brought her to Rockmore Hall. The difference between providing shelter and providing a home was most apparent—and rather significant.

Equally confusing to her was the lack of strife at the convent where calm prevailed most of the time. Rockmore Hall's inhabitants presented much life has to offer, making her think of the delightful Lady Duncamden, and, of course the awful trauma of Rutledge's inexcusable behavior toward those he should honor.

Perhaps the most dramatic occurrence, besides Lord Darnley's stroke, was the discovery of Lady Darnley and that she removed herself from those she loved so as not to be devastated by another loss. These were real people who lived real lives, and Mairéad instinctively knew the problems that arose were worth the effort.

Within the hour, the two women met with Lady Darnley in the parlor. Oils adorned the upper wall space, mostly landscapes, though there were also a few of imperious men staring down their noses, hunting dogs at their heels, guns in hand. The red damask walls made a perfect backdrop for the baroque gilt frames.

Comfortable settees covered in soft yellow and embroidered with the pattern of Ireland's Celtic harp, provided seating in the room. Crystal lamps held candles at the ready for lighting. Rays of sunshine on the dangling prisms threw colors about the room as if dancing fire lights.

Every inch a countess, Lady Darnley swathed in watered pink silk, greeted Mother Abbess. Tea with scones, jam, and little pastries filled with figs that Mairéad knew were Mrs. Hill's pride and joy were laid out, perhaps with the obvious intent of cosseting the nun.

Rigid back, shoulders high, Mother Abbess guarded herself as if ready to do battle. The three women sat at the table. "We were informed Lord Darnley is making a recovery?"

"Which seems rather remarkable as we have been so worried. His constitution is quite strong." Her ladyship's beautiful soft glance shifted to Mairéad, "And, this dear young woman has shown me that quiet and dark are not healing attributes."

Mother Abbess confirmed Mairéad's suspicion about where her determination was targeted when she said, "Now that Lord Darnley is taking a turn for the better, perhaps I can be assured Mairéad will concentrate her full attention on painting. She is not as far along as I considered she should be."

"There may be good cause for that." Lady Darnley dabbed at the corner of her mouth with the linen napkin.

Mairéad wished she could sink into the floor. She knew what was coming and knew of her superior's reaction to frivolity. Lady Darnley continued, "Darnley insisted she learn to ride when she first arrived. He did not want her bent over an easel without some form of outdoor exercise. She has been encouraged to continue on a daily routine. It isn't healthy to work hour after hour without the balance of fresh air and activity."

Mairéad dropped her gaze to clasped hands. To her knowledge no one *ever* talked to Mother Superior like this, certainly never on her behalf.

"That explains why she isn't wearing her tunic and veil." The icy voice scratched Mairéad's nerves. She kept her eyes downcast as Mother Abbess continued, "Attire certainly not fit for riding."

Discovering she could still breathe, Mairéad was loath to look at the nun because she'd no desire to witness judgmental criticism swimming in those piercing brown eyes.

Lady Darnley's cheerful voice was a counterbalance to Mother Abbess. "You have provided her with a wonderful and safe life. She is a lovely young woman. Darnley mentioned to me before he took ill that he intends she become a permanent member of our household."

Mairéad, shocked at Lady Darnley's revelation, could only imagine how Mother Abbess felt, and fearing the worst lowered her gaze.

The nun's voice was as stiff as her upper lip. "I will pray for his return to health more fervently than I have. This has been an extraordinary visit and, in many ways, not what I expected."

"I would not have mentioned it. Except I sincerely agree with Darnley's wish she stay with us, become a part of our household."

Mairéad's chin rose, she glanced from Mother Abbess to Lady Darnley. Her heart hammered, as she took note of the determination on the nun's features, and the sweet, smiling face of her ladyship.

With a deep sigh, Mother Abbess informed, "The secular world is not foreign to me. I was not raised in a cloistered environment as Mairéad has been. I am aware of a young lass' dreams and aspirations. My misfortune was of being a fourth daughter in a household similar to Rockmore Hall."

Fearful of gaping, she held her lips tight as she listened to Mother Abbess. Did any of the nuns know her story? She doubted it, as nary a whisper of such came to her all these years.

Lady Darnley said, "Your dedication to your beliefs must have brought you peace. I commend you for your decision. I withdrew into a solitary world of my own choosing for many years and brought pain to those around me."

She smiled at Mairéad. "This young woman you have so lovingly guided since birth compelled me by her sincerity to reevaluate a decision I made years ago when I was devastated at the loss of my young children."

Mairéad dared not glance at Mother Abbess. What Lady Darnley revealed about his lordship's wishes might be Mother Abbess's greatest fear. Both women were forthright, but how do women cope with such loss? There must be a less dramatic path to take than locking one's self away or taking vows. Mustn't there? Did her mother flounder before making her final decision to leave her infant on a doorstep and be done with it? Or, was her resolve firm, motherhood an accident needing to be hid behind convent walls lest it become a gossipy wisp in the ears of neighbors and such.

Witham entered the parlor. "Mr. Chiley has arrived for Mother

Abbess, my lady."

Tea over, the three women stood. Mairéad owed this nun more than a visit of a few hours, but she did not know how to approach her without causing more regret.

The nun's somber brown gaze drifted to the window as if she reached for an inner calm. Her voice soft and distant, as if she rehearsed the goodbye. "Thank you for your hospitality. We will continue to pray for Lord Darnley's health." Rigid now with her own commitment, she added to Mairéad, "Walk with me to the cart. I wish to have a word with you in private."

Lady Darnley said, "It has been a pleasure, Mother Abbess. You are welcome at Rockmore Hall anytime."

With a nod of her veiled head, Mother Abbess walked out of the parlor, shoulders firm, hands clasped, Mairéad in her wake.

Outside, she stopped before they reached Mr. Chiley's cart. "Did you know of Lord Darnley's intention to keep you?" Her voice stern with accusation.

"Not in so many words. He never actually said so. I believed it more a desire to share his life with me." She wanted to hug the nun, reassure her, but was afraid of rebuff.

Their eyes locked. Mairéad, shorter by five or six inches, looked up, the sun at the nun's back spreading like an aura about her coif and wimple.

Mother Abbess reached out, folding a lock of Mairéad's hair back against her ear, a tender thing to do, considering she never touched anyone. "We will pray Lord Darnley regains his speech. Perhaps his words will unlock mystery and history for us both."

With that, Mr. Chiley assisted the abbess into the cart and snapped the reins of the harness. "Good day ta ye, lass. We'll be settin' eyes upon ye again then." He chastised the mare. "Up the road then, Dinger. Get us back."

As the cart wobbled down the rutted road, she was thankful conversation about Rutledge ended almost as soon as it began. She had no doubt she would be in the cart if the Abbess knew what happened between them.

12

The velvety chocolate aroma and crackle of fire in the grate woke Mairéad. "Good morning, miss." Ryan's lilt woke her more fully. "Will you be desiring to choose your gown?"

"The red plaid and a jacket."

She dressed and hurried into the dining room. "Good morning, your ladyship."

Plate in hand, she scoured the buffet, helping herself to a scoop of eggs, two slices of crisp bacon, and a raisin scone.

Mischief twinkled in Lady Darnley's blue eyes. "Seems you might have plans?"

"Tremaine has asked me to ride."

"That would explain his rushing in, eating, and rushing out. I barely sat down, and he made his excuses. Much like you."

Swallowing a bite of scone, she said, "Then I will hurry."

"You should make your young man wait for you, my dear."

Mairéad looked up, forkful of egg halfway to her mouth. "But he's not my young man."

"Oh, my mistake. I did think otherwise." Sipping tea, her eyes twinkled.

"Have you been up to his lordship yet?"

"I peeked in on my way down. Sleeping peacefully. Yesterday

sitting in a chair watching the birds and the park tired him. He was ready for bed when they returned him to it. There will be more of the same today. When you are done with your ride, you'll have to visit."

Scooping up a last bite of egg, she nodded in agreement.

Her ladyship fiddled with a spoon. "Mother Abbess was not pleased, was she?"

There was no easy way to escape the conversation. Done with eating, she answered, "The Abbess is a strict woman, never bending rules in my favor as I would have liked when younger. She is the nearest thing to a mother I have known. I owe her much."

"However, you did not wear your veil and tunic when you knew she was coming?"

"There is that, isn't there?" A rhetorical question if ever there was one. Why did she deliberately choose not to wear her religious garb? Clearly, she wanted to send a message to the saintly woman. Mairéad sipped her juice and pondered her own actions. Their relationship was complicated. They were not family yet lived as one all these years. They were not mother and daughter, though there was a time or two when Mother Abbess treated her with deference.

How mothers and daughters should act toward each other was a mystery to her. Yet she comprehended the act of abandonment as severing the bond. Lady Darnley kept her grandson from her. Wasn't that the same thing?

She sighed at the confusing behavior of superiors. Lady Darnley leaned into the table, her arm stretching across the linen, palm upward. "Dear child, something has caused you great concern. If I can help, allow me to do so."

Mairéad sighed, "Relationships can be complicated. I know Mother Abbess expects me to return to the convent, and I made it clear to Lord Darnley that I would when the painting was finished. When you brought up the subject that his lordship expected me to live here permanently, I could tell her difficulty in accepting."

"Did they not talk of it when he went to the convent?"

"They may have before coming to my workroom. I don't know, but I declared my desire to take vows, to his lordship. He knows how I feel. I have not changed my mind."

"What I believe you encountered is an old man's desire to make you part of a family he would like." Lady Darnley, in all her wisdom, nodded with assuredness. "Then he took ill. We will work this out. Don't you worry. I'm at fault, hiding away all these years. Shame on me."

The great clock in the foyer chimed the nine o'clock hour. She said, "I am sorry to rush off. Do you mind?"

"Not at all. I would join you if I were younger. Riding was one of my favorite pastimes." As if a child in the nursery, she giggled. "Now, don't keep that young man waiting any longer."

❦

When she reached the stable, Tremaine greeted her immediately. "Are you ready for this?" Rubbing his palms, eyes crinkled around the edges. "Let's not tarry." He put his hands firmly on her waist and lifted her into the saddle. "When you're ready, we'll be off."

She winked at Shamus and put her heel to Caomh's flank. The mare stirred and took off at a trot.

Tremaine's laughter drifted in the air. It took him less than a second to slip his boot in the stirrup and swing into the saddle. Hungas was as eager as his rider.

She knew he would win any race she instigated. His steed was at least two hands higher, with legs to match. Nonetheless, she spurred Caomh to a gallop. The chase aroused the little mare. She reached out, grabbing the rich earth, pushing forward, enjoying the run every bit as much as her rider did. Mairéad's bonnet flew off, and the scarf around her neck flapped in the wind until it, too, sailed away.

With Tremaine fast on their heels, she drew into an estuary, meandering lazily through a copse, and she drew Caomh in until they were at a short trot. Twigs snapped, and branches caught at her hair, which loosened from the pins Ryan so carefully arranged. Tremaine caught up, and she turned in the saddle her bonnet and scarf in his fist.

"You did everything to ensure your win. You are as clever as a fox."

Jumping from the saddle, he lifted her off Caomh, kept his hands on her waist and held her aloft. Craning her neck, she faced skyward, feeling the warmth of the sun and laughed aloud. He gave her a little shake. and she looked down into his blue eyes. Leaning in, her palms slid from his shoulders to his cheeks, and she placed her lips against his, eliciting a murmur of pleasure as his hands increased their pressure.

A wonderful, magical space later, he drew back, slowly lowered her to the ground, and his eyes darkened, his inspection sliding over her features. Slipping her hands from him, she made to step back when his husky voice stopped her. "Finished, are you? I think not."

Her blood thrummed with what she'd done, and she fully understood the want for more. What she said was different. "I can't explain why I did that."

His fingertip traced the ridge of her upper lip then the lower, parting them. His gaze fixed on hers as he slowly brought his face closer. She waited for the thrill of his lips on hers, wanting his kiss more than anything she could imagine.

Instead, he whispered, "*Leannán* mine."

He called her sweetheart.

His eyes smoldered with something she did not recognize, still she freely admitted, "I like kissing you."

He laughed. "So honest, are you? I've not been told that before."

Something must have registered on her face, for he immediately said, "What I meant was, no one has…"

It was her turn to enjoy his discomfort. "I imagine you've heard thus, any number of times."

With a weighted sigh, he declared, "I should never have begun with you." With his hand on her shoulder, his thumb caressed her ear. "'Tis a mighty thing to stop, and I would never dishonor you."

So close, in his arms, the delicious sense of affection existing between them, she asked, "Why should we stop when it feels so grand?" Her misty eyes drank him in.

A grave darkness clouded his handsome features. "You would not understand, *leannán*. Because I do, this madness will cease."

He let her go and dropped to the grass, arms bent across his knees. He patted the space next to him. "Sit with me. Let us converse plainly."

She slanted him a grin as she sat near. Though he took on a serious demeanor, his actions spoke of other intentions.

"I promise to act the gentleman."

A flock of sparrows swarmed above, like a fast-moving cloud twisting and changing shape. They raced well north of the maple and beech forest along the river that fed the small lough of the summerhouse. It was peaceful and lovely, just the two of them, their mounts grazing nearby on sweet grass.

He claimed, "I sensed we would be magic from the first moment I laid eyes on you. I let it go too far with Rutledge that day. I was mesmerized into stupidity, until I woke to what he was attempting and came to your rescue. My apology is late but nonetheless sincere."

Hungas snorted, water rippled over the moss strewn rocks, branches rustled in the gentle breeze. Sunlight dappled through the leaves, mingling with the pungent smell of tree sap in the new summer air.

Tremaine's voice, husky and low, made her yearn for his embrace. "You've led a sheltered life. I apologize for my behavior. For the life of me, it was like lightening. I would not wish it undone, but from now on, I will refrain. You need have no fear with me. I want your friendship above all else. The next time we'll see each other, I will be on my return from Edinburgh in midsummer. And that will be short because I leave again in the fall."

"Why would I fear you?" He puzzled her with his talk after the wonderful moments spent in his arms. "Was it our kiss?" His pensive scrutiny, like sorrow, bewildered her.

His hand covered his heart. "I am grateful you do not, and yes, because we kissed." The darkness lifted from his expressive eyes.

"I desire friendship with you, and I will miss you." Her voice barely a whisper.

His fingers traced her jaw. "You are young, and I am too much in the world. I should have been more considerate."

"It wasn't affection you shared? I kissed you, it is I who should apologize."

He muffled a laugh. "I'm fairly certain *affection* is not a consideration most women ponder."

Her gaze swept his face. "If not, then what?"

He politely coughed into his fist, eventually responding. "You are a rare and priceless young woman, Miss Mairéad."

"That is not an answer to my question." She tugged at blades of grass wondering what he wasn't saying. He hadn't called her sister.

He took her hand and pressed his lips against the soft leather of the glove, then held it to his chest. He confused her, and in such close proximity, the moment was intimate, with a dash of profoundness. She asked, "Do you pay this much attention to all your friendships?"

His laughter seemed brackish after his low tones, as if her question startled him. "What makes you think I have so many friendships?"

"You're charisma and kindness. You surely have many, and you pursue the art of healing. A worthy endeavor."

"Don't think me a saint, for I am not. Just a common man wanting to keep busy with something that uses my imagination. The science of medicine seems to do just that. Although now I seem to have an intrigue of another sort." His gaze slanted toward her.

She quickly glanced away. A butterfly flitted above them, landing on the hem of her riding gown. She stilled until it flew off. "You must be gifted. Lord Darnley certainly thinks so. He spoke of you with respect and admiration. I sensed he wished Rutledge was like you."

"Rutledge is mired in the past and filled with resentment. Until he can put that aside, he will never grow. He refuses to let go of the grudge from early childhood, especially against his father. That poor man stumbled overboard in a storm. That is what set in motion the discovery of Rutledge's identity. His father left a letter with the family solicitors in the event of his death."

He reached for her hand. "It's occurred to me that perhaps it would have been better to leave Rutledge with the cottier. Always sullen and pouty, about four years of age, angry when forced from his cottage. Of course, I enjoyed the wisdom of a nine-year-old and could not imagine why he would pine after dirt floors and potato mash and curdled milk day in and day out."

"Lady Darnley has written to him to return to the estate. He has not yet responded."

"Watch yourself with him. Promise me." He squeezed her hand then let go.

His caring was a comfort. "I will. He doesn't frighten me." She plucked a yellow weed from the grass and twirled it over her nose, then over his.

He sneezed. "I can't imagine how you manage at Rockmore, when you've always lived at the convent." One brow raised he grabbed her hand as she intended to make him sneeze again.

Their gaze locked, and she hoped he would kiss her.

His baritone warned, "Beware, don't tease me. What I seek is unobtainable."

Her brow furrowed, and she was about to say something when he put a finger on her parted lips, as he said, "Allow me to show you something I think you do not know." He stood and drew her up, brushing grass from his pants and the hem of her plaid.

His large hands firmly on her waist, he lifted her to Caomh's saddle, causing her to remember when he had taken her off. Heat covered her cheeks, and he chuckled. "I am thinking the same thing. A memory for when we are apart, yes?" His intense look caused her heart to flutter.

Walking their horses on the narrow path along the backwaters of the tributary, they came upon a domed roof. As they strode the curved path downward, an exposed brick structure with no windows appeared. "What is it?"

"An underground icehouse."

"A curious thing, is it not? Who would live in it?"

As they left their mounts and he led her to the far side, he explained, "Darnley imports ice from England when the winters are not cold enough to freeze the lough. Otherwise, men cut blocks from the lough and store them here between layers of straw."

"Quite clever. We have nothing like this at the convent."

He pointed out the dell, created from a chalk pit. "I would expect not. It is rather labor intensive. The hall stores perishables here. Water from the river runs through, and in the winter hopefully freezes." His hand swept through his thick hair as he grinned.

"So many wonders new to me. I have learned to ride a horse, and Lord Darnley chose me to paint for him." She twirled about, arms out. "I realize how fortunate this time is and will miss all this."

His grin faded. Realizing how momentous her declaration was, she stopped in her tracks. They stared at each other.

"You are thinking, how could I leave?" Her hand waved the air as if she wanted to erase the words that spilled from her. "And, yet, how can I not return to the convent?"

The confusion in her declaration did not echo in his response. He was firm in his belief. "You have no choice but to follow what you think is your path. I know this within myself. When the time comes for me to inherit, even my studies, if I am not finished, will be put on hold."

Water feeding through the icehouse trickled around rocks and twigs. Crickets chirped, and frogs croaked. The wind slid through the tall grass bordering the creek.

She turned toward the sound of rustling. It must be a small animal, not seen, that moved along the water's edge, disturbing the reeds.

He added, "When the time comes, you will return to the convent. You see it as your duty. I am sure of this. I am also certain our friendship will endure."

There was no joy in his voice. His words were more perfunctory than soothing. An invisible wall sprung up.

He reached for her hand, causing her to look up. His lips brushed her palm. He was leaving late this afternoon, and she already missed him.

Walking their mounts back to the stables, savoring what little private time they had left, neither spoke.

Upon entering his lordship's chamber, the first thing noted was Darnley's improved color. Wrapped in a blanket, he sat facing the windows overlooking the approach to the hall. Swans sent ripples floating upon the surface of the lough.

His lordship appeared to have gained more control over the fluttering of his eyelids. His smile, a wee bit wider, though one-sided, was very welcome. Mairéad sat in a near chair. Tremaine stood next to it. Lord Darnley's gaze followed them, and his brow wrinkled. He uttered some sounds attempting to talk, words coming faster than his tongue allowed.

Her ladyship hugged a shawl about her shoulders. She stood near the window and said, "His daily routine is now including several hours in the morning and again in the afternoon in the chair." Relief sounded in her voice, demonstrating her joy in his slow but sure recovery.

Tremaine brought news of his parents, topics he knew would be of interest to Lord and Lady Darnley. Mairéad took comfort in the soft timbre of his voice as he explained his plans and shared what his father had to say. This was much as he told her this morning when they sat on the grass but with more detail for Lord and Lady Darnley.

She was surprised to learn that his mother required two maids to care for her.

Tremaine's younger brother, Cyril, was at Cambridge. His sister, Lady Rowan, was married with three children and lived in County Wexford. Tremaine entertained Lord and Lady Darnley with Lady Rowan's descriptions of her children's antics.

Lord Darnley's eyes closed. When Tremaine stopped talking, he gestured for him to continue. Mairéad's heart filled with comfort as she shared in this time with them, their history that was taken for granted. Her ladyship stood off to the side, a loving and contented look on her face as she folded her arms over a blue woolen shawl about her shoulders.

Tremaine finished with details about his brother's forthcoming engagement when his lordship's mouth opened, and a snore filled the air.

Lady Darnley rang for Tench, saying, "Will you please move Darnley to the bed where he will be more comfortable."

The patient barely acknowledged Tremaine and Tench as they bundled him to bed. Everyone settled after covering his lordship and Tremaine said his goodbyes.

Lady Darnley opened her arms for a hug. "Thank you for spending time with his lordship. When he is better, I know he will tell you himself. Even when you were a little boy, he enjoyed your company. He misses you. When next you write, give your family our warm regard and come back to us soon."

Tremaine, towering over the diminutive Lady Darnley, promised, "I plan to return to Dunraven at midsummer. Be assured I will stop on my way. Please write. I'll leave my address with Miss Mairéad." He brushed back the lock of hair that always drooped across his forehead.

He reached for her hand as they left the chamber. Each step

they took toward the door from his lordship's chamber brought them closer to a good-bye. Alone in the corridor, he kissed her forehead. No words were spoken about this morning and their lovely kiss, but the truth of their affection for each other was explored. It glistened in his eyes as he searched her face, his gaze lingering on her lips, causing a ripple of excitement right down to her toes. She was truly going to miss him.

"Promise me you will write?"

She reached for his long, tanned fingers, knuckles sprinkled with little golden hairs. "I promise." Slipping her hand over his arm, she added, "I already feel the want of your presence. Take care on your journey."

He glanced over his shoulder and then quickly bent his head, kissing her cheek. His warm breath soothing. "I'll write as soon as I arrive in Edinburgh.

His withdrawal created a vacuum. This was a first. Someone to whom she was quite fond of, leaving. This is what you felt when you cared.

His finger traced her chin. "Do not be sad. Our letters will keep us close, *leannán* mine. I wish for you to stay where you are at this moment, so I may keep this picture of you in my heart to remind me of your loveliness."

Watching his long stride take him away, she was surprised when he gained the corner of the hall and blew a kiss. She reached up and grabbed at the air as she imagined it winging its way toward her. She stood a long time holding to the last sight of him.

Later during supper, Lady Darnley entertained with memories of both families, Tremaines and Darnleys.

Mairéad asked, "I know your two families are related, but how exactly did it come about that Tremaine and Rutledge became friends with their age difference?"

"I had already removed myself from daily life. Tremaine was attending Eton. Darnley got it into his head that our grandson might enjoy his company and wrote Tremaine asking if he could spend a day or two with us on his way back and forth from Eton, and so began their friendship.

"Darnley fretted about the disparity in their natures. Though quite serious, Tremaine is always ready to accept the good in others. His nature is to forgive and move on. Rutledge holds grudges. Never able to move forward. When his father died before he could really know him, he blamed us."

"How were you at fault for your son's death? I don't understand."

"Rutledge, poor boy, in his eyes we were the grievous ones. He believed that if his father could not tell us about our grandson, we must have been at fault." She nervously fiddled with the spoon alongside her plate of mostly uneaten food. "Both were situations over which we had no influence."

"As I see it, it's the secrets hidden from you that caused the situation. I know one should not point a finger at the dead, but if you were able to discover why your son could not tell you, it might ease the guilt all around."

"Just so, my dear. The truth of the matter went to the watery grave with him."

Lady Adrianna's soulful glance settled on Mairéad, who responded. "One cannot be blamed for guarding one's broken heart, my lady."

A muffled sob broke loose. Lady Darnley covered her face with the dinner napkin. Mairéad came around the table, kneeling at the elder woman's side. Drawing her arms about the frail shoulders, she was reminded of a tiny bird fallen from the nest. "Shall I ring for Cindy?"

With a final little sob, Lady Darnley gained a modicum of calm. "Not necessary, my dear. I have you by my side."

Mairéad kissed her cheek. "Yes, you do, my lady." Rising off her knees, she reached for the water goblet. "Sip this." Smoothing out her skirt, she added, "I'll pray for your grandson on my next visit to the chapel. Wherever he is, maybe he'll soften and return."

With shaking hand, Lady Darnley managed a sip, then turned

watery eyes on Mairéad. "If anyone's prayers can be answered, they will be yours."

❦

Later that evening, Mairéad contemplated the day as she stood at the windows in her chamber. Moonlight sparkled on the lough's surface. A family of deer grazed out near the summerhouse.

Her last few days were occupied with painting, Tremaine and Lord Darnley which left no time for the chapel. She wrapped the red shawl about her shoulders and slipped down the back stairs and out the kitchen door. The lunar brightness guided her steps toward the small sanctuary. She could feel the dew coming through her shoes. The hem of her dress would also suffer by the time she returned to the Hall.

Deer shuffled and snorted as they fed off the sod, her presence not a hindrance to their occupation. Pulling on the metal latch to open the chapel, something flew above her head, a bird or a bat caught within. A candle flickered on the sill of the window that depicted the two O'Bannon women. Someone had quite recently been here.

Sliding into the last pew, serenity covered her like a blanket. The tiny flicker of the candle filled the air with sweetness. She knew the time was coming when her painting would be finished, and that meant returning to the convent. In this quiet moment, it came to her that she was not ready to leave.

Too many incidents of a puzzling nature inspired her to stay longer than necessary. Above all else, Lord Darnley's illness. She could not leave until he was returned to health. He brought her here to illuminate and opened a world she would never have known. She loved him for that.

She also wondered whether her superior would allow her to continue a friendship with Tremaine. It was doubtful. Though Mother Abbess dealt with peddlers and the occasional traveler seeking refuge for the night, her own life was bereft of friendship.

As far as she knew, the three family members Mother Abbess mentioned, never visited the convent. The nun's passions were prayer, orderliness, and dedication to the Catholic faith.

As she came full circle with her inner warring, a movement out of the corner of her eye caught her attention. A huddled figure stood in the darkness that allowed an outline of less density. A mortal creature, face and upper body swathed in a shawl, shuffled toward her.

The familiar voice surprised her, nonetheless. "Well, now, lass, 'tis good we meet again."

The woman who sang to the stone in the graveyard. Relieved, Mairéad eased back in the pew. "I thought I was alone."

"You've been about some, then. I'll take it you settled a bit?" The woman took the pew in front of Mairéad and sat so that they could converse.

"I have."

"Are you taking to the folks up at the hall, then?"

"They have made me feel most welcome." The woman must have knowledge of Lord Darnley's family. "You live near?"

"Near to the outskirts of the village. 'Tis my cottage." She drew the dark green shawl away from her face enough so that Mairéad caught a glimpse of her features. Lively eyes and a nice smile, tendrils of dark hair streaked with gray curled about her neck.

"When I finish with my work, I must leave."

"That'd be a distance?"

"You mean to the Sacred Heart of Jesus Convent, up on the Suir? Would you know of it?"

The woman shuffled in the pew. It was a bit awkward to talk, sitting the way they were. "'Tis the only convent in these parts."

Mairéad nodded.

"Who would'na know of it, feeding those in need when the cold creeps in. Saved many a body and their souls, over time."

Mairéad leaned in. "Do I know you? I've worked those meals in winters past."

"I know who you are. I've seen you as a wee lass and wearing your nun's wools."

Shutting her gaping mouth, Mairéad's inspection of the woman's face led her to say, "I'm most pleased to meet you. I am Mairéad."

"Call me Nuala." The woman seemed to ponder. "Mother Abbess, a bit tightfisted with the community, I'd think. Rules and all. How do you find her, then?"

The question tickled her. "You know her well. Her good works extend far into our little patch of County Waterford. She's never turned anyone away. Though in the worst of the winter, soup might be watered down."

The woman nodded. "And, yer vows. She's kept you from them, has she? Ye've not the black veil."

Struck with her knowledge of convent life, Mairéad wondered whether she considered taking vows herself. "I intend to do so this autumn when I turn eighteen. She's refused me till I come of age."

Nuala's shawl slipped off her head. She stood, pulling it aright. "Good sense on her part. It's a grueling way of life, and you're too young to begin such." A flash of lightening brightened the interior for a moment, catching them off guard. "It's been a nice little chat. I'll be about the path. Take care, lass. If I leave the candle, will you see to it, then?"

"Gladly. It has been a pleasure to meet you."

An hour later, tucked under the covers, hugging her big pillow, she was so pleased to have met Nuala that tomorrow she would make it a point to talk to Mrs. Atkinson about her.

13

Jonathan, Lord Tremaine, shortened the rein on his dun gelding. The strong, half-bred hunter trotted a bit too fast along the cobbled streets of Waterford. Eve approached, and he planned to greet a few lads, classmates from his years at Trinity. Though they would all take a ferry across the Suir and on to Dublin early in the morning, his travel would continue by coach to Belfast, where he planned to cross St. George's channel then by coach to Edinburgh.

He looked forward to a pint at Dooley's Pub and meeting up with Christopher Curran, a man who shared the same interested in the study of medicine. They met at Trinity, and like himself, Christopher passed the entrance exam after three years at Trinity. Christopher's family came from upriver in Carrick-on-Suir. Periodically, his father conducted business in Hawthorn Village and that's how Christopher became acquainted with the village.

As Tremaine entered the pub, his mates called to him by *Maine*, dubbed early on at prep. He countered with his generous, friendly nature spilling over to each as he wormed his way toward Christopher, who held a pint in the air, waving it at him. "Feared you might not show, as late as it is."

After a swallow and swiping the foam from his upper lip, he

grinned. "I had a full plate, can't just up and leave like you, with nothing better to do. Right?" He took another long swig.

Christopher, confident and ambitious, focused his attention on the sciences right along with his friend. They struck up an immediate camaraderie, both being overwhelmed at the prospect of studying at the prestigious medical university.

"Are you ready to dig in for the next grueling months?"

Tremaine took Christopher's goading in stride, as they were on the same schedule. They discussed opening a clinic in Waterford or Hawthorn Village someday. "I am focused and eager with good reason to do well." He grinned as he drew the tankard to his lips.

Christopher eyed him up and down. "Now, what might that be? Me thinks you're bragging about something."

Tremaine swiped foam from his upper lip. "Not for sharing now, but you'll be the first when and if."

Christopher turned to the group. "He's got a secret, and it's up to us to get it out of him, one way or the other." He held up his pint, splashing a bystander who glared at the young rowdies.

"Oops, sir. Sorry," he said and quickly brushed off the foam and half the pint as well.

Talking over each other, sharing their time at home with family and what was ahead at Trinity for the others, interested Tremaine and Christopher. A storm off the Celtic Sea that came down through George's Channel was the biggest topic of conversation with sailors in the pub. They were a weary lot, glad to be on land for a bit. Winter's last blast, they hoped.

The storm would not deter those heading to Trinity if they sailed across the Suir before it struck. Then by land to Carlow, up through Naas, and be done with it when they reached Dublin.

Tremaine's and Christopher's journey would continue for another ten days or so, depending on the weather. He could think of little else than Miss Mairéad, a brave, kind, impossibly naive young woman who enchanted him. He was thankful the next few months would be chock-full of grinding study. Idle time would make waiting hard. He did not fool himself. He knew she would quite possibly return to the convent, and he did not think Mother Abbess would approve of any visit from him.

Blest with a tenacious nature, however, he planned to overcome the future obstacles, one step at a time, and one way or another.

❦

Early the next morning, after breakfast and before she looked in on Lord and Lady Darnley, Mairéad tapped on Mrs. Atkinson's door. "Have you a minute to spare?"

Setting her ledger aside, the housekeeper beckoned.

"I had an interesting conversation last evening." Taking a straight-backed chair at an angle to Mrs. Atkinson's desk, she leaned over, placing an arm on the desktop. "The O'Bannon woman was in the chapel when I went for vespers."

"Nuala? Surprising."

"Do you know her, then?"

"A bit. She lives in the village, as did I, until Lord Darnley hired me as housekeeper."

"Our paths have crossed before this. She's supped at the convent dinners during wintertime." Her arms laid limp on the oak desktop. "She remembered me from when I was younger and helped serve the meals."

Mrs. Atkinson looked at her, as if she had not said a word. No raised eyebrows, nothing to show she was surprised at this news.

"Don't you think it fairly remarkable? Even a tiny bit?"

"Not really. You would have been the only child amongst all the nuns. What I think odd is her partaking of meals meant for the poor."

"You would know better than me of her circumstance."

Mrs. Atkinson shrugged. "What else did she say?"

"She asked about Mother Abbess. Her frugality. How I got along with her."

"Ah, the Mother is an enigma to many, I would guess. Unless, of course, if you live under the same roof and are Catholic. I've wondered if Nuala is of that persuasion."

"She seemed most curious about my taking vows and is familiar with postulant garb rather than the blacks. It was late, nearing midnight. She had put a candle at the window of the O'Bannon women and asked that I snuff it when I left."

Mrs. Atkinson placed her elbows on the desk and rested her chin on her knuckles. "What do you think of her?"

Mairéad shrugged. "I like that she put a candle at that particular window. You told me she is an O'Bannon. Which might mean she's distantly related to the original landowners. I like that she is motivated to keep them alive, if only in her heart."

Mrs. Atkinson patiently listened to her prattle, her head tilted as if she were interested in every conjecture, until, finally, a brow rose in question. "You've got some interest in her, I think."

"In case you've forgotten, everyone is fascinating. I come from a convent filled with black-robed women. This is like living in a bowl of wildly colored flowers and don't forget the experience comes with chocolate."

As Mrs. Atkinson's office was off the corridor leading to the kitchens and workrooms, Mairéad was aware of the bustling industry just down the hall. "I had better let you get on with your bookkeeping. I promised to relieve her ladyship this morning."

Mrs. Atkinson reached for her pen and opened the ledger. She had already returned her attention to her work, but said, "You've worked a miracle, you know, Miss Mairéad. We are all grateful."

She turned and glanced at the bowed head. Compliments were wonderful nudges to one's heart. "Thank you."

⚜

The only memories Rutledge had of his father were scattered and came from his first four years. He barely remembered the times when his father appeared, and the Molloy's bowing, hands wiped clean, shuffling in obeisance.

His name was Ayden then. The mother would whisper, "Ayden, go," and push him toward the tall man. Ayden bent backward, the man's face far above him. He recalled nose hairs, a jutting chin, and silver threads on his coat glistening from the peat fire in the hearth. He smelled of flowers. A shiny presence amongst the brown and gray clothing of the Molloy clan. With his deep blue eyes, black hair, and great height, he awed the young lad.

Little Ayden, most likely stunned into shyness, was further prodded and shoved against the man's long legs encased in warm leggings. He recalled the softness and even remembered the shoes those legs sprang from all shiny and clean, as if they never walked in the muck. He was a stunning wonder, someone different from those with whom he lived, certainly unlike gruff Molloy.

Once young Ayden understood when the man spoke to him how he was to respond, he enjoyed the questions. Each reunion became a feast of bonding, until the lad got it into his little head that he be allowed to go with the man when the visit ended.

That became a lasting lesson in boundaries. He threw a fit when Molloy peeled his little hand off his sleeve, screaming and crying, kicking at Molloy to let him go. The man brushed off the handprint on his sleeve and never looked back.

The next visit began the same until the man prepared to leave. Molloy scooped the child up, holding him tight. The visitor dropped a packet on the table, ducked under the lintel, and disappeared. Ayden was made to understand that the man would no longer visit if he raised a ruckus.

Rutledge had so few memories, he was a few months from his fifth birthday when he was told the man who visited the mud hut was his father. There were gold buttons on his sleeves and down the front of his frock. A shiny, clean man.

One day, another man arrived, much older, but of the same manner and dress. Ayden's life changed along with his name as if a gale blew across the peat through the decaying mosses, clearing away the old and leaving what? A young lad, bewildered, afraid, and now wanting the familiarity of the woman who mothered him.

The memories cast their pall even now, as he rode toward the hall with the summons from his grandmother in his pocket. His anger was fueled by memories of a father who never took him on his knee and told him of his heritage but left him in squalor and ignorance. Moreover, his grandmother refused to set eyes on him, as if the dirt floor hut was beneath her, as if he would defile her with his presence.

Rutledge's hand gripped the reins of his Arab, much like he would like to lay his hands to his grandfather's neck. If the summons to return to the hall was correct, mayhap the man was already dead. Then he must deal with a frail old woman, who, it seemed, turned her cheek toward him in acceptance of who he was, who he would be when the old man was gone, Garrett John Wallington III, the seventh Lord Darnley.

A high wind at his back, the Suir dark and roiling, sky overcast, he spurred the high-stepping stallion toward his inheritance. Rutledge hoped the convent girl was still there. She would prove entertaining until he appointed a manager and returned to Berkshire to finish up his studies, such as they were.

The first person he encountered was Shamus and, tossing his reins at the stable master he asked, "What news of Darnley?"

"Some improvement, as I understand, my lord."

"Have my bag taken to my room."

As he entered the foyer, the order and quiet of the hall was familiar. He was expected, but no one knew when.

So, Darnley continued to breathe, did he? The old man was in possession of a tenacious will to survive. Rutledge questioned his own desire. There were periods when he was devoid of any reason to go on, as if life was a fruitless venture.

Climbing the stairs two at a time to the west wing of the second floor, he paused at the mahogany-paneled door with its bronze latch and inhaled. As hard as he tried, it was difficult to think of Darnley as his grandfather. Quelling the facts of his past, getting on with a future seemed insurmountable at times. This was one of those times.

Whenever he was in Darnley's presence, the disappointment he sensed scratched every nerve. He would never measure up, never be his father. He was incapable of fulfilling the old man's desire. The profound anguish rode his back with the weight of an elephant. Damn the man! In death, his father had taken on perfection.

Lifting the latch, he stepped into the bedchamber. Darnley's wife was asleep in a chair next to the bed. Her head cradled against the back of the chair, and a soft snore came from her parted lips. His grandfather, also asleep, fingers intertwined with hers on the bed cover. He trod softly across the room, viewing the perfect scene of tranquility, and one, he supposed, might think abiding love and intimacy.

For the first time, he viewed his grandmother in the flesh. Her portrait hung in the library, so her face was familiar, but she was frailer than he envisioned. She wielded a mighty blow with her repeated refusals to welcome him. As a lad, he snuck around her apartment door, hoping for a crumb of recognition. Those days had not occurred after he reached ten, maybe eleven years of age. He realized he was of no importance. Maybe she did not think him her son's child? Perhaps she was imbecilic, not able to make her own decisions. He did doubt that idea. His gaze slid over the bedside scene—hands coupled, faint breathing from the man who allowed the woman to deny his existence.

Driven by the belief he'd been done wrong violence churned within. His fingers and arms flexed, his teeth clenched, and hatred boiled. He desperately needed a drink and walked back across the chamber, silently closing the door behind him.

Stumbling into the library, Rutledge poured a brandy to quell the ever-present panic that sent his blood racing. Downing a second brandy, he stood in the center of the library. Calming with his third, he glanced at the portrait of his grandmother, then his gaze flickered to the one of his father.

KAREN DEAN BENSON

As much as he tried to respect a wispy memory of the man who supposedly sired him, he desperately wanted to know the identity of his mother. His grandfather allowed him to read the letter from the barrister that revealed who he was and where he was living at the time his father drowned. There was no mention of a woman.

He tore his gaze from the portraits, sick to death of searching for answers amongst the brush strokes and vivid colors. One dead, the other as good as dead. It took his grandfather's illness to bring his grandmother from her lofty perch. Who did she think she was, commanding him to return to this hellhole, this shrine to a man who hid his birth? He threw the crystal glass and its contents against the portrait of his grandmother and watched the dark liquid as it drizzled down her face.

The door swung open from the foyer and he spun about. Mairéad's mocking gaze swept over the scene. She asked, "Are you well?"

Fists clenched at his sides, he scowled at her.

"Was that breaking glass? Are you cut?" She stepped into the library, leaving the door ajar.

Turning his back, he intended to collect himself. When he did not hear the door shut, he glanced over his shoulder.

Prim and staunch, hands clasped, she said, "Your grandparents are hoping for your arrival. Have you been up?"

Sweeping his waistcoat aside and gripping his hips. His voice clipped, his head jerking with outrage. "What do you want?" Her intrusion embarrassed him.

"As I said, I heard breaking glass." She glanced about, settling on the portrait dripping of whiskey and then the shards scattered across the marble floor in front of the grate, a smithereen puddle. Her mouth formed an O as realization set in.

Lips curled, he spat, "Get out." He resented her presence in his life and in the manor.

"Not until you talk like a civilized person and act like one." She mimicked his stance, with hands on hips.

Grinding his teeth, he snatched a vase of flowers and threw them at the grate rather than backhand her hard enough to fling her across the room.

That got her attention. She stepped back toward the door, but defiantly kept a wary eye on him.

"Pious woman with your concerns and veils. Who in bloody hell do you think you are?" He snarled, "Coming here, fixing our lives, are you? Think you have the mighty nerve to check on me, do you?" He advanced on her, grabbing her arm. His fingers circled her slender limb. "The two of them so fucking God-struck concerned with each other's welfare. The rest of us can go to hell."

She squirmed, tugging at her arm. "You're hurting me."

"Afraid, are you?"

Skewering her nose, she said, "Drinking a bit early, *aren't you?*"

Realizing she wasn't intimidated he jerked her arm. "You'd do better not to provoke me."

"You're a bully."

Loosening his hold, he staggered back a step, gave a short bow, and spread his arm out toward the door. "You appear to be agreeable to them. Show me the way."

Moving toward the door, her lips clenched as she grabbed at the latch. "In your condition, this isn't a good idea. He is frail, and your grandmother is too gentle a woman to accept your unprincipled manner."

He gave her a tight smile growling with fist raised. "Ah, there's the rub. I have never been acceptable. Either you lead the way, or I'll go alone."

Squaring her shoulders, he followed her measured steps up the staircase.

A maid carrying a basket full of laundry maneuvered her bundle out of Lord Darnley's chamber. Entering the chamber, Mr. O'Reilly was bent over his lordship, listening to his patient's heart. He straightened as they entered. "Lord Rutledge, good day to you," and acknowledged her with a nod.

In response, his lordship's head turned in their direction, his right hand rose off the arm of the chair. Mouth sagging, his left eyelid drooped. His right leg slid outward on the carpet.

Mr. O'Reilly proclaimed, "His lordship recognized you, Rutledge. Appears as though he's happy you've returned." The doctor backed off by the windows, allowing both Rutledge and Mairéad access to him.

Startled at his once vigorous grandparent's incapacitated state, Rutledge hissed at her, "Where is her ladyship?"

"I believe she's discussing food preparation with Mrs. Atkinson."

At a loss for words with the shock of his grandfather's obvious debilitation, Rutledge grabbed her, jerking her close to the chair. "Say something."

She knelt and put her hand in Lord Darnley's. "You are looking rested, my lord. Did you eat all your breakfast?"

His grandfather's gaze slid toward her, his face visibly softening. Rutledge took a deep breath, wondering if this was how you spoke to an invalid. This crumpled shell of the man who ordered him from Rockmore Hall, shouting his disgust and banishing him until he could act like a man. This lump of an invalid would not be speaking to him in that voice now, would he? He was reminded of his last words to his grandfather, *the next time I come back it'll be to put you in a box up on that hill.* It would seem his prophecy wasn't far off the mark.

Mairéad said, "Rutledge has come from school to be at your side."

His grandfather's pale gray orbs shifted to him. Apparently, he still remembered their last moments together, too. His jaw clenched, making the stricken side of his face even more grotesque.

Rutledge felt the doctor's stare boring into him, sensed the reprobation. His ire increased with the amount of liquor he consumed.

She stood, ran her hands over her wrinkled skirt, and glanced at the doctor. In that moment, Rutledge grabbed her about the waist kissing her on the mouth. She struggled, her hands flat against his chest, his strength far out measuring hers.

Mr. O'Reilly reached for Rutledge who spun away. "God's blood. Get out of this room." His strength bulged against the upper length of his waistcoat sleeves, hands fisted.

Rutledge's vulgar laugh filled the air as he slipped a hand over her cheek, cupping her chin. His arm tightened as his gaze turned to the doctor. "You have no authority here. I'm the next Darnley. You get out."

❦

The doctor lunged, separating them. She spun, turning her attention to Lord Darnley, who wheezed with tears dripping down his pale cheeks. She turned his face from the scuffle.

The doctor grabbed Rutledge's upper arms in a firm grip. "You have no authority in this room. As long as his lordship breathes, he is in charge. The look on his face is enough for me to realize you have committed a grave offense against this woman. You are wasted beyond good reasoning. Get out or I'll throw you out."

Mairéad patted Lord Darnley's cheeks and shoulders, cooing as if he were a child, soothing him. Out of the corner of her eye, Rutledge, edgy or nervous, glanced about the chamber, spat at the doctor's waistcoat and slammed the heavy mahogany door on his way out.

The doctor immediately put his attention solely on his patient assessing his heart rhythm with an instrument. Ascertaining his welfare, he then inquired of her, "Miss, are you all right?"

Her hand shook as she stroked his lordship's cheek. "I am fine. Rattled, a bit. Mostly worried about this dear man."

"Sit for a minute." The doctor poured a glass of water and handed it to her. He turned his attention back to his patient, whose labored breathing hissed through his sagging mouth. "Take a deep breath, my lord. You need to calm yourself as best you can.

173

Rutledge is gone, and I do not think he will return." Darnley made a visible effort to breath deeper. "That's it, my lord. Try again. It has a calming effect on your heart."

Witham and Tench burst into the chamber. Witham's worried glance swept the room, landing on his lordship, then he quickly glanced at the doctor, gasping, "Rutledge lunged out through the library doors, making quite a racket. It appears as though he's been here awhile."

Mairéad's hand trembled as she stroked her forehead. "Long enough to..." She stopped from stating the obvious and shook her head. Did the drink make him dreadful? What demons lived inside him?

Witham glanced at the doctor with a narrowed brow and doubt in his eyes.

Mr. O'Reilly nodded.

Under his breath, Witham asked, "Was there trouble?" as if he hoped this was all a mistake.

Again, the doctor nodded.

Mrs. Atkinson and Lady Darnley, followed closely by Cindy, bustled into the chamber. The housekeeper leaned back against the closed door as if Rutledge might thrust it open, though Mairéad doubted he would, thanks to Mr. O'Reilly's threats.

"We caught sight of Rutledge's coattails as he ran across the foyer. Do we know what happened?" her ladyship inquired.

Mairéad's gaze swept past the others, landing on Mr. O'Reilly, who continued to administer to his patient.

Witham stepped close to her, hovering. The concern on his face almost caused her to wilt. Drained, she felt confused and disquieted. This encounter with Rutledge had been much like the first two, rather violent and uncalled for. Distress clawed at her like bestial talons. She turned away.

Mrs. Atkinson moved near, whispering, "Can you tell me what transpired?"

"I'm not sure I understand. He was angry. More than angry, like a vicious animal might come at you. I was on my way up when I heard breaking glass from the library. Though expected, I hadn't realized he'd arrived. I asked if he was hurt, and he told me to leave.

"I should not have, but I mocked him and said I wouldn't leave until he acted civilized. He picked up a vase and threw it. Then of a sudden, he grabbed my arm, challenging me to go up with him to his grandfather." She glanced at Mr. O'Reilly. "If it weren't for the doctor, I fear how Lord Darnley would have..." Her voice trailed off. The picture of him dying crushed her.

Her ladyship came to her, folding her arm around trembling shoulders.

Mr. O'Reilly added to what Mairéad said. "I noted Rutledge watched Miss Mairéad as she talked quietly with Lord Darnley. All seemed rather picture perfect to me, when of a sudden he grabbed her, and well, was unseemly with her person. I interfered such was his strength. Lord Darnley reacted wheezing and gasping for air. I ordered Rutledge out. Thank the Almighty he left."

Mrs. Atkinson and Witham exchanged dark glances.

Witham's lips pressed into a cold, thin line, his gaze locked somewhere above her head.

Mrs. Atkinson cleared her throat. "You need be wary, Miss Mairéad. All of us in this chamber need be. His tempers seem to have increased in violence."

Mr. O'Reilly coughed politely. "We need to clear out this room. No, not you, your ladyship. He needs you near him. And Miss Mairéad, I believe his lordship was looking forward to your reading." Glancing at his watch, he consoled, "I am able to stay for several hours yet. It will give me time to reassess his heart rhythm and color."

Outside the room, Witham closed the door and instructed, "Tench, you stand guard until I determine Rutledge's whereabouts." He glanced at Mrs. Atkinson, "We must all maintain an attitude of moderation. If you should see him, act as if there is nothing untoward."

More sternly than usual, he glanced at her. "No more mocking or teasing."

Her lips formed a thin line as she nodded.

Before she reentered the bedchamber, Witham added, "This might have been his plan all along, you know. We have all witnessed his treatment of Lord Darnley. I don't know about Lady Darnley. As far as I know, they never met."

"You will want to clean the picture in the library of Lady Darnley before she sees it." Mairéad sighed, "Rutledge defaced it."

Mairéad tried to calm anxiety as she read to his lordship the rest of the afternoon. Robinson Crusoe, a book he asked for, about religious undertones of fatherly advice allowed her to wonder if he sought guidance in raising his grandson.

His lordship's head nestled against a pillow on the back of the chair. His eyes closed a light snore whistled in the air. She marked her place and closed the book to read more another time.

Her ladyship reached over and took Mairéad's hand. "Dear girl, I am so thankful for your presence, and at the same time regret the way you were accosted by Rutledge. If you had not been brought here…"

"Shush now. I wouldn't want to be anywhere else, my lady. Except right here between the two of you. I'm fine."

Those bright blue eyes settled on Mairéad. "You're stronger than I at your age. I admire the young woman you are. Your heart is in the right place."

Mairéad glanced at the hand, covered in a lacy fingerless half-glove. Her skin milky white as a dove. "We can pray that the demons chasing him, will cease. I own culpability in that I mocked him. To my shame, I felt no pity. He behaved horridly, and I found it disconcerting enough to deride him."

Cindy arrived with a vase of early peonies, pink, lilac, and white. "To cheer you, my lady, and bring the spring inside."

"Set them where Darnley can enjoy the color when he wakes."

Lively conversation ensued regarding her ladyship's delight in the seasonal budding of prized roses in the formal garden. Mairéad had yet to wander the paths but planned to do so when his lordship progressed in wellness.

She was surprised when her ladyship said, "I intend to dress for dinner."

Lord Darnley's eyelids slowly raised, and there was an awkward slant to his smile.

"You are doing better, my love. I'm encouraged and will leave you in Tench's care."

His dull gaze centered on her ladyship, and the right side of his mouth curved upward. She reached over and dabbed her lace handkerchief at drooling spittle. "Cindy will help you with your broth tonight. She has a story to tell and thinks, with your interest in sailing, her adventure might entertain you. Apparently, she has a friend who took her out on her day off."

He patted his wife's hand, covered in lacy half-gloves as it rested on the arm of the chair. A light blush rose to her cheeks. Thrilled with the privilege of witnessing their devotion, Mairéad kindled the memory of Tremaine's kiss. If she took vows, this kind of love would be beyond her reach. Her devotion to God would take its place.

It dawned on Mairéad what her ladyship had just accomplished. Though her heart must be overwhelmed with her husband's sadness and debilitation, she allowed him a sense of sameness and security announcing she would go down for dinner. She sent him the message that all was returning to normal and in its proper place. Love that strong knows no bounds.

Nearing the dinner hour, Tench arrived with a cloth and warm water to shave his lordship before supper. Mairéad excused herself, leaving Cindy and Tench to care for him.

Rutledge's absence caused Mairéad to believe he must be prowling, intending to cause more mayhem. She prayed for guidance and an open heart. Never in her life had she encountered violence. This was the third time. She needed to grasp the reason behind his anger.

Witham met her in the corridor as she neared her chamber and in a low voice said, "Lord Rutledge has not made an appearance."

"Is it possible he has fallen asleep? I did think he had several of his concoctions."

Witham practically sneered. "His capacity for drink far exceeds several. I believe he has taken himself somewhere. I warn you to be on your guard. He seems to have an unhealthy fascination with you."

"What would you have me do?"

"Lock your door at night." He handed her a key. "Mrs. Atkinson wants you to have this."

She attempted to keep her voice steady. "I'm not afraid of him."

"You should be. You needn't pretend with me, miss. I am quite unnerved by his behavior. It is as if a demon has taken hold of him."

"Put that way, I'll admit his crudity, but I believe he is badly hurt, deep inside. There is something that bothers his soul."

"Take my warning seriously. I have known him since childhood. He has not changed and, in fact, has grown worse over time." His lips grew thin with the declaration as he left her at the paneled door to her chamber.

Mairéad intended to go to dinner so her ladyship would not dine alone. She worried that if Rutledge appeared, it might be her ladyship's undoing. Ryan braided and pinned her hair into a crown, all the while chatting about cook's fussing over curdled gravy. The gossip about Rutledge had not yet reached the kitchen. Otherwise Ryan would have remarked about his arrival, unless, she was putting a stiff upper lip on the whole of the situation.

Where was he? Would he have returned to England after traveling all this way? Surely not. Mairéad said, "Now that Lady Darnley has begun living in her rooms again, it would appear Mrs. Hill is taking particular care of the food she prepares."

"I agree." Ryan stuck one last pin in the crown. "There now, tidy as can be."

Mairéad stood, straightening the sleeve of her pale, yellow gown, and turned toward the door when Ryan called for her attention.

"Miss." She held up the key. "You need to keep this with you."

Astonished she took the key. Not one word had Ryan uttered that would lead her to believe the woman knew of Rutledge's arrival. Then she remembered Ryan's friendship with Shamus and asked, "Might I hope he has taken off?"

Ryan shook her head. "Shamus says no."

"You haven't a clue where he might be?"

"No. You keep an open eye, miss."

14

"Mr. O'Reilly intends to begin therapeutic sessions on Darnley's legs," informed Lady Darnley, "even though the apoplexy extends to only the left, he thinks both legs will benefit. Apparently, therapeutic means massage." Her etched goblet caught the candlelight as she sipped her wine. "I asked him what therapeutic meant."

Mairéad couldn't imagine the weight of her fear. "May I ask how you and Lord Darnley met?"

Her pale blue eyes twinkled with delight. "It was his twentieth birthday. His parents organized a party for him here at Rockmore Hall. People came from all over County Waterford. The afternoon grew into a magical evening, and he asked me to dance near the hawthorn. There was an Irish full moon. The hawthorn was in full bloom. By the end of the dance, many of the guests moved back. We only had eyes for each other."

"I notice his eyes still brighten when you are near."

"We were married two years later," she sighed with the memory.

A footman rounded the table with a silver tray of salmon, another footman followed with a silver dish of vegetables covered in a white sauce.

Sighing, her ladyship added, "I wish Rutledge hadn't caused a scene." A lemony scent swirled in the air as she cut into the salmon. "Darnley was badly shaken and tried to tell me something, but I could not make head nor tails of it. He kept uttering, *a sin*. It sounded as if he mentioned mortal sin, and he kept repeating it. With his slurred speech and anxiety, however, I'm unsure what he was trying to say."

Mairéad dipped a forkful of salmon into the dill sauce with which she'd recently became acquainted. "I agree. All the time I read to him, he kept patting my arm, muttering. I would stop reading, and he would wave his hand for me to continue. Perhaps seeing Rutledge, after he ordered him from the hall, was simply too much."

"I'm too late. My grandson's heart is hardened. Hindsight tells me, I should have left well enough alone."

"Oh, no, my lady. You followed your heart. From what I gather, he is quite troubled about a good many instances in his life. Surely, he can understand your pain. It is, after all, similar to his own."

Lady Darnley placed her knife and fork on her plate, leaving at least half uneaten. "In any case, we believe our son employed the best of intentions in allowing Rutledge to live with the Molloy's. They are honest and devoted to Rockmore Hall, a third-generation family on the land. He meant well. The importance of an education was drilled into him. I think he made the right decision. He was too young to have fathered a child."

Mairéad wasn't sure she totally agreed but kept her assessment to herself.

"Philly has written. She intends arriving by month's end. You will enjoy those two curs. You certainly appeared to when you first got here."

"The closest I've ever been to animals was milking goats. I assure you playing with Sassy and Muffy is a lot more fun."

Mairéad's inner disquiet centered on the two elderly women

should Rutledge still be about. Her ladyship's voice interrupted her concerns.

"... goat's milk. I've not had goat's milk since I cannot recall when. A bit of a sour taste, if I remember. Seems a dab of honey helped." Picking up her fork, she cut into another piece of salmon.

"I prefer cheese made with goat's milk, rather than drinking it. Tastier. I think perhaps it's the salt."

Lady Darnley asked, "After dinner will you stroll to the summer house with me? And return in time to say goodnight to Darnley?"

Like a little parade, Cindy and Ryan trailed behind her ladyship and Mairéad. The evening sun cast a beautiful gold-red glow upon the pastoral scene. A light breeze ruffled their hems as they crossed the park. This historic occasion, Lady Darnley's first walk outside in many years, was not remarked upon.

The evening was mild, the air filled with vanilla scented spring orchids. The sound of a pair of doves atop the chapel steeple completed the enjoyment.

Shamus leaned against the open doors to the stable waving at them. Then, he folded his arms, seeming at ease in the early evening. His presence gave Mairéad a sense of security. Though no words spoken about the topic, she assumed the others shared a bit of anxiety, too. The outrage over Rutledge's behavior and fear of physical reprisal was a wordless, hovering cloud. She sensed he was out there somewhere, watching and waiting.

Ryan giggled at something Cindy whispered. Lady Darnley chastised. "You are flirts. In my day, one did not encourage bold behavior."

Ryan muffled a snort as her gaze fled from Shamus to the grass. The soft, early summer breeze fluttered the gauze wrapped about their coifs. Two long strings of geese honked and whapped across the sky.

After the incident in his grandfather's chamber, a long walk sobered Rutledge. By the time he arrived at the Molloys' dirt-floor cottage, he'd bottled most of his anger. The stooped figure of Molloy was at the pigsty where a sow and piglets set up a racket at the scraps he'd just thrown.

"Good day ta ye, your lordship. Out for a stroll?" Molloy, though having played the role of caretaker to Rutledge early in his life, never forgot the wide berth between them and never failed to be polite. The disparity irked Rutledge more than usual.

Still in his travel clothes, dusty, and dirt-smudged, he was more at ease on this small patch of ground than in the Palladian mansion on the other side of the park. Suddenly, his confusion begged the reason for seeking out this man. Molloy, waiting for an answer, stood at the weather-worn fence as the pigs rooted.

A disturbing pressure to assimilate caused Rutledge to blurt, "How is it my father asked you to keep me?"

Molloy bent to put the empty bucket back in the cart. A bee buzzed around his head, and he swatted at it with his scarf. He deliberately slapped his hands clean of the dirty work, wiped them against his pants, and turned to face Rutledge. His work-worn face, the skin about his eyes wrinkled leather, and with green eyes like chips of stone, he stared at Rutledge. "Is this what ye be wantin' ta know, then? The reason he sought us out, because I can only have a guess."

Rutledge shrugged his shoulders and shook his head. "I don't know. Did he speak of my mother? Were his visits as infrequent as I seem to recall?"

Some of the breath left Molloy. He pulled the scarf out of his back pocket and swiped his forehead. "Well, I would have remembered if he spoke of a woman. I would not have forgotten such as that. As to his comin' by, I'd have ta say ..." His hard gaze fell on Rutledge, locked on him. "... when he was at Rockmore, it was often enough, but when he left for ta continent travelin' as such do, back to university, it would be some time then, wouldna. 'Tis a shame ye didn't have more time tagether. 'Tis a mighty shame. He was good aboot ta larder goods, more than generous, for as little as ye ate as a bairn."

His gaze fell to his crusty hands. A silence ensued except for the pigs slopping and the bee buzzing. He began again. "Ye are wantin' more, are ye not? More of what he was thinkin' ta leave yer babby self with strangers an' all. The missus had as much ta say as anyone aboot yer leavin', but ye weren't ours. Near broke her heart."

The sow grunted in satisfaction, and the piglets squealed and rooted for teats.

Silence hung between them as Rutledge gathered confusing incidents long since put away. He drew a labored breath as memories of that time scattered. Then a hard reflection of a man in fancy clothing shaking and chastising him for clinging to his legs. On the heels of that memory, he said, "I've a memory of Mrs. Molloy handing me over to someone who held me at arm's length. I might have bawled or something because the man dropped me in a chair."

Taking his cap off, Molloy ran an arm across his forehead. "Ye'd be rememberin' rightly. Ye toppled off the chair and cut your head a gash. He'd no way with bairns. Ye must know, most men don't take to it like the máthair's. It's just the way of it, my lord." Placing the cap on his head, he scratched his neck.

Rutledge turned away from him and ran a hand over the rail fence, unmindful of splinters. "I've memories, fleeting images, more of late than not. You covered for him, made excuses. Like you are doing now. It's coming back to me."

"Why would ye think of such? He's gone now. Nigh on thirteen years, is it."

Rutledge couldn't tamp the loathing. He boiled with hatred. Curse the damned demon clawing at his head. The swirl of anger was hot and red.

"I'll say this, if he didna care, ye'd have been put away. He did his best bringin' ye ta us, on your own land an' all. Not far from ta others of your kin."

"You're a blind fool, old man. His disdain for a son he wouldn't declare was clear." *That* was the rub, the sinking in his heart. He stepped near the shocked caretaker, fists clenching. "I believe he took his own life because of the shame of my birth."

Molloy gasped.

Rutledge spat, "Hated the sight of me, he took his own life. 'Tis what I believe."

"Me lord, don't think of it. Lord Darnley's done right by ye. You're learnin' in far off England. You're ta be the next earl. All this will come ta ye, natural like, as should be. If it be the truth, what ye just said, his lordship wouldna taken ye in."

Rutledge's breath knotted in his chest. He could not control the tremors in his arms. He needed a drink but stayed his hand from reaching for the flask in his breast pocket.

With his slop-mucked boots and unshaven face, for some reason this poor farmer earned more respect to his way of thinking than those up at the great manor. Hatred festered, and he could not seem to gain control. His fists clenched with unspent fury, and he caught a dark look of fear in Molloy's eyes.

Rutledge stepped closer, and the man tried to back away. Caught by the fence, his eyes grew large as if trapped. Suddenly, Rutledge realized his affront to this man, and he stumbled off toward the lough.

He walked on past the bog huts filled with families that worked Rockmore Hall's land. At the lough, he climbed a short hill on the far side, the long grasses waving as a slight breeze blew. Plunking down on the ground, he leaned against an oak. Exhaustion overcame him as voices of four women walking toward the summer house drifted on the wind.

Recognizing the convent lass, a common nobody, in company with his grandmother twisted his gut. His lack of history with the elder dredged up the loneliness pursuing him.

Within his pitiable self, a reminder that his grandmother requested he return, he put aside. Too many years spent denying his existence set the pattern of a future relationship. His pain flamed. Focusing inward as his gaze followed the women, their companionship proof how easily he was replaced. Jerking the flask from his pocket, he gulped the amber, mind-numbing cure-all.

Propped against the tree, elbows bent on his knees, he watched as the women crossed the bridge. The maids stood to the side as the girl and his grandmother seated themselves on the bench. Had the little nobody entertained his grandmother. Telling of his tantrum, defacing her portrait, breaking glass, making him a fool to his grandparent?

Pulling another long swallow of his remedy, he cast a sideways glance at the structure on the island. The setting sun cast long golden shadows off the summer house and across the lough. The women strolled back across the bridge. Would his grandmother go to her retreat on the upper floor, or would she return to her long-vacated rooms next to his grandfather?

She could go to hell for all he cared. He took another pull on the flask, allowing the liquid to slowly burn in his mouth and then down his throat as he sought relief. He never fit in here, never been part of their lives. His father took care of that with his suicide. Emptying the flask, he shoved his back up against the tree trunk, the sky burnished with the setting sun. He leaned back and threw the flask as far as he could, not caring if it reached the lough, then he stumbled down the hill.

He should go directly to Madame Fornia's establishment in Waterford. Irish whiskey paled in comparison to her infamous opium lair. His scrutiny traveled the park, falling on the shape of the girl, and he changed his mind.

❧

Witham attempted to make sense of the afternoon. Never, in all his years, was there such an upset. Mairéad looked as though she'd been stung by a hornet's nest, Lord Darnley was as white as a ghost, but on the surface of things, they appeared calm at dinner.

A light knock on his small office door ended his list of aggravations, and he smiled at Mr. O'Reilly.

The doctor had never before been below stairs in the servants' quarters. Witham inquired, "I hope you are not bringing news of a dour nature considering this afternoon's tragic scene?"

"Not directly, this was written in Lord Darnley's own hand to be delivered to his barrister in Waterford." He handed it to Witham.

Surprised, Witham said, "Lord Darnley's hand?"

"Yes. When he calmed, he distinctly, with hand movements and careful enunciation, he was able to request pen and paper. I have added my signature to authenticate I witnessed him write it, and that he is of sound mind."

The doctor added, "He is requesting that the solicitor come immediately and bring a copy of his will. We will keep this information between us, Witham. He does not want to cause any further upset in this household."

Witham's nearly fifth decade at Rockmore Hall, he better than anyone knew Lord Darnley's private way of dealing with matters of great importance. "Rest assured this will be delivered tonight to Mr. Hagadorn."

"Tench is with his lordship for the rest of the evening. Unless I hear from you, I plan to return midmorning." He grimaced and added, "Sorry business this. I will admit we could have lost him in the aftermath of Rutledge's crudity. His heart is not as strong as one would hope."

Attempting to keep his own emotions under control, Witham said, "Fortunate for Lord Darnley you were in his chamber."

Shortly thereafter, Molloy arrived, hat in hand, and asked to speak privately. Mrs. Hill offered biscuits and tea. It was not often the cottagers came to the hall with business.

"No, thank ye. 'Tis a serious business what brought me here. No time for comfort." His tam twisted between work worn hands.

Witham said, "Follow me, Molloy."

When they were settled into wood-backed chairs in his office,

Witham said, "You must have something of import if your face is any indication."

"'Tis Rutledge, sir. He come to talk with me aboot his father and who his mother is, then."

Witham's brows rose. "Does that seem unusual to you? His early memories began under your care."

"Not the way he asked. Evil, like the devil twisted his guts. His eyes all blurry, bloodshot. Had me countin' the minutes left ta me, he did."

"When was this?"

"Mebbey an hour or less, just before sunset."

"What else can you tell me?"

"In his cups he were as I've seen him. An' I've seen him plenty, but this is somethin' more in him, like I said, the devil, somethin' evil." He crushed his tam with his thick, crusted hands. "I've not seen such a madness. In his eyes, it were."

"Did you notice where he went? Did he ride off?"

"He walked toward high hill, but I don't know if it's where he went once he entered the oaks."

Witham played with a pen, tapped it on the desktop. "I ask that you keep this to yourself for now. On your way, will you ask Shamus to come up? Tell him to bring two of his bigger stable men with him."

Molloy stood and, having shared his news, breathed a sigh of relief. As if he passed all his worry to Witham, he could go to his warm wee cottage, sit by his hearth, and enjoy a Guinness and dumplings.

There would be no rest for Witham, however. He must form a plan to protect the people inside Rockmore Hall from its presumptive heir.

❈

Mairéad paced the floor in her chamber. She hadn't drawn the velvety drapes, instead allowed the bright moon to cast its glow upon the carpet where her troubling images fell. The day began nicely then proceeded to crumble with Rutledge's arrival. What was his desperation, truly? His grandparents loved him and encouraged him to fill his life with learning and enjoy an ease most in Ireland could not afford.

A part of her hurt for him. Lord Darnley hadn't encouraged her to befriend his grandson. Her fingertips brushed her lips. She'd no experience with kissing other than Tremaine's wonderful, exciting lips on hers. If that was the way of it, Rutledge's kiss was meant to deliberately hurt and subjugate.

She knew the word *subjugate* from lessons about Ireland's history, and how the English swarmed in, stomping out Catholicism and the Gaelic tongue and ripping the land out from under them. If she hadn't the learning in these things, she would not have knowledge of what his kiss was. He was an angry man, in need of hurting others.

Standing at the large bank of windows, she hoped the deer would show. They soothed, and she needed that. A shuffle outside her door caused her to freeze, until she reminded herself it was locked.

She heard the clink of metal and the turn of a key, then her door opened.

Rutledge.

He closed and locked the door, put the key in his pocket, and calmly asked if she'd anything to drink.

Her mind froze. There was a poker leaning against the fireplace, but she was standing in front of the windows, several yards from the grate. "What do you want?"

"Are you deaf? I want a drink. I suppose you'd not have such a thing in your virginal room." He walked over to her, tucked his hands under his armpits, and took in the scene bathed in the light of the moon.

"No, I would not." Her heart hammered her ears buzzed. She swallowed. "Even if I did, you've had far more than you should."

He stood a head taller than she, lean of body, yet with a wiry, muscular stance. His father would have been a most handsome man. The threat she felt upon his entrance began to ease.

He let out a deep sigh but did not move.

A minute ticked by. The great clock in the hall chimed the half hour. It must be ten-thirty. She dared a glance at him. He was fixated on something beyond the windows, and she followed his line of vision. It was not the deer. There was something else visible against the tree line, changing the depth of the shadows.

He said, "Do you see that old crone?"

"Hmm," she responded. Thankful for his seemingly calm demeanor.

"Been coming for years, as long as I recall."

Mairéad figured she was going to either the chapel or the graveyard, perhaps hoping *she* would be there. "Her name is Nuala. She lives near the village."

He glared at her. She noted it with her peripheral vision. He might wonder how she would know the crone's name, but he didn't ask.

She refused to meet his stare. "How did you come by a key to my room?"

He snorted. "I grew up in this house, didn't I now?"

"Why are you here?" She hoped to appear fearless.

The silence went deep. He did not seem to breathe, nor could she hear the wind in the trees. Partly fearful, she waited for him to say something, but what that would be she'd no fairies' knowledge.

"Because ..." His hands dropped from under his arms. He used them to brace himself against the window ledge as he bent forward. "... because there is ... something here. I've felt it ... but I was not sure ... and I wanted to be ... sure, before ..." The disjointed words came out of him as if he could not believe he said them. His bloodshot eyes grew large, as if his words were a foreign tongue to his own ear.

His sentence hung in the air. He pushed off the window ledge and turned into the room, taking a few steps to the center, leaving her at the window.

She asked, "Before?"

He shrugged and walked back to the windows. "Nuala, she's odd, an old hag, born here like most of us. I doubt any sane person would deliberately come to live in these parts."

Bewildering her with his disjointed conversation, she asked, "Before what?"

He shrugged again his head bowed. "I hate this place."

She almost went to him, but a voice of caution in her head, told her to stay where she was.

He wiped at his face as if tears fell, but she could not tell for certain. "They hate who I am. They have you now."

In disbelief that he would think this, yet put words to it, she said, "I'm the one who doesn't belong here. I'm the outsider, come to paint for your grandfather and will return to the convent soon. How can you even consider that they don't want you? You are flesh and blood to them, their beloved son's child. I am only a someone who illuminates, who is meant to become a nun."

The desperation in his eyes astounded her. Like a drowning man might look going under for the last time. She shook the notion off yet shivered with the image almost as if her heart would stop. "Your grandmother mentioned she wrote to you, begging your return."

"I did then, didn't I?" Between clenched teeth he spit each word vehemently.

Was it possible to reach this man? Did he not see that people judged him by his actions, that how he acted was what condemned him? He swiped at his forehead this time, and she could see the perspiration forming, dripping. His hand trembled as he swiped again. In his obvious misery, he turned away from her.

She slowly crossed the room, reached for the bell pull, and tugged on it as he swung about. His face contorted instant rage bloodied his eyes.

His hands curled into fists as he jumped forward raising them in her face, baring his teeth like a feral animal.

She backed away until forced to stop against the bed. He bent over her, perspiration dripping from his forehead. One hand gripped her throat, the other a fist aimed at her. He forced her to crumble backward onto the bed. She struggled to free herself from his hand clasped about her neck, fearing she was about to be murdered. There was a moment of incredulity when his body tensed, before he jerked backward.

Slamming his fist into the wall, leaving a hole in the plaster where her face might have been. Then stumbled to the door digging for the key. He turned it in the lock and staggered out the door.

Gasping for breath, clutching her throat, she sprang off the bed, chest heaving, her gaze glued to the hole in the wall. With her heart nearly exploding, her ability to speak deserted her as Mrs. Atkinson rushed into the chamber.

"Dear Mother of God, oh, no!" The housekeeper opened her arms as her wild gaze swept the room. Mairéad stumbled into them.

15

The next morning, Witham placed his pen in the inkwell and greeted the barrister. "You are prompt, Mr. Hagadorn. I'll take you to Lord Darnley." The man was dressed in the latest fashion of rolled collar, double-breasted waistcoat, pantaloons, and shiny hessians. A young man with knowledge of legal matters, he had impressed his lordship repeatedly.

Mr. Hagadorn asked, "I understand Lord Darnley has been ill. The doctor's note did not include specifics, but indicated there has been a dramatic change?"

Arriving at his lordships chamber, Witham said, "Mr. O'Reilly will bring you up to date, sir."

With that he opened the door. "Mr. Hagadorn for Lord Darnley."

Lady Darnley turned her attention from her husband. "How good of you to come so quickly, Franklin."

"My lady, I came as early as I thought proper." He took her hand and made a small bow. Witham noted that Mr. Hagadorn showed no sign of surprise upon seeing her ladyship outside her apartments. Over the years, that is where his conferences with the Darnleys took place, upstairs.

Lord Darnley turned to his solicitor. A smile curved on his good side. He nodded in welcome.

☙❧

Lord Darnley waited until Witham shut the mahogany panel. His gaze shifted to Mr. O'Reilly, and he nodded for him to commence with the work to be done.

The doctor said, "His lordship is recovering nicely from a bout with apoplexy. His wishes are to update his will. To save Lord Darnley unnecessary consternation, both Lady Darnley and I will assist in interpreting his wishes as he directs us to do so. You are to understand, it is his speech, not his mind, that presents his communication troubles."

Mr. Hagadorn, whose gaze riveted on his lordship, nodded in agreement. "Yes, my lord. I will be able to work this way with you." He pulled up a chair, forming a little circle with them, and opened his valise.

Darnley sent a questioning glance to the doctor, who answered, "I have notes to write, but I'll also listen to the proceedings and intervene if needed."

His lordship's palm came up as he nodded in agreement.

☙❧

Mairéad entered the dining room early hoping to avoid her ladyship. Ryan chose a gown with a high neck to hide the bruising that formed during the night. She ate quickly and went straight to her workroom. Her attempt to forget last night was fragile, and she needed to bury herself in painting. Mrs. Atkinson stayed with her until she had fallen asleep. The housekeeper promised to keep this between them and would have the wall repaired as quickly as possible.

Yesterday's parchment was now dry, and Mairéad clipped the page with Lord Darnley's W to her drawing board along with the sketch he approved. It now contained trailing vines, to which she planned to add depth with variegated coloring.

Donning her apron and sleeves, she glanced wistfully at the windows, and before mixing her paints, looked out over the park and the stables. A groom walked a colt born the week before, his shiny black coat slashed with a blaze of white on his nose, his spindly legs keeping pace. It occurred to her that Hungas might be the sire. Her fingertip traced the leaded panes framing the beveled glass. The view provided by the windows, and more than that the daylight that spread across the room and the warmth that came with the rays, comforted her.

It was time to leave here. Beyond time. Mother Abbess's notes increasingly mentioned concern for her vocation and that Mairéad needed to prepare herself for the only future she could envision. Wind whipping about the turrets of the convent would once again fill her ears, and she would feel the broken rock underfoot and the damp walls as her hand swept along the corridors.

She allowed herself a moment to ponder life without the comfortable bed and fluffy, down-filled pillow. Life, though filled with challenges, also provided many benefits beyond one's physical pleasure. Most importantly, she owed Mother Abbess.

The altercation with Rutledge was beyond horrid. She was not a coward, but fear set her legs to trembling last night. Nonetheless, through the altercation, she understood that he suffered ills from long ago and harbored grudges against parents he never knew and grandparents who wanted to help him. Yet for some reason he was unable to forgive Lord and Lady Darnley for the sins of his parents.

Why he came to her room talking in riddles she could not fathom and attributed it to his drinking. He was a tortured soul, and she summoned pity for him. Intending to never again be a catalyst for his anger, she would take care during the days to come until she returned to the convent and safety.

Her occupation today included adding volume to the vines and leaves with several shades of green and proceeded to mix the paints. Though she knew religious text was generally exalted with gold foil, and personal drawing with silver, she also intended to use gold on the clothing depicting Lord Darnley. It was her personal preference for him, and Lady Darnley agreed.

❧

Later, but before dining with her ladyship, Mairéad wrote to Mother Abbess telling her the illumination was progressing nicely. She also wrote of Lord Darnley's health and the exercises that appeared to increase his ability to move his leg and arm. Hopefully, she could leave early next week but told Mother she would write again in a few days with the exact date.

Lady Duncamden was expected any time. Mairéad could only imagine her ladyship's excitement to greet her sister-in-law outside the apartment she occupied all these years.

Mairéad was greeted by her ladyship as she entered the parlor regret in her tone, "I'm thinking it will be just the two of us. Do you mind if we go straight in?"

As they left the parlor and started to cross the great hall, noises erupted from the front of the house. She heard the scampering of little paws on marble and turned as Muffy and Sassy ran by as if chased by a wolf.

Her ladyship grinned at sight of her sister-in-law. "I almost gave up on you until tomorrow. We were just on our way into dinner."

With a smile and a twinkle in her eye, Lady Duncamden waved to a footman, "Gather them up. They need a walk, then nourishment."

Lady Darnley laughed. "My dear Philly, do you speak of us? I hope not."

Turning to her ladyship, a hand to her breast, Lady Duncamden gushed, "When...why did you not inform me...did the earth shake, and you fell out of that dreadful tower?"

The footman tried to hold in a grin as he gathered one fur ball under his arm and reached for the other, whom Mairéad had managed to grab.

"My poor husband needed me, more than I needed to be shut away."

The women hugged. Gladdened by their history, Mairéad delighted in the fact that she could witness years of separated living ending this moment. Their shared affection was obvious, and dinner and the accompanying conversation delightful. Not until a vanilla pudding with fresh strawberries was served did Rutledge's name come up.

Lady Duncamden asked, "You brought me up on all the news but have not mentioned my nephew." She picked up her spoon to begin attacking dessert. "I am thinking you are avoiding the topic of him."

Lady Darnley frowned. "As usual, you're assessment is correct. I wonder, Miss Mairéad, would you bring Philly up on Rutledge?"

She would rather not, but recognizing her ladyship's difficulty discussing her grandson, she said, "He seems to have taken himself off somewhere. When his lordship took ill, Rutledge returned from school at her ladyship's summons.

"We were not aware that he arrived until I happened upon him in the library. He was in a fit of anger, throwing a glass into the grate, mumbling and distorted, quite in a stew. It seems he was fortifying himself for or against seeing his grandfather. He took me with him to his lordship's room and behaved...well, in all fairness, I could see how grieved he was at the sight of his grandfather. Appalled, really. The doctor was forced to remove him from the chamber."

Her gaze drifted to her lap, where her hands twisted. It was not pleasant thinking of him, especially after the situation in her chamber last evening.

Lady Darnley interjected. "He will never forgive me, nor does he forgive his grandfather. I hoped, summoning him home, we could begin to restore our past."

Her sister-in-law cut in. "Only he has the power to adjust his attitude. I am sorry to admit he has shown little restraint over the years. Expecting it of him now is a waste."

"He's vanished." Lady Darnley waved her fork in the air. "Gone we know not where."

Shifting her gaze from her ladyship to Mairéad and back again, she tapped her fingertips on the linen, clearly thinking.

Mairéad added, "Witham has men searching the grounds."

Lady Duncamden's keen eye bored into her. "There is more, isn't there?" Leaning near, she said, "What are you keeping from us?"

Unbidden tears welled in her eyes. Embarrassed, she swiped at them. The one thing she did not want to do was reveal the devastating occurrence from last night.

Her lorgnette held against her eye, Lady Duncamden gasped. "Is that a bruise on your neck?"

Mairéad's hand reflexively covered the place that ached from the encounter last night.

Lady Darnley stood so fast the footman barely reached her chair in time. She marched around the table, laying her hand on her shoulder. "He hurt you!" Her shrill voice rang.

Lady Duncamden slapped her napkin atop her plate. "How severe was this attack? Do you need the doctor?"

"No, please. When he would have hit me, he stopped and hit the wall instead. Then he ran out. I had rung for Mrs. Atkinson, who arrived within seconds." The atmosphere grew quiet. She whispered, "His rebellion is rooted in a deep sadness. I pray for compassion that will allow me to accept his character as flawed rather than evil."

"You've a bigger heart than I imagined." Lady Duncamden eyed Mairéad through her quizzing glass, again. A magnified pale blue eye searched what little of her skin showed for telltale effects.

"Harrumph," grunted Lady Darnley. "We'd best have Mr. O'Reilly look you over when he arrives."

Hands trembling, Mairéad entreated, "Please don't. I don't

know why, but in my heart, I sense he's gone. Lord Darnley must *not* know about the incident. I'm sorry to be stubborn on this matter. It means a great deal that this is not spoken of again, to anyone." She laid her palms on each side of her plate, begging. "Please."

Sighs and dour glances were exchanged between the two elders. Reluctantly, they nodded to her request. Lady Duncamden remarked, "It is your safety, not ours that is foremost on our minds." Her brows scrunched with meaning.

After dinner, it was decided they would take Sassy and Muffy to his lordship's chamber and visit until time to retire.

His lordship stroked Muffy's black furry ear as the dog nestled in his lap, and the picture of it brought her contentment. The sisters-in-law chatted about the past, bringing a kind of friendly lullaby to the close of the day.

Mairéad didn't sleep well last night, and it caught up to her now. Mrs. Atkinson assured her she would be safe tonight. Taken at her word, Mairéad did not concern herself about the arrangements to guard her door.

She truly felt Rutledge gone. The instant he raised his fist to her, something flickered in the depths of his gray eyes, an inner qualm that stayed his action. The recall of that moment is what calmed her now, with no sensible reason why. It just did.

The elderly women's chatter about a distant relative living in Glasgow brought her attention back to the present. It was apparent Lord Darnley knew of whom they talked. The eyebrow on his good side rose up and down with the news mongering and prattle.

These loving people drew her so fully into their lives, trusting her with their stories, allowing her the company of a loving family. Why was Rutledge so resistant to the affection of his own family? His startling lack of emotion in the face of near tragedy with his grandfather was shocking. Or, could he be afraid of what his sentiment might reveal, a caring so deep he could not deal with it? She wondered if she wasn't on to something of the truth.

Exhausted, she quit her foolish musing and handed Sassy to

Lady Darnley. "I might fall asleep if I sit here one minute longer. Excuse me, please. It appears I need my bed."

Opening her chamber door, she found Mrs. Atkinson reading a book before the fire. "This is a pleasant surprise." Glancing about the chamber Mairéad inquired, "No Ryan?"

"I'm taking her place. It is a precaution." Mrs. Atkinson closed her book and stood.

"Witham is worried about Rutledge's next move, is he?" Removing the pins in her hair, the dark auburn length drifted over her shoulders and back.

"Witham is certain Rutledge has fixated on you and intended to post a man outside your door at night. Though his horse is gone, no one knows his whereabouts. It might be better to have me here instead. That is, if it is to your liking."

"If your intent is to sit outside my door all night, I'll join you, or you may choose to share this monstrosity of a bed with me." She cast a grin at the housekeeper that deepened to a laugh, as she suddenly realized the heavy cloud she'd been under and relief that she would not be alone tonight. "We could sleep four or five in the size of it."

"Until we are positive we have seen the last of Rutledge, this is prudent, for now at least. And, thank you. I would prefer a bed."

"I am nearly finished with his lordship's biography. A week, perhaps a bit more, and I will be gone, too. I hope my leaving brings a bit more peace to all of you."

Mrs. Atkinson turned away from the warmth of the fire and walked to the window. "Don't be in such a hurry. You have brought joy to us all, despite his lordship's illness and your encounter with Rutledge." She paused a moment. "Lady Darnley left her apartment after many, many years. You have given Lord Darnley a reason to get well. I might be mistaken, but I think you've caught the eye of a certain lord."

She blushed.

"My frankness is a curse." Mrs. Atkinson tilted her head a notch.

Mairéad giggled. "Don't change for me. It is such a lovely experience to have honest communication with others. I will be sheltered for the rest of my life. For now, I would like to bask in the pleasure of friendship between us."

"Does his lordship suspect you're leaving soon?"

"He knew from the start that this was temporary. But, no, he doesn't know how soon. He's like a father figure. Someone special. It's hard to leave before his full recovery."

"Then why?" The housekeeper's attention was directed at something outside.

"What do you see?" She moved to the housekeeper's side.

"The stag and his doe."

"Lovely creatures. They appear almost nightly." A minute of silence between them as they enjoyed the scene, when she added, "Mother Abbess' communications focus increasingly on his return to health and my work coming to an end."

"You are steadfast for one so young."

"I will be eighteen soon. Old enough to choose my future, I believe I know what my path is."

Mrs. Atkinson clapped her hands, "Look, here come the little ones trailing behind. If it weren't for the bright moon, they'd not be noticed."

⚅

A week passed and Rutledge had not made his presence known. Speculation was that he returned to Eton. Each day that passed eased the anxiety at Rockmore Hall. After two nights, the housekeeper returned to her own room.

A letter from Tremaine caused her heart to flip. Ready for bed, sitting before the fire, cuddled up on a cushy chair with a rug over her legs, she passed the envelope under her nose. Fingertips traced the address, her name penned in his hand. As if unwrapping a precious gift, she cracked the wax seal, unfolded the two pages of bold black ink penned only for her. Of all her firsts, this marched to the forefront.

Dear Miss Mairéad, he wrote. She could not explain it, but her name penned in his hand was thrilling. It gave her a keen sense of attachment.

He arrived at his apartment in Edinburgh after ten days of travel. His apartment mate, Christopher Curran, an old friend, journeyed with him. He, too, studied medicine.

They crossed the channel from Dublin, landing at Carlisle. From there the journey by mail coach took fifteen hours due to a deluge of rain that blew across the land. They put up at an inn for two nights because the rough roads were a quagmire of rock and mud. Eventually arriving in Edinburgh, the weather continued blustery with a great blow off the North Sea.

Reading Tremaine's travel adventure, she doubted she would ever write of such a journey? The only person she knew who journeyed any distance was Sister Davideena. Born in America she came to Ireland and took vows. Mairéad knew this because Sister would relate stories of crossing the ocean on the nights it was her turn to put little Mairéad to bed.

Tremaine's description of anatomy class honed an interesting surprise. Knowing little of science, she was enthralled reading about the professor's class on bone structure.

He mentioned looking forward to her first of what he hoped were many letters and sent his regards to Lord and Lady Darnley. He inquired how frequently she was riding, whether she visited the chapel lately, and whether she noticed the old crone in the graveyard. His deliberate posing of questions ensured she must write.

Her fingers brushed his manly signature, *Jonathan*, as if she touched him.

Quill in hand, she began a response. Utmost was Rutledge's disappearance, but refraining from mentioning the altercation in her bedroom, writing instead that it was assumed he returned to Eton. Lady Duncamden and her two little fur balls arrived for a stay of more than a fortnight and the illumination of Lord Darnley's manuscript was nearly finished. He signed his letter *affectionately*, and she signed hers *warmly*.

To Mother Abbess, she wrote of the biography's completion. And mentioned Lord Darnley was adapting to his exercises, thanks to Lady Darnley and Tench who cajoled and coaxed. It was a game eliciting laughter with his attempts to walk from the chair to the window and back again. She ended writing that she looked forward to her return to the convent, a wee little bend in the truth of the matter.

The waxing moon shed a soft glow on the park and the tip of the chapel as it poked through the treetops, beckoning to her. Gathering her letters and a shawl, she proceeded down the stairs, placing the posts on the tray for Witham.

Turning toward the kitchen, she made her way along the lengthy hall to the back of the manor. It was late, and the kitchen, though still filled with the aroma of dinner preparation, now also was scented with berry pie and the musk of yeasty bread rising, tomorrow's feasting.

A light breeze, though warmer than usual for late July, brought a barely discernible scent of an apple-wood fire, probably from one of the cottages. The shawl kept the evening's damp off her shoulders as she took the path toward the chapel. She had grown negligent of prayer. The routine at the convent slipped into laxity. Shamed because of it, she intended to atone.

The latch clinked as she stepped inside. The essence of beeswax lingered, perhaps from her last visit. Lighting a candle, she knelt in the last pew, crossing herself, and began to talk to God.

As her eyes accustomed to the flicker of candlelight and finished with formal prayer, she glanced about the shadowy interior and the windows hardly discernable in the dark. The rendering of the two women, her favorite of all four, reminded her of Nuala and the first time she sang to a stone in the graveyard.

Tremaine also came to mind. She missed his teasing, the sound of his deep, smooth voice when saying, *Sister* Mairéad. She might have to make the decision to give up his friendship. Few nuns, only three that she could recall, received infrequent visits from brothers and fathers. Her palm smoothed across the oaken pew. A cloud passed, allowing a ray of moonlight to spill through the windows. Her gaze settled on the moonbeam backlighting the features of the taller of the two women depicted in the window, the O'Bannon women.

There was no mystery about her life's path once she returned to the convent. It would have but one purpose, prayerful honoring of God and the love of mankind that He taught. Her illuminating would continue, hopefully with improvement. Perhaps, at some point, Mother Abbess would allow her to tutor another, someone with whom she could share the awesome responsibility.

She'd been without her tunic and veil these past months and admitted favoring colors other than gray. A starchy wimple against her cheek would take some personal adjustment.

The soft ruffling of branches high above the chapel soothed her. An owl hooted, and she heard the occasional plunk of an acorn. Her gaze rested on the crucifix high up on the stone wall behind the altar. The crucifix at the convent of the Sacred Heart of Jesus was similar, in that the figure of a tortured Christ hung as a reminder of His fidelity and love. The community of nuns' homage circling the air, a large part of her familiar life.

As her mind wandered, the image of Tremaine's grin and the twinkle in his eyes comforted. He had asked her to call him Jonathan. She decided that when it was just the two of them, she would do so, not entirely artless as to ignore the flutters he stirred when he put his warm hand on hers. She remembered the tender way he brushed a lock of hair behind her ear the first day they rode together, their kiss, the feel of his lips against hers. She drew her fingertips across her lips at the memories.

16

The next morning, Mairéad worked until noon, rode Caomh almost to Hawthorn Village and back, then returned to her chamber.

Ryan helped her into a yellow silk gown with lace at the puff sleeves and bodice.

The picturesque scene in the parlor was of both elderly ladies, cordials in hand and a dog in each lap. Furry little heads raised up beady eyes full of sudden interest. At the sound of her voice, they bounded off the cozy laps and scampered to her, jumping at her skirts.

"Oh, my, what a reception. Good evening, my ladies." As she took a seat, the dogs jumped on either side of her, licking her hands.

"Scat, you naughty curs. Leave her be," Lady Duncamden ordered from her chair. They didn't so much as give their mistress a glance.

"I must take them for a walk tomorrow."

"How is the painting coming?"

"I may be finished." She cast a sideways glance at Lady Darnley. "They will be dry tomorrow. Lord Darnley can decide if they are to his liking?"

"I can't imagine him not liking anything you do, my dear."

That comment was the second time she'd heard it. The first coming from Mrs. Atkinson. She answered her ladyship, "If he agrees, it will be time for me to return to the convent. Mother Abbess wrote that I should not tarry when finished. There is work waiting for me."

Two women, frowning at her remark, turned their gazes to the cordials in hand. If she did not know better, she would expect them to speak the same words in unison, so alike they appeared. With one exception, Lady Darnley was a softer, kindly spoken woman. Her sister-in-law exhibited more of an edge, saying exactly what was on her mind.

Offered the lime drink made especially for her, Mairéad, hands full of furry wigglers, nodded for the footman to set it on the table at her elbow. A thoughtful gesture as was everything in this household and these dear, lovely people.

The picture of the two sitting across from her, scowls gone, sipped sherry and caused Mairéad to blink back the threat of tears. "This time with you has been wonderful. You welcomed me with open arms. I'll never forget your kindness and expressions of generosity. But I made my choice a long time ago."

She kept both her hands busy rubbing fur and receiving licks, hoping to not embarrass herself. It was almost as if the dogs understood. It took an inner courage, but she cast a grin at Lady Darnley, saying, "I'll be leaving you in good hands. Her ladyship is rather forthright with her brother. She'll certainly drill him on his recovery."

That brought a snort from Lady Duncamden and a giggle from Lady Darnley, who said, "The lass knows you almost as well as I do."

Witham announced supper. A footman gathered up the dogs, one under each arm, and the three women progressed. The elder ladies did not chatter, and the rustle of silk and padded steps on the carpet caused Mairéad to ponder her departure, though she knew not what to do to fix the mood.

The next morning after breakfast, Mairéad returned to her workroom and gathered up the dried pages. If his lordship approved her illuminations, she would attach them to the manuscript.

He must have been waiting for her. He waved her inside as she stood in the doorway. Tench was cleaning up a side table. From the looks of it, he just finished shaving his lordship.

Lady Darnley stood near the bank of windows and nodded to her. Mairéad bent to give him a kiss on the cheek. "I see you must be feeling quite well this morning."

His gaze dropped to the package she carried. She said, "I've brought you the finished product for your inspection before I rebind it."

Lord Darnley said, "I … am … sad."

She took the seat next to him and leaned her bundle against the legs of the chair. She noticed that the muscle in his left eyelid appeared to be gaining strength. When they rode that fateful day, she was not been sure this day would arrive.

Placing her hand over his, she leaned in. "Your recovery is the answer to prayer, my lord." She searched his eyes as he listened. "I hope my painting is worthy of the trouble you have gone to bringing me here."

"Grateful … for … you."

She reached for the bundle, opened it on her lap, and held up the first page of his manuscript. "The W, of course, is your family initial." She pointed to the ivy vine. "This is a symbol of the Wallington heritage. To illustrate your family, the vine trails downward amongst the script." She held up the next page. "I've extended the vine across each page of the manuscript."

Though his arm was a bit shaky, he was able to trace the vine with a fingertip then lightly patted the page curling his fingers to indicate the next.

Turning the next page, she said, "My intention was to manifest the Wallington lineage with the vine. It is an impressive family, my lord. I embellished the green vine with touches of gold, thinking it reflects a sense of pride for the generation's past. You have devoted an enormous amount of research to your ancestry."

Lady Darnley leaned over her husband's shoulder to better view the pages. "You are not only gifted in your painting but most clever with the use of a vine rather than a tree. It flows through the pages, and the gold overlay glistens and brightens." From behind Lord Darnley, her slender hands cupped his shoulders, and she put her cheek next to his. "She has given us a treasure, my love. Has she not?"

Flecks of blue in his gray irises seemed to spark. He slowly blinked, and his fingers tightened on her arm. "Stay ... with ... me ... us." His vigorous grasp reflected his intention.

At such praise, the sting of emotion threatened tears. She breathed deeply, her head scrambling with thoughts of vows, Mother Abbess, the convent. Her ladyship's features, as she stood behind her husband's chair, were full of expectation, brows raised in question.

Mairéad blurted, "I cannot. My time with you has been exceptional, but I have an obligation to fulfill."

Lady Darnley placed her hand on her shoulder. "He knows, child. He is wishing 'twas different, but may I ask why you feel this intense obligation?"

Mairéad cupped her hand over Lady Darnley's, as her other was in the grasp of his lordship. For a single moment, the world stood still. She savored the love and caring these two embodied. "I believe I was left on the convent steps as a gift from my parent to the church. It is my only link to that parent."

Lady Darnley said, "You are a strong, young woman. Most your age do not have the insight and judgment you possess."

Her Ladyship's words gave her strength for the duty that lay elsewhere. The moment ended. Her thirst for this life could only endure as a memory.

Lord Darnley sputtered. His hand gripped her arm with a shake. "No vows. A ... a ... letter ... Mother ... said ..." He did not or could not finish.

Mairéad knew of what he spoke. "Mother Abbess told you about the note that was in the basket with me."

He nodded, his hand gripping her arm.

Years of unfolding the short note, searching the words for hidden meaning from a parent or parents she would never know, caused her to say, "I have held that note in my hand, read and reread it any number of times. I assume one of my parents penned it. As I've grown, I feel this decision is mine to make, not theirs. They gave me up. Mother Abbess forbade my taking vows before I come of age. This September I will be old enough, and the choice is mine."

His lordship squeezed her arm and drew his hand back to the armrest. "You … are … determined."

The conversation at dinner was all about her illustrations. Lady Duncamden was more than excited to read her own shared history. Mairéad perused snippets as she worked her way through the parchment that dated before Henry VIII created the Earldom of Darnley, bestowing it on an Englishman, Wallington. A solicitor and politician who became the First Lord Darnley. He was born Robert Garrett Wallington in England in June 1510.

The part that fascinated Mairéad, though she had not read it in the manuscript, her ladyship explained at dinner. "The First Lord Darnley was awarded title and land, referred to as Carrigmore Hall, including the graveyard and chapel. The first lord anglicized it to Rockmore Hall."

She knew *carrig* meant rock in Gaelic, and already knew the history of the little church. "I met a woman who lives in Hawthorn Village, Nuala. She told me a little of the history. Her family has settled here since time began."

Lady Darnley sipped her wine. A moment passed, and it was obvious she mulled an idea. "As long as I can recall that woman has come to the graveyard. In my younger days, I used to walk the chapel path beyond the graveyard. Weeded and cared for, I knew it was not Flahertie. He keeps the grounds meticulously, but he refused to enter the graveyard gate. Fairy stories are as much a part of him as are his Catholic beliefs."

"His rose garden almost exceeds mine in loveliness," offered Lady Duncamden with a sly smile. "His superstitions do not surprise me. I find it is not only the gardener with silly notions. I caught my cook throwing salt over her shoulder. Can you imagine the waste?"

Mairéad giggled. "Nothing riles Mother Abbess quicker than folklore. The muttering and discontent that follow one of her reactions to such *decay of the mind*, as she refers to it, is comical. We try to stay out of her line of vision when it happens."

Casting a side glance at her, her ladyship said, "Our Irish is steeped in lore. What I have come to recognize as I ease into my elder years is that we English are more Irish than we think."

Mairéad considered the tiny heart etched into her chest, and her superior's reaction to such abomination, calling it a ritualistic deviltry of paganism and was forever grateful the mark would remain secret. "Have you heard of the cricket's song?"

Lady Darnley shook her head, but her sister-in-law said, "Yes."

"Then that tells me ..." with a knowledgeable grin, Mairéad added, "... that you have a dirt hearth in your kitchen. It was believed that crickets chirping in the hob of the hearthstone brought luck. A dwelling without their song was a sad place, indeed. And, if you killed one of them, they ate holes in your clothing."

Lady Darnley asked, "What has a dirt hearth have to do with it?"

Lady Duncamden giggled. "Finally, after all these years, I know something you don't." Her big blue eyes winked at Mairéad. "I will tell you how I learned of the cricket's song. When Duncamden received his title, we took up residence in his ruinous inheritance. It was drafty and old and had a dirt hearth in the kitchen. We kept his father's staff. After all, they knew more about

Duncamden than either of us. I did not think of it, but, over time, I noted bits of food on the floor at the hearth when I ventured into that area of the castle.

"One day I asked about the sloppiness, with bits always at the hearth. Cook told me in no uncertain terms that without the cricket's song, the castle would fall down, and the owners would die because all luck left with the chirping."

Clearly surprised, Lady Darnley said, "You never told me that story."

"Part of me believed it, so intense was cook in her telling and her assistants bobbing in communion with her." Again, she winked at Mairéad. "You can believe me when I say, we left a good patch of earth around that hearth when we put in slate flooring. Another reason to think of us being as Irish as the Irish. We clearly bought into the fable."

"The convent has a patch of dirt about our flagstone hearth as well," said Mairéad. "I am always surprised when the bits of crumbs are gone in the morning."

"Mice," snorted Lady Darnley.

They laughed and continued with the meal. At the start of supper, Lady Duncamden's sweet tooth always evoked an answer about dessert from a footman. The anticipation of delicious raspberry custard topped with whipped cream and sprinkled with chips of shaved chocolate hung in the balance of the meal.

Later, as the setting sun cast a golden, pinkish glow against the clouds, Mairéad gathered up her shawl and made her way to the park, thinking either to settle in the gazebo or to go on to the chapel. Mikey, the groomsman, waved at her as he slid the stable door closed for the night. The day she met him seemed so far away. She effortlessly fell into the rhythm of this lovely place.

Memories here and there would be easy to forgo. Not so chocolate and mayhap even riding. The larger gift of living here was another matter. Lord Darnley, a man testing her from the beginning, opened a way of life she would never forget. As far as Rutledge went, she already devoted prayer in his name for recovery from the demons that plagued him. Lady Darnley was her own gift when she quite literally came down out of her tower and joined her husband.

The servants in the hall kept their distance, but Mrs. Atkinson treated Mairéad as an adult, showing kindness and a respectful understanding of her unique circumstance, somewhere between household staff and guest.

Then there was Lord Darnley's sister. The more time she spent with her, the more Mairéad loved her. She was comfortable, approachable, and accepting of things with which she might not exactly agree.

Mairéad's reflections brought her to the edge of the pond, ripe with the scent of fresh-cut grass. The path to the left continued to the forest and the solitude of the quaint chapel with the glass windows and the musk of incense and beeswax. She wandered to the left.

As she neared the structure, a faint flicker of candlelight caught her eye. When she opened the door, Nuala glanced at her from the middle pew. "Now wasn't I wanting you to come."

Delighted at sight of the older woman, this was exactly what she'd been thinking. She genuflected and made the sign of the cross before the crucifix on the wall, then stepped in and sat near her. "I am leaving day after next. It was hoping to say good-bye. I've enjoyed our chats."

The woman folded her shawl back, revealing her searching gaze. "I think you will be missed something sorely up at the great house. It's been whispered about how well you get on."

"I'm but a painter."

The woman reached over and drew Mairéad's hand from her lap. Her calloused thumb rubbed the young, softer skin, then she glanced at the tips of her fingers. Mairéad was a teensy bit reminded of Tremaine when he was first introduced to her, bowing over her hand. "It shows, then, you do paint. Such a fancy thing to be aboot. I'm thinking then you are good at it. Would I be right?"

"Well, it sounds boastful, but both Lord and Lady Darnley

were pleased with my efforts. It is the reason I was brought to Rockmore Hall. Now that I've accomplished what was set out for me to do, I must return to…"

"It'll be the Sacred Heart for you." She let go of Mairéad's hand and turned in the pew to look more directly at her. "Right?"

The woman then asked, "What have you pondered of our little village and the land the hall sits on, then?"

"The gardens are breathtaking. The fountain at the front drive, I've not seen the likes of." She glanced about the chapel with the candlelight flickering against the oak pews and the stained window to the right, casting the rest of the interior in shadow. "This has a special place in my heart."

Mairéad's hand drifted to her throat. "I'm glad we met. I will remember you as time goes by, and you will be a part of the history of these months."

"Then you'll think of me, 'tis a comfort you give."

Silence cloaked them as they sat together. The luster of candlelight bathing them in its golden circle with the honeyed scent of beeswax and a light wind rustling the treetops.

A moonbeam filtered through the west side of the tinted windows.

It was curious Nuala appeared so at ease. Usually she fidgeted and only stayed for a few moments before she was off. Though it was dark, Mairéad's gaze darted to the bowed head, the large, capable hands. Could she be a nun who left the convent.

"May I ask …" The bowed head rose up, dark eyes meeting hers. "… were you a member of the sisterhood?"

Nuala's gentle smile, beautiful really, nestled in the soft face. "I could'na. I needed to care for my parents. There was no one else. All gone now, and I'm about my own pursuits, aren't I."

Mairéad reached over and patted the cupped hands. "I suspect you keep a busy life, and I think you most likely have many friends."

"Thank you for that and thank you for the visits. I'll do the same and recall the lass that warred with becoming a nun rather than marry."

Quite surprised, Mairéad asked, "What makes you say such?"

"Words that live on the wind, amongst the hills and loughs of the good ol' sod, and plenty of talkers going on about this and that, now don't cha know?"

"Nuala, I would not have guessed you a gossip."

Nuala stood wrapping her shawl about her dark hair streaked with gray. "I'll be getting back to my place now, lass. You'd best do the same. May your journey be quick and without mishap. I'll see you when the cold comes, and I'm in search of a hot meal."

She was out the door so quick Mairéad's good-bye trailed off into the dark, leaving only the flicker of the golden glow against the stone wall and silence.

17

Nearly packed, with Ryan's assistance, Mairéad turned to her next task, the workroom. Mrs. Atkinson was directing a footman to dismantle the easels. A slight vapor of turpentine twitched her nose as she spotted some rags left in the corner atop a stack of old newspapers. The sleeves Mrs. Atkinson gave her were draped over an easel.

The trunk, with *Sacred Heart of Jesus Convent* stamped on the side, yawned ready to receive brushes and paints. The workroom at the convent, with its walls of dark wood and windows high upon the outside wall, did not allow for the same abundance of light, making the miniscule work of illuminating difficult. She scoffed at the uncharitable idea, it made her seem whiney and dissatisfied.

The fireplace gaped, devoid of ash and not reset. Its warmth kept her fingers and toes warm as she had worked. Trailing her hand across the windowsill, she glanced back at Mrs. Atkinson, who'd not uttered a sound since she entered. "You are quiet this morning."

The housekeeper's attention diverted from the maid, who folded clean rags about the bristles of the paint brushes. "Seems like a light is snuffing out."

"I feel it, too." Her voice was barely a whisper as her finger trailed over the empty easels.

The silence spoke to them.

Mairéad stood at the bank of windows, drinking in the loveliness, etching it upon her brain. The stable doors flung wide. Shamus walked a colt with white stockings. That nervous little man, Molloy, followed close behind. Did the colt belong to his mare? She remembered him from the day Lord Darnley was struck. He approached her asking for news of his welfare and that they were praying for him. Later, she learned he was the cottier Rutledge lived with before he was brought to the hall.

It occurred to her that Rutledge might have gone to him with his troubles. She turned from the window. That was none of her concern now.

The maid, a hand to her back, straightened, then brushed at her skirts. "I believe all is right and ready to be sent back with you, miss."

"Thank you for packing. I apologize for my laziness. I simply don't know what has gotten into me. All I seem to want to do is think about what I'm leaving."

Mrs. Atkinson crossed the room and stood with her at the windows. "Change is a good thing. It shakes us out of our lethargy. Though, perhaps your change, coming to the hall, was overly so."

Mairéad laughed outright. "You think maybe it was a great leap, then? I'd agree. I also agree change allows us to look at what we have and what others have. I'll always be grateful that his lordship needed an illuminist."

"Surely it was providence."

"It certainly allowed me association with Lord and Lady Darnley, and you. Nuala was at the chapel last night. We each hoped the other would be there. That could be considered providential. She hinted that she might come by the convent for a hot meal this winter."

Mrs. Atkinson scrunched her brow, as if something didn't strike her as believable. "I'm not surprised you made friends." She picked up the rags in the corner and handed them to the maid, "Give these to laundry, please. On your way, will you inform a footman the trunk is ready for the carriage."

To Mairéad, she said, "I will see you off in the morning but wanted to say something privately. You changed their lives, you know. I'm deeply grateful. Your vocation as a sister of the religious will be near miraculous if what you accomplished in this household is any indication."

※

Sassy and Muffy pulled at the leads, causing Mairéad to skip across the park. The fur balls headed straight for the bridge and the gazebo. They scampered across the wooden bridge, jumped up on a bench and barked at the reeds standing tall, swaying in the breeze. Shushing them did not work, and she simply gave up and let them whimper and yap.

Holding tight to the leashes, she glanced out over the pond and beyond to the wide, bubbling creek that fed it and recalled the day Tremaine showed her the icehouse. Her heart skipped a beat at the tickle of memory, the strength of his arms about her as he lifted her off Caomh, his face so near, the lean lines of his cheeks dipping to his square jaw, and his warm breath as his lips touched hers. Tender, dear, and lovely. A sigh spilled from her lips. Would she forget him if she could not be here and feel him near?

An egret flapped its wings and took flight spooking the dogs, and herself. The large bird soared heavenward, a fish in its beak. She clutched the leashes, lest Sassy and Muffy attempt to fly off the bench and most assuredly into the pond.

The instant their leads jerked, she stumbled, and their attention returned to her, skittering over her prone self, licking and trampling. Jumping to her feet and scolding the busybodies now running in circles around her ankles, she felt lighthearted.

That evening in the parlor, Lady Duncamden greeted her with a cheery, "Come sit by me," and patted the yellow silk cushion.

Indicating a portrait of a stern-looking gentleman, a riding crop in one hand, two hunting dogs at his feet, she stated, "That imposing figure is my grandfather, the Fourth Lord Darnley. He was born in Drogeda but lived during his formative years in England. A famous solicitor and politician, it nearly broke his heart when his eldest daughter, Elizabeth, married and sailed to America with her husband."

Lady Darnley intoned, "You give Mairéad a history lesson when she leaves on the morrow? She's likely to forget all about us."

Mairéad was about to protest but was prevented when the elder's scrunched brow turned on her sister-in-law. "I believe she has an interest in all things, whether leaving or not." She grabbed up Mairéad's hand and shook it. "Tell her so."

Not wanting to get in the middle of one of their friendly snits, Mairéad asked, "Elizabeth moved to America before the English revolution?"

"Yes, well before. A few of her missives exist somewhere in this mausoleum."

Her ladyship's eyes narrowed. "Your knowledge about the revolution is greater than I would have thought."

"Sister Davidenna was born in America and came to County Waterford to take vows. I learned a bit about the history from her."

Witham announced dinner. The two ladies seemed to be conspirators of sorts, whispering on the way as Mairéad trailed behind. When they entered the dining room, Lord Darnley was sitting at the end of the table in his usual place, grinning widely on the good side of his face. His soft gray eyes twinkling with delight.

Three footmen, stiff and formal as always, pulled chairs for them. His lordship patted the place setting on his left and curled his hand to Mairéad offering her a place of honor with his wife and sister present.

A knot tightened in her throat, and tears stung. His effort to be part of her last evening at Rockmore was so thoughtful. He appeared most pleased with himself. With his left arm, his lordship raised a toast. "To…you…my…dear."

Tears, held in check until this moment, bit her eyelids. His grand effort to show she mattered was beyond her ability to remain impartial. She swiped her cheeks. In the years to come, this is the memory that will warm her heart, his caring.

Dinner finished, his lordship, with footmen on each side, made his way to the foyer. At the bottom of the steps, the footmen joined arms, gathered him up, and carried him to his chamber, where, no doubt, Tench waited.

Having already said goodnight to the delightful trio, Mairéad encountered Ryan folding the top coverlet down to the foot of her bed. Her satchel lay open and ready to receive her few possessions.

No more having her hair brushed and braided at night. No more overly fluffed pillow.

Ryan stooped to pick up a book that had fallen off the bedside table. "It will be a bit of a struggle to be sure."

Mairéad sucked in a breath. Did the maid read her mind?

Ryan added, "You have been the master of your time. I suppose that will change."

"Don't remind me. I'll get all weepy."

"Well, miss, I did observe the Mother Abbess when she visited. She did not seem to be one that allowed anything less than the perfect order of the day. I think you enjoyed your own rhythm as you went about your duties here."

Mairéad overcome with emotion, practically fell into the chair in front of the grate. "I might be in trouble then, to be sure. Between now and tomorrow, I am going to have to work on my attitude. It simply will not do for me to appear anything less than obedient and accepting of my future."

The next morning, Mairéad awoke even before the maid lit the grate. She stayed beneath the eider quilt, snuggled in with her own warmth. Her cheeks felt a nipping chill. Tomorrow morning, she would no longer have the luxury of basking beneath a thick quilt, waiting for a maid to light her grate. No indeed.

Nor would she begin the morning with a steaming cup of chocolate. Her lips quirked. What would Mother Abbess say if she knew about the pampering? Mairéad fully enjoyed a space of time filled with learning new things, dining with conversation, new people to meet, dogs with which to romp and play, and love in the air. Love? Did she really think it was love? Surely, the warmth in her heart directed toward Lord and Lady Darnley was akin to such.

Love? She felt her cheeks curve with a smile. She was not thinking of just Lord and Lady Darnley.

A maid entered white cap bobbing in silent good morning. She set a tray down and bent to the grate. Within a few minutes, warmth curled through the chamber. Mairéad slipped out of bed, wrapped a shawl about herself, and stood in front of the fire, cup in hand, enjoying the smooth creamy texture of the chocolate as it slipped over her tongue, knowing it was the last she would have.

Ryan arrived with her tunic and veil. The early morning was slipping away. As if it were a lifeline she was unwilling to let go, she turned to the large bank of windows that originally overwhelmed her with the panoramic view of the park. Growing accustomed to such luxuries was not appropriate. It was disloyal perhaps weak-willed, too. She focused on the steeple peeking out of the treetops. It seemed to wink at her in the hazy early sun.

Ryan handed her a letter that arrived late yesterday. Mairéad knew instantly it was from Tremaine and slipped it into her pocket to read tonight in the privacy of her little room. Hopefully, the nub of a candle would be available.

Within moments of her entering the dining room for breakfast, Lady Duncamden arrived, gasping as she slid into her chair. "I do wish you'd not worn a reminder of where you are going. It grieves me so."

Practically on her heels, Lady Darnley entered and cast a scowl at her sister-in-law. "What grieves you now?"

"Look at her." Using a triangle of toast, she pointed at

Mairéad. "Ready for the rest of her life, or so she would have us believe." She bit into the toast slathered with what looked like her favorite blackberry jam.

Lady Darnley kissed Mairéad on the forehead before taking her place at the table. "She's cranky until she gets her sugar. You will be spared her moods."

"Breakfast will never be the same without you both. Beginning tomorrow, it will be different."

"How is that?" barked the elder as she lifted her tea.

"Always porridge. Quieter, and no blackberry jam, except sometimes on Sundays."

Her placid features broke into a wide grin. "I'd no idea my friendship with you was in competition with blackberry jam."

Lady Darnley set her utensils down and focused on Mairéad. "His lordship has developed a deep fondness for you. We wish to ask if we invited you to visit on occasion or come stay for a time here and there, would you be agreeable?"

"Why, yes, of course. If I am allowed, that is. I have not known any of the sisters to leave except for a death in the family, and even then, it seemed almost too much to ask."

Lady Darnley, palms on the tablecloth, leaned forward, "You are aware of the many years I closeted myself with a grievous heart." Glancing at her hands, in a shy gesture, she added, "I had a fear of loss. That is something I've been able to overcome, largely due to your involvement in my life."

Taken aback, Mairéad said, "You give credit where it is not deserved."

"Tch, tch. I'll be the one to decide that. My point is to encourage you to visit us in the years to come. Surely, Mother Abbess will allow you that. I intend to direct my pleas to her. Perhaps, I'll be influential in forcing her hand."

Lady Duncamden patted her hand on the linen tablecloth seeking their attention. "There will be a package for you in the carriage, and you are not to open it until you visit. Is that clear? You must promise me?"

She looked from one to the other. "You have my promise, but whatever have you done, my lady. I am most curious."

"Tut, tut, all I need is a promise, and that I've got. No more to be said."

❧❦❧

Immediately after breakfast, Mairéad knocked on Lord Darnley's chamber door.

The narrowing of his somber eyes at sight of her postulant's garb was noticeable, Tench, with his usual stoic demeanor, said, "He is waiting for you."

Lord Darnley was positioned in his comfortable chair near the window facing the front lawn. She guessed he intended to watch her drive off. She cast a quick glance at the Celtic harps carved into the crown moldings. They were but one of many distinguishing insignia throughout the hall glossing her memories. She had counted them while sitting with the unconscious lord. There were forty-six embellished into the plaster.

"Come…come…" He waved his hand.

Her arms outstretched, she bent over and hugged him, brushing her lips against his receding hairline. "I am going to miss you terribly, my lord."

Pursing his lips, he nodded in assent. Gripping her hands in each of his, he showed off the strength he was gaining. A gentleman, he did not indicate resentment at her choice of clothing. Having met her at the convent, perhaps he alone understood to what she returned.

He said, "We've…come…long…way…"

Taking the chair next to his, she said, "The first hour I met you, I was wary of your intent in taking me from the convent. I have never been so wrong about anything my whole life."

His eyes twinkled. "Whole…life…?"

"A long time to me," she said and flashed him an impish grin.

222

"If Mother Abbess allows, I will visit. Once I take vows, if she hesitates, I'll argue my point."

He tugged on the hand in his clasp. "Ha…my…lass."

"If I return, hopefully the haws will be ready, and I'll make you the best jam you have ever tasted."

"The…hawthorn."

"Those little red fruits should be ripe by the end of next month. I will ask to return for a short visit."

His eyes brightened at that. She could not leave him without a promise, or was the promise for herself?

When he drew her hand to his lips, she could have cried and quickly said, "Huet is bringing the carriage around. I mustn't keep him waiting." Cupping his cheek, she added, "Thank you for giving me the whole of this spring and summer with you."

Quickly, she rubbed her cheek against his and heard him whisper, "Love…you."

She stood and immediately turned from him for the door, stung by emotion.

Tench reached for the knob just as she swiped at the tears on her cheeks. "God bless, miss," he said as she passed into the hall.

Her heart ached with self-sacrifice. Her obligation to the Catholic Church and her superior drove her down the grand staircase and out the massive carved doors to the waiting carriage. Settling back against the velvet cushions, the carriage pulled away from the front, taking the turn at the pond with the spouting fountain. She was afraid to look back and find a dear man waving his goodbye.

She turned anyway.

Lord Darnley stood in the upper floor, drapes pulled aside, waving. Lady Darnley was at his side, her arm around his waist.

She should never have looked back. It served no purpose. One must always look forward to the bright, wonderful future. The knot in her throat was difficult to swallow.

18

The late August sun at midday shone brightly on the rolling hills, lambs frolicking alongside grazing ewes. The carriage ambled past swaying bog grasses. Preparing herself for life at the convent, Mairéad took comfort in the clip-clop of the workhorses. The rhythm made her think of the first time she sat in this velvety interior, across from his lordship, knowing nothing of what lay ahead.

Boasting was not a good trait, but she was proud of her work on Lord Darnley's biographical manuscript. It might just be her finest illuminating. It pleased her tremendously that Lady Darnley drew attention to the gold highlights of the ivy she used to indicate the branches of his family.

Glimpses of the River Suir glistened in the sunlight. An ancient ruin, one of its towers still reaching the sky, caught her attention. The scene reminded her of the convent, which once was a Norman castle.

She could feel the pull of the conveyance as it teetered atop a small crevice, then downward amidst shouting and cursing. She grabbed at a strip of leather near the window. Huet yelled at her to get down. Tossed aside as if a rag doll, the great boxy carriage leaned to one side then crashed to the earth, coming to an abrupt halt. The pair of horses screeched in pain and horror.

She lay still a moment, waiting for the earth to fall in, terrified.

Braying, honking, and shouting came in waves, and then her world turned black.

A hand shielded her face from bright sunlight. "Stay quiet, lass," Huet's voice quivered. "You've no broken bones, but ye may have a bit of a concussion."

"What happened?" It hurt to talk. A fierce pounding had taken up the space in her head.

"We encountered a herd of bull-headed, jack-ass donkeys. Excuse my anger. Smack in the middle of the road, they were, as we came down off the hilltop. Spooked the team, it did." His hand lifted a bit off her eyes, and the brightness hurt. "Sorry, lass. I've a scarf to cover yer eyes."

An angry voice shouted at them. "Don't cha' be sayin' who carried ta fault. Ye were at a fine rate of excess comin' down off that cliff."

Huet, muttering in an awful anger, grunted up off his knees.

Her stomach was queasy. The pain in her head throbbed. She lay still with his kerchief over her face.

The cries from the team seemed to have stopped. She hoped they were all right and tried to lift her head. Severe discomfort rent her shoulders and arm.

Huet's voice boomed. "It isn't about the speed of your horses, my good man. It's about the damage done. *You* can be grateful the horses survived. We'll see how the Right Honorable Earl of Darnley takes ta having his carriage ruined, won't we, now?"

A growl accompanied the answer. "Will his lordship pay for the two donkeys who've seen better days? They were my income, now, weren't they?"

She lifted the scarf off her eyes, allowing her a bit of a glance at the men's boots. She knew which pair belonged to Huet, as the rest were older and greatly muddied. All the dirty boots shuffled about while Huet's remained still. His calm voice inquired, "I've a young woman who needs to get to the Sacred Heart of Jesus Convent. How do you suggest that is going to happen?"

Grumbling and shuffling caused her to lower the scarf back to her eyes.

"Can she sit a donkey?"

Her head swirled with fogginess, but her ears perked up at that. A donkey?

Huet's voice was sharp with impatience. "With a bash to her head, and you would suggest such a thing?"

She lifted the scarf again, peering upward a bit until the sun brought a crushing torment to her head. Huet's hands curled.

"Give it a moment, sir," the other man sardonically intoned. "I'll get me wife's chariot for ye." One of the other pair of dirty boots nudged close to the one who spoke. He grabbed hold of the other's arm and shook him. "Leave go. What in the name of the Almighty can I do?"

Gruffly, Huet suggested, "If the young lady is able and willing, she and I will ride donkeys to the convent. When I am satisfied she is comfortable and in good hands, I will return with one donkey. If at that time you have not repaired the carriage, I will ride the donkey back to Rockmore Hall and get help."

"What's become of me second donkey, then?" The man's face was red, and it wasn't from the sun. His thumbs tucked into his belt.

"I see it as an offering to the convent for the suffering and inconvenience to one of their own." He leaned in with seeming confidence he would win the battle.

From beneath the scarf, three pair of dirty boots moved, sticks in hand, shuffling the herd onward, continuing their drive to the previously interrupted destination, she supposed.

Now there were two pair of boots, Huet's and the man with whom he argued. Glancing to the other side, she could see his lordship's carriage, two wheels at odd angles and tipped over. It was ruined, from what she could see. However, did they get her out? How long was she unconscious? The horses, unharnessed, were now tethered, nibbling grass.

The other man sighed, a long, weary sound. "Lord Darnley ye say?"

The driver nodded his head, wiping his brow.

"If the daft thing wasn't at such an angle, me men could stand her upright. It's the loss of the wheel that'll be trouble. I'll take the horses to me shed. Me place is over ta next pasture. Ye see the chimney smoke?"

Nauseous, she dropped the scarf back over her face.

"When I return, we'll figure something out. Right now, I need to get the lass to the convent."

Fortunately, they were less than an hour by donkey. Mairéad knew Huet felt responsible. She needed the kerchief wrapped about her eyes. The light was painful. Throbbing in her left shoulder sharpened with each jagged step.

Huet was doing his utmost to get her to the convent, and she stilled as best as she was able.

"I will deliver your trunk and valise first thing in the morning, miss. I am so sorry for the inconvenience to you."

"Are there many accidents of this nature?" she asked, suddenly realizing her veil was still in the carriage.

"It is not unusual. A man does have to get his flocks and herds from one patch of grazing land to another. I should have slowed coming over the hill. I just thank the Almighty you were not hurt worse."

"What about you, atop the carriage? How did you manage to escape injury?"

"As it tippled, I jumped clear."

"Seems to me, this might have happened once before?"

"Possibly. Our land is noted for sheep, but they usually scatter right quick at the approach of a carriage."

"Not donkeys, obviously."

"Not too many years ago, the Emperor Napoleon traded donkeys for our wonderful Irish horses, and wouldn't you know, it didn't take long for the stubborn animals to multiply. 'Tis rumored they are intelligent. We saw the farce in that now, didn't we? Stood like rocks in the middle of the road, looking as if nothing a'tall was coming at 'em."

She tried not to laugh, knowing the poor man was beleaguered by the accident. He let her know when they neared the convent. She peeked from beneath the kerchief at the tall rampart of the old castle housing. It would not be long now.

Though her heart was heavy, she would be glad to get off this long-eared animal. Her legs and head were reeling with the effects of the accident, but she was grateful the queasiness in her stomach abated. She pined for her room at Rockmore Hall and Ryan's assistance pulling down the quilt. A sense of sliding beneath the silken sheets and drifting off took hold of her imagination. Her desire for comfort surprised her, possibly because the aches in her bones were increasing.

Mairéad drew off the scarf as Mother Abbess opened the heavy door. "What in the name of the Saints?" She flung the door wide. "Come, come." She glanced from Mairéad to Huet and back again.

"Our carriage incurred an accident. He borrowed donkeys for the rest of our journey."

"Pleased to meet you, Mother Abbess" Huet said, turning his hat in his fists, quiet obviously nervous at having to explain the whole of their troubles to this holy woman.

They entered the cool interior. Sisters Boniface and Constance came forward from the recess of the stone-walled hall, heels clicking on the slated floor, rosary beads jingling with urgency.

Mother Abbess directed them. "We'll sit in my office. Bring a refreshment." She glanced at Huet. "Have you taken nourishment?"

He was a bit startled but answered, "Earlier this morning."

She nodded assent to the sisters and guided Mairéad and Huet along the hall to her office. The strong scent of candle wax and incense reminded her of the life to which she had now returned. Though the chairs in Mother's office were not padded, it was a relief to sit on something other than the bony back of a donkey.

She cast a weak smile at Huet, who appeared more uncomfortable than astride the four-legged animal.

"While we wait, tell me what brought on such turmoil." Mother Abbess sat behind her desk, rested her arms on her desktop and folded her hands.

He cleared his throat. "We were coming over Gibbet Hill and encountered a herd of donkeys smack in front of us. Now what was I to do?"

The nun's gaze shifted to Mairéad. "Looks as if you took quite a shake-up. Your face is developing a bruise."

Mairéad's hand went to the place that hurt the most. She winced.

Mother Abbess added, "And without your veil. Tch. Tch. I hope you did not encounter anyone on your way here."

Which was funny—because they encountered a herd of donkeys. And, *without your veil*. She slipped her hand back to her lap, sat straight in the chair, and said, "Just animals. Fortunately for us, we were able to get back to our journey rather quickly." She turned to Huet. "Wouldn't you agree? Other than exchanging words with the donkey herder, we spoke to no one."

Huet quickly nodded. He was unfamiliar with Mother Abbess's disquiet over Mairéad's improper dress.

In his desire to comfort, Huet spoke up, "You need not worry. If you mean the lass' headpiece, I take responsibility. We were mightily distressed with lifting her outside the overturned carriage, and I must confess, my concern was more for her than anything."

"Hmm." The nun's gaze swept her face, looked her over, came back to the bruise. "I suppose your mind was elsewhere."

Huet blurted, "She was blacked out, ma'am. It took a few minutes to bring her around."

Her dark brows, so distinctly framed by her pale skin and black veil, scrunched in disbelief.

The pain in Mairéad's head brought on confusion. She ached to lie down, but daren't ask.

Sister Davideena entered with a tray laden with steaming tea and scones. Mairéad's stomach roiled as if she might be sick. Mother Abbess allowed Sister to pour the tea and distribute the cups and saucers.

Huet's hand shook as he held the little cup and drew it to his lips. She felt sorry for him. He was truly out of his element, no doubt feeling a heavy responsibility. It was not his fault at all.

Mother Abbess's demeanor was snippy as if she wanted to blame someone for something.

Mairéad's voice whispery as she said, "Huet struck a bargain with the herder, allowing the convent to receive the donkey I rode. Is not that a good thing?" She could only hope Mother Abbess would agree.

Mother Abbess's inspection shifted to the large driver, whose thirst must be great, as he finished his tea straightaway. "Another mouth to feed," she stated in complaint.

"I recall you wishing for just such an animal to transport the produce to market in Portlaw when Mr. Chiley is too busy." Mairéad reached for two scones and placed them on Huet's saucer, then added, "Have things changed so much since I've been gone?" The exchange cost her a blinding pain, and she rubbed her brow hoping the buzzing would cease.

Mother Abbess's gaze narrowed on her. "I am remiss. Thank you for reminding me." Her tone did not match with sincerity.

❧ 19 ❧

The next morning, Mairéad woke to the tingle of *Prime* bells. When she threw off the cover, her body rebelled. Every bone ached, most of all her head throbbed. She fell back on the cot, remembering her superior's stern reaction to the lack of a veil and most of all, her expectations now that she was back where she belonged.

Sliding her legs over the side of her berth, her feet touched the cold slate floor. Her head pulsated, a cascade of dark auburn hung over her face and arms, and she waited for the dizziness to abate. She considered how grateful she would be if Ryan came into her room right now.

A knock at her door, and with eyes shut, she whispered, "Come in."

A voice said, "I've been sent to get you." The door closed, and a rosary swished as Sister Davideena crossed to the cot. "You've overslept, then."

"It appears I have." Her eyes remained closed.

"You need assistance. May I help?"

Mairéad's arm lifted off a length of hair, exposing her face. The nun gasped. "All that is holy." Her hand gently touched the bruise. "What has happened to you?"

"From the accident yesterday." Her jaw ached to talk.

"What's this of an accident?"

"Our carriage overturned."

"Does Mother know this?"

"Yes." Her fingers lightly trailed over her cheek. The swollen place was especially sore. No wonder her jaw hurt.

"You poor thing. She knows and demands you attend *Prime*? How can she be …?" She bit her lip to stop the flow of criticism.

"We both know her code of behavior is harsh at times."

"I don't see how you can attend prayer."

"I'll do my best. I suggest you go on ahead, or you will be late. No sense both of us breaking the rule."

Sister Davideena reached for Mairéad's arm. "You need assistance and I do not mind bending her command to assist you, nor the result of such."

Mairéad chuckled softly. "Well, then, please fix my hair." Her eyes closed against the pain, she added, "I would appreciate it if you ruffled through my drawer for a veil."

Minutes later, the two slowly made their way along the slated corridor. The bell chimed at the front door, and Sister Constance passed them on her way to answer.

The two continued to chapel. A man's deep voice drifted through the small portal Sister Constance would have opened. The voice sounded familiar, but Mairéad's discomfort at walking seemed to dominate her thinking. Dizzy with movement, she said, "Go ahead. You'll just make it. I'm holding you back."

Conflicted, Sister Davideena shuffled ahead, then turned as she reached the door and glanced back. Mairéad waved her on.

Moments later, intending to lean a moment against the wall, Mairéad collapsed.

How many minutes later, she did not know, but several voices drifted through her muddled brain. One belonged to Mother Abbess, and the others sounded familiar.

Someone scooped her up and asked which way to the

infirmary. The distinct voice of Mr. O'Reilly assured her. "You'll be fine, lass don't worry."

The solace of his words allowed her to return to oblivion.

❦

A sharp smell caused Mairéad's eyes to open. Mr. O'Reilly leaned close with a great toothy smile, so close the black rims around his irises and his thick black lashes were most apparent once her eyes focused. "Good morning, young lady."

He stood up and put a cap on a vial. "How do you feel?"

"Cozy. Warm. Maybe a bit hungry."

A twitter bubbled up from a corner, and she realized she was in her little room, her head comfortably nested on a pillow. Huet peered over the doctor's shoulder. "It is grateful I am, miss. Truly grateful your eyes are open. Truly."

Her gaze returned to the doctor. "Your presence is surprising."

"It appears it was in the nick of time. Yesterday when Huet returned to Rockmore and Lady Darnley was informed of the accident, she called for me to ride with Huet and see to your health. There you were, sleeping on the floor."

His attempt to lighten the mood brought a grin. "A blackness came over me." Her cheek hurt with the effort, and her fingers brushed the soreness.

A slight cough came from the corner, again. The doctor glanced over his shoulder. "Would you like to come near, Sister?"

Sister Davideena held tight to her rosary beads as she crept close to the cot. "I am horrified to have left you. Such a precious young woman you are to all of us, and we'd no idea what happened to you. That–that the carriage overturned with you in it. Oh, Mairéad, forgive me."

"There is nothing to forgive. It was an accident." Her glance shifted to Huet. "He is the one who needs consoling. He could have broken his legs, jumping as he did."

Sister Davideena said, "Will you eat something?" She turned to the doctor. "Can she eat?"

"Probably something soft, tea, a porridge. Her jaw is quite sore."

She nodded and left as Mr. O'Reilly said, "You might be in for a visit. Lady Darnley is beside herself with worry over you."

"What of the carriage?"

Huet answered. "'Tis our next stop. If I'm right ta think so, the herder might have attached the wheel and taken the carriage to his place, for we didna see it on our way here. I'll return with your trunk and veil and valise later."

"The horses?"

"No broken bones, thank the Almighty. Right as rain, I'll warrant. If the leads hadn't snapped in two, it could be another story altogether."

Mr. O'Reilly said, "It appears you took the most injury, Miss Mairéad. You will need bed rest for at least a week. Your head sustained quite a knock as the carriage tumbled. All indications are you received a concussion to your brain. You could pass out again, and you need to stay safely in bed and allow the swelling to recede. You will be back to yourself in time. I intend speaking with Mother Abbess and will see that my orders are obeyed." He winked at her as he returned his examining tools to his black valise.

"That won't be necessary, doctor. I overheard your diagnosis and will see that your orders are carried out."

The doctor and Huet spun about. Mairéad could not see Mother Abbess, but the voice she heard was the voice of authority she had listened to all her life.

Two weeks later, Mairéad returned to her workroom and the illumination projects that were waiting for her. Mother Abbess continued taking orders for painting all the while she'd been at

Rockmore Hall. There was enough work to keep her busy through the end of the year.

The swelling on her face was down, her jaw no longer ached. The pain in her shoulder eased, and life at Sacred Heart was back to normal, or so it appeared.

Sitting atop her stool, overlooking the easels filled with work already begun, Mairéad sighed with resignation. The accident had taken a lot out of her, far more than she knew at the time. Two weeks was a long time to stay abed.

Since her return and forced recovery, her superior remained cool toward her, and she did not understand why. Laying abed, puzzling over what she might have done to create the chasm between them yet knowing Mother Abbess' innate manner was strict. Still, she sensed a deeper rift. Gnawing at her to such a degree she decided to speak with the Mother Abbess.

Several sisters, sleeves rolled up to their elbows, skirts tucked into their apron ties, toiled in the garden. Vegetables were ripening daily in the late August sun. She waved as she crossed the path leading toward the main part of the convent. As if on cue, the donkey brayed, a satisfying sound since she knew Huet's quick thinking made the gift possible. The convent also acquired two more pigs, with a litter expected any day. A gift from an unnamed Waterford benefactor.

Mairéad padded along the slate floor. She heard women's voices in Mother Abbess's office. Not wanting to intrude, Mairéad was about to retreat when she overheard her name and could no sooner continue than she could order a bolt of lightning to strike inside the convent. Halting midstride, she blatantly listened.

"We wish to see how she's recovering."

Mairéad slapped a hand to her gaping mouth, the voice sounded exactly like Lady Darnley's dulcet tones.

"If you had written and arranged a time, we would be better prepared for your visit. As her workload does not allow her leisure at this time …"

Mother Abbess's strident voice horrified Mairéad. No one in

this convent dared brook her authority, but, Lady Darnley was not a person to be spoken to in that tone. Torn between rushing headlong into the office and turning away, her hand shook as it rested against her mouth. She leaned against the stone wall, damp with the morning rain.

"I think it an abomination we are denied a visit. How will we know for certain she has been restored to good health?"

Mairéad's lips spread in a smile. Lady Duncamden. With that, she spun on her heel and knocked on the carved panel as she entered.

Two little ladies in all their finery, sweet smiling faces, feathers in their bonnets, turned at the intrusion.

At sight of Mairéad, Mother Abbess' shoulders slumped. Averting her face, she muttered and tucked both hands beneath the sleeves of the tunic.

Delightful *oohs* and *aahs* accompanied Ladies Darnley and Duncamden wrapping their arms about her. Giddy with their presence, she soaked up the caring and concern heaped on her until she sensed a pair of eyes burning into the back of her head, from a rigid, domineering force.

Drawing back from the embraces, holding each by a hand, her gaze feasting on their loveliness. "How can this be, both of you here? I am awed." Suddenly, it dawned on her Lady Darnley may have just experienced something she hadn't done in years. "Is this your first carriage ride?"

Lady Darnley chuckled. "You were worth the adventure, my dear."

Her sister-in-law spouted, "It was exhausting listening to her go on and on about this and that, as if she had come from a dark cave."

The grumbling brought a chuckle from Lady Darnley, who said, "One could consider that is exactly what I came from."

Mairéad forced herself to gaze at the woman on the other side of the desk, certain she would meet censure. What caught her breath was the nun's head tilted to the side, a frown creasing her brow.

Lady Darnley gushed. "This is such a pleasure. We are grateful Miss Mairéad could escape her duties."

Lady Duncamden added, "We have a little gift for your community, Mother. Can someone have our driver carry it to your office?"

Mother Abbess beckoned to Sister Catriona, who stood at the door. "Will you see him in?"

Within minutes, Huet followed the nun into the office, hefting a large crate that he set on the floor. "Will that be all, my lady?"

The last time Mairéad saw him, he had accompanied Mr. O'Reilly and delivered her trunk and valise. She asked, "See any donkeys on the way?"

He chuckled, pursed his lips, and shook his head.

Lady Darnley thanked him and turned her attention back to Mother Abbess "This was one of Mairéad's favorites, and I know she will delight in sharing with all of you."

Mairéad bent to the crate and took out one canister, among many. "Is this what I think it is?"

Mother Abbess, her tone not exactly rigid, asked, "What might that be?"

"Chocolate."

As Mother Abbess nodded in recognition, the ends of her black veil drifted from her shoulders. "I recall from my childhood. A treat like no other." A tiny smile broke the severity of her features.

Mairéad handed the tin to her. "Well, now, you can once again enjoy."

Accepting the canister, she admired the elaborate decorations. "A most generous gift and a lovely tin. Tole, is it not?" Without waiting for an answer, she added, "There is enough to last all of us a long time."

The nun's delight brought an inward sigh. Awkwardness, it seemed, was washed over with a gift, if not from the Magi then from two darling elderly ladies.

The visit lasted into the afternoon as Mairéad toured her visitors about the convent, including her room and workroom. The three of them were almost of a matching height, and their conversation picked up and changed direction as fast as the words came, the ease of their banter bringing laughter. With serious concern, Mairéad inquired, "Was Lord Darnley told of the accident?"

"Not intentionally. Tench, of course, overheard and asked if there was any more news, inadvertently alerting Darnley. He took it rather well, considering," her ladyship answered.

Lady Duncamden said, "Aside from our great interest in you, he ordered us to visit and bring back firsthand knowledge of your recovery."

As they strolled through the garden on the way to her workroom, Mairéad noticed Mother Abbess peeking out the window of her office. She declined Lady Darnley's invitation to stroll with them. Noticing her now, sorrow tugged at her. The woman's inability to mingle was sad. She pleaded work, but Mairéad knew the truth behind her refusal.

The feminine side, the heart side, of who Mother Abbess was never came into the light of day. Mairéad's forgiveness toward her grew from guessing she must have endured rejection or serious hurt during early life. The compassion she held for the nun overrode a conflicted sense of right and wrong. She quite easily excused her stern control in all things, even if she didn't understand it.

The infant left on the convent steps knew that deep within Mother Abbess there must be love. Otherwise, what would have become of that child? She was indebted to her benefactor for the life she lived, another reason she committed to the taking of vows.

Seven Months Later, February 27, 1817

The *Haggart*, once a proud warship fitted with forty or more fixed guns and no less than eight mid-shipmen and two minor officers, sliced through the roiling, storm-ridden waters of the Celtic Sea, intended for Bristol.

Rutledge spent the last seven months, or much of it anyway, in the company of one of the barmaids along the quay in Waterford. Stumbling between the warm bed of an Irish woman, Dervila Murdock, and Madame Fornia's opium den. Time passed in a fog of anger, self-pity, and blessed oblivion. Repeating a pattern common in the last few years, Rutledge eventually came to his senses and drying out with the hard-core assistance of Mrs. Dervila Murdock was now returning to Eton. Once arrived on England's shore, a hired carriage would take him to Berkshire. The *Haggart*, demoted to a supply hulk several years previous, transported travelers between Wales, Ireland, and England.

Rutledge kept to his cabin, warring against returning to school. The question was, where would he go? This was his graduation year, and he could not shake the weight of expectations from his grandfather. There were choices facing him, curriculums to choose for the coming year at university, which meant he must choose a school. The expectation was Trinity. His father, grandfather, and great-grandfather had all graduated from the esteemed university in Dublin.

The restraint of his grandfather's vision was a lead cape. The lady in the tower, as he thought of his grandmother, the unapproachable woman guarding her heart, remained aloof, until her urgent summons had caused him to leave Eton before finishing his exams.

He had no more desire to succeed his grandfather than he did to enter university. If forced by his grandfather's ill health to return permanently, he would hire a manager the moment the old man died. Furthermore, he would not take up permanent residence.

Stretching his right hand out, massaging the knuckles he might have broken when he'd slammed his fist into the wall seven months earlier, he sulked and cursed. He'd obviously done serious injury to the knuckles. Leaning against the ship's rail, he concentrated on the whirling mass of black below. What in the bloody hell made him do it? The look on Mairéad's face haunted him, poor little nun-to-be. What possessed his grandfather to hire her to illuminate that meaningless batch of paper? Over the years, his elder read sections of it to him, who begat whom, boundless travels to unearth this or that.

His grandfather continually urged him to consider his lineage, even to the point of force-feeding him passages of this and that ancestor. It mattered not a bloody damn. The seed that created him was not strong enough to instill a sense of belonging. His weak begetting did not propagate a sense of himself. He knew more about where he did not belong than where he did.

He clutched the rail as the wind blew his hair into disarray. Curls swept down over his brow. The ship's bell rang, indicating that a storm brewed, and all on deck were ordered to their cabins. He moved closer to a pile of rope, where rain barrels were lashed in place. Angry waters of the Celtic Sea pummeled the vessel, sea spray spewed upward dousing him soundly.

He guessed the ship's speed was upwards of ten knots, possibly more. Standing portside aft, the wind at his back, sails full, he would see Bristol earlier than he wanted. He despised the return to Eton more than he could put to words. He was not accepted at the hall, and he was also no longer accepted at school —something he needed to come to grips with.

The *Haggart* plowed the dark waters, and white froth flew into the wind. The ache in Rutledge's hand brought him back to Miss Mairéad. What stayed his fist? The look on her face? His reaction to his own fury, hot and intense enough to want to bash her, pummel her, awakened something in him.

Uncapping the flask in his pocket, he gulped the contents, finishing off the last of the fiery liquid. Abhorrent to the point of disgust, he punched the air with his right fist pitching the flask into the sea. He looked at his hand as if it was not a part of him, an evil appendage.

A bolt of lightning scratched across the dark clouds, accompanied by a simultaneous clap of thunder. Another bolt zapped, closer this time, and he hoisted himself up on the rain barrel, raised his arm, waiting for the next strike of God's revenge.

The ship lunged in the waves, and Rutledge lurched from the barrel top, sailing through the air, his arms outstretched, reaching for the mercy for which he hungered. The icy sea caught his breath, and within seconds, the bitter chill encased his lungs.

March 25, 1817

Sitting at his desk, Darnley took pleasure in the winter scene and how the sun shorn off the bare branches of the hawthorn. His longing for Miss Mairéad was considerable, and he tried not to dwell on her absence. Her vows to join the religious life were completed last fall. At least she was safe and sheltered from the world's strife.

Every day now he progressed, managing the stairs by himself, though Lady Adrianna firmly announced that Tench must be in front of him when he was going down, and behind him going up. Grumbling did no good. Tench was far more concerned for Lady Darnley's good will than for that of his lordship.

Lord Darnley enjoyed allowing her certain attitudes. He did not need his butler, and Tench knew it, too, but humoring Lady Darnley was a pleasure after all the years of separation.

His writing would probably never be as legible as it once was, but if he wrote slower than was his wont, it was decipherable. His intention was to write to Mairéad. It would be his first letter in his own hand since she returned to the convent months ago. Seven months, to be exact. He reminded himself that it was March, after all.

He turned in his chair, dipped the quill into the ink, holding it above the paper until a drop of ink plopped. Returning the quill to the inkpot, he muttered and reached for the blotter. A bell tinkled somewhere in the far reaches of the Hall, and the pad of footsteps beat a path along the marbled foyer.

"Captain Besaw, my lord."

Darnley pulled himself up and out of the chair, his knuckles bent on the desktop for stability.

The captain, a large hulking man, graying mutton chops, and eyes with a perpetual squint, walked into the library. Though Darnley had never met the man, an ominous chill seemed to hover about him. "What can I do for you, sir?"

"Lord Darnley, I've come with news. It is not of a pleasant nature, and I am compelled to deliver it in person."

"Sit, please. Would you like a drink or tea?"

"Perhaps a sherry. I've been on the road since early morn." He sat in the chair his lordship indicated.

Darnley nodded to the footman, who poured the refreshment and handed it to the captain, then left the library with a click of the door.

Darnley waited as the captain took a sip and set the small

242

crystal on the desk. "I have brought news of your grandson, Rutledge, my lord."

A sigh gusted from him. In his heart, he knew someday a scenario like this would unfold, pulsating like the beat of the death drum. He waved for the man to continue and almost dropped into his chair.

"On the twenty-seventh of February, Lord Rutledge sailed with us on the *Haggart*, traveling from Waterford to Bristol. As usual, when the ship docks, passengers gather their baggage and go ashore. It was not until the next day that Rutledge's things were discovered still in his bunk room. Yet, it included no identification that we could use. The manifest listed an Ayden Wallington. When all avenues to locate that name in Bristol were exhausted, I hired an investigator to interview the passengers in the cabins on both sides of Rutledge's cabin. This took a great deal of time, as the single gentleman on one side lives in Manchester, and the elderly couple on the other side live in Nottingham."

Darnley held on to the instant mortification, sucking in breath. His grandson traveled under the name his father gave him.

The captain asked, "Are you well, my lord?"

Hands flat upon his desk, Darnley rasped, "Continue, please."

"We did not realize Ayden Wallington was not his name and were getting nowhere with his identity. The investigator first traveled to Nottingham, where the elderly couple said little, next to nothing about Rutledge. Then the investigator went to Manchester, to talk to the single man who had spent an hour earlier on the last day in conversation with Rutledge. *Wallington* mentioned he was on his way to finish up his last year at Eton.

"That piece of information led the investigator to Eton. In cases such as this, we attempt to find out the destination of the traveler and verify whether he or she arrived before alerting the family unnecessarily, although leaving one's baggage onboard does not bode well."

"I take it you discovered his identity at Eton, or you would not be here now." Lord Darnley leaned forward, his hands clenched, prayer like.

"Well ..." Captain Besaw met his lordship's intense gaze. "It took the investigator a good month to determine what Rutledge's destination might have been. When he was able to make his way to Berkshire and talk to the officials at Eton, a problem arose with the name he used on the manifest. Eton did not have a student named Ayden Wallington. However, there was a student who had not arrived for the new term, Lord Rutledge.

"Adding up Lord Rutledge's family address and the fact he boarded in Waterford, it became apparent they were one and the same young man. At this point, the investigator began to suspect foul play might have figured in his disappearance. The headmaster did mention, after coercion, Rutledge's troubled attendance through the years, a fact that might explain why the school did not contact you when the new term began. At that point I asked the headmaster to hold off, considering that I wanted to speak with you in person."

Lord Darnley focused on his clasped hands. He already concluded his grandson's demise. "What happened next?"

The large, brawny man stood and raked a hand through his red hair, as if nervous. He moved across the floor to a bookshelf turning to Lord Darnley. "It is difficult to share what was passed on to me by the investigator. However, under the circumstances, I believe you would want to understand his frame of mind."

Lord Darnley suddenly inquired, "Have you family? Children?"

"Three sons, twenty, eighteen, and twelve."

Darnley's voice rasped. "Rutledge was-is-would be eighteen now. A troubled young man that no amount of privilege or caring seemed to satisfy. We were always lacking with him. Carry on, captain, please. Unfortunately, I do not think you are going to shock me."

The large man marked his distance, as if he needed the space to lay out his words and not allow the fracturing of them, the immense hurt, closeness could cause. "He was in his cups, walking the companionway, talking to himself, and some of his words were legible to the occupants of the cabins. All three occupants shared the same memory of that evening. He mentioned his father, and apparently he related an encounter with a young woman, one he fiercely regretted, according to the occupants."

The captain shoved his hands in his pockets, clearly resistant to what he needed to impart. "The lone, male passenger, Mr. Bingham, realizing the young man was distraught, invited him in, but the offer was declined. He noted Rutledge's eyes, as if he could not focus. Frenzied is the way Mr. Bingham described him. He assumed the young man was upset over the rising storm. Ship's bell rang, and several stewards went about signaling my order to stay in their cabins. This was the last Mr. Bingham saw of Rutledge. The evening met with a high wind, with waves splashing upwards against the hull and the boat rocking to and fro."

Darnley had difficulty absorbing the events the captain described. He allowed a gut-wrenching vision to wash over him. His precious grandson, whom he could never convince of his love and ultimately of what his existence meant to him.

He knew he must have appeared visibly shaken, because the captain strode across the room. "Shall I ring for someone, my lord?"

The words came from a tunnel, far, far away. A place where a five-year-old ran, laughing, chasing after a colt, his little legs scurrying, his hat long blown off. That is how Darnley remembered his beloved grandson, happy, vibrant, and wonderfully alive. A fresh breath of life after the death of his own son, the lad's father.

Darnley sighed, fixed his eyes on his twiddling thumbs. What was this life supposed to be about, if not the future? He wanted to ask this man a question. He was not quite sure how to phrase it. An ominous fear caused his voice to stumble. "Did you-would you-is it your belief he took his own life?"

Captain Besaw returned to the chair across from Darnley. "Our conclusion, considering we know he did not walk off the ship, is that he drowned. As to taking his own life, we cannot be certain. That beast of a storm makes us think he might have slipped and been thrown as the *Haggart* listed. According to Mr. Bingham, he noted Rutledge walking toward the rear of the vessel as he closed his own portal, apparently well in his cups, and my guess is he lost his footing."

The captain added, "Rutledge was on his way to school. To my way of thinking his motivation suggests he did not take his own life."

Darnley's agony burnt his heart. His last words to his grandson banished him from the Hall and now from his life.

The captain added, "There was no note in his cabin. Nothing to indicate this was deliberate. I left his bags with your butler, so your grandson's belongings are returned to you. The headmaster asked me to return what was in his room at Eton."

"You said this happened on the twenty-seventh of February?"

"Yes, my lord. Our destination was Bristol."

"He left here in late July. This begs the question, where was he?" He sighed deeply, his gaze on the captain. "I am grateful for your time and investigation, the effort you put forth. It cannot have been easy to come here."

The two men shook hands, and as the captain left the library, Darnley sank back in his chair.

What now?

Another trunk with the belongings of another son returned to the family estate. For safekeeping? He would not dig into it looking for answers as he did with his son's things so many years ago. He could not endure the pain. He dared not linger on the last time they spoke, as he ordered his grandson from the premises. The memory of that grievous scene penalized the fibers of his soul.

With heavy heart, Darnley sought refuge in his library,

dreading the task ahead. He sent a footman requesting his wife and sister come to him.

Feminine chatter floated along the hallway as they approached.

"Have we a treat in store, Darnley? Something foolish and delightful?" His sister took a chair in front of the fireplace, her dogs settling about her skirts. He stood at the mantel watching them in their pretty, soft-hued day dresses, floating like flowers over the carpet.

His wife's smile and lovely head of white hair beneath a lacy cap bobbed at him in greeting. Taking a seat next to her sister-in-law, she said, "Yes, dear, you have aroused our curiosity."

He could not help but observe the likeness between them. Smiling, faces glinting with mischief that within moments would shatter.

Lady Darnley's brow narrowed. "What is wrong? Something's amiss. What is it?"

He nodded and pushed away from the mantel. "Unbelievably sad news."

He formed a circle with the women as he sat. "Our grandson —" he choked on the words and began again, "Our grandson is gone." The word *dead* he could not say.

Philly reacted instantly. "Gone? You sent him away. He has gone to school. Have you forgotten."

Her ladyship extended her hand to her sister-in-law's arm, but her gaze was on her husband. "Gone as in …"

He nodded, his features hard, his chin set firm. Words failed him.

Both women gasped, eyes wide, palms to their bosoms, as they assimilated the obvious. A horrid intrusion, dark and ugly, circled as understanding soaked their hearts.

He wished with all his might and love that he could spare them. His own grief welled, and he tried to swallow the pain, gulping with discomfort. How does one stop the downpour of sadness, of overwhelming pain? His hands shook, and he could not catch his breath. It clustered in his chest like a rock.

His wife stood, woodenly. Barely able to move, she turned toward him, saying, "No, dear God, no."

Gasping to breathe, he reached out with a shaky hand.

Philly yanked the bell pull. Within seconds, Witham, Mrs. Atkinson, and several footmen rushed into the library, immediately ascertaining the urgency of the situation.

Witham ordered one of the footman to fetch Mr. O'Reilly. Mrs. Atkinson bent to his lordship ordering the footmen to carry him to his chamber. Once they laid him upon the bed, Tench loosened his cravat and waistcoat, and a maid arrived with a cloth and a bowl of water. Tench mixed a dose of powder in a glass of water, asking Witham to raise his lordship's head. Mr. O'Reilly had left instructions for its use, should he have an attack.

Darnley's eyes fluttered. Tench said, "My lord, if you could manage a sip or two." Able to sip then, his head lolled, and Witham laid him gently against the pillow.

The two women stood at the foot of the bed mumbling prayers, hands firm upon the foot rail, as if their grip could return his health. This could not be happening. Not again.

In less than an hour Mr. O'Reilly burst into the room. Placing his black bag upon the bed, he drew out his measuring tool, which resembled a funnel, and placed it over Lord Darnley's chest, then put his ear to the other end. The room quieted, everyone holding their breath, praying that Mr. O'Reilly was a worker of miracles.

He moved the funnel to the side of Lord Darnley's chest and again put his ear to the other end of the device. Then he took a deep breath and placed the funnel on yet another piece of exposed skin.

He closed his eyes for several long moments, concentrating, then raised his head as he drew the funnel off. "We can thank God. His heart is strong."

A united gasp filled the room. Witham, stoic in any situation, swiped at his left eye. Mrs. Atkinson turned into a corner, her shoulders shaking.

Tench pursed his lips. "Gave us a scare, my lord."

Lord Darnley's eyes fluttered open. A smile quirked at the corner of his lips. He glanced at the end of his bed, where his wife and sister stood, their faces shadowed with a mixture of grief and relief.

Mr. O'Reilly held the glass Tench used to mix the potion. "How much did you administer?"

"I would say two ounces. Seemed about all he could manage."

"It proves to have worked. His heart's rhythm is normal. I recommend the day abed." He glanced at his patient. "You may resume activity tomorrow, my lord. No riding, of course," he said, a wry grin chasing the gravity from his features.

Returning his instrument to the black bag, he spoke to Tench. "Here is another dose of the foxglove. You did just as I asked and most likely saved him from a great disability."

Tench accepted the small vial as if it were the Holy Grail. "Thank you."

Lady Darnley followed the doctor out the door, and he waited for her. "Darnley was imparting sad news to us when his attack came on." As the doctor's brow rose, she added, "Our– Rutledge is dead."

His eyebrows rose to his hairline and his mouth gaped.

Afraid of bursting into tears, she nodded, dabbing at her eyes with a lacey handkerchief.

"How?" Grasping her arm, he drew her over to sit on a bench.

"He was so overcome he could not finish the particulars. We are uncertain at this point. I shall be afraid to inquire further."

The doctor grew pensive. "One might argue that purging the information, sharing it, if you will, is a good thing. Relieves the body of a measure of grief. Such a tragedy, my lady." He pondered a moment. "Lord Darnley's heart is strong. He is recovering rather nicely from his apoplexy. I suggest you make yourself available to him. Perhaps he will finish telling you of the sad news. He needs to talk of it, not hold it in. Do you know how he came by this news?"

"Witham mentioned he had a visitor. A Captain Besaw."

"Ah." He reached for her hand, patting it in reassurance. "You have my sincerest regards, my lady. Your family has suffered through the years. I will return in a few hours and check in on his lordship to give you peace of mind. I do feel he is going to be fine in body, if not otherwise."

Lady Darnley returned to her husband's chamber. He was sitting up in bed, a sad, weary look to him. Philly in a chair next to the bed, lifted her brows in question. Lady Darnley nodded with the briefest smile.

Witham asked. "Tea?"

"Yes."

The butler gave a slight nod and turned toward the door.

Lady Darnley followed both he and Mrs. Atkinson out into the corridor. "I need a moment."

They stopped and waited until she composed herself. "We have suffered another loss." She drew out the damp handkerchief from her pocket and dabbed at the tears that began to sting, her composure slipping.

Mrs. Atkinson asked, "Can it wait, my lady? You're quite distressed."

"Best said, Mrs. Atkinson. Although I have not fully accepted it myself." A deep sigh accompanied her words. "Rutledge is dead." Like stone statues both, they barely breathed. She quickly added, "Darnley's visitor was a Captain Besaw. I am thinking Rutledge must have been aboard, perhaps returning to us. Darnley was about to reveal the specifics when he was taken with this— this episode."

Witham, stoic as usual, said, "We will keep this to ourselves until further notice from you, my lady."

"I think it best, at least until Darnley regains his strength."

Mrs. Atkinson asked, "Is there anything I can do for you, my lady?" Her face was wreathed with sorrow.

"Nothing right now. I must stay close. I fear for the future." Having said that, Lady Darnley knew Witham and Mrs. Atkinson could run Rockmore Hall with or without her direction. She returned to her husband's bedside. His sister seemed to have soothed him. His eyes were closed, and he looked quite peaceful though his face was pale.

The women moved to the windows overlooking the pond and its fountain. Lady Darnley whispered, "What is to be done, Philly?" She took her sister's-in-law hand. "I am so grateful for your presence. Tell me what to do."

She cupped her sister-in-law's cheek. "Take care of yourself, my dear. This will sort itself out in time." Her pale-blue gaze lingered on Lady Adrianna's face. "He was a tortured soul. Though young, life used him up. He never knew ambition like someone of his age should. It was as if he lived in another time but was forced to reside in ours. Perhaps he never resigned himself to the circumstance of his birth?"

"That was most apparent. Abandoned by his mother, left with the Molloys, his father in an early watery grave." Her whisper died out. Silence ensued. They looked out upon the park and its spewing fountain. Swans, graceful and serene, glided effortlessly, unburdened by the cares of the world.

In a broken voice, she admitted, "I refused to set eyes on him, refused a friendship. I withheld a grandmother's love because I was afraid someday I would lose him." She sucked in a breath. "I am so ashamed, Philly."

෴

A week went by. The news of Rutledge's demise, like the early morning mist, curled with heartbreaking disbelief over the landscape and through the countryside. There was no stopping the whispers in the kitchen. Did he take his life, as his father did? Did you hear the ruckus the day he stormed out of here? Bad words between him and his lordship, that day in late July. Not a word from him all this time, and now we know why.

Immediately upon hearing the scandalous remarks, Witham addressed the issue at the staff's evening table demanding loyalty.

He reminded the servants on whose estate they resided, who fed them, and who paid them.

Proud of Witham's swift response, Mrs. Atkinson silently applauded his stern criticism of their backhanded remarks. She'd not likely forget Mairéad's wild-eyed, fearful response to Rutledge's rage, almost as if she unwittingly played a role in his tortured life.

Mourning seeped over the estate. There were no remains, which was an act of cruelty for those who grieved. Her ladyship took her sorrow to the chapel daily. She also mourned the loss of Miss Mairéad, perhaps even more so because her presence filled this great Palladian manor with a winsome loveliness, a fresh and spirited outlook that was sorely lacking.

Sometimes Lady Duncamden accompanied her on walks to the chapel. Most often, however, she wanted to hover over her brother, who fell to melancholy far too quickly.

Today the women and the curs meandered past the graveyard, stopped at the wrought-iron fence and glanced at all the markers. They needed to add Rutledge's stone, but hadn't the heart or desire to make the last, final gesture of his death.

Slowly and surely, healing crept in on silent cat-like paws, unsuspected, until they occasionally laughed at an old memory or took delight in a tart lemon pie.

The days, weeks, and months passed. Lady Duncamden was grateful she stayed through the holiday season. It allowed her to be of some comfort to her brother and sister-in-law.

She spent some of the time absorbed in putting a puzzle together in the parlor, until it was finished late in February. The wind whistled in the chimneys, and bare limbs tinkled with the shiver of the blow. Gray days followed gray days, until slowly more of the sun appeared than clouds, a metaphor for those living in the Hall.

The warmth coaxed dense, cylindrical spikes of early orchids, blue spring squill, and bright yellow globeflowers from their winter hiatus.

Spring also brought the certainty that life went on. Each in their own way, Darnley, his wife, and his sister healed to some degree from the devastation. Mixed in with their grief at the loss of Rutledge was their sadness at the lass' choice to take the vows of convent life.

I n the new year of 1817, April came and went, with its blustery winds clearing the branches of their dead leaves. Bog rosemary crept like evergreen, its new growth lime-green, shiny, and leathery in the marshy woodland. Depending on where one walked, orchids, dull pink and scented of vanilla, dotted the forest floor.

Unfurling ferns and the earthy scent of spring enhanced by continual drizzling rain, reminded of the summer to come. Lady Duncamden packed her bags and her Pekingese on a bright day in early April and left after breakfast. Lord Darnley took part in the meal to wish his sister safe travel.

The warm spring sun brought the promise of a delightful journey midst the verdant rolling hills. Wooly sheep nibbled clover, and puffy white clouds pushed along with the wind in the cerulean sky.

Lord and Lady Darnley walked with her to the waiting carriage, Sassy and Muffy snuggled on either side of her, the coachman provided a footrest upon which she could stretch out her legs in comfort and nod off for a good bit of the travel.

Waving her off, the Darnley's returned to the interior of ·Rockmore Hall and settled comfortably in the library. Lord

Darnley intended to write two letters, one to Tremaine at university and the other to Miss Mairéad. He reminded himself that by now she would have taken another name that began with Sister. Nonetheless, he wanted to tell her of Rutledge's death. Then he corrected himself once more. *She would want* to know. She was that kind of young woman. He missed her vibrant nature, her inquisitive loving self.

"What is to be done, Wally? Will your title sit in a drawer in the King's dusty archives? And, what of the inheritance of Rockmore Hall? What will you do?"

Bemused, he gazed at his wife as she stitched on a frame near the sunlit window. Returning the pen to the inkpot, he stated, "As it stands right now, Charles Burke Wallington, Lord Tremaine is the heir presumptive."

"Jonathan's father? Hmm. I guess I let that slip my mind over the years." Her attention was on a knot and the untying of it.

"He's younger by less than a score. I have no plans to give up the ghost for a decade or more. So, do not *hmm* me, madam."

A burst of laughter shot from her. "Your demeanor these weeks got me thinking you were bent to the thought day and night. It's heartening to realize I am dead wrong."

"Ouch."

Her cheeks puffed with a wide smile.

His attempt to sound harsh failed. "I have communications to write, madam. You keep me from my endeavor."

"Then change what's on your mind, because I can read it from where I sit." She stabbed at the taut linen with her needle.

His gaze narrowed. "Then you understand what I am thinking at this moment, right?"

Again, she rejoiced, the jar of grief near fully emptied. "I am reminded why I love you."

He seemed faraway at the moment.

"She would want to know about Rutledge. You hired her to work for you." Her arm stretched out, tugging on the thread as it pulled through the fabric.

"She was more than an illustrator, to all of us. Why think of her as hired?"

"Darnley, really. Your relationship with her mystified me. That is true. She is a lovely young woman who is and was completely dedicated to the nunnery. I think your writing to her is a grand gesture. I do believe she would want to know of our loss, but the truth is, she painted for you, and you made a generous donation to the convent on her behalf."

"I won't argue the point, but weren't you drawn in by her even a bit?"

"From the beginning she was to be temporary. When Mother Abbess visited, it was exceedingly clear to me Miss Mairéad would return to the convent." Setting her embroidery hoop down, she gave him her full attention. "I am not like you, dear heart. I have not the capacity to allow people in and then out again." Her eyes misted, and she blinked, trying to avoid emotion that welled in spite of her attempt to ignore it.

He came over and sat with her, putting his arm about her shoulders. "I know. You have suffered far more than your share should have been." He squeezed her shoulder, drawing her toward him. "Thank you for the delightful conversation and laughter that brightens your eyes. I needed that." He planted a kiss on her cap, its ruffles causing him to sneeze.

"Sorry about that." He drew a handkerchief from his pocket and wiped his nose.

"I think you did that on purpose."

"I did not. I came over here to comfort you."

She smiled. "I hope to never find out what life would be like without you."

He patted her arm. "Another reason the lass is special. She drew you out of that confounded apartment and back where you belong."

"There is that, to be sure." She adjusted her cap and peeked over at him.

In all sincerity, he said, "I imagine our emotions will be up and down for a time, until we get used to his absence."

"Similar to when Garrett passed." She turned a loving glance to her husband of forty years. "I wasted so much of our time together all because I was afraid of the pain of death."

"I understood that, my dear, and you weren't all that far away." He chuckled. "Two flights of stairs."

"You always find a way to make it right."

"Perhaps, but in this case, I'm certain we will not discover another grandson hiding in a cottage on the grounds." Before he stood, he placed a tender kiss on her cheek. "I must get my writing off before I decide a nap would be better use of my time."

She picked up her sewing, "And I need to work the flowers into the center of this doily."

As he settled down to write his letters he hoped Mairéad and Tremaine wrote to one another. There was an inkling of a friendship between them. He noted it before his unfortunate attack.

His missive to Tremaine was not as delicate as the one he wrote to Mairéad. Hers was a superficial rendering of the facts of Rutledge's last hours and the storm aboard the *Haggart*. He ended with his and Lady Adrianna's affections and saying that if it were possible for her to leave the convent, he would send a carriage, she was simply to mention the day. Omitting the fact that they needed her presence, he implied it in a way that he felt she might be able to convince Mother Abbess to allow her to come. Any length of time she could manage would gratify them deeply.

To Tremaine, Darnley detailed the specifics given by the *Haggart*'s captain. Tremaine would not have settled for anything less. Darnley treated him like the second heir apparent that he was. After all, he was next in line after his father and, therefore, would someday inherit the title and lands of Rockmore Hall as well.

Mairéad was working when Sister Davideena brought a post from

Lord Darnley. Wiping her hands, she broke the seal, read, and reread every word.

An unnerving sense had come to her a month or so earlier. She was already abed, and the rustle of wind in the trees quite strong, to the point of creaking limbs. Hardly a star visible through her window, she remembered lightning strikes flashed across the black heavens crackling with the storm. That night she dreamt Lord Darnley was a victim of an accident. But could it have been Rutledge's death, and she mistook the omen?

His lordship did not mention how Rutledge died. He probably omitted the fact thinking her too sensitive. She surmised it must have been an accident because Rutledge was healthy and strong.

What the letter did impart was how they hoped she could find it in her schedule to come to them. He didn't reference her vows other than to say he hoped Mother Abbess would allow the visit.

Knocking on her superior's office door, she asked, "Have you time for me to share a post that's just come?"

Mother Abbess unloaded an armful of books onto a ledge, intending to return them to their rightful place on the shelves. Swiping her hands of dust, she indicated a chair to Mairéad and sat next to her. "I trust it is not bad news."

"Lord Darnley's grandson, Rutledge, has died."

Remorseful, Mother Abbess sighed, "So young. Did his lordship mention particulars?"

"It apparently happened February 27. Lord Darnley doesn't say how, just that he is gone. I expect they are hardly coping. He asks if I could visit. I think as a comfort, though he does not say so." She folded the missive in her lap, settling her hands atop.

Mother Abbess lowered her chin, piercing her with a knowing look. "What is it you want to do?"

"Go to them, stay awhile. I remember how lonely Lord Darnley was though I do suspect things have changed since Lady Darnley returned to her own rooms." She glanced at her hands covering the letter. "They came to mean a great deal to me. I hope to help them through this somehow."

"I believe returning to Rockmore Hall will reinforce the decision you made about your future. Your vocation is decided, and you are not the same young woman that you were."

A soft breath puffed as she agreed, confident she could provide comfort and diversion in the Darnley's' grief. "I will send word straight away. I have two illuminations that need to be finished before I leave. I could be ready by the end of next week."

"April ..." Mother Abbess mentioned "A lovely time in the gardens, as I recall."

Mairéad returned to her workroom contemplating how Tremaine would handle Rutledge's death. He acted the big brother time and again through Rutledge's offenses. Such a shame, Rutledge was too young and had much to accomplish.

Returning to her workroom, she glanced at the easels of pages drying. She could not rush the process, which was integral, but still should be able to leave by the end of next week.

🕮

Jonathan, Lord Tremaine, sank into a chair in the lounge of Edinburgh University's marbled medical library. The announcement that Rutledge was dead brought a swift, stinging pain. Pinching his nose, he hoped not to embarrass himself in such a public place. He took a deep breath, attempting to control his fiery emotions. Forming a stiff upper lip, he reread the unbelievable news. He pressed the note against his chest as if he could hold his childhood friend near. Tremaine was troubled about Rutledge almost from the first time they met. His grief weighed heavily.

After several long minutes of ruminating through the past, he bolted from the library and walked across Drummond Street south on Bridge. A mix of sleet and rain this morning when he picked up his mail, turned the day dreary. The news from Lord Darnley changed his current plans. After tomorrow morning's final exam, he would be free until next fall. He needed to talk to Christopher about leaving earlier than planned.

It always made sense for them to travel together, but Christopher would be hard to convince. He had fallen in love. With a young woman, Miss Hammond.

They met at a botany lecture. She had captured the interest of his friend straight off. Tremaine did agree her knowledge of botany appeared rather impressive. Anyway, the point being, as he argued with himself, he wasn't sure Christopher would be willing to leave by the end of the week.

A picture of Mairéad flashed. They wrote all these months, but not once had she mentioned taking vows. He finally quit inquiring, realizing it must be such a sacred event that he was not worthy of details. It was simply gratifying that she continued to write.

Still painting, she recently acquired obligations involving the secular world in as much as she was the spokeswoman for ordering supplies for the convent. Textiles, blankets, books, ink, her list was long. His distinct impression was she reveled in her new position. Mother Abbess must have finally grasped Mairéad's depth to promote her.

The convent was self-sufficient to a degree. The kind of spending Mairéad wrote about suggested a wealthy benefactor. Her recent letters imparted an excitement that he'd not noticed in their earlier writing. Happy for her, he knew she deserved the best life offered. Perhaps they would meet again someday. It seemed fruitless to visit her at Sacred Heart, but the idea of never seeing her again, regardless of her vocation, saddened him.

Her heart was honest, even with the challenges she'd faced with Rutledge, she was compassionate toward him. Her eagerness to learn about the world and perspective about the future were insightful and challenging. Which he considered surprising, considering she lived a sheltered life. Above all, she embraced a deep belief in humankind.

His musings got him nowhere. He wanted someone who wanted a life devoted to God.

Stomping muddied boots on the threshold of the apartment he and Christopher shared, he entered the foyer, calling out, "Chris, are you here?" His coat and hat weren't on the peg. Hanging his own outdoor articles, he added a bit of kindling and tossed a log on the coals in the grate and hoped the latest blast from the north would cease in a day or two. As he hung the kettle on an iron arm and swung it over the fire his apartment mate entered.

Christopher said, "I didn't expect you back this early."

Tremaine pulled two cups off the shelf and fixed tea leaves in a sieve. "I received a letter from Lord Darnley. Not good news."

Christopher stopped, arms in midair, while taking off his woolen scarf. He looked at Tremaine with great interest.

"It's Rutledge. He has died. Fell overboard on his return to Eton."

Christopher hung the scarf over his coat and moved into the kitchen area. "I am sorry to hear this. I know what he meant to you. Is there anything I can do? You must be in a quandary, what with your essays tomorrow."

Tremaine turned to his friend as he leaned his hip against the counter. "After tomorrow I could leave for Ireland, but I think you've committed yourself through the week."

The fire crackled to a nice blaze, heating the room. Sleet pelted the windows.

"Damn miserable out there," Christopher said. "I've made plans with Miss Hammond. The next time we'll see each other is September. I hate to break them."

"Would it be disloyal of me to go on ahead?"

"Not at all. Perhaps I should cancel my plans." He grabbed up a thick pad and took the kettle off the fire, filling their cups.

"There are a number of things needing attention that encourage me to return quickly. Lord Darnley wrote expressly asking that I spend a few days with them on my way to Dunraven."

"One of them wouldn't be Sister Mairéad, would it?"

"She's immersed in convent life. With her pure devotion, all I can hope for is a friendship, and I'll be grateful to get that."

Christopher sipped his tea and made a face. "Bitter. Is this the batch from old man Hegas?"

He shrugged, "I don't keep tabs on tea like you."

"He enlarges the batch with senna. Comes down to pence with him, old bugger."

Handing him a jar of honey from the cupboard, Tremaine said, "You would not mind if I go on ahead, then?"

"Not at all. I know what the Darnley's mean to you." He stirred the thick golden sweetener into the cup. "If you are free tonight, we are attending a lecture by Sir Michael Comrie at the Royal College."

Lost in musing, Tremaine caught the last part of Christopher's invitation. "Let me see, to engage both of you, it must be a discourse on the life phenom of a plant that grows ..."

Christopher guffawed as his friend blathered on.

"... I must decline. A paper on leprosy cases and causes, and new cures for fevers, and the added attraction of available pharmacopoeia will be my reading tonight."

Christopher grinned over the rim of his tea. "Our focus after all the combined years of study is beginning to culminate in the vision of a fine clinic in Waterford."

Tremaine grew serious. "With Rutledge's death, I hate to think it, but it's entirely possible my father will be named the presumptive heir to Rockmore Hall and the Darnley title, which translates to my inheritance someday. Hopefully that will be many years in the future. All the studying in the world won't change that, but if we set up our clinic well before, I'll be content. With you in charge, I feel comfortable about our future."

"Great misfortune being born first. I suffer for you, old boy." His caustic remark made Tremaine laugh.

Sleet pinged against the windows with a consistency that indicated it would not soon abate. Christopher added two more logs to the grate. "These late last blows of winter are unnecessary. Brr."

"You can't oversee the weather *and* study."

"Now that we are homing in on the last of it, I'm beginning to get excited. Not that far off, is it?"

"If I pass my exams tomorrow, I'll be on schedule to graduate a year from now."

"Drat weather." Christopher rubbed his upper arms. "I've got you beat, old man. I met with Mr. Terrian. He said I'll have enough to graduate after fall classes. Sometime in late December."

"Then it will be up to you to find a place in Waterford that will serve us well."

"Speaking of, have you given Hawthorn Village any consideration?"

"It's crossed my mind. I don't spend enough time looking when I am at Rockmore Hall. I'll make a point of it this time."

By the second week in April, all of Hawthorn Village was aware Lord Darnley's heir passed. News traveled toward Waterford, seeping along Greyfriars amidst the quay and in and out of pubs he frequented. Doolan's was a favorite, built along the old eastern flank of the Viking triangle.

Rumor was Rutledge spent many a night with Dervila, an Irish woman abandoned in Waterford when her husband sailed a tall three-mast vessel bound for New Guinea.

By the end of the second week in April, gossip settled, for the most part. The carriage Lord Darnley sent for Mairéad earlier in the day pulled up at Rockmore Hall. The sun began to drift toward the western sky as the carriage wheels crunched on the gravel approach.

As a footman took her bags, Witham presented himself and greeted her with a smile, something rare of late, to be sure. "Welcome back, miss."

"Thank you. May I go directly to Lord and Lady Darnley?"

"They are awaiting your arrival, miss, in the parlor with Lord Tremaine." He walked across the marbled foyer and opened the door, announcing her.

Flickering firelight in the grate blazed, warding off the April chill. An ornate blue and white porcelain vase spilled with pink roses, no doubt from the hothouse, a lovely sight to behold this early spring.

Both men stood. Her ladyship stayed seated across the room. Mairéad's heart fluttered as she exchanged a bright smile with Tremaine. His flaxen hair curled about his impeccably knotted cravat. How she had missed him these many months. She'd forgotten how tall he was. He appeared restless judging by his wrinkled brow and his eyes dark with discomfiture.

With Lady Darnley's open arms beckoning Mairéad leaned in, "I am grieved for your loss, your ladyship."

Lord Darnley said, "We need reminding of the good things in life." She received a buss on each cheek from him. "We are grateful the two of you have time to spare us."

Lady Darnley insisted, "We want this to be a gathering of easy hearts, not that we aren't incredibly sad and broken hearted. Darnley and I need your youthful interest in life. Your gay perspectives. Please."

Lord Darnley whispered in Mairéad's ear, though loud enough for the others to hear. "Your duty is done." He pivoted her by the shoulders to face Tremaine.

Tremaine's smile wavered as he stepped forward, "Though a sad circumstance calls us together, it is wonderful to see you." His lips brushed across the hand she extended.

Her skin tingled at the touch of his hand. "Mother Abbess was most obliging, given the circumstances." Turning back to Lord Darnley, she added, "She sends her condolences and will offer a Mass for the family."

Lady Darnley's voice was laced with profound sadness. "We have yet to discover where he was from the day he departed last July until the captain informed us of his death in February."

Lord Darnley knew his wife could not let go of the fact that many months passed before Rutledge returned to Eton. "Adrianna, we need not dwell on what we cannot understand."

It was crushing to witness her ladyship's anguish as she

admitted, "We are coping, but there are no remains, which grieves us so. Just like his father."

Mairéad turned to Lord Darnley. "In your letter, you didn't mention how he died."

"We were just about to enlighten Tremaine when you arrived. Please make yourselves comfortable."

Lord Darnley took the chair next to his wife, leaving Mairéad and Tremaine the settee. The timbre of his lordship's voice indicated his return to near normal. He'd many months to recover, but this news, coping with Rutledge's demise, she prayed wouldn't force a setback.

Once seated, Tremaine turned to her with a pensive expression knitting his brow and asked, "Would you be up for riding this afternoon?"

"If time allows," she said, "I certainly am."

"Good then and thank you for your letters, Sister Mairéad. They were always eagerly anticipated."

She knew he called her *Sister* because she deliberately did not answer his questions about vows. Although she wasn't wearing her habit, but she hadn't worn her habit during the months she lived here, either.

As if reading her mind, Lady Darnley said, "As much as we honor your decision to take vows, my dear, Lady Duncamden and I did so want you to look as we remembered when you visited. It seems the gown we chose was perfect. Soft pink suits your coloring."

"I had refused her offer. But she won the effort, didn't she. Sneaking it into the carriage like she did." Mairéad folded her hands in her lap and gave a side-glance to Tremaine. He appeared subdued, a finger rubbing his lower lip.

Lady Darnley, whose emotions obviously crossed between despair and resignation, perked up. "Luncheon is planned, but shall I ring for tea until then?"

Mairéad nodded, which sent Witham about his business. She

turned to Tremaine and asked, "You must be on your way to Dunraven? How long will you stay at Rockmore?"

Hands clasped on his knees, a slow smile filled his square jaw as he turned to the Darnley's, "If it is all right, I would like to spend several days here with you before going on to my family."

Mairéad itched to put her hand in his. Did he mean *you* as in her, or did he refer to the three of them?

He added, "I have the entire summer to do as I please. Next fall will be my last at university." He relaxed against the settee, placing his left arm along the back. She could sense the nearness of his fingers. She did not have words to explain what his proximity meant to her.

Witham returned, a footman following with the tea tray. Mairéad asked of her ladyship, "May I?" And at her nod, began serving. When she handed Tremaine his cup, their fingers touched.

Tremaine's brows pulled in. "Excuse me."

As Witham and the footman closed the parlor door, Lord Darnley began the story of Rutledge's demise. "I deliberately kept some information from the letter I wrote you, Mairéad. I didn't want to upset you more than necessary. Our lad drowned on his return to Eton. It was during a storm, and he'd been drinking, according to the interviews conducted with travelers on either side of his cabin. His eyes were glassy and red, and he rambled."

Mairéad felt a cold chill ripple her skin. Her breath caught. Tremaine took the cup from her trembling hands.

Her ladyship chastised her husband. "You were rather abrupt. Could you not have told her in patches, a bit at a time?" Her lips tightened with angst. "Wasn't it you who said we want to keep this gathering light, not dwell on the…the, oh my…it's done and said."

It was quiet for a minute, the four of them trying not to suffer but all feeling it, nonetheless.

"As usual, my dear, you are right." His mournful gaze lit on Mairéad, "Forgive me. The whole purpose in telling you this was to get to the part where he was quoted talking about a young woman, saying, *how could I harm someone I care for*? That is the part I wanted you to know. How sorry he was, because obviously he was referring to the altercation with you."

Her heart felt as though it skipped a beat. Her palms pressed together, prayer like. "I don't know what to say."

He died in a similar way to his father. Was it planned? She kept the question to herself.

The parlor grew quiet, allowing her to absorb the latest news. She asked, "He fall overboard?"

"According to the captain, there was a horrid storm, and at one point the ship listed enough that if he was not steady on his feet, he very well could have been swept overboard. The death certificate reads an accident."

An ache rent her heart. How and why he died seemed less deliberate and more accidental. The loss of him was devastating, especially considering the altercations that preceded it. Though both events were months apart, they were linked in her mind. Not realizing how struck she was with his death, she was grateful when Tremaine's large hand cupped hers, easing the clench of her fingers.

Everyone fell silent absorbing the declaration of Rutledge's death, the sadness of losing one so young. Their beloved grandson, despite the troubling times raising him.

Tremaine shifted the mood to a lighter topic. "Sister Mairéad, tell us about your ceremony. The taking of vows. I waited letter after letter, yet you did not answer my questions." He was smiling, she could see, but behind the smile was something else, a dark and deeper meaning to his question.

If she was going to talk of it, now was her chance. Taking a breath, easing the pain clenching her heart, she turned her full attention to him. "Well—"

The door swung open, Witham stepped inside, followed by Mrs. Atkinson, he announced, "My lord, a woman from Hawthorn Village requests to speak with all of you. Nuala O'Bannon."

Dressed in dark blue wool, hair caught up with pins, and shoes covered with dirt and grass, the woman obviously walked from the village. Appearing edgy, her shoulders squared, she refused to sit declaring she would rather stand.

Mrs. Atkinson stayed back from the group, against the wall. A soft smile played on her face. It appeared she was immensely satisfied with the woman's unexpected presence.

"What brings you to us, Nuala?" Lord Darnley inquired.

"I'd like to get right to it, my lord, now wouldn't I." Her chin rose a tiny bit. "I have come to declare that I am Mairéad's mother."

Lady Darnley dropped her cup and saucer. Mrs. Atkinson went directly to the mess.

Lord Darnley shook his head as if he hadn't heard her rightly.

Tremaine scanned the room, and then his gaze settled on Mairéad. His hand squeezed hers, reminding her of his strength and friendship.

Mairéad's breath caught, until Tremaine gently shook her into taking a deep gasping breath.

"I beg your pardon!" Lord Darnley said loudly as he sat on the edge of his chair.

With all eyes on her, Nuala repeated in a matter-of-fact voice, "I am her mother." With a nod to Mairéad, she added, "And there is more."

Extremely agitated, Lord Darnley spoke with a vengeance. "What more? What more folly could there be?"

Mairéad froze like a statue.

Nuala raised a wrist to her mouth, her eyes reddened with turmoil. "Never in all these years have I vowed this to a soul, but I do so now. There were two."

His lordship gaped. As if the air went out of him, he fell back against the chair, groaning, "I knew it."

Finding her voice, Lady Darnley asked, "Knew what, Darnley?"

The look he turned on Nuala was one of dire confirmation. "You speak of Mairéad and Rutledge, the two of them." His arms drooped off the chair dangling in resignation.

Nuala added, "I kept my daughter, and Garrett kept his son."

Lord Darnley's chin drooped to his chest as she said the last. He squeaked, "Ayden."

She nodded, as if his lordship's recognition of the truth emboldened her.

Lady Darnley's voice thick with incredulity. "My son had twins. Oh, my. Philly is going to be furious she left."

Lord Darnley growled at his wife. "In a manner of speaking, it is women who have them." A heavy cloud of regret blanketed him. Years of suffering smothered him. This woman's declaration near took the life from him. And now learning his son could not see his way to tell him about this momentous twin birth shook him to the core.

Like an ill-wind, shock turned to anger. He glared at Nuala and demanded, "What proof have you of all this? Why speak now, after all these years? Do you really expect us to believe you? It was common knowledge that Rutledge was our son's child. They favored each other. Any woman could come in here and claim to be the mother."

On trial now, Nuala did not appear cowed as she raised her chin and met his lordship's stare.

Nuala's revelation beginning to sink in, Mairéad's truth was in the life she led since birth. This skeptical and angry woman dared to come here, bring up her past like she was hanging wash on the line to air. She needed more than proof. The years of suffering, the needless separation of parent and child. She squeezed Tremaine's hand grateful he'd not let go.

Lord Darnley demanded. "Speak up, woman. Why now?"

Nuala armed herself with a deep breath. "I was aware of your grandson's anger and resentment. Afraid I would make it worse for him, I kept silent. Look at me. Who am I?" She held her hands palms up in supplication. "Your son loved me enough to marry me. He could not see the difference between us, but I was firmly aware, wasn't I? I needed time to conform, adjust. I needed to ready myself to be brought before you. For Garrett's sake, I prayed you could accept the truth of our love for each other.

"Then almost immediately we discovered I was *ag iompar clainne*. My parents were ailing. The care of them fell to me, their only child. I was duty bound. 'Tis the way of it for our kind. Garrett intended returning to university. His obligation as heir important to him. I'm believing you need to fathom that fact, if you do not already."

Lady Darnley asked, "What did she say? I know so little Irish."

Lord Darnley growled, "Pregnant, my dear. She discovered she was with child."

Nuala continued, "We planned that after our wedding we would live with our respective families until the time came when this might happen. We were shocked when two *babaís* were born then, were we not, and totally unprepared. He took our son to the Molloys, and our daughter stayed with me. I intended to keep her. We desperately prayed the penal laws would loosen between the Protestants and the Catholics. Naturally, our *nai onáns* changed that. We agonized over it."

Lord Darnley leaned over to his wife, "*Infants*, my dear."

Continuing, her fingers twisted with her tale. Her shoulders stiffened, and she shuffled from shoe to shoe, perhaps because of his lordship's gruff manner. "My parents worsened, and I worried over the health of my precious child. Garrett arranged her baptism and afterward straight away left for university. I took her to the nuns up on the Suir. Eventually my parents died, and my beloved Garrett died as well. I did write to him of Mairéad and where I placed her. I was not sure he received my letter. In the end, with his death, I knew she was safe in the convent."

Wordless, Mairéad waved the air in a gesture meant to dismiss Nuala. Her heart squeezed shut.

Lord Darnley noted Mairéad's ashen face and glanced at Mrs. Atkinson. "Show her the door."

Shoulders sagging with resignation, Nuala turned to leave.

Mairéad's mind in a state of shock and disbelief, her gaze

shifted to the retreating woman, the hem of her blue wool gown stained with mud.

Sullen and angry, provoked to reveal a deep-seated war that raged within her, Mairéad spewed, "My experience of a mother is one bent toward a stern matriarch with rigid leanings. A woman who cannot show kindness nor love. A woman incapable of forgiveness toward others." She sprang off the settee, arms crossed as if she tried to control her rage. "I am trying to piece together our conversations in the chapel and reconcile you more fully. You are a softer, more understanding woman than the one who raised me, but that does not signify you as a mother."

As Mairéad's raspy words spilled across the room, Nuala glanced over her shoulder. Anxiety creasing her face. "My darling. I wronged you in my feeble attempt to protect you."

"You could have come for me. We could have been mother and daughter. You tell a convincing story, but I find it extraordinary to believe after eighteen years." Her sense of betrayal overwhelmed her. "We-we sat in the chapel together, talking. Why not then? Why now?"

Nuala's shoulders sagged with the loss of credibility. Regret thickened her voice. "At the time, I knew you would be eighteen soon, the twenty-first of last September. Was it not better to wait for you to belong to yourself?"

Disbelief crowded Mairéad's ability to accept the excuse. Rutledge was her brother? Could that be true? There was a tiny ring to it, something he said that night in her chamber when he was angry and drunk. Something about how he came to tell her the truth. The tingling, the tightness in her chest caught her breath. She glared at the woman who said she was her mother.

Nuala's posture straightened as if taking pride in her disclosure. Maybe relieved at loosening the hold on her secret after eighteen years? It was hard to read her soft features. Her dark eyes flashed with her story, and her fingers clutched near white.

Nuala's voice barely a whisper, she admitted, "I often lit the candle on the window of the two women and prayed for courage to tell the truth. I prayed, fearful because you'd not know our ways, our heritage."

The parlor grew quiet, neither of the Darnleys disallowed Nuala her disclosure. The woman's confession impacted them as it did her. The blood flow of truth—if it was the truth.

The woman's voice picked up strength. "Mairéad, your name has come down through the centuries on this land on which Rockmore Hall is built. Rockmore, though mightily changed and enlarged, was called Carrigmore Hall, wasn't it, back in the day, then." She paused, keeping her dark questioning gaze riveted on the lass.

"You've my mother's name. As does each generation of women in my family. I, Fionnuala, have my grandmother's. The O'Bannons go back centuries on this land that was taken from us by that mighty king and given to the Wallingtons in the sixteenth century."

This woman withheld far more than her paternity. Mairéad's bitterness extended to her voice. "You lit candles under the window of the picture of the two women. Never have I seen my name anywhere, yet it is on the window, and all the time, you saw fit not to tell me." Tears streamed down her cheeks her arms folded defensively across her chest. She sneered at the woman. "Do you have any idea how heavy my heart has been with no family of my own? I've dreamt of being a part of someone's life. People to whom I belonged, who were mine?" A great sob, born of years of longing poured from her, spilled across the short distance between them. "How could you keep me in ignorance?"

Nuala stepped from side to side, obviously anxious. "We wronged both of you. Wasn't what we intended. None of this sadness-sorrow-wasn't a'tall. I'm grieving with you, my dearest."

The parlor reeked with confession the inhabitants stunned at the disclosure.

Mairéad's voice hardened as she locked her gaze on Nuala. "If what you say is true, you would have me believe I have a surname? I've been reminded bastards do not have surnames."

"There is a signed certificate proving our marriage. It bears your last name. You were born a Wallington." She turned to Lord Darnley. "Garrett gave you a copy, did he not?"

"It could be forged. The one I have revealed only the initials F.O. Hardly proof in my estimation." Lord Darnley continued to sit, his hands gripping the arms of the chair as if he might spring forward and force her out.

Mairéad hugged herself. Tremaine reached for her, and she shied away, turning her back to them all, tears spilling down her cheeks. The handkerchief he handed her was put to good use.

He stood back, ready at a moment's notice to support her, showing no signs of skepticism. She found his trust shocking. What did he know of the years spent in the convent? Her heart clutched with grief.

She heard Lord Darnley stand and turned about to face him.

He said, "The decision is yours," he said. "What say you, lass? I'll have her escorted out if you wish it."

Nuala's brow wrinkled with confusion. What was it Mairéad discerned? Though the woman stayed grounded on the carpet where she turned back from leaving, was there an inkling of truth in what she confessed?

Mairéad focused hard on the woman. "'Tis hard to reconcile what is truth and what is mockery."

Nuala unfolded her hands, stepped forward, causing Mairéad to retreat, as if the woman was deranged.

Tremaine put his hands on Mairéad's shoulders. "I'm here."

Nuala stood firm with a voice to match, "If you are my daughter as I've declared, then you bear the mark of a heart on your chest. You were but a wee day old when I did that so that I would always know that you are mine should you disappear from the convent. I deemed it an eternal way to identify my daughter. I carved my chest as well, to match. I also carved a heart on the wall of Dark Castle, the place of your baptism."

Mairéad's palms slid to the cambric of her bodice that covered her left breast, fingers fanning out as she stumbled backward.

Tremaine's strong hands caught her.

Mother Abbess's sensibilities were disgusted about the mark on Mairéad. It caused the nun to occasionally rail about heathen rituals and the barbaric and unchristian symbol on Mairéad's body, leaving Mairéad with the sense she was devil spawn.

This woman declared it to be a symbol of love, a way to find her daughter in the years to come. A gasp and then sobs wracked her to the point that Tremaine's strong arms held her as he whispered words of comfort.

Lady Darnley grumbled at his lordship. "Enough. End this. Look at our darling, pale as a spirit. This is too much for her."

Nuala admitted, "I've never in my life revealed what I did until this moment. As God is my witness."

Mairéad twisted the handkerchief. "I-I was told it was the mark of an evil ritual that heathens performed on my body." The anguish of her sobs filled the room. "After all these years ... you say it is not so."

Grateful for Tremaine's strong arms, she would crumble without his firm grasp.

"It is clear you have lived without even a whisper of who you are. I could not allow Garrett's daughter to live in a dirt floor cottage with one window, now could I. You are *grá mo chrai*, Mairéad Wallington. I did it for you."

Mairéad's tears quieted, and now were again in full force. Nuala called her *my beloved*, yet, Mairéad's body was unwilling to release the devastation of being left on a doorstep because she was unwanted, unloved. The fear this was a lie, kept her rigid.

Lady Darnley held up her hand as her husband was about to translate for her. "I am familiar with the endearment."

Mrs. Atkinson spoke up from where she stood against the wall. "I just realized I practically witnessed your baptism, Mairéad. When I was quite young, I walked past Dark Castle that day. The sun was low in the sky. I saw the priest and Lord Rutledge as they left separately, then a woman carrying an infant came out. It was the twenty-second of September. After they left, I snooped inside and found a warm candle and a tin of frankincense, and, yes, the heart carved in the wall."

Nuala's eyes widened with amazement. "You were Shanna O'Key, curious and meddlesome, I recall. You stood off the road, watching us leave my daughter's baptism. I prayed you did not recognize us. All these years we've been in and out of each other's lives, in the village and when I visited the chapel and Garrett's stone. I was afraid you would begin to suspect the ties that bound us."

"Only recently did the likelihood unfold," said Mrs. Atkinson, a weak smile of admittance playing on her features. "When you came to me this morning seeking this audience, I wondered at the possibility."

Lord Darnley asked his housekeeper, "What brought on your suspicions?"

"Well, in those days, I admit being a bit into everyone's business, and took note of Lord Rutledge and Nuala together in the village. Exchanging happy glances, made me wish I'd such a handsome suitor. To my young self, she was the luckiest colleen alive. After Rutledge's tragic death and her visits to the graveyard began." Glancing at Nuala, she continued. "She always visited the chapel, but after his death she began visiting the graveyard, too, singing to the air around his stone."

A shrug of her shoulders, and a glance at his lordship, she went on. "It all began to add up. When you, my lord, announced your grandson some years ago, I immediately recalled the memory of the bundle Nuala carried from Dark Castle so long ago. Never would I have suspected two babies."

As Mrs. Atkinson spoke, Mairéad searched Nuala's face, locking on her dark eyes. This woman came here in faith. Perhaps her heart is broken, too. Losing her husband when no one even knew they were married, save the Protestant reverend and the rogue priest. In those days, a Catholic priest would be hard pressed to lie, and yet he would have been forced to if he valued his life.

Silent, Nuala stood, hands clasped, resignation etched on her features.

Mairéad softly inquired, "It must have taken great strength to come here today and reveal yourself."

A curt nod attesting to the truth was all she offered.

Mairéad added, "The truth is I do have a tiny heart on my breast."

Her hands prayer like, Lady Darnley gasped, "Oh, my dear." Tears began sliding down her face.

Her husband, hands folded across his stomach, looked as if his whole world opened up.

Mrs. Atkinson swiped at her nose and eyes with a linen kerchief Tremaine handed her.

He, having stood the entire time, leaned toward Nuala. "In today's world your marriage certificate holds credibility. The penal laws are less stringent, thankfully."

Lady Darnley catching her breath sweetly declared to Mairéad, "You are an O'Bannon, then? A direct descendent. What a magnificent history."

Witham stepped inside the parlor, no doubt waiting for the right time to announce luncheon.

His lordship stood slowly, "Witham, allow me to introduce Fionnuala, Lady Rutledge. Turning to her, he said, "It would be our honor if you will grace us with your presence at table."

Lady Darnley scolded, "You'll have to have the papers legitimized before proclaiming anyone anything. Much like you did Rutledge's birth."

"Ha, that will go smoothly as I already had the marriage certificate authenticated when we found out about Ayden. Which authenticated his mother, though she was only known as F. O. The discovery of Mairéad's lineage will be merely a formality, mark my words." He glanced over the top of his glasses. "Fionnuala, Lady Rutledge, get used to it."

It took her a moment before she realized his lordship addressed her. Mairéad noted the questioning in her dark eyes, the puzzled brow. Whatever this woman expected from her grave admissions, a title and dinner were obviously not in her wildest dreams.

Mairéad went to Nuala, taking up her hands and pressed her lips against the workworn knuckles. "Please say yes, máthair."

Nuala's eyes filled with emotion as she nodded to the invitation, obviously not trusting herself to speak.

Tremaine stepped between the two, holding out an arm to each, and the threesome followed the Darnleys down the hall.

Lord Darnley leaned over to his wife. "She said—"

"Yes, yes, yes. I know máthair," she said as she lifted the hem of her dark green silk.

By the time they reached the dining room, Witham had added one more setting.

Lord Darnley waited until all were seated. "I want to say a prayer." Clearing his throat, all eyes upon him, he bowed his head. "Dear Lord, thank you for Nuala's strength in *You* that led her to come here this day. Though I suspected the truth, we now know we have a granddaughter and a daughter-in-law, both of whom we would never have known. Thank you for the gift of family and for this food."

A chorus of *Amens* followed.

Tremaine teased Lord Darnley. "You slipped it in while invoking the Almighty that you suspected the truth all along. Not very humble, my lord."

Her ladyship laughed. "He gets high and mighty sometimes, needs to be settled back into place."

Darnley cast his gaze to the ceiling as if in despair. "I have a defense. I began to suspect when Witham discovered a batch of letters in Garrett's old room. One began with mention of putting *Mairéad* into the convent, with no explanation of who *Mairéad* was. All the letters were signed F.O. I did recall the marriage certificate was signed F.O."

Nuala spoke up. "Garrett was concerned about our precious daughter. He knew the trials ahead with my parents and suggested the convent as a temporary placement. He was not—well, neither of us were—ready to face the consequences of what we'd done. If our family hadn't begun so quickly, we might have handled our decisions differently."

Tremaine added, "Isn't it remarkable how a few years can change society's attitudes?"

Her ladyship said, "The hatred bred for centuries because Henry VIII wanted to divorce his Catholic wife and remarry."

"A toast," Tremaine said, raising his glass, his attention across the table at Mairéad "To Nuala's forbearance, without which we would not have true knowledge of her daughter."

Mairéad reached for her mother's hand as tears again stung their eyes.

A delicious stew with maize dumplings followed by roast leg of lamb with apple and mint jelly, yeasty rolls with spun butter, and stuffing filled with raisins, walnuts, and apples. Dessert, served later in the library, was to be a lemon sorbet with sugar cookies that would end the extraordinary day.

Mairéad noticed Nuala was rather quiet and inquired about how she was feeling.

She whispered, "I never gave it an inkling to be called máthair."

Her shyness caused her to appear pitiably vulnerable. Mairéad could hardly imagine the strength it took to tell the story of her marriage and all the tragedy that followed. As much as Mairéad yearned for a family, this woman gave up both children, and then lost her husband, and almost at the same time, her parents. The depth of her solitude and pain was unimaginable.

Lord Darnley gestured for Witham. "Inform Shamus that Lady Rutledge will need the carriage when she is ready to leave."

The look on her máthair's face caused Mairéad to whisper. "Quite the title, when you most likely would prefer Nuala."

Lady Darnley grinned. "You'll get used to it."

Mairéad whispered, "I believe they are more than pleased you were inspired to reveal yourself."

"I turned back twice, then, surprising myself, I turned about, putting one foot in front of the other, thinking I might be heading toward hellfire, not Rockmore. Do or die it comes down to. What put a spur in my walk was knowing you had come back and might leave again. I did not want to chance that. I was heartbroken when you left last fall, and I didn't have my nerve up." She glanced about the table, grown quiet as she spoke.

"It is all right, máthair." That one word caused her throat to tighten.

Lady Darnley said, "You brought us a future. We share the losses, and we will share the happiness."

Mairéad gasped, "*Seanmháthair* and *Seanathair*. I just realized.*"

Lord Darnley leaned toward his wife. "She said—"

Lady Darnley held her hand up. "I know what she said. I have been sitting through this meal, waiting for it to come to her." She cast a devilish grin at Mairéad. "I am partly teasing, my dear," and tried to wink, instead batting both eyes.

Tremaine stood and raised a toast to Mairéad. "To a young lady who found something she wasn't even looking for. Family. Not only are you a Wallington but an O'Bannon."

She was toasted with laughter and love.

Lady Darnley remarked, "Philly will never forgive me."

Tremaine, who took a backseat until now, turned to Mairéad. "I am curious. You have not once mentioned taking your vows—"

A shriek rent the air. Nuala, who sat on the other side of Mairéad, squawked, "No. No. You did not, tell me quickly, I need the knowing." Her wrist covered her mouth, and her eyes grown big as saucers. "I did not mean to scream, but there was a note in your basket, and I did not think the nuns would go against my wishes for you."

Lady Darnley's fork was halfway to her mouth. Lord Darnley's wineglass held in midair.

Tremaine's hand brushed hers. Mairéad realized how important her vows were to this newly acquired family.

Shaking her head, she said, "It was selfish of me, but in the end, I could not do so."

An audible gasp rent the air, with a few grateful *thanks* whispered.

All eyes were upon her as she added, "I was incapable of making a commitment that would not assure me enough freedom to be with all of you."

His lordship lifted his crystal goblet, the red wine sparkling in the candlelight. "Did you suspect your ancestral ties?"

"Not an inkling, though Rutledge said something quite unusual the last time we were together. He said he would have told me a deep, dark secret, but that my flippant manner changed his mind."

"That didn't spur your interest?"

"Of course, it does now, but how would he have known? He probably referred to something else."

Nuala said, "There were times in the past when Rutledge stood across Market from my shop. I spotted him through the windows as I worked. I knew who he was, of course. Now that you mention he held a secret, it does beg the question, did he know? If so, how would he have come upon the knowledge?" She leaned in with both arms on the linen, pondering questions never to be answered.

Each of them seemed to digest this and rue the circumstance that took Rutledge to his end. Secrets can destroy, and he most likely was just such a victim. Mairéad slipped her hand into her máthair's. No words were necessary.

She knew what not taking vows meant to Tremaine. She also knew what that meant for her. Her heart flip-flopped as she met his piercing blue gaze.

"We have to talk, you and I." His pensive expression gone his words wrapped in a silky baritone.

Her skin tingled at the masculine weight of his voice.

23

Before she left, Nuala invited Mairéad and Lady Darnley to tea the next day. Lady Darnley had not been to Hawthorn Village since before her self-imposed seclusion. Adding to her excitement was seeing first-hand many of the changes of which Darnley kept her abreast.

After luncheon, Nuala left.

Tremaine suggested to Mairéad, "In view of all that has happened, I think riding this afternoon might be out of the question."

"Do I detect a man concerned he might be outridden?"

Glancing at his watch, he asked, with a glint of mischief in his eye, "Does half past two agree with you?"

At the appointed time, Tremaine met Mairéad at the stable where grooms waited with Caomh and Hungas. Lord Darnley expressly asked Tremaine if he would ride the stallion. As they raced toward the village, past low land filled with bog cotton, Tremaine reined in Hungas.

Jumping off his mount, he lifted Mairéad off the saddle. Her gloved hands spread to his shoulders and their gazes locked. The horses nibbled at the sweet grass, and a gentle wind ruffled the leaves of scrub hawthorn and oak.

A breathless moment overtook him. A future with this woman was now a possibility. "All this time I thought you'd taken vows."

She cupped his cheek, and her lips tenderly touched his, stirring dormant passion. Slipping an arm about her waist, he held her close. She traced his nose and brows with a fingertip, then his lips.

"Kiss me," his gravelly voice directed.

"Allow me to enjoy your handsome features. I've dreamt of this moment for months. Don't rush me."

His laugh muffled at her scrutiny when she pressed her lips to his. His hand tightened on her waist the other slid to the back of her head.

A groan trilled from his throat as he quickened the embrace. Moments of gilded possibility swirled until he drew back and gently kissed her eyes and cheeks, his warm breath mingling with hers. She stilled his face and forced his lips back to hers. A whirlwind of passion engulfed them until Tremaine deliberately stepped back, causing her to sigh.

Her radiant smile teased him. "Do you see stars when we kiss?"

"*Stars*? I'm besotted with you." His voice low and thick, he cuddled her in an embrace, "Are you willing to marry me after I graduate?"

"You never left my thoughts these past months." Her voice muffled against his woolen riding jacket a brass button tickled her nose. "I'm quite willing."

"You're muttering into my waistcoat."

Glancing up at him she teased, "If I must repeat myself, it will cost you another kiss."

He picked her up, twirling them about. "You're rather bossy."

Her laughter caught in the slight breeze as he grabbed her by the waist and kissed her again. Eventually drawing apart they sat on the grass and he declared, "I will ask your grandfather for his blessing."

She twirled a blade of grass between two fingers. "Of course. I have family now, and he is the head."

Tremaine chuckled. "You could not have a more noble and loving family."

Silence set in as they pondered the moment, until he commented, "This place makes our proposal more fitting, don't you think?"

Her gaze swept over the rolling hills, and the stone wall where she'd dismounted that fateful day...a year since now. Picking at another wildflower she reminisced, "It's a good thing I didn't take vows. I would be without a handsome proposal now, wouldn't I?"

He chuckled, "Have you a grain of compassion for what you put me through? I nearly failed my last exam my mind was in such a frenzy. Why?"

"Why I ignored your questions about taking vows?" casting him a side glance, a lilt of teasing salted her voice.

He nodded.

"If you cared enough, you would not falter. I was right, now wasn't I?"

A glower in the set of his chin, he agreed.

"If there was going to be anything between us, I needed us to be face-to-face. I hoped it would be just the two of us if you were to ask again."

"If I hadn't, what then?" He turned away, but not before she caught the twitch of his lips.

"Probably fainting. Sister Davideena says faint if all else fails."

He leaned close to her. "I was the object of gossip at the convent?"

"I told no one about my feelings, but Sister Davideena has an uncanny intuition."

"As a medical man. That little trick of fainting might have worked."

"What would be your remedy, Lord Medical Man?" she wheedled.

His arm lowered to her back. He turned her into his elbow and lifted her chin. "This." His eyes searching her face as their lips met.

There came a moment in the passionate embrace when he deliberately drew back. His palm caressing her cheek. "You are a precious composite of child and woman. Your heart brims with love for all. You are kind and caring, yet stubborn and can be roused to ire. Material wealth pales in comparison to gathering people about you. You fascinate me to the core."

Her emerald eyes glistened, "Lovely words, my lord. Why do I feel there's something unsaid."

His fingertip tapped the end of her nose. "Precisely my love, which is why we've embraced enough for now. I'm but a man, who *wants* you in all ways."

As enlightenment dawned, the heat of a deep blush spread over her cheeks. Without words to express, she turned away from him.

His warm hand fell to her shoulder. "Are you going to faint?"

She couldn't look at him just then. "No."

He chuckled, "Good."

A burst of giggles shot from her as she gave him a brilliant smile.

He said, "You're a clever pippin. I believe I've just received my first of many lessons in the working of your mind?"

Her brows rose. "Don't you have a sister? Seems you would have already known about women."

"Rowan is a bit older than I. Married with three children. I don't remember her at your age."

"Oh, well then, if I must, I'll take on the responsibility of acquainting you." Her tone utterly serious until she burst into laughter at the dour look on his face.

A tense moment passed before his eyes rolled, and said, "It's worse than I thought, is it?" He got to his knees and pulled her up with him.

On the return to Rockmore Hall, they walked the horses awhile and rehashed the life-changing revelations from this morning.

The sun, beginning to lower, cast a soft golden glow, dappling the forest and path they strode.

She mused, "Do I really have a mother? Is that really my ancestry on the window in the chapel? Are Lord and Lady Darnley truly my grandparents? Did my máthair marry again? Do I have siblings?"

"I thought your silence was in pondering our kiss."

"In a sense, because of you I'm thinking about my own life. I know who you are, a solid, strong man, secure in your life. My ground shifted this morning like the earth quaking."

He reached for her hand, squeezing. "So, it did, my lovely. Your many questions, no doubt will be answered tomorrow?" He shortened his steps.

"It is what I intend."

A few minutes later, on the path leading past the graveyard, he asked, "Don't you think it a little odd that Darnley said, *I knew it* when Nuala announced there were two babies?"

With lips pursed, she contemplated the last evening with Rutledge, and nodded. She could not speak ill of the dead, of a brother, her twin.

"I am honored to have been a part of her revelations. Watching you work through disbelief, anger, and then slow acceptance. I wouldn't have wanted to be anywhere else." He stopped walking and faced her, "You are so much more than I already knew. A woman of grace and strength."

She glanced at this handsome man who would one day be her husband, admiring his warm smile, a lock of flaxen hair that always seemed about to fall over his brow, and his eyes, a dark blue at the moment, filled with a mischievous glint. "It matters a great deal to me that you were by my side."

⚜

Her ladyship swept through the foyer on her way to breakfast in a glorious display of bright blue skirts and lacy bodice, complimented with a short strand of pearls. "How is everyone this morning?"

Taking her seat, she gave instructions to a footman: "Tea and one piece of toast lightly buttered and a pot of strawberry jam. And two pieces of ham." Then turned her attention to Tremaine. "Do you have plans while we visit Lady Rutledge?"

"Lord Darnley and I are discussing a Mr. Stephenson, who has developed a system with the potential to move goods and people from one place to another."

She set her cup in the saucer. "He devours *The Freeman*. Has it posted to him and the *London Times* as well, though it's a week old when it arrives. He looks for information on a—I think it is a locomotive. Do you know enough to keep him entertained?"

"It is the talk. Could be a revolutionary endeavor, from what I hear."

Lady Darnley's finger traced the rim of the saucer, as she expressed, "I am thankful he has recovered to the point he is interested in something."

Mairéad mentioned, "His conversation is normal. Prayers do get answered."

"You might hear a lisp now and again. He continues to rely on the cane for support. Minor from what Mr. O'Reilly has seen in other patients."

"Darnley has always shown a keen attitude for industry. I will do my best, but the probability is, he will know far more than I." Tremaine turned his attention to Mairéad. "I'll be interested to know how your visit goes. I think you are in for a real surprise from what we witnessed yesterday."

⚅⚄⚅

Tremaine knocked and entered Darnley's inner sanctum. His nose buried in the newsprint just as predicted, Darnley folded the paper and nodded, "How are things in Scotland?"

"Quite well. If all goes as planned, I should graduate next year at this time."

"Remind me of the name of your colleague?"

"Christopher Curran."

"That's the one. Do you continue to plan a medical center in Waterford?"

Tremaine crossed a leg over his knee and sat back in the chair. "Yes. In fact, Christopher will be returning to Ireland by the end of next week and has made arrangements to talk to several people about a building that would suit us."

"Have you considered Hawthorn Village rather than Waterford?"

"We talked about it. Waterford has a doctor in residence. With the population growing, the town could easily support two more, but we did discuss Hawthorn. The decision isn't final."

"The last I knew the village mayor is promoting the need for a medical man."

"Christopher graduates this winter. I will make sure he is aware."

"Your father does not attempt to dissuade you?"

Tremaine kept his voice neutral. "He would like to, but I don't see a hindrance when the time comes for me to inherit. That is where your questioning is leading, am I right?"

Darnley chuckled. "Since Rutledge's demise, I'm forced to think of the future. Your father is, of course, heir presumptive to both title and land. I believe you know that."

"He wrote."

Darnley said, "Then you are aware of your responsibilities in the future?"

"You are referring to my dedication to medicine?" At Darnley's nod, he continued. "I see no hindrance. Christopher is aware of my other duties in the far distant future. He would not expect anything less of me. I am not good at dawdling, sir. I need to be involved."

"You've set yourself quite a course. I do think your abilities are your strength. Since you were a young lad, you've proved yourself. Though heartbroken over the loss of my grandson, I could not be more grateful it is your father, and then you, who will inherit."

"Yesterday's revelations must have given you and Lady Darnley a great deal of comfort. All these years, so close and yet so far beyond belief."

"We talked for hours. Once we began, well, I certainly can be forthright. It wasn't just Nuala's revelations. Garrett's deliberate passing and the discovery we had a grandson, Lady Darnley's isolation for nearly twenty years. You must recall, it was the initial tragedy that spiraled her out of control. To top off all the drama, Witham's discovery of those old letters of Garrett's put me in a spin. Though they left no real clues to anything, I perceived a monumental curiosity about an infant named Mairéad who lived in a convent.

"And what have we now? A granddaughter, a daughter-in-law. And most of all, promise for the future." Lowering his chin and glancing down the length of his nose, Darnley locked his gaze on the young man.

Tremaine leaned forward. "I need to say how sorry I am that I didn't try harder with Rutledge."

"What happened was a tragedy to be sure, but one I am convinced was in the making for years. Do not berate the friendship you offered. He was a tortured soul. We can only hope he has found peace."

The morning was cloudy, a bit of mist in the air. The carriage taking Mairéad and Lady Darnley to Chadwick Lane gently swayed as they progressed toward Hawthorn Village.

The first time Mairéad rode in this carriage, her grandfather had taken her from the convent.

Rockmore Hall was almost directly north and a bit east of the village. The distance between was scattered with a cluster of mud huts built in the cutaway of a bog, several with a goat or two standing in the doorway and hens pecking in the loamy ground as their carriage rolled past.

Straight ahead, the lough came into view, its surface rippled with an April wind. Fish jumped, snapping at mayflies in early hatch. Two boys on a raft busied themselves with lines, hoping to surprise their mother with dinner, no doubt. Overcast with a gray sky, the scene appeared dark and gloomy.

Lady Darnley turned her gaze from the lough to Mairéad. "This is my first visit to the village since before …"

"Since you retired to your apartment," Mairéad suggested.

"Yes, my dear. I am curious about the shops. Market Street was lined with them. I need some thread for my cross stitching. I'm sure Nuala will know where I should look. It's a quaint village. Hardly anyone is a stranger as I recall."

The carriage slowed, drawing their attention to the surroundings. Little bells tinkled as sheep scattered. A black and white patched herder dog barked commands, nibbling at the stick-like legs, forcing the plaintive, bleating animals to move forward. Far off, they could see the shepherd on his perch atop a rocky embankment, staff in hand and whistle at the ready. It was amazing that he could work his herd from so far away, using a whistle to command the dog, who, in turn, controlled the herd.

Within minutes the road cleared and Huet snapped the reins and off they went. Soon to come upon a group of men cutting turf and setting the blocks to dry. The convent used peat for heat and cooking fires. Mairéad was quite familiar with the red smoky flame and strong scent. Modernized, Rockmore Hall used coal brought in by the wagonload and kept in the back of the stable and then carted into the hall as needed.

Further on, the curl of chimney smoke off in the distance and dark clouds, heavy with rain, against the backdrop of sheer beauty as the landscape rolled toward the Suir.

"Oh, my." A gloved hand went to her cheek as she turned to her grandmother.

"What?"

"Mother Abbess will be speechless."

Her grandmother reached over and squeezed her hand. "You will handle her with all the respect and love you have always shown her, my dear."

The carriage turned onto Forge Street, where a horse and carriage stable on the right seemed a prosperous business. As they rode past, a board above the large entrance read *Carnahan's*. They turned onto Chadwick Lane, one of the few cobbled streets, passed over Strawberry Hill, then Rocky Lane, and eventually came to a halt in front of a two-story cottage surrounded by a stone wall about four feet high. A red gate and cobbled path led to a matching stone entryway with an A-frame roof on the front, perpendicular to the cottage roof. A matching red door with brass bell was inviting. Stucco plastered walls, and red shutters were quite charming. The rustic thatched roof, a symmetrical design woven into the reeds, and smoke curling from the chimney was most welcoming.

It dawned on Mairéad the woman who sang to an empty grave was far more of a gentle woman than she originally thought.

24

Huet tossed the reins to the page and clamored down from his seat. Their arrival appeared to cause a bit of a commotion on the lane with neighbors' curtains ruffling as they satisfied their curiosity.

Nuala, Lady Rutledge, stood on the threshold, red door wide in hospitality. Wearing a light green day gown trimmed in lace, her hair pinned in braids woven into buns over her ears, and a welcoming smile on her face, was not the woman Mairéad knew from the chapel.

Warmly greeting them, Nuala offered Huet the hospitality of her kitchen, also suggesting Maher's on Sister's Lane or the Black Pig on Stoney Batter, which he readily acknowledged was a favorite. Placing a cap on his head and leaving the page to tend the horses, he strutted on down the road.

Struck by the reality that she was in her máthair's parlor, Mairéad devoured the portraits of what must be her mother's parents above the hearth and flanked by silver candlesticks. White lace curtains on the windows facing Chadwick Lane allowed for privacy. Whitewashed walls were a neutral backdrop for a lovely carved mahogany cabinet filled with odd bits of memories. Many fine pieces of furniture filled the room for leisure and function. A thick carpet, woven into a pattern of pink and green vines and flowers, covered the hardwood floor.

The room opened into a dining area through a large curved entry. The outer wall lined with leaded windows allowed an easterly view of a well-tended garden. She did not know what to expect, certainly something humbler. Noises and conversation drifted into the parlor from the kitchen at the back, indicated servants at work.

With a cheery voice Lady Darnley said, "I confess, I am delighted to be here, my lady. You are full of surprise."

Mairéad was in a bit of a daze. Her máthair, this lovely cottage, presiding over tea, directing servants, the normalcy confounded her. She squelched a giggle. Normalcy? This way of life wasn't normal to her not so very long ago.

Tea and watercress sandwiches were served by a maid in starched cap and apron.

Lady Darnley asked, "Is this where you lived with my son?"

"We never really lived together. It was originally my grandparents' dwelling, added onto during my parents' life. Garrett returned to school shortly after our marriage. When I wrote the news of expecting, he arranged to stay here late that summer until after the birth before returning to university. That was when we made our plans. And, it was also the only time we lived together."

Lady Darnley asked, "Do I recall he didn't seem in a hurry to get back to University?"

"He was concerned about me and worried I would over do. The problem was my sickly parents. Sight was taken from my father, my mother nearly so."

Mairéad was consumed with interest. *Her máthair* was talking about the time before her birth, hers and Rutledge's. All these years she craved this—to listen to her *máthair* talk about an unknown past. It took on the aspects of a miracle.

"Your son was very kind and loving. He arranged for a couple to stay with my parents the last several months while I moved to a small cottage on the outskirts of Portlaw." Her soft gaze rested on her daughter. "It was there the *nai onáns* were born. We were so proud, and no one with whom to share our fortune. The decisions did not come easy and were intended as a temporary solution until Garrett graduated. He found the Molloy's willing. He quickly arranged for Mairéad's baptism and then immediately returned to school. I took her to the convent the next day and returned to the care of my parents."

Lady Darnley finished, "And Garrett sailed for the university?"

Nuala's gaze fell to her hands. She did not look up as she nodded.

Glancing at the saddened Lady Darnley, Mairéad said, "And you retreated to the fourth floor of Rockmore."

A collective sigh filled the air.

Mairéad asked, "Was my brother baptized?"

Nuala took in a deep breath. "When Garrett took him to the Molloy's, he asked that they have him baptized. I assume they would have, but don't know what faith."

Lady Darnley's soft voice filled with wonder. "I may shock you both, but it doesn't matter which faith, as long as he was baptized. We are survivors. United through my son, we are not alone, nor ever shall be again. I am convinced of your love for him. Through the years, I can't count the number of times I saw you walk to the chapel, quite a distance. Now I understand why."

A blush spread on Nuala's cheeks. "I enjoy the stroll. Especially in the early evenings, day almost done. A time of reflection as the sun sets." She glanced at Mairéad. "I think you enjoy the evening stroll, too."

Enchanted with her máthair, she was eager to have similarities.

Lady Darnley set her cup aside. "I must say, the two of you are alike. None more obvious than your facial structure. With a wee bit of imagination, I see sisters."

Nuala chuckled. "No offense, but ye'd have to stretch that imagination all the way to Hook Head and back, my lady."

"What have your neighbors and friends to say about finding your daughter, and your marriage to Garrett?"

Her brow knit as she took a moment to reply. "The truth of it, I've never put voice to any of it. Mainly because I've held it for so long, telling others seems an odd thing to do."

Her grandmother nodded in understanding and sipped her tea, long since cooled with all her questioning.

"I have something to share." Nuala went into the dining room and returned with an oil painting. "Garrett—I should ask, do you mind that I call him Garrett?

"Heaven's no. He was your husband, after all."

A sweet smile of relief swept over her features. "He painted this for me." She held up a self-portrait.

Gasping, Lady Darnley held fingertips to her open mouth. "Oh, my. Himself, with his favorite, Gunnar." She turned to Mairéad. "Your father's Arabian black. He was a beauty and would let none other ride him, and that's the Wallington Crest in the corner." She fell silent, admiring her son's likeness.

Nuala leaned the portrait against the arms of a chair, where they could enjoy looking at him.

Her father was truly handsome with his black hair drawn into a queue and deep-set blue eyes. His blouse loosely tucked, one hand on the reins and the other on his hip, he appeared self-assured. A slight grin filled his face, as if Nuala, off in the distance walked toward him.

Lady Darnley said, "Look at the likeness between Garrett and Rutledge. Oh my, they could be brothers."

Nuala offered, "Would you like the portrait?"

"No. no." She fidgeted with her gloves as if embarrassed, "I could not take it from you, but I would know your reason for keeping it out of sight."

"My neighbor's questions, now wouldn't they have a bundle of them? I do take it out at night, after I visit his stone. I sip a bit of mulberry wine and think of what could have been."

Lady Darnley's face crinkled with sadness. "My dear, dear woman, I can't imagine your suffering."

Nuala lightly touched the frame, as if to caress him. "I have lovely memories." Glancing at Mairéad, she added, "I always knew where my daughter and son were, safe and cared for."

Lady Darnley tapped Mairéad's arm. "A number of Garrett's works hang at Rockmore. I'll have to point them out to you."

Mairéad said, "Perhaps that is where my interest in illuminating came from. Do you think that possible?"

"I would not discount it, my dear. Artistic endeavors have been known to follow through generations." She lifted her chin, sheepishly grinning at her granddaughter. "If 'tis the case, you acquired a useful talent."

Nuala said, "You just reminded me of something I know you will be interested in. Excuse me again, please."

For the first time in her life, Mairéad sensed she had a father. She also comforted herself with the knowledge he was a good horseman. Perhaps she inherited that trait as well.

Nuala eventually returned to the parlor with a small box. "Garrett made one for me and one for our daughter." She dangled two lockets from gold chains.

Lady Darnley sighed, "You are reminding me of his tender heart." She dabbed at a bit of wetness in the corners of her eyes.

Mairéad knelt before her grandmother. "You loved him so. Nuala makes his life real for both of us."

She dabbed at her nose with the lacy kerchief and patted her granddaughter. "I have you to thank I am not stuck in that apartment."

Her máthair's gaze widened, and Mairéad explained, "She took refuge on the top floor of Rockmore Hall for many years after his death."

Nuala settled her loving gaze on the older woman. "Ahh. We each loved him, and it was difficult to reconcile when he was no longer."

Lady Darnley waved her damp kerchief. "Show me what you have there. My curiosity has taken over."

"I did not intend to make you sad, my lady."

"No, no. It's my age, I think."

Nuala laughed outright. "I would rather believe it's your loving heart."

She showed one locket to Lady Darnley and the other to Mairéad. "If you open them, you'll see how precious they are."

Already overwhelmed with the visit, Mairéad gasped. "His hair! For me? My athair did this for me?"

"You were newly born, and he'd not left for university yet. Seeing as how one was a boy, we didn't think a son would want a locket. What of the likeness? Fairly well done, do you think, my lady? He used a mirror in a room upstairs to pose when painting."

Lady Darnley was busy using her kerchief once again. "He truly loved you, and that brings me a great deal of comfort, because now that I've found you, I'm not letting you go. Fionnuala, Lady Rutledge." Her pale blue eyes lit with mischief as she spoke. "There, I've said it and dearly wish that he could hear me."

"Ah, my belief is that he can, my lady." The doorbell tinkled, and the maid scooted past the parlor archway, then announced, "Mrs. Bedford, ma'am."

The neighbor charged into the parlor on the heels of the maid, shoving a plate of sugar cookies with cherry jam into her hands. "I simply must talk to you about the linen purchased yesterday, its quality."

Indicating the plate of still-warm cookies, Nuala said, "Thank you. Allow me to introduce you to Lady Darnley and her granddaughter, Miss Wallington. My neighbor, Mrs. Bedford."

That was all the neighbor needed, and she promptly took the remaining chair in the parlor. "It's a beautiful day for a ride into the village, is it not? I regret my intrusion but find it necessary that Nuala know her linen is by far the best I've purchased, including some bought from Houlihan's in Waterford. I always say, if you have something pleasant to say, you need to share, and she has done exceptionally well."

Lady Darnley and Mairéad exchanged glances and raised eyebrows. Nuala, obviously flummoxed, said, "I have a shop and sell textiles." She turned to Mrs. Bedford. "Thank you for the compliment."

"Think nothing of it." Licking her lips, enjoying her intrusion, she inquired of Lady Darnley, "I am sorry to learn about Lord Darnley. Last summer was it now?" She did not wait for an answer. "He is recovering?"

"Yes, thank you. His lordship has always been robust."

"I didn't realize there was a granddaughter. It's a pleasure to meet you, Miss Wallington. Are you visiting?" She must have been exerting herself, as beads of perspiration covered her upper lip, and she dabbed at them with a linen kerchief.

"Yes, ma'am." Mairéad realized Mrs. Bedford was on a hunting expedition. Nuala remained calm, yet she sensed an undercurrent of regret that the woman barged in uninvited. "I wonder, Mrs. Bedford, what is it that you particularly like about the linen?"

"Tight weaving, no holes and the color she coaxes from her dyes. I don't know how she does it. I needed a periwinkle, and that is exactly what I received." Her vivacious, pink-skinned face turned to her host. "You didn't charge me extra to redo the last batch. It's why I brought over my famous sugar-jam cookies to thank you."

Lady Darnley gathered the locket into her hand, as did Mairéad. Mrs. Bedford might ask about them, and it wouldn't do. They intended to protect Nuala's story until she decided otherwise. Their shared history was too new to all of them. The village gossip, uncharitable as it sounds, will have to remain uninformed.

Huet's deep voice traveled the hallway from the kitchen. He must have had his fill of the Black Pig's camaraderie and now was in search of a tidbit or two from cook.

Mrs. Bedford, full of compliments, said, "O'Bannon's is the best dry goods store this side of the Suir. I would include County Kilkenny, too."

Lady Darnley realized the scope of the compliment, "I need needlepoint thread."

Mrs. Bedford interrupted. "Well, no finer place. Have your driver skip over to Market and Stephen's. It's on the corner. O'Bannons painted in bold letters across the lintel. You can't miss it."

Perhaps feeling as if she fulfilled her social obligation, Mrs. Bedford stood. "I must go. St. John's dinner tonight, and I'm in charge of supervision. I'd give ye a bit of neighborly advice, Nuala. You need to get out and mingle with folks. It would do ye good, as hard as ye work." Turning to Lady Darnley and Miss Wallington, she added, "I am pleased to make your acquaintance. Now I can put names to faces."

As she turned to leave, her gaze fell on the portrait in the chair. "My, my, a handsome man. Who might he be, then?" Her gaze swept the three faces staring at her.

Mairéad saved the day. "A wonderful man who has gone to his eternal reward."

Mrs. Bedford's mouth shaped like the letter O. As if a question was forming it in her mind.

Nuala, having her fill, grasped Mrs. Bedford by the elbow and led her to the door. "We appreciate your cookies. Thank you for your kindness. I do hope your evening at St. Johns is enjoyable."

Closing the door behind her, quiet gathered like a soft shawl and then twitters began.

"It seems a wind just blew through your parlor," Lady Darnley said, a faint smile on her lips.

Mairéad could not hold her curiosity in check another moment. "Tell us about your dry goods store. It must be quite an enterprise."

Settling into a chair, she said, "My life changed drastically when both parents died within days of each other. Suddenly, all the care, all the managing stopped. Like a door slams shut. Your father and I talked of our dreams. After my life settled, I took comfort in sitting by his stone, asking for guidance, didn't I? What was I to do with my life?"

Mairéad near whispered, "It would have been awkward to bring your children home."

"If ever I was to do so, that would have been the time. But the questions about the father...and I feared the gossip that would spread. Would folks believe me? And without having met you..." she glanced at Lady Darnley, "...I was uncertain what Garrett may have revealed in letters to you. I knew my *ba bais* would be safe and well cared for."

Running a palm over her lap, Nuala admitted, "Providence played a part. The next day Mrs. Dooley asked if I would be interested in her store? I used to weave with wool, cotton, and then linen fabrics. I liked trying out new dyes. Nothing fancy or exotic. It seemed God was providing me with a future with my carding combs and spinning wheel. I suppose it was my way to get on."

Lady Darnley set her cup down. "A remarkable story. You are truly a wonder. Darnley will be quite pleased to learn of your industry. I can hardly wait to tell him."

"You're certain he'll take to it? Some men, so I've found, think a woman is the one to sit at the hearth, stirring the fire."

"Pish posh. A wee man might be frightened. A real man would be proud. He mentioned last evening just before bed how grateful he was to have found you, a bit like bringing our son back to us."

Her máthair turned a quizzical gaze on Mairéad. "Speaking of real men, did I notice you are of particular interest to Lord Tremaine?"

Uneasy about the question, Mairéad turned to the windows rather than answer.

"Aha, I've hit a ticklish nerve and will pry no further. Though, I believe I have my answer."

Lady Darnley picked up her quizzing glass, inspecting Mairéad from across the way. "Is that a blush?"

"You expect me to share an intimacy with a grandmother and a mother who were not known to me less than twenty-four hours ago?" She grinned at both, and then took a bite of one of the sugar and cherry jam cookies the maid set on the table.

Tremaine waited for his lordship in the mahogany paneled library. He slowly made his way along the bookcases showcasing many artifacts from travels and awards.

The focus in this room was a giant Hawthorn that stood outside the bay of windows behind the desk. For as long as he could recall, Tremaine received numerous scratches playing in the branches. It was a majestic symbol of Ireland's past. And harbored memories of a childhood shared with Rutledge.

Darnley arrived with his brow puckered in question. "I expected you to be riding this time of day."

Tremaine neared the desk and took a seat. "I've something of import I wish to discuss with you."

The frown disappeared with raised bushy brows. "A mystery."

Tremaine tried to relax, but for some reason could not. What if Darnley somehow fixed it in his mind that it was not a good match? A puff of breath escaped. He straightened in the chair. Crossed his legs, uncrossed them.

"Get to it, Tremaine. You've got me on pins and needles."

"I wish to marry your granddaughter." A long slow breath followed.

"About time you got around to asking. You're sluggish as a turtle."

"Wha…!" Palpable relief swept over him.

"I am not blind, nor is Adrianna."

The weight of the world flew off his shoulders. "Does this mean you do not object?"

"Hardly, young man. It's a dream come true. We could not hope for a better match for either of you."

Tremaine shot out of his chair and leaned across Darnley's desk, hand out. "Thank you, my lord. Thank you. Thank you."

Darnley grabbed the hand in a firm shake. "Did you think we would be against a marriage between the two of you?"

"I wasn't certain. Considering my father is your heir

presumptive, it did occur to me you might want fresh blood."

"What occurs to me foremost is with Mairéad's marriage to you, she will live on the estate where her family was born. Rockmore title, land, and estate are entailed, and you know she could not inherit.

"Because she is my granddaughter, your declaration sweetens the pot. She will be safe and cared for by a man clearly in love with her."

The women's chatter from the foyer allowed that Lady Darnley and Mairéad returned from their visit. Cheeks rosy from the ride and gaiety spilling from constant conversation, they entered the library.

"Well, well, what have we here? Two chatterboxes. I would think your gossip would have run out by now," Lord Darnley exclaimed. With a smirk he added, "Anything that can be repeated?"

Tremaine remained standing as Mairéad and Lady Darnley tugged their ribbons, drew off their bonnets, handing them to a maid who followed close behind.

Lady Darnley said, "I can tell you Nuala is the owner of O'Bannons. Did you know that?"

"I suppose if I was into knitting or some such, I might, but it never occurred to me."

Tremaine cast a slanted look at Darnley, which caused her ladyship to spurt, and open palm to her heart. "Something has happened?"

His lordship said, "You have a suspicious mind. What makes you go to the dark side?"

Lady Darnley scowled, "Wally, don't fluster me. Tell me this instant."

With a grin the size of a quarter moon, he conceded, "Well, my dear, if you must know, a young man whom we have known his entire life has asked to wed our granddaughter."

Lady Darnley squeaked. "What has she to say about this?"

All eyes turned to Mairéad as Tremaine approached her. "Will you so honor me? Wed me for all the years to come?" He would have drawn her hand to his lips, but she cupped his cheek and stood on tiptoe, lips pursed, and he could not refuse the invitation.

Highly vexed, Lady Darnley said, "I will never finish writing to Philly. Every single day something happens, and I keep adding to the letter."

"You poor dear." Lord Darnley voiced with a decided lack of empathy.

"It's already eleven pages. Whatever will she think when it arrives? That I've sent her a batch of lace kerchiefs? No telling how long it will be, considering I have yet to write about today's excitement."

Tremaine and Mairéad burst out laughing. Lady Duncamden could definitely be a force.

Mairéad said, "the news will be a thunderbolt to Mother Abbess. I need to inform her in person."

Tremaine asked, "Shall I go with you?"

"This is something I must face alone but thank you for the offer."

"We will sort it all out, dearest," her grandmother said as the tea cart arrived. Lady Darnley declared, "We will announce your engagement at a ball."

Lord Darnley opened his mouth to voice his opinion, and she cut him short. "I'll brook no disagreement. I have waited my entire life for an event such as this, and nothing will stand in my way." Sheepishly, she glanced at the young couple. "I hope you both agree."

Tremaine led Mairéad to the settee.

"I believe you have bossed them into silence," Lord Darnley said in a low voice tickled with humor.

"Shush." Lady Darnley's attention was fully focused on the young couple.

Tremaine leaned close to Mairéad, "My experience with my sister's marriage taught me that your grandmother's question is meant for you." He drew her hand to his lips.

"Won't it be a lot of fuss? The nuns are the only friends I have. Of course, you have many. I can't dance, and isn't that what people do? I'm frightfully awkward about it all. Truth be told, though we talked about getting married, even now, with my grandfather's consent, I find it difficult to grasp."

The three of them stared at her. Of course, she would have absolutely no experience or even the simplest knowledge of engagements, nor a notion regarding the preparations that would lead up to the actual nuptials.

With minimal knowledge of his own, Tremaine offered, "We'll take it in steps, no pun intended. How is that? The first involves contacting those we love, to let them know we are engaged. As for dancing, we can begin with lessons in the parlor for the next two days before I go on to Dunraven."

"I think it grand if you taught me. Will we need music?"

Lady Darnley offered, "I haven't played the pianoforte in years. I'll brush up."

His lordship's deep voice bellowed. "What a honey-fall, my sweet. I've longed to hear you play."

Lady Darnley blushed a deep pink. "Don't make much of it, I said I'd try."

Tremaine said, "Have I mentioned My mother and your grandmother are friends of long standing."

Mairéad asked, "Do I understand there is a family connection?"

"Your great-grandfather, Robert Garrett Wallington, 5th Earl of Darnley is my grandfather."

His lordship quizzed Tremaine, "Have you thought of a date for the wedding?"

Tremaine leaned in elbows on his knees, "We've not discussed a date." He reached for Mairéad's hand, "Unless, of course, you would consider a hurry-up affair, and then move with me to Edinburgh while I finish my last year and graduate."

That left a huge silence hanging over the tea that turned cold before anyone chanced a drink.

25

Two days later, Tremaine left for Dunraven immediately after breakfast. He was eager to break the news to his parents. As he prepared to go, he assured them his mother would no doubt be issuing an invitation. More than anything, Mairéad looked forward to meeting his parents.

As soon as the dust settled with Tremaine's leaving, Mairéad ordered the chaise to deliver her to the convent. Though she and Mother Abbess understood her decision not to take vows, Mairéad convinced herself the nun would be resistant to all that Mairéad imparted.

She received a post from Sister Constance the day before, informing her of the sow gifted to the convent late last summer. She was bloated horridly, and they feared its demise.

Mairéad arrived at the convent and rather than investigate the commotion in the yard, went to the office. She wanted this time to be private with Mother Abbess. At the very least, she owed her that courtesy. She was thankful for the commotion that was providing diversion for the rest of the nuns.

As she glanced about the austere, wood-paneled room, the familiar Crucifix high on the wall. The only color in the room was an oil painting of the Blessed Mother, her arms in prayer, a red and gold crown on her long brown hair with doves at her feet. No matter where one sat or moved in the room, her eyes appeared to be watching. When Mairéad was quite young and in for a scolding, it was as if the painting knew what she'd done.

With the pat of sandals and swish of beads, she recognized the Abbess's stride and turned to the door as it opened.

A note of concern in the web of her brow, Mother Abbess breathlessly exclaimed, "This is a surprise. You are the second this morning." She came forward, pointed to a chair, indicating Mairéad take a seat. "We've ten piglets," a little smile chased the frown away. "We were prepared to lose her. Instead, we have piglets to sell. Once weaned, Mr. Chiley suggests three to four weeks. The mystery is how she got that way?"

That said, she glanced at Mairéad, all business, though politely so, arms resting on the desktop, hands folded. "Now, tell me, what has brought you back here earlier than expected?"

Mairéad didn't know where to begin and just blurted, "I've found out all about my past and my parents."

"You are referring to Fionnuala O'Bannon, I take it."

"You knew." Her voice cracked.

"I suspected. Someone was donating generous sums, and I began to consider Nuala because the money was on my desk the days she came for winter dinners. She seemed the most likely of all the folks. It took me a while to discern the why of it, and then I suspected you might be the reason."

It hurt her to think Mother Abbess would not have shared the supposition. Though she knew it wasn't her way. "There is one thing you should know. My máthair put the symbol on my chest. She has an identical one. She marked both of us when I was newborn. Her hope was that it would identify us—me if we were separated."

"Hmm."

That was it? That was all she could summon. "It is not a pagan symbol with evil intent. I especially wanted you to know the truth."

The holy woman continued to stare at her, clasped hands, waiting for more. Of what? Her lack of excitement was disconcerting. Mairéad added, "I am to be married. There will be a ball to announce our engagement. We would like you and the sisters to attend. Invitations will be sent after the date is decided."

She leaned over and took up her reticule and gloves from the vacant chair next to her. "It would please me a great deal if you attended."

Mother Abbess pushed her chair back and stood. "We will see what the future holds. Is it Lord Tremaine to whom you are betrothed? The young man who interrupted us in your workroom?"

Determined to make the best of her short visit, she was overcome with compassion for this woman, despite her unemotional reaction. She nodded as she stepped toward the door. "Yes. He asked, and Lord Darnley agreed. My grandfather, as it turns out, and I also know who my father was, Garrett II, Lord Rutledge."

"Fionnuala was married?" Her brows rose high on her forehead, almost pushing the wimple upward. Finally, a reaction.

With a heavy heart, Mairéad glanced at the nun. "I have seen the document signed by Father James Deane on the ninth of November 1798."

"A renegade priest. I recall tales of him, going about the countryside performing mixed marriages and bestowing a Catholic blessing. She did well for herself, didn't she? With him coming from a wealthy Protestant family. It explains why you were left on a Catholic convent step." She folded her hands across her chest, hiding them within the wide sleeves of her tunic.

Mairéad heard past the animosity in the nun's voice to the woman beneath and felt sorrowful for her. It was plain she wanted something else for herself, another kind of life.

Mother Abbess challenged, "I am sure you know how your father died. Suicide, it was whispered. You will do well to not question the rumor to your newfound grandparents."

Barely nodding a goodbye, Mairéad lifted the latch and fled to her chaise. In the solitude of the drive to Rockmore Hall, she chastised herself for thinking badly of the woman. She should have hugged her. Mairéad understood that if she had taken vows, it would somehow confirm the nun's own secular life. She allowed that Mother Abbess's unresolved hurt kept her from being charitable.

⚜

By the end of the week, a letter arrived inviting Lord and Lady Darnley, Miss Wallington, and her mother to a weekend at Dunraven, Wednesday next, the second of May.

It took a lot of coaxing to convince Nuala to accept the request. In the end, a daughter's persuasion won, and they all rode in the Darnley's carriage toward the foothills of the Knockmealdown mountain range where Tremaine was born. Mairéad harbored a longing to discover more about the man to whom she gave her heart.

The first item of conversation as they traveled in comfort was the addition of springs beneath the floor of the cab. Carnahan's forge completed the work within the five days Lord Darnley allowed. It tickled Mairéad, when at dinner the day the invitation from Dunraven arrived, her grandfather teased about a four-hour carriage ride with three women. Perhaps he considered a smoother ride might be conducive to naps along the way.

Her heart swelled with gratitude and thankfulness. Family!

⚜

Lord and Lady Tremaine and Jonathan, Lord Tremaine, greeted the carriage as it swung up the winding road to the front of Dunraven. An outrider announced their imminent arrival, and all was at the ready. Lady Darnley brought her maid, Cindy, and allowed that her granddaughter would need Ryan. Lord Darnley

308

could not go anywhere without Tench. Nuala, Lady Rutledge, with an air of independence, did concede that perhaps she would borrow Ryan if the need arose. The three servants sat in a second carriage with trunks strapped to the back.

Dunraven, a classic Palladian consisting of a central block with wings on both sides, nestled against the backdrop of the green Knockmealdowns and presented a sense of peaceful grandeur. A beautiful garden circled nearly a half-acre and a pond spilled outward toward the forest of trees to the east and west.

Tremaine introduced Mairéad and her máthair as Miss Wallington and Fionnuala, Lady Rutledge, to his parents.

Inside the manor, Mairéad beheld a striking black and white marbled foyer with a two-story ceiling and massive mahogany stairs. In the center of the entrance, an elegant chandelier with hundreds of prisms dangling. Dunraven was as elegant as Rockmore Hall.

After tea a refreshing walk appealed to them all. The women fell in together, leading the men toward the garden.

Tremaine held Mairéad back with a question about Mother Abbess, his ulterior motive being one of private time with his beloved. "I've missed you. It's pure suffering to be parted."

The sound of footsteps in the hallway caused him to step back from the kiss he was about to bestow. Knowing his intent, she giggled at the interruption. The footsteps faded, and she placed her hands on his arms. The intimacy of the touch was most pleasing.

Her chin rose. "Now, if you please."

He traced a fingertip across her brow then down her lovely, dainty nose. "More than anything, I want to, but …" The fingertip reached her upper lip and spread itself across her slightly parted lips. "… we have no privacy, and I'm not sure I could pull away, once I start." The finger tapped her chin and closed her gaping mouth.

"Oh," she murmured, her disappointment clear. Struggling to straighten her shawl, he drew it over her shoulders.

Pressing his lips against her brow, he whispered, "This is a safe kiss."

"I prefer the other kind."

Taking her by the hand, he said, "Before we join the others, I want to give you something."

"A present?"

"More than that. Something that will seal our bond, but it is not new."

"Jonathan Tremaine, you tease me with riddles."

"Ah, I do. How clever of me." He pulled a circle of gold from his pocket. "My mother has bid me offer this to you as an engagement gift. A token of her love that you will be her daughter."

He held the ring. The center piece a sapphire, encased in tiny diamonds.

Awed, her fingertips trembled at her lips. "It's stunning."

"She wants you to have it. It was her mother's, and I believe even her grandmother's. It is meant as an engagement gift, to seal our troth."

She touched the smooth, unblemished surface. "It's breathtaking."

He slid it onto her finger, then kissed her palm.

"I will treasure your mother's gift. I hope to prove worthy to her."

He drew her chin up, his eyes searching hers. "You don't have to prove anything to anyone. My mother honors me as well in wanting you to have this. She is telling me you are also her choice."

"Did you know one day she would give this to your wife?"

"I was quite taken by surprise. I can't remember a time she has been without it. Come, let's join the others."

"Not just yet." Her arms circled his waist. She snuggled tightly against his solid, inviting self and lifted her lips to his.

In all, they were gone half an hour. Lord Darnley glanced at his watch as Tremaine and Mairéad, hand in hand, joined them at the gazebo.

"There's a look of mischief on your faces." Her grandmother's voice reminded her of Lady Duncamden.

Lady Sarah teased, "Something you might share with the rest of us?"

Mairéad held up her left hand, "This."

Lady Darnley glanced at her old friend with surprise. "I've never seen you without it."

"I'm thrilled with his choice. It completes our circle." Her watery eyes glistened with contentment as she glanced at her dear friend of many years.

Liveried footmen approached the gazebo with trays of sliced ox tongue, liver pate on bread squares, strawberries, black and green olives, shrimp, and butter cookies made up the finger food. Tea and cherry cordials were also presented.

Sunlight dappled off the Koi swimming about like butterscotch candies. The pond circled the gazebo, much like at Rockmore Hall.

Lady Sarah mentioned to her son, "Whenever we travel to Waterford, I insist your father take me to O'Bannons on the way through. The finest linen in Ireland is there, as far as I'm concerned." She glanced at the object of her praise, noting the high color on Nuala's cheeks. "You deserve the compliment, my lady. 'Tis well earned."

Nuala's composure melted with the praise, "It is kind of you to say so."

Charles, Lord Tremaine, perhaps ten or so years younger than Lord Darnley, shared the same stout and robust build. Tremaine's mother and Mairéad's grandmother were most likely about the same distance apart in years, although the women appeared younger than their husbands.

Nuala's cheeks flushed with the acceptance. Mairéad sat next to her on the cushioned seat, leaning against the railing, sharing her liver paste and fresh fruit. Clouds lazed in the bright sky. A hawk soared as the two women conversed about the garden of which Lady Sarah was so proud.

Tremaine walked back over the bridge to the edge of the pond, a drink in hand, glancing about the landscape. Even from a distance, she was struck by how handsome he was, flaxen hair caught in the breeze and his coat tails swelling a bit with gusts of wind. He warmed her heart. One more year and he would be a practicing man of medicine. Steadfast, a man of moral integrity, kind almost to a fault, Mairéad hoped to be worthy of him all the days of her life.

Lady Sarah drew her back to the present when she asked, "What plans have you considered for your engagement ball?" Mairéad glanced at Tremaine on the other side of the bridge.

"From what I understand, it must be held on the evening of a full moon, so carriages leave by its light. Do we know when that might be?"

Charles, Lord Tremaine scrambled to answer. "I keep a daily calendar, and of last eve the moon was waxing in its first quarter."

"What of a June ball?" her grandmother inquired.

"That doesn't allow enough time if it's already in the first quarter. You will need a good month, mayhap six weeks," sensible Lady Sarah decried.

Nuala joined in. "Then July would work perfectly."

When Tremaine returned to the group, his father, Charles, offered, "We are discussing a night of a full moon for your engagement ball."

Smiling, Tremaine bent over and kissed Mairéad on the top of her head. "Do we know when that will be?"

Lord Darnley dove into the particulars. "Since last evening's moon was brighter, but only in its first quarter, it means we have two to three weeks. That is not enough time. Therefore, July has been suggested. This would bring the ball at about the third week."

Nuala mentioned, "A gibbous moon is a time to learn and prepare. 'Tis appropriate, do you not agree?"

"A thoughtful saying," Lord Darnley leaned toward his wife. "I am imagining the undertaking. What one of you doesn't think of, the other will."

She turned a fixed stare on him, "You no doubt will disappear into your inner sanctum and bury yourself in paperwork through it all."

Lady Sarah spoke up. "Keep me informed. Anything I can do while at Dunraven, you must ask. When Rowan married, of course that was a few years ago, but it does require a great deal of planning."

"Ma'am," said Tremaine, "this is an engagement, not a siege?" He glanced at the circle of women their mouths pursed in skepticism. "Really?"

Lord Darnley smacked his knee. "The preparations will open your eyes to what the tender sex can accomplish. To say nothing of the cost. Lesson number one on the path to wedded bliss."

The elder Tremaine elbowed his old friend. "He might as well know the ropes from the beginning. Isn't that how it was with us? Gad about days became a distant dream."

◌⁊⁊

Dinner was in the grand style, even more so than at Rockmore. Mairéad assumed it was the occasion and not necessarily the norm. The menu included stuffed quail, oysters roasted in the shell, brown bread, carrots and peas in a cream sauce, and scalloped potatoes crusted with cheese. For dessert, moss pudding so delightful one could swoon.

Candlelight flickered on the crystal. Conversation was lively. Nuala was radiant. She borrowed Ryan to braid her long dark auburn hair into a crown of sorts.

Beloved Tremaine sat directly across the table from Mairéad, fully engaged in conversation with her máthair. Her grandparents were engrossed in a tale of some sort that the elder Lord Tremaine enthusiastically told as he waved with a fork in hand, a piece of meat stuck in the tongs. His wife corrected him on some fine

313

point. As if he were a racehorse with blinders, he didn't allow her comments to deter him.

Mairéad was suddenly overwhelmed. Emotion flooded her, and her eyes watered with the overflow of happiness.

"What's wrong?" Tremaine asked, ready to push his chair away from the table.

She lifted her hand. "I'm fine," and dabbed at her cheeks with a napkin.

"But …"

"I'm so happy." Burying her face in the napkin, she was able to regain composure. As the room quieted, she lowered the napkin, revealing a tremulous smile. "I used to wonder what it would be like to have a family."

Lady Sarah's fingers covered the lower part of her face, her eyes watered. Nuala swept a finger along her eyelid. Lady Adrianna's cheeks pinkened.

The carriage ride on their return to Rockmore was pleasant enough to allow the passengers quiet reminiscing about the last four days. Mairéad was grateful for the opportunity to spend time with her future in-laws. Her mother was captivated and exhausted, as were her grandparents.

The afternoon sun glistened off her stunning sapphire, a deep purplish-blue gem. With the fateful turns in her life, would she measure up?

As the carriage gently swayed past the emerald landscape, and Lord Darnley's eyes closed, she glanced at her mother and grandmother, asleep, too. Her family. She never in her wildest dreams thought of a future such as she now found herself.

When the carriage reached the halfway stop at an inn, Lord Darnley referred to them as his sleeping hens, and mentioned he'd taken watch over them. Chuckling to herself, she knew he was one of the napping hens.

Nuala and Lady Darnley were now ready to discuss the guest list. Lord Tremaine had consulted his diary before they left, he predicted with certainty that Saturday, July 27, 1817, promised a full moon. Satisfied that the date was far enough in the future, they now had sufficient time to prepare.

Nuala asked, "How many of the good sisters do you think might attend?"

"Counting Mother Abbess, Sisters Davideena, Constance, Helen, Boniface, and Catrina, six. Though with the opportunity to witness a festivity of this sort, I can't say with certainty who would wish to be there. It's quite possible all of them might beg Mother Abbess to allow them."

"Darling, it was yours for eighteen years. I am quite sure there will be more if Mother Abbess agrees."

"I will write to her of the date and ask for a number."

Lord Darnley let out a puff of breath. "Will they all be like Mother Abbess?"

Her grandmother's brows rose imperiously, "I hope you meant that in the nicest way."

He turned his attention to the landscape lest she see his grin. He did like to stir things up.

The tone of his voice reminded Mairéad of the first time they met, and so she inquired, "Tell me, grandfather, when you first saw me, did you believe I was your granddaughter?"

He admitted, "I prayed you were, but the letter that sent me to the convent did not identify you, only your name and where you were. I must say, the moment I set eyes on you, I did not think there was any similarity to either Rutledge II or Rutledge III."

He glanced at Nuala, sitting across from him. "You, my dear lady, wrote that prophetic letter to your husband. Without it, none of this would have happened."

"Truth be known, my lord, I did fidget about saying something, even before you brought Mairéad to Rockmore. I always seemed to have excuses why I should not."

Mairéad said, "My máthair came to several of the dinners the convent held for the poor. We met, as I was a server."

Nuala added, "It was a convenient ruse for me, to pretend to be needy. I craved the sight of my daughter, how she looked as she grew. I must admit I disliked the veil and tunic, but I could say nothing. I believe she didn't suspect me. Though I worried once."

Nuala took hold of her daughter's arm. "You were five and dropped an armload of dishes. Do you recall? I overreacted, jumping to your assistance a bit too quickly, looking you over for bits of shard. I could feel Mother Abbess' dark eyes on me. Who was I to tend to you? I stayed away from the convent for the rest of the winter."

"That was you," wonder in her voice, "you were so kind, washing my arm. I remember you ripped off part of your petticoat to wrap it. You were an angel in my dreams."

"I knew Mother Abbess to be stern. She tsk-tsked that I spent far too much time fussing over the cuts, and I could not say that you were my child."

Mairéad said, "In the end, she did own up that she suspected you of being my máthair. Admitted to me she began to note the secret donations left in her office were on the same days you came for a meal. For a long time, though, she didn't realize I was the reason."

"'Tis a mighty good thing to put behind us, for sure." Nuala fanned herself with a glove, "No more worries on that score."

"She never showed partiality. When I announced my decision to forgo vows, there was no reaction. I know I hurt her with my decision. She clung to a dream that I would follow in her footsteps."

Lord Darnley agreed with Nuala. "That's the woman I encountered the day I showed up at Sacred Heart. Firm. Quiet resolve. I reasoned with myself that she oversaw a community of women, but there was nothing of a motherly sort about her, no nurturing of those in her care."

"I will always revere and love her. She told me of being one of many daughters, and the only path open to her was the convent. There was no other choice."

Nuala agreed. "At that time, Penal Laws were so strict. She would have been jailed or murdered if discovered. Her first years were clandestine, not only in keeping her vows from the English but also living under the stringency of the Catholic Church. She and the other nuns frequently moved from one safe place to another. They could not wear religious garb and were forced to take in boarders to cast off any hint of cloistered living."

"Ghastly," intoned Lady Darnley. "I was in my own little world." She nodded with finality. "Never you mind if all the sisters in the convent come. Please make sure Mother Abbess knows."

Her father must have loved her mother very much to marry even though he was raised Protestant. She even considered that her father's return to university must have been empowered by the desire to follow in his father's footsteps. And care for his new wife. He must have loved her greatly to plan as he did.

Mairéad asked, "Is it possible to erect a stone for Rutledge? He is my brother after all. We need a place to go, like Nuala has had all these years."

Her grandfather reached for his wife's gloved hand. "We've discussed the need and intended bringing it up. When Tremaine asked for your hand in marriage, we agreed to postpone the sad conversation."

"You see, dear ..." said her grandmother, "... so much has happened in such a short time, it's better left off for a while."

"What I would like ..." Mairéad started to say.

Her grandfather interrupted, "Oh, oh, she's at it again."

Begging, she said, "Hear me out, 'tis all I ask. If we arrange for his stone, couldn't we, his true family, see to its placement? When July 27 comes around, all his friends will be at the engagement ball, and they will be able to visit his special place, where they can perhaps leave their grief."

Nuala dabbed her eyes but said nothing. Lady Darnley's keen

glance fell on her daughter-in-law, though she became uncharacteristically quiet, too.

Mairéad watched as her grandfather rested his chin on his chest and sighed. "I do need to make peace with my soul. Our last argument is what led to his death."

The women all protested his statement, and he glanced at each of them, a bit of a smirk curving the side of his mouth. "Gracious, ladies. What a ta-da over the truth of it."

Nuala reached over and patted his hand as it rested on his knee. "My son had his demons. No one's to fault. I kept as good a watch on him as possible, considering he didn't know me. Even I know he was shadowed by a banshee."

"I don't believe in folklore but thank you for comfort."

"My lord," cautioned Nuala, "I would very much like to bring you peace. We all were aware he was hounded by something not of your doing. I don't truly believe in banshees, either, but it does give a name to his demons."

Lady Darnley finally piped up. "I like your idea, Mairéad. Made more appropriate because you shared the same womb. You must have an innate tenderness for him, or you would not have such a brilliant idea for a stone when the coming weeks should be devoted to your ball."

Mairéad ran a thumb and forefinger down a pleat on her skirt, not knowing how to respond to the high compliment.

The carriage hit a rut, and even the newly installed springs did not protect the passengers. Huet let out a garbled word from his lofty perch outside, not distinguishable, but the tone certainly was. Even the footman in the rear seat squawked.

"Well, then, let it be so." Lord Darnley straightened. Glancing at each of them, his deep regret for the lost grandson etched on his face. "We will mourn him as is his right as your son, your grandson, and your twin. I will see to the engraving, and the four of us will concoct a ceremony."

"What of a man of the church? Holy water," asked his wife, her chin rose with a firmness often seen when she challenged him.

"Certainly. I'll speak to Reverend Walker." His gaze swept to Nuala as he added, "He resided over Rutledge's service at our chapel thirteen years ago. Perhaps he'll agree to come out again."

Nuala said, "I believe he is still in charge at Christ Church."

"Ah, you know him?"

"Doesn't everyone? He's been around for decades, since before the new construction."

A twinkle in his eyes, Darnley challenged, "I mean as a Catholic, you acquaint yourself with Presbyterians?"

She could not help but grin. "My lord, in our world today, we must all get along."

He nodded the truth of what she said.

The carriage, drawn by four bays, slowed as it took the corner onto the long drive beneath the sunlight-dappled tunnel of green oak. The hall lay at the end, like a welcome fortress of love, arms spread wide. The outrider alerted staff ahead of their arrival. From this distance, a line of little people in black and starched white, hands folded, could be seen waiting patiently.

Nuala asked to go on to the village. She'd never left O'Bannons before and needed to assure herself operations proceeded without her presence. Hugging each in turn, she stepped back into the carriage.

The next day, Mairéad wrote to Mother Abbess, telling her all about the grand visit with Tremaine's family and included the date and the need for numbers for the engagement ball. Sealing the letter, she dropped it on the silver tray for Witham to post along with a rather fat letter addressed to the Most Honorable, The Countess of Duncamden. Her grandmother either rose early or went to bed later than usual. Mairéad couldn't help but giggle, thinking of the faces Lady Duncamden would make as she read about each occurrence that happened since her departure.

26

B y mid-May, the hawthorn was in full bloom, a lovely pink cloud of blossoms framed by the bank of windows in Lord Darnley's library. Little more than a year has passed since Mairéad arrived at Rockmore Hall.

Leaning on a bentwood cane, Reverend Walker descended from his carriage to officiate at Rutledge's memorial service. In his acceptance to do so without a coffin, he'd written to Lord Darnley, "Funeral services are for the living, not the dead." His sympathy for the family was genuine. Two watery graves in one family was a significant tragedy.

The Molloys received an invitation to join the family at a short graveside service. As the small group gathered around the gravestones, the Molloys, holding hands, quietly came across the park and stood inside the wrought iron fencing. Tremaine had arrived the day before.

Reverend Walker donned his robe and scapular in the chapel and made his way to the graveyard, leaning heavily on his cane. Two deacons accompanied him, one carrying a silver pail partially filled with holy water.

The reverend read two passages from his well-worn Bible,

then took the silver aspergillum, sprinkling holy water over the grass and Rutledge's stone.

At this time, Lord Darnley stood, hands clasped, head bowed, and said, "Dear God in Heaven, we pray our grandson, son, brother, and friend has found comfort from his earthly search for answers, which plagued him his short life here on earth. We love him and shall always miss him. God bless us all. Amen."

Afterward, Reverend Walker could not stay for refreshments, pleading another ceremony at Christ's Church. "I am grieved you find yourselves again having lost a loved one. Your grandson was far too young." Mairéad noted that his eyes were pinkish as he turned an intense gaze on her. He was emotionless during the short ceremony. Perhaps he suffered from an affliction.

"Allow me to introduce you to Rutledge's sister, Miss Wallington," said Lord Darnley.

"I heard there was a pair." His brusque inspection almost made her toes curl. "And is the rumor she's been in a Catholic convent valid?"

Darnley's breath caught. When he spoke, his voice was edged with declaration. "It was not a rumor." His chin rose as if he expected the reverend to respond.

"Harrumph. Papist." His cane thumped the ground. "Next time you get to Hawthorn, Darnley, stop in. Don't wait too long. As you can see, I'm aging faster than I like."

Lady Darnley pressed a hand to his as he grasped the cane. "We can all see how age is affecting you, Reverend. Thank you for coming. You have eased our minds and hearts, allowing us time to reflect. We are appreciative."

The reverend's carriage was brought up to the gravel approach, and he did not have far to walk, his deacons assisting. The Molloys added their condolences.

Mrs. Molloy approached Mairéad. "A little something about your eyes reminds me of him. Though his were gray, they were rimmed with the same black as yours. As a young boy, he was cheerful and playful. Not like he grew to be. It warms me to know about you. He is not lost altogether then, is it not so?"

The remark gave Mairéad pause, her breath caught, as the rest of the small party walked back to the estate. A bittersweet sadness capable of imparting a sense of peace. "I thank you for saying so, Mrs. Molloy."

Mr. Molloy approached his wife, and they quickened their pace to catch up with the others.

Mairéad sympathized with her mother who continued to stand near the stone where Rutledge's name and dates were etched. She watched as the woman removed a small vial from her reticule. Of a sudden Mairéad understood and approached placing a comforting hand to her shoulder as she sprinkled Catholic holy water on the place where her son's memory would rest. The superstition that holy water was different for each religion was ingrained.

Finished, she intoned the Our Father and Hail Mary. Mairéad's voice joined hers in prayer, and then she said, "You've done a fine thing, máthair. Truly, he will rest in peace now."

"I am plagued by those occasions when he stood across from O'Bannons in the afternoon near time to close."

Mairéad marveled, "He knew who you were."

"It is what I believe."

"You suffer now for not walking across to him?"

"What would I have said? What would I have dared to admit to? If your father had lived, my son might be alive now."

Mairéad listened to the tone of her voice; fear, tinged with deep sorrow. Nuala's shoulders rounded. Her gloved hand swiped across her eyes.

With sympathy for her regrets, Mairéad said, "I think the grace you showed came from a woman with a loving heart, not a wicked nor self-indulgent person."

Mairéad stood beside the woman as she attempted to regain control. "You have not lived as a married woman, and the children you bore were sent elsewhere. Your dear husband lost from you."

Nuala fisted her gloved hands and dug both into her eyes as her daughter spoke. She desperately needed to be rid of condemnation.

"This I promise, máthair, our lives will change. We have each other and the regard of my grandparents, and though I know how difficult an adjustment it is for you, time will heal."

Nuala swiped a gloved finger under her nose. She shuddered and quieted, finally lifting a blushed face and red eyes to her daughter. "I never believed it could happen, but you have come back to me, haven't you?"

❦

Nuala refreshed herself in her daughter's chamber. Her face no longer blotched, and the red in her eyes faded. Mairéad knew how dearly the blessing of Rutledge's stone with holy water meant to her.

Her grandmother's luncheon arrangements comforted, too. With an impish grin, her ladyship concluded, "After the reverend's remark about a papist, I'm rather glad he could not stay."

Molloy sat next to his wife, nodding in agreement. Mairéad supposed they practiced Catholicism as well. Most people in this part of Ireland clung to the old faith rather than change.

Tremaine added, "He lives in another time with his religious leanings. We must show patience toward bigotry."

Lord Darnley challenged, "If you were in a crowd in Dublin or even Dooley's in Waterford, would you admit to your feelings?"

Tremaine's face broke into a wide grin. "Ha! Questioning me, my lord? I'm not the least abashed to admit how I feel on the subject considering our marriage will be a Catholic Protestant union. If you love and respect each other, there is no space for aversion to the other's chosen way to live. With Christ in your heart how can you possibly go wrong."

"Here! Here!" Lord Darnley stood, raising his glass. Delighted,

323

everyone followed suit, the Molloy's clinked their glass with a fork.

Her grandmother kept the meal casual, instructing everyone to go along the sideboard and fill their plates.

Nuala sat next to Mrs. Molloy, and their conversation mostly consisted of Rutledge as a youngster, which appeared to bring Nuala a great deal of solace. Lord Darnley's conversation with Molloy included snippets of discussion on produce, fencing, and two new litters of piglets. As she glanced about the table, Mairéad's gaze drew to her beloved. He winked as if he read her mind.

જીરું

By the time June neared its last days, Lady Darnley gathered all the names of those to be invited and hired a special secretary, whose hand at script was well known, to write out the invitations. The list of names came to 110, counting seven nuns from the convent. Mr. Chiley made himself available to escort them in his cart, freeing Lord Darnley of sending a carriage for their transportation and allowing Mr. Chiley to join the servants of Rockmore Hall in their own celebration in the kitchen below stairs.

An instructor hired to show the women the newest dance steps kept Nuala, Mairéad, and even Lady Darnley involved. Poor Tremaine wanted to show his beloved the graceful moves, but when her grandmother and máthair showed interest, the dance master won out.

Amid all the preparations, Lady Duncamden arrived. Sassy and Muffy, off their leads, scurried into the parlor, sniffing about, tails wagging, probably in delight at having been released from the carriage, their mistress attempting to follow, but in no way able to keep pace. Mairéad noted a miniature tail wagging from under the woman's arm. "What have we here, my lady?"

Feigning surprise, her ladyship said, "Good gracious. How did

324

this one manage to escape?" She held the puppy with one hand, a tiny replica of its dame and sire, a black swatch across one eye, otherwise white like its dame. She handed the sniffing little cur to Mairéad. "An engagement present, my dear."

Mairéad squealed in delight at the tiny dark eyes, the twitching nose, and the wagging tail full of vinegar. "What will I call you? Are you a lad or a lassie?"

"Patch seems suitable. It's a bitch."

Her skirts swishing, Lady Darnley hurried into the parlor, having become aware her sister-in-law arrived when footmen began running about corralling Sassy and Muffy. "If it's a gift, you should allow Mairéad to name her. How many in the litter?"

"Just two, the other didn't survive." Lady Duncamden's hand swept over the little backside and tail. "I would have kept her, but if my niece lets that handsome Tremaine go off to Edinburgh alone, she'll need to keep occupied."

Mairéad nuzzled the puppy's nose, and a tiny pink tongue gave her a scratchy lick. "Well, then, welcome to Rockmore Hall, Patch."

Leaning on a cane, her fingers sparkling with diamonds, Lady Duncamden mumbled, "Fiddle-faddle! I've got something to say, and I want this young woman to listen to me."

"When have you not something to say?" questioned her brother as he entered the parlor.

Mustering herself, she glared at him, then turned her pale blue eyes on Mairéad. "I want to be referred to as something other than Lady Duncamden, my dear. Do you think you could refer to me... as perhaps, great aunt? Does that suit?"

Mairéad hugged the woman, cane and all. "I am honored, my dear great aunt."

"She bribed you with a cur?"

Ignoring her brother, her great aunt waved at the footmen to take the dogs away, and asked, "Have you decided when to set a date?"

Reluctantly, Mairéad handed Patch over. "Tremaine is in

Waterford. Something to do with a site for their clinic. He's meeting up with Christopher Curran. I know you've met the man in times past. He graduates this winter, ahead of Tremaine, and intends to open up on his own."

Lady Darnley asked, "He isn't interested in the village?"

"He is, they both are. They are weighing their options. Which is why Tremaine's gone for a couple of days. Procuring a building is important. The decision is where."

Her great aunt, full of questions gushed. "Am I to understand you have not discussed moving to Edinburgh?"

Sighing, Mairéad delayed her answer a moment. "I'll know more when he returns."

"Good enough, my dear. Now, let me see your left hand."

Mairéad rolled her eyes in pretend disgust. "If I must."

"Gorgeous." Her great aunt's fingertip tapped the sapphire. "Befitting your future as Baroness."

※

Tremaine returned two days later just as Mairéad, Lady Darnley, and her great aunt practiced a form of the quadrille, more like a waltz, with the instructor being the fourth person. At least it looked like a version of the dance as he knew it. He watched from the hall as the four turned gracefully with the steps while attempting to keep an eye on the teacher as he held to Mairéad.

Her swan-like movement was not surprising. Tremaine's memory recollected that Lady Darnley loved to dance. Lady Duncamden noticed him and coaxed, "Come over and help us. Free Mr. Watson from dancing so he can give us music to learn the steps."

"A pleasure, my lady." He gave a nod to Mairéad and took her hand. "Shall we?"

She smiled up at him. "Our first dance."

His smile melted her. "So it is, my darling."

Mr. Watson, fingers poised over the ivory, began with a three-quarter-time piece perfectly suited to the steps he taught. She counted to herself, one on the right, one on the left, turn, counting out the steps.

"Your brow is scrunched."

"Shush, I'm concentrating." He twirled them as the sisters-in-law stood to the side watching.

Mr. Watson suddenly stopped playing. The women clapped. "Well done."

Tremaine and Mairéad weren't near ready to quit.

The dance master gave a slight bow, "I have another appointment and must be on my way." He quickly gathered up his music sheets.

Lady Duncamden, did not disappoint with her many questions, "Did your search in Waterford prove enterprising? Did you come to an agreement?"

"Indeed, my lady. I will enlighten you at dinner, if that is all right?"

"Certainly, though I like my gossip fresh." A glint in her eyes brought a chuckle. She was a determined elder.

Ryan delivered Mairéad's shawl, then she and Tremaine were out the door. "You will be pleased to learn my great aunt has given me a gift."

He glanced down at her as they slowly ambled across the park. "Should I guess?"

"A puppy from Sassy and Muffy's litter."

"One of those yappy little critters? Always jumping and sniffing?"

She laughed at his teasing as they approached the gazebo and sat on a bench. "Yes, one of those."

Sandhill cranes fished amidst the reeds at the edge of the pond. He stood at the railing as if contemplating the lanky birds. His low baritone sounded hopeful. "I'm sure you've given some consideration to marrying before I leave for Edinburgh."

She studied his posture, tall, proud, and yet unassuming in

authority. "A year is too long for us to be apart. If you were to return for Christmas, it's still too long."

"Are you saying yes, then?" He swung about, his face brightening.

"If you believe a wife won't be a distraction with all your studies, can we not marry just before you leave for Edinburgh?" Though we will go against convention with Rutledge's death only a few months in the past?"

"Not if it's small. I think Darnley will approve. I'll get a special license, though there is time for banns to be posted. We would need three weeks. Either way, we can manage to be in Edinburgh a week before classes begin. That will give us time to settle in."

"I suspected this was the reason you pulled Reverend Walker aside." A sudden flap of the cranes' wings took her attention for a moment as they flew off. "I wasn't sure with our mixed religions what might be the procedure or possible hindrance."

"There is nothing to stop us, except perhaps the authentication of your birthright, and I can't see how that will stand in the way. Your máthair has the documented marriage certificate."

"My father left one with the lawyer, too. It is how my grandfather was able to have Rutledge declared legitimate."

"The English rule is that the Protestant ceremony must be first then the Catholic."

"I know just the priest," she said. "Father Fitzums. The convent is one of his weekly duties. I'm sure with Mother Abbess on our side, he will accommodate us."

Tremaine teased, "Can we be sure she is on our side?"

A side glance from Mairéad declared her determination and increased his humor. Was it to be an easy fix considering two centuries of imperious governance. He would marry her with the blessing of a druid if he thought she would allow such a thing. He craved her in his life, by his side, loving him, having his children, growing old with him.

27

Swooping her up, Tremaine twirled them about the gazebo. "You've made me exceedingly happy, *mo stór*. The sooner our future is begun, the better."

Returning to the bench, his arm draped about her, he added, "I was deeply concerned about taking you from family, thinking perhaps it is too soon for you to leave after all that has happened."

She gazed into the sincerity and goodness gleaming from his handsome self. "I have come to realize what love is through all of the months missing you and pretending it was something else. I know devotion. I've watched women shower it upon God daily. I also know about love. These same women pledged their lives in the name of love," she brushed his cheek with her lips.

He swallowed and blinked back emotion.

A lock of flaxen hair drifted over his brow. She combed her fingers through the thickness, settling it back in place, and said, "You quicken the beating of my heart. I want my life to blend with yours forevermore."

A beautiful sense of right surrounded them.

He drew her hand to his lips. "I dislike banishing this wonderful moment."

She raised an eyebrow in question.

"I need to return to Dunraven until the engagement ball."

"Three weeks is a long time. I will miss you, but it makes sense to accompany your parents and sister. I need to learn to share you with others who love you, too."

His arm tightened on her shoulders. "A ball in July, a wedding in September, each will be here before we know it and never more will we part." He placed a kiss on her brow. "I plan to show you Scotland as you could never imagine, and when our year is up, we will return and make our lives here in County Waterford, near family."

She interrupted, "You will become a grand practitioner of medicine, perhaps even after you are elevated to earl. Though, I dread thinking of it."

"I expect to be an old man, walking stick and favorite chair, before that is a part of our lives. No fear. Your grandfather, and my father, are hearty sorts."

As they strolled across the park, he said, "Well, now that we've settled our future, we have *fresh gossip* for your great aunt, et al. Let's tell them at supper tonight, and I'll inform my parents when I return to Dunraven. September it is."

৩৶৩

Tremaine clinked the side of his glass for everyone's attention. "We have decided on a wedding date and it will be sooner than later. Mairéad has agreed to accompany me to Edinburgh while I finish up my last year."

Lord Darnley asked, "What have you in mind?"

"September first, if at all possible. I need to be back at University on the 18th."

Great aunt did not disappoint, nor did Mairéad's grandparents and máthair, who took to dining with them, due largely to the fact Lord Darnley sent his carriage for her each evening. The *fresh gossip*, now fact, was received with joyous approval.

Her great aunt's raspy voice enlightened them all. "We have plenty to accomplish before July. How I love planning." She quickly turned to her niece, "I know, I know, it will be a small affair. My goodness, I haven't this much fun in years."

Her soft blue eyes settled on Mairéad. "I've been to Edinburgh, twice. I suspect the route has improved in the past forty years, and with a guide such as Tremaine, you'll not want for social interaction."

Tremaine leaned near, whispering loud enough for everyone to hear, "The voice of approval."

Nuala, breathless with excitement said, "I envy you Scotland and Edinburgh. Your letters will be greatly appreciated."

Lady Duncamden's voice piped up again, "Will you take Patches with you?"

Mairéad, quite surprised by the question, said, "I hadn't given the pup a thought."

Her máthier offered, "If not, I'll be glad to care for her if it helps."

Lady Duncamden lifted her eye piece, "Well said, Nuala. I have an even better thought. You keep Patches, and by the time Mairéad returns, I'll have another pup waiting for her."

Lord Darnley shook his head. "See how she wheedles and connives. She's been at it all her life."

After the laughter died down, Tremaine glanced at his future mother-in-law. "We would enjoy your company, if you are able to visit. I hope to have procured a fitting place with guest rooms."

"What about your valet and Ryan?" Her grandmother inquired. "My granddaughter's gotten used to a maid. It would be difficult for her."

"All taken care of. Not an hour ago, I wrote to my solicitor, listing our needs and gave him instructions to hire a cook and a small staff with the hope Hix and Ryan accompany us."

Lady Darnley asked, "What is the news of your infirmary? Waterford is it?"

"Christopher and I settled on a building not far from Ring Tower."

"Along the quay then?"

"Further east up on Catherine Street, closer to Johns River."

Lord Darnley mentioned, "'Tis a shame there was nothing suitable in Hawthorn Village."

Setting his wine aside, Tremaine responded, "We looked earlier in the day. A nice little place on Sisters Lane appealed to us, but someone else is interested in the building, and the owner is duty bound to wait for his answer."

"Another doctor? There's been a strong need for doctors, and now we will have three more to assist Mr. O'Reilly?"

"I don't believe the person interested is a doctor. He is looking at the building as a warehouse of sorts."

"What happened to that monster...Martin, was it? The bloodsucker?"

"Philly, honestly," intoned Lady Darnley. "Rumor is, he packed up and took his practice to Dublin."

Tremaine added, "He did, but the medicine practiced in that metropolis is progressive. He won't find many who will agree with his old-fashioned cures."

Lord Darnley turned the topic back to the infirmary. "Will Curran keep after the possibility in the village?"

"He will, since Hawthorn is our first choice. The clinic in Waterford needs another source. The population is growing. An infirmary in Hawthorn would do nicely, and as its three blocks from the lough, ready access to ships. There appears a constant flow of injuries off the ships. Which makes me wonder why they don't keep a doctor on board."

Lord Darnley chuckled. "They do. It's often the cook."

❧

Readying for bed, Mairéad glanced at Ryan's reflection in the mirror. "Have you pondered living in Edinburgh?"

Ryan kept her attention on the pins she pulled out of Mairéad's hair. "Not until I have tried to picture you living there."

"Would you consider giving up a year to accompany me after I marry?"

"Oh, miss, in a heartbeat. My answer is yes."

Their eyes met in the mirror, both grinning. "Wonderful. Truthfully, I don't know what I would do without you."

❧

The next three weeks were a blur of convulsive preparations. Thank heaven for staff. Witham and Mrs. Atkinson, each controlling their different branches of efficient domestic retainers kept a firm grip reporting to Lord and Lady Darnley each morning after breakfast.

Lady Darnley woke the morning of the twenty-seventh of July excited that the *day* finally arrived. Mrs. Atkinson drew back the drapes, and Cindy placed a tray of chocolate and biscuits on the side table.

"Will there be any last-minute instructions, my lady?" the housekeeper asked.

"All appears in order. How is my granddaughter?"

"Ryan wasn't below stairs before I came up."

"Do we have word when the Tremaines are arriving?"

"Their outrider had just given a note to Witham as I was on my way up."

"Most likely midday, then. Thank you."

❧

As predicted, at midday the entire Tremaine entourage arrived and settled into the rooms on the second floor of the west wing.

Houseguests included Tremaine's family, Lord and Lady Tremaine, and his sister Rowan and husband George, minus their three children. Of course, there was also great aunt, who came prepared to stay for a good length of time even before any of these activities were known. There was Tremaine's long-time friend and future medical partner, Christopher Curran and Rutledge's childhood friend from Waterford and Eton, Lord Innisbeck, who seemed at a bit of a loss.

Invited to stay the weekend, Nuala declined because her dear friend, Constance McGrath, was also invited, and this allowed Nuala a traveling companion between Rockmore Hall and the village, what with Lord Darnley's carriage at their complete disposal.

First to arrive for the family dinner, preceding the actual ball, was Mr. Chiley's cart filled with Mother Abbess and Sisters Constance, Davideena, Helen, Catherine, Boniface, and Catrina.

Dinner also included twenty family and friends, all beginning to gather in the formal parlor.

Nuala whispered to her friend, Constance. "I peeked in on my daughter before coming down. She is breathtaking in soft pink silk."

"I am happy for you, Nuala. All these years I've wished the best for you. How you kept such secrets from me is mind boggling. If I wasn't standing here proof of what you've told me, it would be hard to believe."

"Wait until you see my daughter."

"I think I'll keep my eye on Tremaine, if you don't mind. He is a golden god with his flaxen hair and deep blue eyes. When he bent over my hand, my breath left my body."

Nuala shook her head at her friend's excess. Chatter filled the parlor, footmen walked amongst the guests offering libations. The sound of violins drifted from the ballroom. A hush rippled near the doorway. She craned her neck and spotted her daughter. Her thoughts immediately included her husband and son. What a family they could have been.

Tremaine waited for his beloved, knowing full well Ryan would have detained her, giving her the advantage of an entrance. Mairéad would not have given it a moment's consideration.

Even from this distance, he watched her green eyes widen as she became aware. Her gloved hand lifted to her lips and just as quickly returned to her side as she closed the steps between them.

Fully aware of how extraordinarily fortunate he was that he followed his heart, he wanted to scoop her up and kiss those full lips and feel her close warm, and enduring.

Instead, placing one arm behind his back, he bowed, brushing her hand with his lips and whispering, "Welcome to our engagement fest."

She reached up, touching his cheek, not taking her eyes from him. "I have not spoken with your mother yet. Will you take me to her?"

Tall as Tremaine was, he spotted his mother and sister halfway toward the back of the ballroom.

Mairéad greeted the woman with a kiss to each cheek. "I am grateful you made the journey. I want to say thank you for the wonderful son you raised."

Lady Tremaine gulped and clearly struggled not to cry, rapidly blinking her eyes. Tremaine knew Mairéad's declaration overwhelmed her. Even his sister, Rowan, appeared touched.

Lady Duncamden stood within the tiny circle. "You are getting quite a young woman, you know. A rarity."

Mairéad turned to her great-aunt. "Please."

"Ha! I'm of an age where I can say what I want." Pursing her lips, she smiled at Tremaine's womenfolk. "Far too long a time. Ten years, is it?" Without waiting for an answer, she continued, "Rowan a married woman, with how many children, three? Am I right?"

The women settled into a catching-up conversation. Tremaine led his fiancée to her mother, and then he went in search of Innisbeck.

With the later arrival of ninety more guests responding to the invitation for dancing and a late-night buffet, the announcement of the engagement of the Darnley's' granddaughter, Miss Mairéad Wallington, to Jonathan, Lord Tremaine, was planned for an hour after dancing began.

With music in the background and conversation floating above it all, Mairéad, her máthair in tow, quickly cornered Mother Abbess. "I wish to introduce Fionnuala, Lady Rutledge, though I know you've already met."

Mother Abbess, hands tucked within the sleeves of her tunic unfolded them. "Lady Rutledge. We meet again over a meal."

Nuala grinned impishly. "It seems we do, Mother."

The Abbess said, "Knowing what I now know, I am fairly certain you were the benefactor of several quantities of pound notes through the years."

Gowned in a becoming green watered silk overlaid with black lace that complimented jet earrings, necklace, and bracelet, Nuala noted the shock on the Abbess's face. She said, "I've no idea to what you refer but let me say it is certainly nice meeting again under such a pleasant circumstance. It appears you've raised a lovely woman. From my heart, I do thank you for your care of her these years."

Mairéad, inundated with a barrage of questions from the dear sisters of Sacred Heart, left Nuala and Mother Abbess to finish their conversation. As it was, a lump caught in her throat. Their love for her, each in their own way, was a grounding legacy.

As she turned her focus to the special person who taught her to illuminate, Sister Boniface mentioned, "A busy bee, missy. So sorry, I think of you as one of ours, probably always will. I should address you as Miss Wallington."

"I couldn't bear it. You may always call me missy."

A crooked smile lent itself to her sweet nature. "Well, then missy, are you illuminating?"

"Not since I finished up at the convent before returning to

Rockmore Hall. There has been little time. There is to be an announcement later, but I can mention to you. We will have a small family wedding in September. Our plan is that I accompany Tremaine to Edinburgh while he finishes up his studies."

A wistful look clouded the nun's face. "The only good thing about your leaving the convent is my return to the art room."

"You are exactly where you belong. Painting was always a struggle for me. You are a natural. When your work is seen by others, orders will increase the convent's income."

Sisters Catherine and Catrina were in a corner of the parlor, glancing upward. Mairéad knew most of the nuns came from families of means, but usually without prospects for their daughters. She did not doubt these two women were familiar with the elegance of the ceiling, the plasterwork of a Greek key bordering a riot of design.

Sister Helen slowly toured the perimeter of the parlor with a cup of punch, stopping at Mairéad's side. "I'm excited about dinner. A culinary adventure. I hope we are served oysters. I haven't tasted them since I was twelve and left my family for the convent."

Sister Davideena overheard. "You getting your hopes up? Better think before you do, sister. Though I expect the finest will be on your plate, no doubt about that." She grinned widely at Mairéad. "When Lady Darnley and Lady Duncamden visited the convent after your accident and brought the big box of chocolate, do you remember it was as though the earth moved. Even the sisters with picky appetites, who should have turned up their noses, did the exact opposite. Something they missed from childhood." Her gaze slipped about the room. "I'm thinking tonight will bring back a little of that to us all."

Witham announced dinner, and with Lord and Lady Darnley, and Tremaine and Mairéad next, everyone fell in line according to rank. Each pairing passed beneath the Corinthian door casing framed by columns on both sides and a pediment above as though they walked into an entirely different world. Elegantly placed vases of pink and red roses, babies' breath, and ferns were centered with candles that flickered off crystal goblets against the crisp white linen.

Three hanging chandeliers swathed the room in a golden glow. Delicious scents increased the effect. Delighted to have the dear sisters in attendance, Mairéad was certain Mrs. Hill's culinary expertise would be up to Sister Helen's longings from an earlier life.

Footmen, smartly dressed in green and white livery, seated the guests and served course after course. As the meal slowly progressed to dessert, conversation began to dim with the hum of violins, flutes, a harp, and a pianoforte that drifted along the corridors from the ballroom.

A full two hours later, supper over, and everyone refreshed. Witham, stoic and fully aware of the arrival of another ninety guests, gathered those who needed to be in the receiving line, directing them to the rose and gray marbled foyer. Mrs. Atkinson stood in the corner, near the drapes framing a smaller parlor. Mairéad went to her. "Nothing amiss?"

"No, I'm merely trying to keep Witham calm."

Mairéad could have laughed. "You do have that effect on him so I've noticed."

"May I add my congratulations on the pending announcement this evening?" She tried not to raise her brows, and the effort caused Mairéad to burst with delight.

"Sorry. I'm all aflutter. Thank you. Say a prayer I do not giggle when my grandfather makes the announcement. I'm so excited and I want to appear calm."

Mrs. Atkinson must have sucked in her cheeks because she turned her head toward the wall to keep a straight face.

"Well, aren't we a pair," Mairéad whispered. "I wish to thank you again for everything that will happen tonight. If not for you I'm rather sure my máthair would not have come forward. It has come to my attention, Shana O'Key, you suspected many things but with no real proof of any of it. Yet you never wavered."

Witham snapped his fingers, and Mrs. Atkinson turned to him with a nod. "That's my signal. You are right, Miss Wallington. I'll always treasure our talks when you were Mairéad the little nun-in-waiting." She reached out, pressing a hand to her, as she quickly turned toward the butler.

Mairéad glanced about for her máthair and Tremaine. She noted Ryan tucked in the shadows of drapery. The maid was still all aflutter at being asked to accompany her to Scotland. As she neared Ryan, the chamber maid said, "Just wanted to make sure your hair wasn't mussed, and your gloves are not dusty." She held up a clean pair.

"You will hover in Edinburgh?"

Ryan was unsuccessful in an attempt not to grin.

Witham, straight as an arrow, chin held high, glanced at her. This was her cue, as if a beginning, except in some respects it was a conclusion. Not a sad one, just who she was, and now who she is. She rather liked it. A lot, in fact.

She glanced along the receiving line. Her grandparents, grayed, a tiny bit round-shouldered, heads high, proudly assuming the role of nobility and what was to come. Her máthair, obviously waiting for her, saving a small space where she would stand between her and her beloved. And lastly, Lord and Lady Tremaine.

For a moment, she glanced into the ballroom, doors flung wide, music tumbling outward, chandeliers brilliant with candlelight. The Sacred Heart nuns lined up in chairs, perfectly willing to endure an evening of people watching as they perhaps hadn't done since childhood.

Lovely music by Haydn filled the ballroom. The orchestra Lord Darnley settled on was composed of eight professionals. Fiddles, a harp, violins, flutes, and pianoforte all joined to create a pleasing sound. Mairéad found herself counting the rhythm and measure now that she had focused on learning to dance.

Emotion welled, she felt the pull of Tremaine's gaze, the most natural thing in the world, and she turned toward him. His magnetism would draw her even in the dark, in sadness or joy, in health or sickness. She was instinctively drawn to him. His outstretched hand beckoned to her now to come and take her place beside him.

And she did.

THANK YOU FOR READING

※

Don't miss out on your next favorite book!

Join the Satin Romance mailing list
www.satinromance.com/mail.html

※

Did you enjoy this book?

We invite you to leave a review at your favorite book site, such as Goodreads, Amazon, Barnes & Noble, etc.

DID YOU KNOW THAT LEAVING A REVIEW...

- Helps other readers find books they may enjoy.
- Gives you a chance to let your voice be heard.
- Gives authors recognition for their hard work.
- Doesn't have to be long. A sentence or two about why you liked the book will do.

ABOUT THE AUTHOR

Karen Dean Benson gained a love of history from travels that took her into many different cultures around the world. A voracious reader from an early age, she loves research, history, and tales of complicated lives. Her stories, woven against the backdrop of a by-gone era, present numerous plot twists.

Her first series, *Ladies of Mischief,* is about women who find themselves enmeshed in mischief and mayhem spiced with charm in the 18th and 19th Centuries.

Her second series, *The Prickly Hawthorn:* Southern Ireland in the early 1800's where the inhabitants of Hawthorn Village's lush emerald hills and breathless azure heavens find adversity and acceptance along the banks of the ancient River Suir.

She lives with her husband Charlie in Florida on a golf course.

www.karendeanbenson.com
http://freshfiction.com/author.php?id=40966

f facebook.com/Author-page-for-Karen-Dean-Benson-1415121542104941

g goodreads.com/karendeanbenson

BB bookbub.com/authors/karen-dean-benson

Made in the USA
Monee, IL
24 June 2020

34654408R00208